COLD AS
THE GRAVE

JAMES OSWALD
COLD AS THE GRAVE

WILDFIRE

First published in 2019 by WILDFIRE
An imprint of HEADLINE PUBLISHING GROUP

1

Cataloguing in Publication Data is available from the British Library

Hardback ISBN 978 1 4722 4988 3
Trade Paperback ISBN 978 1 4722 4992 0

Typeset in Aldine 401BT by Avon DataSet Ltd,
Bidford-on-Avon, Warwickshire

Printed and bound in Great Britain by Clays Ltd, Elcograf S.p.A.

Headline's policy is to use papers that are natural, renewable and recyclable
products and made from wood grown in well-managed forests and other
controlled sources. The logging and manufacturing processes are expected to
conform to the environmental regulations of the country of origin.

HEADLINE PUBLISHING GROUP
An Hachette UK Company
Carmelite House
50 Victoria Embankment
London EC4Y 0DZ

www.headline.co.uk
www.hachette.co.uk

For all those fleeing violence, oppression and war

1

If only it wasn't so cold.

She remembers a land of sun and heat, desert sand spreading away from the city in all directions. Night could be freezing, out beyond the ancient walls, but home was always warm. Narrow cobbled alleys, the smell of spices and street food. Dawn prayers called from a thousand minarets, bringing life to another new day. These and countless other happy memories taunt her as she huddles in the dark corner, shivering, alone and afraid.

It's coming for her, she knows. The bogeyman, the afrit, the djinn. A hundred different names for a hundred different nightmares. Her life since the anger came to her world, since the explosions began, since the bombs started to fall and they all had to flee.

She hugs her knees to her chest, wraps herself tight against the wind that whistles through this old building. So unlike the places she knew growing up. What's left of them now? No more than rubble soaked in the blood of her friends and family.

Around her neck, the amulet hangs like a dead weight. She remembers her grandmother's solemn face as she gave it to her, remembers the words she spoke: 'Keep this with you at all times, littlest one. It will summon protection when you need it most.' There have been many times since then when she has needed its protection, and yet none has ever come. Still, it is a reminder of home. The only one she has left.

A noise like thunder, and lightning chases away the darkness as a door on the other side of the room is kicked open. She clamps her mouth shut against the chattering of her teeth, longs for the sun and the warm breeze blowing in across the desert. Longs for a place where the air doesn't freeze your breath, and the rain doesn't turn to ice as it falls from a sky painted purple like a bruise. She is so cold she thinks she will die here, long before the demon claims her soul. Knowing that those are her two options forces a tiny sob from her throat.

'I know you are here, my sweet little thing.'

It speaks in the language of her dead father, the words of the Imam, the voices of the hard-faced men who jostled her and her mother onto a tiny boat and set it sailing into the wide sea. It is all the people who have promised her freedom while taking it away. She shoves one hand into her mouth, bites down on her knuckles and tries not to breathe. The other reaches for the amulet, its ruby crystal warm to her touch as if a fire burns within it.

'Come out now, child. There is no point in hiding.'

It is closer now, she can hear. Its tone is beguiling, but she knows better than to believe its lies. She has heard too many now to fall for them again. All she can do is sit motionless, hoping against hope that it won't see her in the gloom. And now she can smell it, too. The sickly-sweet musk of rotting bodies, the sharp tang of freshly spilled blood, the sting of gun smoke. She hardly dares breathe lest its stench make her sneeze. She must not be found. She cannot be found.

'You are close, my pretty. I can taste you on the air. So much fear.' A pause, and she hears the animal grunts as it sniffs out her scent. 'Why do you fear me so?'

She almost answers, such is the power behind its questioning.

2

Tears run through the dirt on her cheeks, snot dribbles from her nose but she dares not wipe it away. She is petrified like the ancient statues her father took her to see in the desert. The old city ruined, reclaimed by the sand. Is that how they came to be stone? Did this demon exist even then? Steal their souls like it will surely steal hers? She grips the amulet tighter still, feels the thin cord around her neck snap.

A floorboard creaks, shifting under weight. It's close, she understands. Too close. She sees the door through which she came, a thin strip of light making the shadows even deeper. She ran here across an unfamiliar city, following her instincts, trusting them to take her to safety. How foolish to think it would be that easy, after all this time. The demon knows her intimately, has her scent. She can't hope to escape it. Not now, not ever.

She sees motion in the darkness, and it turns its head towards her, a black shape even darker than the shadows. Twin circles of dullest red hover in the air. Like iron heated in the forge until it begins to glow, they smoulder and smoke. They move slowly, passing over her once, twice. She almost believes she has escaped, but then they pass a third time, stop. The iron glows bright and all she can see is flames.

'Ah, my sweet little girl. There you are.'

She cannot move, cannot scream. There is no hope for her, and no protection comes. There is only the amulet falling from her grasp, tumbling to the stone floor and smashing into a million pieces. And if they billow into a tiny flame before vanishing altogether, she does not see.

She is already dead.

2

Tiny flakes of snow fluttered down past the glass window that made up one entire wall of the third-floor conference room. Detective Chief Inspector Tony McLean knew that he was meant to be concentrating on the meeting, the profile reports and photographs spread out on the table in front of him, the slide show of mugshots projected onto the screen that hung from the ceiling. He was finding it hard to care.

It wasn't that Operation Fundament was a waste of time, far from it. Closer work with uniform was important too, so this was exactly the sort of modern policing he could get right behind. It was simply that his unwanted seniority meant he would be stuck here at headquarters overseeing things, not out there in the field doing some actual detective work. Hard to muster much in the way of enthusiasm for driving a desk.

'You still with us, Tony?'

He looked away from the rooftops outside, focusing back on Detective Superintendent Jayne McIntyre. Another one recently promoted above where she wanted to be.

'Sorry, Jayne. Zoned out there. Late night, and it gets a bit stuffy in here with the projector going.'

McIntyre narrowed her eyes, not convinced by his excuse but neither too fussed to make anything of it. 'Almost done, anyway. Was there anything you wanted to add, Tom?'

All eyes turned to the man sitting at the head of the table. The flow of replacement senior officers from the old Strathclyde region had slowed of late, which might have explained how they'd ended up with Chief Inspector Tom Callander running the uniform operation in the station. A Dundee man born and bred, he'd worked all his life in Tayside, but seemed to be fitting in just fine in Edinburgh.

'No, I don't think so, Jayne. We all know what we're doing here. Hopefully this demonstration will be peaceful.' He looked towards the window McLean had been staring out of. 'Who knows? If the weather stays bad they'll probably cancel anyway.'

'Chance'd be a fine thing.' McLean picked up the first of a pile of photographs from the report in front of him, studied the face staring out at him from the paper. Eyes too close together, floppy blonde hair on top, shaved to the skin around the ears, a single black swastika stud in the left earlobe. Andrew Chester could do with losing some weight if he wanted to become one of the master race, as could most of his unsavoury colleagues. Flicking through the rest of the photographs, McLean saw a bunch of young men with too much time on their hands and a seriously misplaced sense of grievance. But he'd read the reports too, knew what drove them to demonstrate, agitate and at times militate. A few snowflakes weren't going to dissuade them.

'Well, if they come we'll be waiting for them,' Callander said. 'Chief Constable's sanctioned the cost. Christ knows where he got the money from. I'm inclined to agree with him though. These wannabe Nazi loons want to come up here and kick up a fuss, we'll be ready and waiting.'

The meeting broke up without any more discussion. It wasn't necessary: everyone knew what their roles were. McLean didn't get up, comfortable in his chair and still staring at the angry, piggy expression on Andrew Chester's face. There was something in that expression, his defiance mixed with disdain, that suggested a fuss was exactly what Andrew and his bunch of neo-fascist idiots were looking for.

A low buzz of conversation filled the CID room when McLean entered half an hour later. He stood just inside the doorway, waiting to see how long it would take for anyone to notice him, pleasantly surprised at how busy everyone seemed to be. It still wasn't the full house he remembered from his detective sergeant days: first the creation of Police Scotland, then the endless austerity cuts, and finally the drain of the best and brightest to the Crime Campus over on the other side of the country. The permanent plain-clothes team in the station was a pale shadow of its former self.

'Looking for anyone in particular, or just lurking?'

McLean turned to see Detective Sergeant Laird standing beside him. From the set of his shoulders, it looked like Grumpy Bob had been there a while.

'Just thinking, Bob. Where did everyone go?'

'And here's me thinking we were just about back up to decent numbers. Might as well enjoy it while it lasts.'

'Still grumbling about having to retire?'

'Maybe. A wee bit, aye. Should be plenty still to keep me busy down in the basement with Dagwood, mind.'

'Anything exciting going on right now? I feel kind of out of the loop up on the third floor. It's all strategy meetings and finance meetings and God knows what else.'

Grumpy Bob's face crumpled into a smile, and he put a fatherly hand on McLean's shoulder. 'That's what happens when you clamber too far up the pole. Ambition always has a cost.'

'You know I was bounced into taking the position, Bob. Christ only knows who they'd have foisted on us if I'd refused.'

'I know. Just kidding. As for anything exciting going on, I was just coming to collect a few detective constables. We need to get down to the Royal Mile soon. Spread out a bit so it's not obvious we've all come from the same place.' He glanced at his watch. 'Whole thing kicks off in an hour and a half.'

McLean thought about the meeting he'd just left, the mug-shots of the usual suspects they were hoping to spot in the crowd. Everyone was briefed for the operation, and looking across the CID room he could see most of the detective constables were dressed for the part too. Fewer dark suits, more casual winter coats and heavy walking boots. He'd put his own pair in the back of his Alfa before coming in to work that morning.

'Reckon an extra pair of eyes would be helpful?'

Grumpy Bob's smile widened, and he shouted across the room to where the unfeasibly tall figure of Detective Constable Blane loomed over everyone else. 'That's a tenner you owe me, Lofty. Looks like the boss is coming with us after all.'

3

'**Y**ou got a moment, sir?'

McLean had been on his way to the canteen, a cup of coffee and possibly some cake. Anything to distract himself from his ostentatiously large office on the third floor and the endless round of reports, staffing rotas and other management bollocks he had to attend to. There was no point in him going to the march until later, so he needed something more appealing to fill the next hour. Coffee and cake were good, but a 'You got a moment, sir?' from the duty sergeant had the potential to be much better.

'What is it, Pete?'

'Gentleman in Reception. He's . . . well, it's hard to say, sir.'

'Hard to . . . ?' McLean shook his head. 'Never mind. I'll have a word.'

Something like relief passed across the duty sergeant's face. 'Name's Billy McKenzie, sir. Says he works in a sandwich factory and one of the girls there's missing. Seems a sandwich short of a picnic if you ask me, but there's something about him.'

They both walked through to the reception area at the front of the station, Sergeant Dundas nodding in the direction of a row of seats where a young man sat in the one nearest the door. Shaven-headed, he had a woolly hat in his hands and was twisting

8

it this way and that as if it were a wild beast he needed to choke the life out of. McLean was reminded of some of the photographs he'd been looking at earlier, the far right Nazi sympathisers who were expected to join that afternoon's march. The heavy Doc Martens boots, skinny jeans and padded jacket only added to the picture. He seemed not to have noticed them coming in, fixated on a spot on the floor a short distance from his feet.

'William McKenzie?' McLean approached cautiously, aware that Sergeant Dundas had retreated into the relative safety of the small office behind the security glass. The young man looked up as he heard his name, almost flinching. His face had a pale bloodlessness about it, and his eyes were so dark it looked like he was wearing make-up. When he spoke, his voice was quiet and higher-pitched than McLean had been expecting.

'You a detective?'

'Detective In—. . . Chief Inspector McLean. Sergeant Dundas said something about a missing girl?'

McKenzie stood up, still clutching his woolly hat as if it were a shield against the world. 'You have to find her, aye? You can do that?'

'First of all I need to know who she is. Who you are, for that matter.'

Confusion wrinkled McKenzie's brow, spreading up and over his bald head. Then the penny dropped. 'Oh, aye. Right enough. See, it's like this. The girls at work, right, they're all foreign, like. Don't know about the polis here an' how they're no' as bad as back home, see?'

McLean didn't, but he knew that standing in the draughty reception area wasn't going to make things any clearer. He held up a hand to stop McKenzie from speaking.

'Why don't we go and have a seat somewhere a bit warmer and quieter, eh?' He turned to the glass screen. Behind it, Sergeant Dundas looked on with a slightly puzzled expression.

'Buzz us through, Sergeant. I'll take Mr McKenzie to one of the interview rooms.' McLean waited until the click of the door unlocking, pulled it open. 'Oh, and see if you can't rustle up a couple of coffees, aye?'

'It's a sandwich factory, right? We make sandwiches.'

McLean sat in a hard plastic chair on one side of the wobbly table in interview room two. Across the scratched Formica surface, Billy McKenzie was talking as much with his hands as his voice, waving them in the air excitedly as he spoke. His work was clearly something he took very seriously and about which he was quite passionate.

'Sandwiches?'

'Aye. Sandwiches. Ye ken? Two white slices an' a slab of ham. Cardboard carton and off you go.' McKenzie swept the air, bringing his palms together and then apart again in a motion that as far as McLean could tell had nothing whatsoever to do with the making of sandwiches. He paused for the time it took to drink some of the coffee Sergeant Dundas had brought up from the canteen.

'And where exactly is this factory, Mr McKenzie?'

'Oot Newcraighall way. In the industrial park, aye?'

That was another thing about McKenzie, McLean noticed. Everything was a question.

'I'd never given it much thought, but I suppose sandwiches have to be made somewhere.'

'Aye. See, if you buy a sandwich from a garage, like? Or maybe the wee corner store for your lunch? Chances are that's me's made it for youse.' McKenzie pointed at his chest with both hands. 'Me or one of the girls, ken?'

'Your co-workers? Is it one of them who's gone missing?'

McKenzie paused a moment before answering, that frown creasing from his eyes right over the top of his shaved head again.

'Aye, well, no. See, most of the girls is foreign, ken? Immigrants, refugees? Mr Boag, he's the boss, ken? He says they make the best workers. Too much to lose if they kick up a fuss. It's no' right, ken? The things they've seen, the stuff they've had to put up wi'. An' they never complain, aye? Just do the work.'

McLean took another sip of his coffee. Not as nice as Grumpy Bob's brew, but not bad, considering. He was all too aware that the only reason he was listening to this man was so that he didn't have to deal with paperwork. No amount of wishing or distraction would make that go away, though. Still, there was something about McKenzie that fascinated him, even if he couldn't quite put his finger on what or why.

'Do you have a problem with them? Immigrants, I should say.'

'Me?' McKenzie's confusion at the question couldn't have been faked. 'No way, man. They's as much right to a job as the next, aye? See the work they do? There's no' many folk'd do it for the pay and no' complain.'

'But you do, though. You make the sandwiches, I take it?'

'Aye. On the line wi' the rest of them.'

'The migrant workers.'

'Aye.'

'And one of them's gone missing.'

'Aye.' McKenzie stopped a moment as if his thoughts were having trouble keeping up with his mouth. 'Well, no' one of the workers. But her sister, see? Akka. That's her name. An' she's got this wee girl. No' sure if she was born here or came over on the boat wi' her. Thing is, Akka's wee girl has disappeared. Nala. That's her name. The wee girl, see?'

McLean wasn't sure that he did. Keeping up with the natter wasn't easy. 'So there's a little girl gone missing, that what you're trying to tell me?'

'Aye, that's right.'

'And has her mother reported this to anyone?'

'That's the thing, ken? She won't. She don't dare. Thinks youse lot'll lock her up and send her back where she came from.'

'And where's that?'

'Syria, ken? She . . . Well, I probably shouldnae say, but I don't think they came here legal like, ken?'

McLean tried to suppress his sigh, although he may have failed. Migrant workers were one thing, and brought their own set of unique problems such as an ingrained mistrust of authority. Illegal immigrants were another deal altogether, and needed a far lighter touch. Especially if there was a missing child involved.

'Let's take this from the top, Mr McKenzie.' He fished in his jacket for a notebook and pen, opened up on fresh page and started to write things down.

'Who do we know in Immigration these days?'

McLean had seen a slightly bewildered Billy McKenzie out of the station with a promise to look into things, then spent the best part of fifteen minutes searching the station for someone to whom he could delegate the task. Officers were thin on the ground, most preparing themselves for the afternoon's march and Operation Fundament, no doubt. He had finally tracked down Detective Constable Sandy Gregg in the empty major-incident room, cleared out and unused since the city centre truck crash in the summer.

'Immigration or Specialist Crime?' Gregg had been sitting at one of the tables, a mountain of papers and books spread around her, but she stood up swiftly at McLean's words.

'Specialist Crime, for preference. Need someone to look into something without going in heavy-handed. At least, not yet anyway.' He repeated Billy McKenzie's story, unsurprised to see the confusion spread across Gregg's face.

'Is this something we should be getting involved with, sir?

I mean, it all sounds a bit . . . I don't know . . . vague?'

'There's a child involved, so I can't let it go. McKenzie seemed on the level, but you could maybe check him out too.' McLean took out his notebook, opened it at the page where he'd scribbled down the scant details he'd managed to get from the man. McKenzie had been happy enough to give his full name, date of birth and address, which was one more reason to take him seriously. Gregg took up her notepad, flipped over pages of neatly written notes to a clean sheet and copied what she could.

'Not going to the march?' McLean nodded at the books spread over the table.

'Shift's over, actually. Thought I'd use the peace and quiet to get some studying in.'

'Sergeant's exam?' McLean picked up one of the books. 'I'd have thought you'd have no trouble with that.'

'Never been very good at tests, sir.' Gregg shrugged. 'I know all this stuff, but as soon as I have to write it down? Poof! It's gone.'

'You'll be fine. We could do with a few more half-competent sergeants, too. Going to miss having Grumpy Bob around when he goes.'

Gregg made a noise that might have been a cough, but sounded suspiciously like a laugh. 'Don't think I've ever seen him do a day's work in all the years I've been here, sir.'

'And yet, somehow the job gets done. There's not many times he's let me down. That's always been his skill.'

A short pause, and then Gregg waved her notepad. 'You want this looked into now?'

'Soonest would be best, but if you're off shift I'll find someone else.'

'No, you're OK. I'll pass it on to one of the Immigration team. Probably Dougie Naismith. He's reliable, if not the sharpest pencil in the box.'

McLean wasn't sure he knew who Dougie Naismith was, but he trusted Gregg to get the job done. 'Thanks. I owe you one.' He waved a hand at the table and the books. 'Good luck with that. Not that you need it.'

Gregg grimaced. 'Aye, well. We'll see.' She hesitated a moment, as if deciding whether to say something or not. Apparently settling on yes. 'You'd be better off going straight to DCI Dexter about this, mind.'

'Dexter? But she's Vice.'

'Aye, but that's where you'll find most of the illegals, right?' Gregg's scowl described eloquently how she felt about the situation. 'Either that or picking fruit and veg up in Fife.'

McLean couldn't deny she had a point, but raising it with Jo Dexter meant having to explain why he was interested, and since he wasn't entirely sure himself, that wasn't a conversation he wanted to have right now. It didn't help either that the last time they'd worked together on a case it had gone spectacularly badly.

'Just see what your man Naismith can come up with first, aye? Shouldn't be more than a couple of phone calls. Then we can see if it needs more serious attention.'

4

In theory it should have been a peaceful protest. A few thousand well-meaning people, Scots-born and incomers both, marching against the rising tide of intolerance that seemed to have gripped the world. It was a well-organised event, and the police had been planning how to manage it for months, working with the organisers to keep everything tidy. McLean was even sympathetic to the cause behind it all, although he knew better than to voice his feelings on the matter. He also knew that it was inevitable the very people the march was supposed to be against would try to infiltrate it, agitate and cause chaos.

Operation Fundament had been cobbled together between the Anti-terrorism task force, uniform and what was left of Edinburgh CID, which meant too many meetings, but also meant shared intelligence and a degree of preparedness he wasn't used to. McLean wasn't so naive as to not see the conflict of interest though. Uniform wanted a peaceful outcome, with everyone going home after a day in the cold walking down the Royal Mile to the parliament building and chanting slogans. Anti-terror wanted agitators to try something on, at least seriously enough for them to be able to arrest some people and shake them down for yet more intelligence. Being the majority of the plain-clothes bodies on the ground, his team was always going to be caught in the middle.

'Wasn't sure whether we'd see you or not, sir.' Detective Constable Janie Harrison had dressed for the weather. Her cheeks were rosy below a woolly hat pulled down to meet a chunky knitted scarf. Along with a red nose, they were about all of her exposed to the chill wind blowing in off the Forth

'So I understand. Some of you lot were even running a sweepstake.'

'Not me. That was Lofty's idea.'

McLean looked around the crowd gathering outside the castle gates. It didn't take long to see DC Blane, looming over the more normal-sized people. Over in the distance, a couple of organisers were handing out banners, and as soon as they were done the rally would start. Everyone would march down the Royal Mile to Holyrood, or dive into one of the many warm pubs along the way. Those that remained would listen to speeches, shout and applaud, and then go home. Quite what it was all supposed to achieve, he could only guess. A mention on the evening news perhaps, a few column inches in the papers hardly anyone read any more.

'Everyone here, then?' He glanced at his watch, trying to remember what time things were supposed to kick off. As if reading his mind, a nearby tannoy squawked into life and a high-pitched female voice started giving out instructions.

'Everyone's here, aye. You'll no see them, if they're doing their job right.' Harrison pulled one hand out of its thick skiing glove and poked around in her ear. McLean could just make out the wire for her earpiece, the connected Airwave set no doubt hidden underneath her padded coat. He didn't have a set himself, not having intended joining the march. Now he was here though it felt like a much better prospect than trudging back to the station and working through the stack of reports awaiting his signature.

'Mind if I join you then?'

16

Harrison merely shrugged, pulling her glove back on. McLean shoved his bare hands into the deep pockets of his overcoat, hunched his shoulders against the wind. The thin flecks of snow were getting thicker, which would probably weed out the less zealous of the demonstrators. He was about to mention it to the detective constable, but before he could speak the chanting began and the crowd started to move. The march had started. Operation Fundament was go.

It was never going to be a long march. The Royal Mile was, after all, just a mile long from the castle to Holyrood Palace. A few thousand people in a bunch necessarily move slowly, but downhill and with the weather closing in the pace soon picked up. Taller than DC Harrison, McLean was able to look over the crowd, spotting faces and keeping an eye out for any suspicious behaviour. Even so, it was she who spoke first.

'Think I see one of our boys there.' She tapped at her earpiece and muttered something into a microphone hidden away in her scarf as McLean looked off in the direction she had pointed. He saw DC Blane's looming form struggling through the crowd, and then a couple more plain-clothes officers converging on the same spot.

'Shit. There's at least a dozen of them and it looks like they've come for a fight.' Harrison must have heard something over her Airwave, as McLean couldn't see anything. She barked, 'On my way!' into her microphone, then pushed through the crowd. McLean followed her a couple of paces, and then she stopped.

'You wearing a stab vest under that, sir?' She nodded at his overcoat, not waiting for him to answer. 'Didn't think so. Best you stay out of the way. Divert people round us if it gets nasty, aye?'

He didn't have time to answer before she was away again, pushing through the marchers with polite but firm 'excuse me's and 'coming through's. Some of the protesters on the march had begun to notice something unusual happening, and as a body they began to drift towards the other side of the road. McLean found himself carried with them, away from what was beginning to look like a very one-sided fracas as a dozen or more plain-clothes and uniformed police officers descended on a group of angry young men. Trying to keep his eyes on them, he tripped on the pavement and almost fell into the tightening crowd. Shouts of alarm mingled with the chants, echoing off the tall stone buildings, and before he knew it, he was stumbling into a doorway a half-dozen steps down a narrow close leading off from the pavement.

Like much of the Old Town behind the tourist facade, the doorway had seen better days. Piled high with discarded rubbish, lightly silvered by the increasingly heavy snow, the stone steps were worn in the middle by the passage of centuries of feet. The door itself looked like it had only been painted once in those many hundreds of years, and that right at the start. Layers of festival posters peeled from it like eczema, covering over the old keyhole. There was no handle, but someone had fixed a hasp and padlock. Someone else had levered it open with a crowbar, splintering ancient wood in the process.

Looking back at the march, McLean could neither see nor hear Harrison and the other officers. Just a few feet and a couple of steps down from the marchers, he could have been invisible for all the attention they were paying him. He slipped one hand into his jacket pocket and fished out his phone, unsurprised to find it had virtually no signal. Well, it wouldn't be the first time he'd gone into a crime scene without backup, and by the look of the rubbish on the ground this door had been jimmied open a while ago.

It creaked reluctantly to his push, jamming slightly less than halfway. McLean paused, straining to hear whether there was anyone inside. Might as well try to hear a bird singing on a motorway embankment during rush hour. Stone steps carried on down into a basement room, pitch black save for an arc of light coming from the open door. It fell over broken furniture, a table on its side, chairs piled one atop another as if they'd been thrown there.

He switched on the torch function of his phone and played the meagre light over the rest of the room, surprised to see that it stretched back a good distance from the front of the building. Stepping down to the floor, McLean sniffed the air, taking in the scent of cold, damp stone, dust and something else. A sickly-sweet musk that had the hairs on the back of his neck standing upright.

'Anyone here?' He knew there wasn't, but said it all the same. No answer came back, and his words were swiftly swallowed up by the darkness. He swapped his phone light for a proper torch from his pocket, sweeping the more powerful beam over a room filled with discarded furniture. Most looked like it had been broken long ago, but the centre of the room showed signs of more recent activity. The table he had seen lying on its side had obviously been tipped that way, leaving a space where it had stood. Other items had been flung further towards the corners as if some giant had pushed its way through, flinging things aside as it searched for something.

Shards of broken pottery crunched under his feet as McLean trod a careful path through the mayhem. There was generations of rubbish piled up in here, as if people had begun discarding unwanted things into this basement from the moment the building above it had first been built. Hundreds of years of old boxes, broken pieces of furniture, ancient bicycles and piles of old clothes. There was even a large rag doll, leaning against the back wall as if it had been abandoned by a child grown too old for such things.

He approached it with caution, noting the heavy coat and long rag dress over what looked like woollen leggings. The doll's head had lolled forward, hair falling into its lap. It wore dark leather gloves, hands fallen to each side, palms up, and it gave off that sickly musk that he had noticed when he'd first entered. Damp rotting away at the sawdust and horsehair that no doubt filled its fabric body.

McLean played his torchlight back and forth over the scene, taking in more detail with each pass. Everything in here was old, forgotten, rimed with ages of dust and neglect. Why would someone break in, move furniture around as if searching for something? Perhaps there was an entirely innocent explanation. The owner had simply lost the key and jimmied open the door to fetch some long-forgotten piece of furniture. He wasn't convinced. If that had been the case, then they would have been more careful. There wouldn't have been broken china on the floor, and he'd have expected there to be more method to the search, more careful rearranging of the mess. This room had been cleared in a frenzy, a line from the door almost directly to the doll.

Which had no dust on it.

A cold sensation settled in his gut that had nothing to do with the freezing temperature. McLean carefully stepped closer, crouching down in front of the still figure. Close up, its hair was black and wiry, that same dark texture to its skull as its leather-gloved hands. Only, as he played the light on one of them, he saw that it wasn't a glove. The whorls and lines of fingerprints and the deeper creases of palm lines showed clearly. Not a glove, but a hand.

Not a doll, but a child.

5

She was dead, of that he had no doubt. She had probably been dead for many years, hidden away down here in the dark. McLean pulled out his phone to call it in, but there was no signal in the basement. Popping his torch in his mouth, he tried to take some photographs, all too aware that the forensic team were going to be pissed off with him for contaminating their crime scene. The camera on his phone wasn't very good, and, if he was being honest with himself, McLean had to admit he had only the barest understanding of how to use it. A couple of snaps were enough to show the exact position of the body as he had found it, but he knew he should leave now, secure the scene and call it in.

For long, silent minutes he simply crouched there, motionless. The wall against which the body leaned was made of rough sandstone blocks, much like most of this old part of the city, its crumbling lime mortar littering the floor in powdery heaps. Some of it had fallen into the girl's hair, and a few bits sat on her shoulders like dandruff, but nothing like as much as lay on the ground, and on the old pieces of furniture piled around her. Quite apart from the very fact of there being a dead body lying here, there was something wrong about the scene. Her physical condition suggested she'd been here a long time and only recently uncovered, but other little clues made him suspicious of leaping to that conclusion.

There was too little light to see anything clearly, so McLean stood back up again, joints creaking in protest, and played the torch over the room once more. There were no windows, and no obvious sign of an exit other than the door through which he had entered. He backed up, retracing his steps as best he could.

Outside, the snow had begun to fall in big chunks, and most of the march was gone. Just a few stragglers following on. A police transit van had parked on the far side of the road, its blue light flashing slowly. Its rear doors open, a couple of uniformed officers pushed miserable-looking protesters inside. McLean checked his phone as he climbed the stone steps back to street level, hoping for enough of a signal to call it in.

'There you are, sir. Wondered where you'd got to.' Detective Constable Harrison trotted over the road towards him, her ruddy face beaming, eyes wide with excitement or adrenaline, or both. Her breath misted in the chill air, and she'd lost her woolly hat. 'That was a bit of a barney, I have to say. Wee shites tried to put up a fight. Guess they didn't see Lofty coming. Still, nobody hurt, and the anti-terror boys'll be well chuffed.'

'Good to hear it. You got your Airwave on you?'

There must have been something about his expression, as her smile ebbed away, taking her enthusiasm with it. She shoved a hand into her coat pocket and pulled out the chunky receiver. 'Aye, sir. Something up?'

McLean recalled the scene just a few feet behind him, shivering as much at the horror of it as the deepening cold. 'Back there.' He hooked a thumb over his shoulder towards the door. 'I've a nasty feeling life's about to get complicated.'

'You sure this is the route you took to the body, Inspector?'

Not for the first time in the past hour, McLean regretted ever having come out to join the march. If he'd stayed back at the station and just got on with the paperwork like he was supposed to, he wouldn't be trying hard not to shake with the cold that had seeped deep into his bones. Heavy boots and overcoat or no, the basement room was somehow even colder than the snow-filled street outside. Even the hastily erected arc lights hadn't managed to lift the temperature, or the gloom. The air directly in front of them steamed, but everywhere else was as cold as the grave.

'I can show you exactly where I went if it helps. Of course, that'll mean going there again.'

'Best if you just point it out, aye?'

Standing a couple of feet inside the now fully opened door, McLean tried his best to show the white-suited crime scene manager where he'd been in the room. A team of busy forensic technicians had laid out a pathway to the body that was more or less exactly the route he had taken. At the end of it, two more white-suited figures crouched low, heads close together in conversation. After a moment, they both stood up, one more quickly than the other, and trod a careful route back to where he stood.

'You do find me the most interesting cases, Tony.' Angus Cadwallader, city pathologist, pulled back the elasticated hood from his overalls and scrubbed at his thinning hair with a still-gloved hand. Beside him, his assistant, Tracy Sharp, raised a critical eyebrow.

'Your glove, Angus.'

'Eh?' The pathologist frowned, then looked at his hands. 'Oh, aye. Right.'

He snapped off the gloves, handing them over while McLean looked on and tried not to laugh. He'd known Cadwallader almost all his life, knew the open secret that was the pathologist's relationship with his assistant. Despite the difference in their ages, Tracy and Angus made a good couple. He needed someone to look after him, and she enjoyed a challenge.

'What's the story then, Angus? You reckon you can give me a time of death?'

Cadwallader cocked his head to one side, shrugging his shoulders. 'You always ask, Tony. I'll get you something more accurate once I've had a chance to look at her in the mortuary, but I'd say some time around 1995. Maybe a bit earlier.'

'Nineteen . . .' McLean's brain was processing the number as a time of day, thinking somewhere around seven the previous evening. Then he caught up with the pathologist's words. 'Ninety-five? You mean she's been there, what? Years?'

'She's been somewhere that long. Can't say without a doubt that's where she died, although from the way she's sitting it feels likely. Otherwise someone's gone to a lot of trouble to pose her. That's not a position you'd end up in just being dumped.'

McLean recalled the scene as he'd found it, the small amount of mortar on the body compared to its surroundings. Could someone really have thrown all the furniture aside just to carefully place a decades-old body there for him to find? It seemed unlikely, but then stranger things had happened to him in the past.

'How can she be like that? Down here?'

'Your guess is as good as mine. She's mummified, I can say that much. Her skin's like leather, hair's brittle. It's like I said, you always bring me the most interesting cases. I doubt this lot will find anything interesting in here though.' He nodded in the direction of a forensic technician as she stepped past carrying a large aluminium case.

'Are you . . .' McLean was about to say 'sure', but he stopped himself, shaking the word away. Angus was the most qualified and experienced pathologist in the city, and, while everyone got it wrong once in a while, there was no good reason to doubt his initial assessment. Except that it didn't feel right. There was no way that this room could have been unvisited in decades. The door had been forced recently, for one thing. And there was still the matter of the furniture seemingly cast to the corners, clearing a direct path to the body.

'We'll get a better look at her on Monday morning.' Cadwallader patted McLean on the arm. 'No point worrying about it just now. She's been dead a while. I'd stake my reputation on it.'

McLean watched the pathologist and his assistant leave, then took another look around the room, trying to fix it in his memory even though the popping flash of the crime scene photographer meant there'd be plenty of images. With the door wide open and the arc lights bright, he could see much more of what was clearly a storeroom where old and broken furniture went to die. Some of it had been stacked neatly, old chairs piled in a corner, tables neatly squared away. But whoever had last been in here had just thrown stuff from the doorway, or at least that was what it looked like.

He ignored the intake of breath and quiet tut from one of the forensic technicians as he stepped away from the door and went to examine the table he had seen lying on its side when he had first entered. Thick planks made up the top, warped and cracked. Woodworm holes covered the legs, crazing the surface with tiny exposed tunnels. Dust covered most of it, and the timber had darkened with age, except for a long split in one of the planks. Fresh new wood showed up against the old surface.

Once he'd seen that, other signs started to show. Some of the chairs jumbled in the corner had fresh scratches on them, and the floorboards were scuffed, dust rubbed away by something that didn't look like feet. Bending down to look closer, McLean spotted something lying on the ground under a chair that had escaped destruction. He looked around, seeing the white-suited photographer close by.

'Over here, can you?'

The photographer shuffled over, her overalls clearly not fitting well. 'Aye?'

'Under there. See? Can you take some photos before I fetch it out?'

'What is it?'

'I don't know, but I'm not going to move it until it's been recorded, am I?'

'Probably shouldn't move it at all. I'll get one of the techs to bag it.' The photographer rattled off a dozen or more pictures in quick succession, detailing the area, then shouted over. McLean stood up, retreated back to his spot by the door and let them get on with it. He should have just left them to process the scene, but some deep sense of disquiet kept him there. As if he knew deep down that something was going to happen and he needed to see it for himself.

'Here you go, sir. Good shout that. We'd maybe not have found that for a while, what with all the action happening back there.' The crime scene photographer handed McLean a clear plastic evidence bag as she nodded in the direction of the far wall, where they were getting ready to remove the body. 'I'd better go and get that.'

McLean watched her tread carefully along the marked route, camera at the ready, then turned his attention back to the bag. Holding it up to the light, he saw something that at first looked like it might have been a dead rat. For a moment he wondered if that was all it was, and when he was going to get shouted at by the technician for wasting their time. Then what he'd thought was fur resolved itself into something synthetic. The dark colour was smudged here and there, showing lighter fabric underneath a layer of dirt. It had whiskers and a short, stumpy tail, true enough. But the eyes were beady because they were made of beads. Not a rat, nor a mouse, but some handmade stuffed animal of indeterminate variety. A child's toy.

6

McLean wondered whether he was ever going to feel warm again. He'd left the basement room as soon as they'd carted the girl's body off to the mortuary. It wasn't far back to the station, so he'd walked, thinking the exercise might shift some of the cold from his bones. Instead, the snow had returned with a vengeance, borne on a wind that cut right through him, so that by the time he reached the back door and had been buzzed in, all he could think about was the canteen and a hot mug of coffee. He was on his second, and considering another slice of cake, when DC Harrison found him.

'Heard you were back, sir. Any news?'

'Post-mortem some time on Monday. Angus reckons the body's been there a while. Probably one for Dagwood and the Cold Case Unit, but we can get the preliminaries in place. Find out who owns the building and bring them in for interview. We need to know when that basement was last checked, that sort of thing. Might be some CCTV footage of the area, but without a timeframe it's hard to know what to look for.'

Harrison hadn't sat down, McLean noticed, and she was doing that fidgeting thing with her hands that meant she wanted something.

'How are you getting on with the hoodlums?' he asked.

'Got them all processed, just about. Public-order offences, carrying weapons, that sort of thing. We'll get a couple for assaulting police officers, too. And resisting arrest. The anti-terror unit want to start interviewing as soon as possible.'

McLean cupped his hands around the mug, leaching the last of the warmth out of it. He was still cold, but he couldn't hide down in the canteen for ever. He drained the last of the tepid liquid, grimacing at the bitterness, and struggled to his feet. 'OK. Let's go and see who these knuckle-draggers are.'

'Your listed address is in Manchester. What brings you to Edinburgh, Mr Seaton?'

McLean stood in the observation booth, looking through the one-way glass at interview room three, where a Mr Matthew Seaton was being interviewed by Detective Sergeant Peterson from the Anti-terrorism Unit. He hadn't met many right-wing activists, but the thing that struck him most about Seaton was how ordinary he looked. Take a walk down Princes Street on an average day and you'd see a thousand men just like him. He wore clothes that were normal, didn't have any visible tattoos, sported hair not much longer than McLean's own, and was clean-shaven. He fitted none of the stereotypes. And yet when they'd arrested him, he'd fought and screamed like an animal by all accounts. A couple of hours in a cell had calmed him down, but it explained his rather unkempt appearance, the bloodshot eye and angry graze on one cheek.

'My client does not wish to answer that question at this time.'

It was a familiar refrain. Sitting beside Seaton, his dark-suited lawyer fitted all of the stereotypes associated with that profession. He'd appeared not long after the last of the detained men had been processed, which suggested to McLean that they'd not got all of them. Thin-faced, pale as a vampire and

28

with Bela Lugosi slicked-back hair, he wore a suit which must have cost more than Seaton earned in a month. Maybe even a year.

'You attended the march down the Royal Mile this afternoon. Are you a keen supporter of immigrant rights, then?' DS Peterson didn't even attempt to keep the sarcasm from his voice, but Seaton didn't rise to the bait.

'I only ask because we have a list here of members of a neo-Nazi organisation, the Sons of Enoch. Would that be a reference to the biblical prophet? Only you don't look the religious type to me.'

Seaton opened his mouth to say something, but his lawyer placed a hand lightly on his arm, silencing him with frustrating effectiveness.

'Sons of Enoch isn't a banned organisation, Detective Sergeant.' The lawyer's voice was as thin and pale as the man himself, a whiny mixture of nasal and sibilant that must have been popular at school.

'No, it's not. But it's associated with several organisations that are. And this isn't the first time you've been in trouble with the police, is it, Mr Seaton?' Peterson fiddled with the sheaf of papers in front of him, not really consulting them, McLean could see. 'Seems you have quite a habit of turning up at peaceful marches and causing trouble.'

'My client denies your allegations. He is nothing but an innocent bystander caught up in a police sting operation.'

'Aye, I thought you might say that. It won't stand though. We've all the evidence we need for a conviction, and given your record you'll be serving a stretch inside. Quite a long one if I have anything to do with it.'

McLean was watching Seaton rather than the detective sergeant, so caught the flicker of anger that tightened his eyes, the swift sideways glance at his lawyer. 'Might want to get someone in there,' he said to Harrison. 'Reckon it's all about to kick off.'

Harrison opened her mouth to speak at the same time as Seaton lunged at DS Peterson. His face had turned bright red, a snarl ripping from his mouth and leaving trails of spittle behind. The lawyer fell off his chair in his haste to get out of the way, crashing to the floor with all the dignity of a dead bat. Peterson dodged Seaton's badly thrown punch, grabbed the man's arm and had him face down on the table in seconds. The young detective constable with him piled in just as swiftly, and in a few moments Seaton was being bundled out of the interview room by three large uniformed officers.

'We'll just add assaulting a police officer to the list, shall we?' Peterson said as the lawyer struggled to his feet. 'He'll be up in front of the sheriff on Monday, but I think we'll be keeping him here until then.'

McLean flagged down DS Peterson as he was leaving the interview room a couple of minutes later.

'Nicely done,' he said. 'There weren't many signs he was going to explode like that.'

'I thought at least one of them would lose the rag, sir. Hoped one would. All the rest were quite quiet by comparison.'

'You get anything useful from them?'

'Only confirmation of what we already knew. Same old faces turning up over and over again. It all helps to build the bigger picture. At least we know who's talking to who. And after that little outburst there, Mr Seaton's not going to slip away from us, no matter what his solicitor might say.'

'Don't think I've had the pleasure of his acquaintance before. Shifty fellow. Looked expensive.'

'Oh aye, Kennedy Smythe. He's a right slippery wee bugger and no mistake. And not cheap, no.'

McLean looked up and down the corridor, half expecting the

lawyer to still be hanging around like the bad smell that he was. 'You know him?'

'We've crossed paths before, aye. Made a name for himself over on the west coast, getting gangsters off the hook on technicalities. He's a partner at MacFarlane and Dodds.'

McLean recognised the name of the firm, recalled a case a couple of years back where he'd encountered one of their junior partners. That hadn't gone well for anyone involved. 'I thought they were corporate law, not criminal.'

'They're that big I reckon they've departments covering everything under the sun. Smythe's a pain in the arse. Sharp as they come. I'll give you good odds he'll get them all bailed and away before the sheriff's even sat down.'

'All of them?' McLean nodded his head towards the still-open door to the interview room.

'Aye, well. Young Mr Seaton's done us a wee bit of a favour there. Attempted assault on a police officer. Plenty witnesses, and we've got it all on tape too? No, I think he'll be kicking his heels in Saughton until his time comes round to see the judge. That's something Kennedy Smythe's no' going to be happy about.' DS Peterson didn't look like he was too bothered about the lawyer's state of mind.

'You know what he does for a living?' McLean asked. 'Seaton, I mean.'

'File says he's a security systems expert. Fits alarms to office blocks and stuff like that.'

'Not his own business though, I take it?'

Peterson consulted the sheaf of papers he'd brought for the interview. 'He's self-employed, apparently. Sole trader. But it's all contract work as far as I know.'

'Pays well, then, the security business. If he can afford a sharp suit like your man Smythe there.'

'Aye, I thought that too. Smythe's representing all of them, and he's not known for working pro bono. He turned up pretty sharpish, too. It's not like we had to bother the duty solicitor or anything.'

'Too much to hope we can find out who's footing the bill, I suppose.'

Peterson shrugged. 'We could ask, but I'd not hold out any great hopes.'

'Maybe not right now. But give him a couple of weeks in prison and he might be a bit more forthcoming, aye?'

Peterson tried to suppress the smirk, hiding it with a wipe of the hand across his mouth. 'That's kind of what I was hoping, sir. Just need to make sure he gets the right cellmate when he arrives at Saughton.'

'I'm sure I don't know what you mean, Sergeant.' McLean hid his own smile with a nod of the head. 'Keep me up to speed on any developments, OK?'

7

The ceiling lights flickered as McLean clumped down the stone steps into the basement, as if the ghosts of villains past were haunting him. The station had been built on top of a much earlier building, retaining the Victorian stonework below street level. Most of the old cells weren't considered fit for incarcerating felons any more, and had instead been pressed into service as stores. The evidence lockers were down here, and so too was the Cold Case Unit. He often wondered whether it had been put there in the hope that nobody would want to work in it for more than a couple of months, but if that was the case then they hadn't reckoned with the sheer bloody-mindedness and thrawn of ex-Detective Superintendent Charles Duguid.

'Anybody home?' McLean asked as he stuck his head in through the open door. At least the CCU room was large, and the arched ceiling was too high in the middle for him to reach with an outstretched arm. The only natural light came from two narrow wells in the stonework that pointed up towards the car park at the rear of the building. They hardly worked in the height of summer; winter left the room in a state of perpetual gloom.

'Thought I might be seeing you down here soon enough.'

McLean turned to see a figure emerging out of the shadows.

Clutching a heavy archive folder in one hand, Duguid threaded his way through the empty desks.

'You heard about the dead girl?' McLean knew that the station gossip travelled fast, but it was only a couple of hours since Cadwallader had told him he thought the body had been around for a while.

'Word is she was mummified. Might have been there twenty years or more. Sounds like a cold case to me.' Duguid shuffled around and sat down at his own desk, pulling the anglepoise lamp closer and placing a pair of spectacles on the end of his nose. In his tweed suit he looked more like a teacher than a detective.

'Aye, well. Post-mortem's Monday, so we'll know better what we're dealing with then. Meantime I've got DC Harrison chasing up the details on the building. Hard to believe a basement room off the Royal Mile hasn't been used in all that time.'

'You'd be surprised.' Duguid took his spectacles off again, the folder on his desk still unopened. 'Look at this place, after all. Some of the old cells in the lower basement probably haven't been opened in a decade, and this is a working police station. Stuff gets shoved away and forgotten. People get old and die. You know how it goes.'

McLean remained unconvinced. 'Well, I'll get Harrison to work with Grumpy Bob on it anyway. He's down here more than not these days, but if it does turn out to be something else, he's not retired just yet.'

Duguid opened the folder, pulled out the top sheet of paper and peered at it myopically. Then he grabbed his spectacles again, shoved them on and frowned. 'That all you came to tell me about?'

'Pretty much. Actually I was just going to leave a note. Didn't think you'd be in at the weekend. Certainly not this late.'

'Mrs Duguid has her bridge club tonight. I prefer to stay away. What's your excuse?'

From anyone else, the question might have been innocent, just a simple retort. McLean knew the ex-detective superintendent better than that. He knew himself better too. With the Anti-terrorism Unit looking after the men they'd arrested on the march, and all the tasks relating to the dead girl delegated to reliable junior officers, there was no reason for him to be still here. He should have gone home an hour ago, possibly more. He glanced at his watch, knowing that the later he left it the worse it would be.

'You're right. I'll be off then. We'll keep you in the loop on the dead girl investigation. Might appreciate your insight.'

Duguid made a noise halfway between a grunt and a growl, shoved his spectacles up his nose and started reading. McLean knew a dismissal when he saw one. There was no getting away from it, he was going to have to go home.

Snow made the drive across town tricky, and not just because a multi-car accident meant he had to take a different route to normal. McLean could remember a time when every winter brought snow, when the icy cold air fell on the city from the Pentland Hills to the south, chilling him through as he built lonely snowmen in the garden of his gran's house. Childhood memories were not the best to rely on though, and he knew those deep winters had been few and far between. More recently the mild, wet weather had stretched on through spring and into summer as climate change wreaked its predictable havoc, but the past two years had seen something of a return to the seasons he remembered. It was hard to view the white chunks tumbling from the sky and smearing themselves against his windscreen with the same naive wonder he had as a child.

All these thoughts and more occupied the rest of the slow journey through a city turned into a hellish orange-white landscape. At least the heating worked in his Alfa, and he'd even remembered the little dial that toned down the performance to make it easier to drive in the conditions. As he pulled up the drive and parked outside the back door, the snow began to fall in fat chunks, filling in the rectangular patch of clear gravel where a car had been parked until recently. So she'd gone again. He couldn't really blame her.

The hot engine pinked and clicked as it cooled. McLean sat there, hands still on the wheel, motionless as he stared through the windscreen at nothing. At everything. The months since Emma's miscarriage had been cruel. He'd tried to reach out to her and been rebuffed, tried to support her as she threw herself into work even though he knew well enough she was using it as a distraction. An excuse not to talk about what had happened. It was what he did, after all. Easier to keep moving than sit still and let the grief catch up with you.

The thought spurred him into action. He unclipped his seatbelt and climbed out of the car, hurrying to the back door as the snow fell ever thicker. A last glance back showed the space where Emma's car had been was almost covered now. McLean shook his head. Not an omen. He had no time for such things.

'Just you and me then.' Mrs McCutcheon's cat eyed him with feline disdain as he entered the kitchen. At least Emma had left the lights on for him this time. No note, though. McLean stared at the magnets on the fridge door for a while, then opened it and peered inside. Last night's takeaway curry was about the most tempting thing in there. He pulled out a beer and popped the top off, considered drinking from the bottle and then fetched a glass instead.

He sat and leafed through the various reports and other useless paperwork he'd brought home while the microwave went about reheating his meal. It wasn't perhaps the most exciting way to spend an evening, but at least the kitchen had the benefit of no distractions. Not for the first time, McLean regretted giving in to Deputy Chief Constable Stevie Robinson's insistence on promotion back in the summer. Detective inspector was a level of responsibility he didn't exactly feel comfortable with, detective chief inspector even less so. There was never time to concentrate on anything properly. Too much chasing targets, squaring budgets, going to endless meetings about performance where none of the others present could see the irony of them wasting so much time not doing the job. He began to understand now why Duguid had been such a crabbit bastard in the years until he retired. Maybe that was why the ex-detective superintendent was being nice to him now.

The ping of the microwave interrupted his musing. McLean struggled to his feet and crossed the kitchen, surprised to find it still whirring away, the countdown minutes yet to go. His confusion was cut short by a second ping, this time from underneath the report on resource efficiency monitoring that he'd not been reading. Picking it up, he saw the screen of his phone lit, a text displayed. It disappeared before he could read it, but he knew it wouldn't be important. Just Emma telling him not to wait up for her. Again. He dropped the phone back down on the table as the microwave pinged for real. Food was more important right now. He'd get everything ready for Monday and then he'd worry about whether or not he still had a relationship to salvage.

A freezing fog hangs thick in the midnight air, making dull orange circles of the street lamps and swallowing the winter trees whole. It muffles all sound, a silence so total it seems as if the city has simply stopped. All is still, not a car moving, not a person to be seen.

Billows swirl and eddy on hidden currents, thickening and thinning as the frozen air churns. Monsters form in the mist, fight each other and are absorbed again unseen. For a moment, soft headlights pierce the darkness, form a perfect tunnel bound by white like ectoplasm in a Victorian medium's parlour. And then the low thrum of diesel engines shudders into hearing as, one by one, the trucks trundle through.

The city never truly sleeps any more, but this one night there is nobody out to witness as the convoy slows, pulls off the glistening, icy tarmac and onto the snow-crusted grass. Insect-like, they circle. Headlight eyes struggle to pierce the fog, and yet without any sign of direction they find their allotted spaces. The chutter of engines dies in steps, each massive rig shuddering into silence. And as the lights wink out, so the fog reclaims the meadow, the barest outline of monoliths in the swirling, swallowing white.

Soft noises float through the air, the clink of hammer on iron, thwap of canvas unrolled, rip of rope pulled taut. Occasional voices mutter and moan, the odd curse thrown out to the weather gods or the wind or the cold. And, all around, the city rumbles on, unaware of what is unfolding at its heart.

8

McLean yawned and rubbed at his face, felt a roughness under his fingers where he'd missed a bit shaving that morning. It was always the same; Sunday off pretending to relax had left him sluggish and unfocused. He'd spent most of the day trying to find a way to talk to Emma that didn't sound either needy or patronising. In the end his suggestion they maybe go out for a meal had met with a noncommittal shrug, and now he felt bad for not pushing the point. They'd eaten separately again, her perched on the sofa in front of the television with a healthy salad, him in the kitchen with Mrs McCutcheon's cat and cold leftover pizza he couldn't remember ordering.

'Rough night, Tony? Thought you had the day off yesterday.'

He looked up to see the smiling face of Detective Superintendent Jayne McIntyre. She stood in the open doorway to his office, clutching a heavy folder under one arm.

'Eh? Oh. Not really. Just can't seem to get my head in the game today.'

'Too much paperwork and not enough street time?' McIntyre stepped into the room, and for a horrible moment McLean thought she had brought him yet more to wade through. She kept hold of the folder though, slumping into one of the armchairs at the far side of the office that wasn't nearly as comfortable as it looked.

'Too many distractions and not enough getting on with the job.' McLean looked at his watch. 'Still, Angus is going to be doing the post-mortem on that wee girl soon. That's my reward for dealing with all this.' He picked up one of several reports lying open in front of him.

'Thought you'd given that case to Grumpy Bob to follow up. Seeing as it's likely to be the CCU who take it on anyway.'

'You know what Bob's like with post-mortems, Jayne. And this one feels kind of personal, given that I was the one who found her.'

McIntyre leaned forward in her chair, folder on her lap, arms crossed. 'About that. How was it you came to be in that building anyway? What were you doing in the close? You were meant to be here overseeing Operation Fundament, weren't you?'

'Thought I'd get a bit of street time like you suggested.' McLean told the superintendent about his last-minute decision to join the marchers, leaving out the bit where Grumpy Bob won the bet that he would. ' You're right though. It looks like it might well be one for the Cold Case Unit, and Bob's working there more than with CID these days. Easing himself into the position in time for his retirement, I guess.'

'Another experienced officer we can't really afford to lose.' McIntyre drummed her fingers against the folder for a few moments before getting to the point she'd clearly come to make in the first place. 'So you don't think this wee girl's going to be a problem then? I mean, it's tragic, for sure. And we'll have to investigate it as thoroughly as we can. But if she's been dead a long time . . .'

McLean closed the folder he'd not been giving his full attention to even before the detective superintendent had come in. 'I know. Budgets are tight and we can't afford to waste too much time chasing down a decades-old crime. Best-case scenario nobody knew she was in there, and she died of something natural. Let's wait until Angus has a few more answers for us though, aye?'

'It's an interesting case. Not often I see a body so well preserved. Things left in basements in this city tend to rot, not cure.'

McLean stood in the examination theatre, a few paces back from the stainless-steel table where Angus Cadwallader carried out his grim task. He'd long since lost count of the number of times he'd been in this position, but he could count on the fingers of one hand the times the subject of the examination had been this young. The girl's body seemed even smaller and frailer for having been stripped, the table too big for her.

'Preserved?'

'Well, I can't think of any other way to describe it. Her skin's like leather. Dried-out leather. She must have been treated with something after death, but damned if I can tell you what. I'll take a sample and send it off for analysis, of course.'

'Any indication of how she died?'

'Patience, Tony. I'm getting there.' Cadwallader bent close to the cadaver, sensitive fingers running over the dead girl's skin. He picked up her hands, one at a time, turning them this way and that as he inspected her fingers under the powerful overhead lights. McLean had watched his friend perform this ritual many times, but he couldn't remember ever having seen him take quite so much care, quite so much time.

'Hmm. That is interesting. Can't think how I missed that before.'

McLean took a step closer, getting a full view of the young girl's face for the first time. He could see what Cadwallader meant about her skin. It had a leathery quality, but apart from her hands, neck and face was like old beeswax. Not the pasty white of native Scots; there was more yellow to the tone than that. Except where she had been exposed to the air of the basement where they had found her. There her skin was the colour of day-old milky coffee, stained darker here and there with blotches like liver spots.

'A scalpel please, Tracy.' Cadwallader had reached the girl's head. Doctor Sharp placed a scalpel in his outstretched palm, and McLean stepped back before he had to witness any cutting. He was comfortable enough with being here, liked to discuss any important findings as soon as they were discovered, but he felt no need to witness the innermost secrets of the dead being revealed.

'Ah. Right. No.' Cadwallader placed the scalpel down on the stainless-steel tray his assistant held out for him, and took an uncharacteristic step back from the body.

'Is there something wrong, Angus?' McLean could tell without asking that there was.

'I'm afraid so. Very wrong. Very wrong indeed.'

'How so?'

'I thought this poor wee thing had died years ago. Examining her at the scene, everything pointed to that.'

McLean knew a 'but' when he heard one, and this came with an all-too-familiar twist of cold in his gut that had nothing to do with the snow outside and the artificial chill of the mortuary.

'It's the eyes that give it away.' Cadwallader took a step back towards the examination table, then stopped. 'Her lids were closed, dried up like the rest of her skin. I must be getting careless in my old age, but I just assumed . . .' He tailed off, waving a hand at the body. McLean leaned forward until he could see what the pathologist was indicating, then wished he hadn't. The girl's face was still blotchy and leathery, but a neat scalpel incision had lifted one eyelid to reveal a staring eye beneath. Not shrivelled with age and white with cataracts, but clear and shiny and round.

'I'll need to open her up.' Cadwallader made it sound like the most terrible thing in the world, which in a way it truly was. 'But I don't think she died years ago at all. I don't know how, Tony, but I think this girl's been dead no more than a few days.'

'Sorry to bother you, sir, but there's something I think you need to see.'

McLean had barely stepped through the door to the station before being accosted by DC Harrison. Her face was red with exertion, her words breathless as if she'd run all the way from the CID room. Clearly whatever it was she had to say was important, but so was the revelation from the post-mortem on the dead girl.

'I have to find McIntyre first. Do you know where she is?'

'Umm. I think she was going over to Gartcosh for a liaison meeting with the Serious and Organised Crime Unit, sir.'

McLean had been striding towards the stairs, but he stopped so suddenly Harrison took two steps past him before stopping herself. He'd forgotten McIntyre mentioning the meeting when they'd spoken earlier. He'd also forgotten that as a DCI he was well within his rights to direct the investigation into the young girl's death. He didn't need anyone's permission to set things in motion.

'OK. I need you to find DC Gregg, Grumpy Bob and DI Ritchie if she's about. We'll need to set up an incident room.' There were so many unanswered questions, it was hard to know where to start. The more he thought about it, the more each question posed another dozen.

'Incident? Is this still about the dead girl, sir? Only . . . ?' Harrison held up her hand, clutching a clear plastic evidence bag. McLean stared at it, unable to make out anything other than black.

'What is it?'

'It's the dead girl's dress, sir.' Harrison turned the bag over, and McLean could just about see pleating in the dark material.

The reflection of the overhead lights in the plastic bag didn't help.

'Go on,' he said. Harrison wouldn't have brought this to his attention if it hadn't been important and relevant.

'I've not opened it, but I couldn't help noticing the label, see?' She pointed at a white tag poking out of a fold. It bore a logo that meant nothing to him. 'My wee niece is mad about these clothes. They're cheap, right, but dead trendy.'

'And this dress is from a recent collection. This year's style, am I right?'

McLean felt a little bad for stealing Harrison's thunder. She'd done a smart piece of detective work, after all. It was worth it for the look of disbelief on her face.

'How'd you . . . ? How could you possibly . . . ?'

'Really, Constable, I'm not that old.' McLean almost smiled, then remembered whose dress this was. 'That's why I wanted to see McIntyre, why we need to get an incident room up and running. This might have been a cold case an hour ago, but it's just got a lot hotter.'

9

The buzz was addictive. This was what he'd been missing. They'd taken over one of the smaller incident rooms, clearing out the detritus of the last investigation and setting up to do it all over again. McLean watched as a team of detectives began bringing together all the information they had so far on the dead girl. It was depressingly little – they didn't even know her name yet. Forensics had been sent back for a second look at the basement room where she had been found, but there wouldn't even be an interim report for hours yet.

The lack of anyone else meant taking on the senior investigating officer role himself. Technically he could have handed it over to a detective inspector, or even one of the senior detective sergeants. No doubt when she got back from her strategy meeting at the Crime Campus over in Gartcosh, Detective Superintendent McIntyre would tell him to do exactly that, go back to his office and start shuffling the budgets to pay for this new case. She wasn't here, though, so for now McLean was going to do it his way. Which was why every plain-clothes and uniformed officer he'd been able to rustle up at short notice was now packed into a room really too small for them all, awaiting instruction and hoping for overtime.

'OK. Can I have your attention, please?' he shouted above the hubbub, and the room fell swiftly silent. That was a first.

'Right. As you know, we discovered the remains of a young girl in a basement on Saturday afternoon. The door had been forced, but early forensic examination suggested the body had been there some considerable time. Years rather than days. The plan was to hand it over to the Cold Case Unit once the initial examination had been carried out.'

'Is it true something sucked the life out of her like a vampire?'

McLean couldn't see who had spoken, but the voice was male. He glanced briefly at DC Gregg, hoping she might be able to identify the perpetrator. Her minimal shake of the head suggested she had no idea.

'If anyone has any evidence of vampire activity in the city, please bring it to my attention after this briefing.' He waited for the uncertain laughter to die away. 'In the meantime, I can confirm that as of the post-mortem examination on the body this morning, we're treating this as a murder and a recent one at that.'

A murmur began to swell in the room as officers reacted to this information. They must have known already, hence the vampire comment. No bigger gossip than a policeman, either. Still, this was confirmation for some that there'd be plenty of work to go around. McLean glanced over the heads of the nearest constables, looking for someone a bit more senior. Detective Inspector Kirsty Ritchie picked the wrong moment to enter the room.

'DI Ritchie will be coordinating house-to-house enquiries,' McLean said, earning himself an angry scowl. Fair enough, he should probably have briefed her before this meeting. 'DS Laird will be leading the team trying to identify the victim. Somebody's got to have noticed this young girl's missing. DC Gregg will tell you which team you're allocated to, and I shouldn't need to remind you that this is not for discussion with any of your friends in the press, OK?'

'Is there a scheduled press conference, sir?' DC Harrison asked as the meeting disbanded and the assembled officers went to find out what they were meant to be doing. It was a fair enough question, and McLean had no doubt the story would be out soon enough. Given that more than twenty-four hours had passed since they'd discovered the body, he was surprised it hadn't already, but then most of the news cycle over the weekend had been taken up with the march and the counter-protest.

'We'll have to put something together for later today. Let's get the scene processed and see if we can't find out who the girl is first.'

'Thanks for dropping me in the deep end there, Tony.' Ritchie pushed her way through the throng to join them.

'Sorry about that, Kirsty. I wasn't sure if you were back in town until you came through the door. Grumpy Bob not brought you up to speed?'

'Last I heard it was a cold case. How did it suddenly become a murder enquiry? Do we know how she died?'

'Angus is working on that. It's not a natural death, for sure.' McLean saw the image of the girl laid out on the mortuary examination table, her skin preserved as if she were some modern-day mummy prepared for an eternity in the afterlife. 'All we know is there's no match with local missing persons so far. Bob's going to spread that net a little further, and we might get a ping from the DNA database if we're lucky. Meantime I want you to canvass the locals. Someone must have seen something, heard something.'

Ritchie turned slowly, looking over the assembled officers and support staff. Lined up and attentive, it had seemed a reasonable number, but now they'd dispersed a bit the shortage of manpower was all too evident. 'This all the bodies we can get? Going to be stretched a bit.'

'You know how it is. There's never enough people to do the

job properly. I'll see what Jayne says when she gets back from Gartcosh. Maybe we can steal a few more from uniform to help out.'

'I can help with the door-to-door, ma'am,' Harrison said, sounding a bit too eager even to herself if her blush was anything to go by.

Ritchie raised a non-existent eyebrow. 'Ma'am? What am I, your teacher now?'

'Be nice, Kirsty. You used to call me sir, remember?' McLean turned to the young detective constable. 'You find out who owns that basement, Harrison?'

'Er. Not yet, sir. I made a couple of calls, but we handed everything over to the Cold Case Unit.'

McLean suppressed a sigh. The first twenty-four hours were the most crucial in any murder investigation, and they were already up.

'Never mind. You can come with me. We'll do it the old-fashioned way.'

The weekend's snow clung to the pavements, waiting patiently for more to come and join it. McLean trod carefully as he walked from the station back to the Canongate and the tiny close he'd stumbled into. Approaching it from downhill this time, he realised with a start that it was only a few yards away from the antiquarian bookshop where Donald Anderson had plied his gruesome trade so many years ago. It wasn't as if he'd consciously avoided this part of town, and yet somehow he'd failed to notice that the shop had been redeveloped and was now a café.

'Is there a problem, sir?'

DC Harrison's question woke McLean from his stupor. He'd stopped walking, staring at the clear glass and the happy customers inside. Did they know what had happened here? Just below their feet?

'No. Nothing.' He shook his head. Chances were they had no idea. Harrison probably didn't know either. How old would she have been when it happened, after all? That was what time did, erased the horror. Except for those who had witnessed it first-hand, of course.

Without the hordes of marching protestors, it was easier to get a sense of the layout of the crime scene. The close down which the crowds had pushed him was little more than a narrow passage, ending abruptly about twenty yards back from the street. A uniformed constable stood on guard at the entrance, keeping the public away as a procession of white-suited forensic technicians trooped in and out. Was Emma one of them? McLean couldn't see any features behind the face masks and hoods, and no one met his gaze. She was probably back at the labs, or it might even have been her day off.

Like much of this end of the Royal Mile, the house in whose basement they had found the girl was narrow-fronted and tall, rough-cut stone set with lime mortar. Smooth worn steps led up to a heavy wooden door, a single bay window overlooking the cobbled street. A shiny brass plaque by the door had been polished so often the letters on it had all but disappeared. Beside it, a more modern but less aesthetically pleasing sign told him that this was the office of a registered charity called House the Refugees. Through the window McLean could just make out a darkened room, some office furniture and a wilted pot plant. Faded leaflets stood in cardboard stands on the windowsill, surrounded by dead flies. When he tried the door, it was locked.

'Anyone spoken to them?' McLean looked around for a doorbell, finally spotting one hidden under the brass plaque. It looked old and dysfunctional, but he pressed it anyway. In his imagination, an elderly chime sounded.

'Not sure, sir.' Harrison pulled out her phone and swiped at the screen. 'I can have a look online. See if I can find a contact number. Doesn't look like there's anyone in, though.'

McLean climbed back down to the pavement, then craned his neck and peered up to the top of the building: four storeys high, a pair of windows on each floor, each reflecting the slate-grey sky like dead eyes, empty. He was about to turn away, debating with himself whether to go and see the basement again or leave it for the forensic team to finish rather than upset them, when a light came on in the top window.

'Hang on a sec. Think there might be someone at home.' He trotted up the steps again and pressed the doorbell. Still the only sound was in his imagination, and then footsteps clumping wearily down stairs. A pause, followed by a rattling of locks and chains and finally the door swung open.

'Yes?' A man peered out through the narrowest of gaps. His thin face looked like something from a cartoon, scraggly white hair sprouting from his scalp and fuzzy white bristle from his chin. McLean couldn't quite be sure, but it seemed as if he was wearing paisley-pattern pyjamas underneath a heavy wool dressing gown.

'Detective Inspector McLean, Police Scotland.' He pulled out his warrant card and held it up for the man to see. 'Do you live here, Mr . . . ?'

'It says Detective Chief Inspector on there,' the man said. His voice was as thin as his face, although there was clearly nothing wrong with his eyesight.

'Right enough. I'm still not used to that. Could we have a word please, sir?'

The old man paused for longer than was perhaps polite, eyes widening as he looked out onto the street and saw the forensics van and white boiler-suited technicians. Eventually he turned his gaze back to McLean.

'Aye. You'd better come in, I suppose.'

★ ★ ★

50

His name was Peter Winterthorne, and judging both by the way he introduced himself and his look of disappointment when neither McLean or Harrison reacted, he had once been important. Or at least used to being recognised. He led the two of them up four storeys and into a surprisingly large but cluttered living room with a view over the city people would pay good money for. They'd probably pay even more for the astonishing collection of old artefacts, small statues, framed papyri and other trinkets that showed a passionate interest in ancient Egypt and the Middle East. Dominating one wall, a series of carved stone panels the equal of the Elgin Marbles must have taken some effort to bring up the four flights of stairs.

'Quite the collector, Mr Winterthorne,' McLean said as he studied a photograph showing a younger version of the man standing beside a fallen statue in a desert.

'What? Oh. Not really. Just a few things I've picked up on my travels.' The old man shuffled over and peered at the photograph with rheumy eyes. 'Ah, yes. Dura. That would have been the late eighties when I helped out with one of the excavations. Doubt there's anything left of it now, after ISIS and that bloody civil war. Such a shame.' He paused for a moment as if lost in thought. 'But where are my manners? Can I get you a cup of tea?'

'Thank you, but I don't think that will be necessary. I just needed to ask a few questions.'

'Of course. Please, have a seat.' Winterthorne settled himself into a leather armchair that was older even than him. 'What can I do for you?'

'Were you here on Saturday afternoon, when the march came past?'

'March? No, no.' The old man shook his head just in case they didn't know what the word meant. 'I've been away, what? A month now it'd be.'

'But this is your home, right?'

'Oh yes. I bought this house in the sixties. Rest of the band said I was mad, spending my money on something like this. Theirs all went on booze and drugs, so look who's laughing now.' Winterthorne's laugh turned into more of a cough, and he thumped his chest with a frail hand.

'You were in a band?' Harrison asked.

'Aye, lassie. You'll have heard of us, I'm sure. Loopy Doo. They called us the Scottish Beatles.'

Judging by her expression, the name meant nothing to the detective constable, which was hardly surprising. The old man tried to hide his disappointment.

'Ach, well. It was a long time ago. 'Fore your folks were born, I'd guess.'

McLean racked his brain for a moment, trying to remember. There was a song his mother had liked. 'I used to have a copy of "Falling Angels, Rising Stars",' he said, and was rewarded with a smile and a nod. 'Not listened to it in a while though.' Mostly because all his old records had melted into slag in the fire that had destroyed his flat in Newington some years back. 'For now though, if we could concentrate on this property. Do you own the whole building, or just this flat?'

'Oh, the whole building. Used to live in it all, too. The parties we had. But I don't need that much space, and I spend more time out of the city than in it these days.'

'Yes, you said. You've been away. I take it you rent out the ground floor to the charity? What was it called? House the Refugees?'

Winterthorne had been staring at McLean, but his focus shifted as he thought before answering. 'Aye, that's right. Sheila Begbie. Bonny lass. She cares about folk, which is more than most do these days. She has the ground and first floors. I live up here and the floor below. Suits us both fine.'

'And the basement?'

A frown creased Winterthorne's brow, and he tilted his head slightly as he looked back at McLean. 'Don't think I've been down in that basement in years. I'd be hard pushed to tell you where the keys are, if I'm being honest.'

'Can you remember the last time you went in there?'

'No, no.' He shook his head again. 'Is that what this is all about? All those young laddies in their white suits?'

'I'm afraid so, yes. I can't go into details, but someone broke into there recently. It's very important I speak to anyone who might have seen or heard anything unusual in the close in the past few days.'

Winterthorne shrugged. 'I only got in last night. Been up country visiting old friends. I don't get to see them as much as I'd like. Most of my lot are dead now, anyway.' He thumped his chest again, coughed, and for a moment McLean wondered whether he was going to choke, or spit out phlegm onto the floor. He also wondered how the man had managed to get back into the house without one of the constables on watch duty noticing him. That was a question for a sergeant to deal with.

'We'll need to take a full statement from you anyway, Mr Winterthorne, and I'd be grateful for some contact details for this Sheila Begbie if you've got them. And anyone else you can think of who might have seen or heard something.'

'Of course. Anything I can do to help.' Winterthorne struggled out of his armchair and shuffled over to a small desk, rifling through drawers until he found a little black address book. 'Here's her number. But she'll be here soon enough. Usually gets in around ten.'

10

A group of forensic technicians were peeling off their white overalls and chucking them into a bin liner in the back of the battered old Transit van parked across the road. McLean looked for Emma among them, but couldn't see her. Too much to hope that she might speak to him at home, but he'd hoped he might get a word in at the crime scene. He'd much rather speak to her face to face than send endless texts.

'What the bloody hell's going on here? Why can't I go inside? It's my bloody office.'

McLean turned swiftly, wincing as a stab of pain shot through his hip. A few paces up the road, a short, round woman was remonstrating with one of the uniformed constables guarding the front door and the entrance to the close. Harrison moved swiftly down the steps to meet her.

'Ms Begbie?' The detective sergeant's approach was more tactful than McLean would have managed, but even so the short woman turned on her with an angry scowl.

'Aye, an' who're you?'

'Detective Constable Harrison, ma'am.' Harrison held up her warrant card. 'Edinburgh CID. And this is Detective Chief Inspector McLean. He's in charge of the investigation.'

Begbie's eyes widened in surprise as she looked at McLean.

No doubt she'd seen enough detective shows on the telly to know that a DCI was someone to be taken seriously.

'What's this all about then, Inspector? This fellow won't tell me anything.' Begbie waved dismissively at the constable. 'Won't even let me in my own front door.'

'I'm sorry about that, Ms Begbie. This is a very serious investigation, though. Can you tell me, do you have access to the basement?'

Unfeigned surprise wrinkled the woman's brow. 'The basement? Is there one?'

'Around the corner there. Wooden door with a padlock on it?' McLean pointed at the entrance to the close as a white boiler-suited forensic technician came out with a heavy aluminium case in both hands, waiting for a car to pass before lugging it across the road and into the van.

'Never much go down there. Just for the bins, aye? There's no way out at the end.'

McLean suppressed the urge to say that was why it was called a close. He stamped his feet and rubbed his hands together to emphasise the cold. 'Perhaps we could go inside, then?'

'That's what I was trying to do, only this wee scunner here wouldn't let me.'

The constable shrugged. 'Crime scene manager said no one in or out till you got here, sir.'

'Well we wouldn't want to upset him now, would we?'

'She, sir.' The constable shook his head. 'And no. We certainly wouldn't.'

'Would I be right in assuming you re-home refugees here?'

McLean stood in the middle of a room that took up most of the ground floor of the building. If there was a theme to the decoration it was threadbare: second-hand furniture; drab paintwork peeling around the cornicing; a fine collection of dead flies on the windowsill. Sheila Begbie struggled out of her overcoat and hung it on a hat stand by the door. She wore sensible clothes for the weather, a woolly cardigan over a long skirt of some dark material that merged into black tights so thick they might better be described as leggings. Only the small pink Converse trainers on her feet were incongruous, and rather inappropriate given the snow outside.

'We do our best, aye.' Begbie pulled out the chair from behind the desk and sat down. She hadn't offered seats to either McLean or Harrison, nor tea.

'And what are your office hours? Are you here often?'

'Depends on what's going on.' Begbie switched on an ancient computer that wheezed like an asthmatic as it powered itself into life. 'Summer's usually busier 'n this.'

'Oh? Why's that?'

'You fancy crossing the Med in a wee boat in the middle of winter? Not much fun trying to hitch through Europe when the weather's cold either.'

'So the refugees you deal with, they've not necessarily come in through normal channels then? More asylum seekers?' McLean resisted the urge to say 'illegal immigrants'. He'd met women like Begbie before.

'They've no' done anything wrong, Inspector. If anything it's the other way round. We made the bombs that ruined their cities, armed the rebels who turned their lives to misery.'

'I'm not here for an argument about immigration, Ms Begbie. As an officer of the law, I can't ignore rule breaking, but as an individual I can only agree with you, and what you're trying to do here.'

She stared at him with an intensity he was more used to turning on others, and for the first time in a long while McLean thought he might have met his match. In the end, they both looked away at the same time; Begbie to her computer as it pinged into life, him out the window, where he saw Emma pulling down the hood of her white paper overalls and chatting easily with some of the other forensic officers. What he wouldn't give to have her talk to him like that again.

'You know, I think I believe you, Inspector. There's not many in your profession would say the same, and I've had a fair few officers through that door over the years.'

'You have?' It made sense, given who she was dealing with. 'How long have you been doing this?'

'There's a question. Fifteen years, maybe? More?'

'Always from here?'

'Aye, I think so. Why?'

'And yet you didn't know there was a basement down there?' McLean waved his hand at the floor, covered in a carpet that might once have been some vibrant colour but was now varying shades of beige and grey. Patches had been worn smooth by the passage of countless feet, a trail leading to a narrow door at the back of the room.

Begbie shrugged. 'Never gave it much thought, but I guess there'd be something under here, leastways to the back where the close drops down from the street. Then again, there's all manner of hidden rooms and stuff in the Old Town. It's been built over that many times.'

She had a point. They weren't far from the Vaults, and Mary King's Close wasn't much more than ten minutes' walk, even in this foul weather. 'So there's no other way into here but the front door there?' McLean hooked a thumb over his shoulder.

'No.' Begbie shook her head. 'Well, aye, there is but . . .'

'But what?'

'But see for yourself.' She pulled open a drawer and rummaged around a while, coming out with a key on a piece of string. It fitted the lock on the door at the far side of the room, and she opened it to reveal a small kitchen. A chipped old sink sat under a narrow window that looked out onto the close, the green stain under one tap showing where it had dripped for the best part of a century. Cupboards not much younger ran along the far wall, then tucked away under the stairs up to Pete Winterthorne's flat. At their far end, they almost butted up against a simple wooden door, leaving just enough space for it to open.

'There used to be a door through to the hoose at the back of the close, see?' Begbie pointed at the wall directly opposite the door, where a noticeboard above the counter was covered in leaflets, notes and other detritus collected over the years. Nothing looked like it had been touched any time recently except the kettle, coffee jar and stack of mugs on the draining board beside the sink, but when he took a step closer McLean saw that what he had taken for a noticeboard was in fact a heavy plank door.

'Don't know why they left it like that, but it's never been opened in all the years I've been here.'

McLean pulled aside a few of the leaflets for a closer look. Thick paint sealed the gap between door and frame, covered the ancient hinges. Even so he could see that it would open into the room if it could. The cupboards stopped that from happening, and there was no sign they'd been moved in decades. It was an odd way to do up a house, but he'd seen worse.

'What about in here?' Harrison's voice came from the other side of the room, and he turned to see her reach for the door under the stairs.

'That's just a cupboard. We keep the cleaning stuff in there, aye?' Begbie took a step back to the door through to the office as Harrison opened the cupboard door and peered inside. From where he was standing, McLean couldn't see much, but he heard the voices from below clearly enough.

'. . . get this lot shifted out of the way then we can start looking at the ceiling properly.'

One stride was enough to see over Harrison's shoulder as she peered into what wasn't as dark a space as he had been expecting. Bright arc lights shone on the underside of the wooden stairs from a hole at the back of the cupboard. Not large, but big enough for an undernourished child to crawl through. He turned back to where Begbie still stood in the doorway. Her face suggested she knew nothing about this, but knew exactly where it was going to lead.

Daylight had long since gone, the evening turning rapidly to night by the time McLean parked his car outside the house and switched off the engine. He'd meant to come home earlier, but realistically that was never going to happen this early into a murder investigation. That the victim had been a young girl meant everyone was that little bit more stressed. He'd spent most of the afternoon arguing for more resources, and going over a mountain of useless information gleaned from DI Ritchie's door-to-door interviews. They still didn't know what had killed the girl, or indeed who she was. That last fact bothered him more than anything. How could anybody have not noticed that their child had gone missing? There was nothing from the schools, nothing from Social Services, and Missing Persons didn't have anything on file that matched either. DNA would take time, and even then it wasn't going to be as much help as he would have liked.

At least Emma's car was parked in the driveway this time. That was a clue that she might be home, although he could never be sure these days until he actually saw her. Inside, the kitchen showed signs that somebody had been cooking, and Mrs McCutcheon's cat wasn't in front of the Aga. McLean dumped his briefcase on one of the chairs, then went through to the hall. The library door stood slightly ajar, a thin strip of light fanning out across the black and white chessboard tiles and illuminating the small pile of mail on the sideboard. He grabbed it, knowing full well that he was only using the letters as a shield in the coming encounter. Pausing for a breath first, he pushed open the door and stepped into the library.

'Hey, stranger.' Emma looked up from the sofa, reaching for the remote to mute the television. She stood up, stretched and yawned, and for a moment it was as if the past few months had never happened. She'd even lit the fire, although inexpertly, and the room was pleasantly warm. Mrs McCutcheon's cat lay on the threadbare rug in front of the hearth. She glanced up, giving him a look of minimal interest, then went back to sleep.

'Sorry I'm late in. You know how it is. Saw you at the crime scene on the Royal Mile earlier, but you were busy so I left you to it.'

The frown was a familiar sight on Emma's face now, but at least this time it was short-lived. 'Thanks. It wasn't an easy one to process. Not when I knew what had happened there.' Her gaze flicked from his face down to the collection of envelopes he'd brought in from the hall. 'What've you got there? Anything interesting?'

McLean sifted through the collection of bills, junk mail and other rubbish. 'The usual. Oh, hang on.' He extracted a heavy envelope from the pile, its weight more to do with the quality of the paper than any contents. The address on the front was hand-written in elegant copperplate script, and there was no stamp, just a simple 'by hand' added in the corner where one would have been. Turning it over, he found it sealed with wax, the design stamped into it too detailed to make out in the poor light.

'Let's have a look then?' Emma reached out and took the envelope from him, studying it with younger eyes less tired from a day staring at dry reports. She peered closely at the wax seal. 'It's letters, I think. All curly so you can't really read them. Maybe I-L-B? No, that's D, I reckon.'

McLean felt a knot of chill in his gut and made to take the letter back, but Emma snatched it away from him and tore it open, obliterating the seal in the process. Inside was a thick rectangle of card, an invitation.

'Detective Chief Inspector Anthony McLean and Miss Katrina Emma Baird.' Emma's frown wrinkled across her brow again. 'How the fuck does anyone know that?' She fixed McLean with a stare more familiar to him from the past months. 'Did you tell them?'

'Tell who? And "Katrina"? I didn't even know you had another name, Em.'

'Here. You deal with it then.' Clearly the revelation of her true first name was the most hurtful thing to happen to her in years. Emma shoved both crumpled envelope and invitation at him and slumped back into the sofa, flicking the sound back on the television. Her sudden mood swings didn't surprise him any more, even if he wished he knew how to help her. He'd tried everything else though; all he could give her now was time.

Turning his attention back to the invitation, McLean felt that cold tension in the pit of his stomach again. On the face of it, there was nothing unusual about his being invited to a charity fundraiser. He was senior enough within Police Scotland to be on those kinds of guest lists now, and he was a wealthy man. He'd donated money to many charities, most recently the re-building of the church roof, even though religion wasn't something he subscribed to. No, what bothered him about this invitation, apart from the fact that someone knew more about Emma than he did, was the name of the person hosting the event.

'Jane Louise Dee. I thought she was dead.' Images of an explosion in the darkness, falling too far, deep snow softening the impact, his body pumped with enough drugs to stun an elephant. Memories of that time were hard to pin down. 'At least I hoped she was.'

He flipped the card over, half expecting there to be something cryptic and personal scrawled on the back. It was mercifully blank, and when he raised the card to his nose it gave off no scent more exotic than expensive stationery. Reading the details again, he saw that the event was less than a week away, held in one of the swankier hotels in the city centre. Apparently it was to raise money for something called the Dee Trust. He didn't care. He wasn't going. And if he never met Jane Louise Dee, the enigmatic Mrs Saifre, ever again, it would be too soon. That she was back in town was worry enough.

'It's no matter,' he said more to himself than anyone else. Emma was completely absorbed by whatever was on the television. Sliding the stiff card back into its expensive envelope, he walked over to the fireplace, shifted the guard and consigned the invitation to the flames.

11

'How the hell can a body get that way so quickly?'

Early morning and McLean found himself in Detective Superintendent Jayne McIntyre's office, along with a hastily gathered group of the more senior detectives still based in the station. Detective Inspector Ritchie had put in a welcome appearance for a change, and Grumpy Bob was there too.

'The short answer is I don't know. I'm still waiting for Angus to get back to me on that. He's been talking to some of his old university friends, wants to run some tests.'

'So he doesn't know either.' McIntyre didn't voice it as a question. 'OK then. What do we know?'

'At the moment, very little.' McLean was going to leave it at that, but the questioning eyes of the other detectives around the table prompted him to fill the silence. 'We've no ID on the girl yet. She wasn't carrying anything with her, and her clothes are a mix of cheap and old. That suggests to me charity shop or possibly even handouts. At the moment we're working on the theory she got into the basement through a small hole in the floor of the charity offices above. They deal with refugees, so it's possible she's foreign. That would explain why Missing Persons haven't got any matches.'

'The charity.' Ritchie flicked through a copy of the very basic summary DC Harrison had prepared for everyone. 'House the Refugees. We know anything about them?'

'I've spoken to the woman who runs it, name of Sheila Begbie. We'll be getting her in for a full statement, but the office was closed over the weekend. We're checking her out, but she seems legitimate.'

'And her clients? The folk she was finding homes for? Any of them missing a child?'

McLean rubbed at his temples, head aching after a poor night's sleep.

'Not the ones we've managed to track down so far. The addresses we've got aren't exactly permanent, and a lot of them have moved on recently. It's a hostile environment for immigrants and refugees out there. And they're not the sort of people who leave paper trails.'

'You want to shake down this Begbie a bit harder? We found a body in the room under her office. It's not going to be hard justifying a warrant to go through all her records.' McIntyre opened her hands wide as if the paperwork was already there to hand over.

'I thought it would be more productive to work with her, Jayne. The people she's dealing with, they don't have a very good relationship with the police. Not here, and certainly not in the countries they've fled from. We go in heavy-handed and everyone we need to talk to will just disappear.'

McIntyre's scepticism was written all over her face, but she kept quiet.

'What about children, then?' Ritchie asked. 'Do we know if any of her refugees had kids with them?'

'Lots of them, and all different ages. It's not like we could show her a picture of the girl though.' McLean reached out across the table and picked up one of the photographs he'd brought to the meeting. A head and shoulders shot of the dead body as it was laid out on the examination table, it showed all too clearly the strange damage that had been done to the girl's skin. She looked almost like a body taken from a bog after thousands of years' slow pickling, except that she wasn't the dark leather colour that peat tanning gave. Her pallor was more orange, her features waxy. Her thick black hair reminded him of nothing so much as an elderly sofa, its stuffing burst from some tear in the fabric. There was an artificiality to it, more like a wig than real, which was why he'd thought her a doll to start with.

McIntyre's heavy sigh broke through his musing. 'What do we know, then? How did she die?'

McLean put the picture back down on the table, face up so that he could still see it. 'What we know from the post-mortem so far is that she died two or three days ago, from what appears to be massive and rapid organ failure. The basement where we found her hasn't been used for anything in years. It's full of rubbish, old chairs, tables, pretty much a lifetime's worth of forgotten things. According to Winterthorne a lot of the stuff was in there when he bought the place at the end of the sixties, and, having seen it, I can believe him.'

'Winterthorne?' Grumpy Bob had been doing a good impression of a man not paying attention up until that point, but he leaned forward. 'Pete Winterthorne? As in Loopy Doo?'

'The same. Apparently he's not been home for almost a month, didn't get in until Sunday night. We're checking that, of course, but he's an old man. No way he'd be able to break down that door, let alone move any of the furniture in the room. Right now I don't think either Begbie or Winterthorne are likely suspects, although it's possible Begbie inadvertently let the girl in.'

'How do you figure that?' McIntyre asked.

'Forensics found a small toy underneath some of the discarded furniture, and a carrier bag with food in it. My guess is she was trying to escape something, went there to hide until it stopped looking for her. The only way she could have got in was from the offices above, and they were locked when we got there.'

'So you reckon what? She snuck in during office hours, hid somewhere until Begbie locked up, then found her way down into the basement?' Ritchie arched a non-existent eyebrow. 'Sounds a bit far-fetched, doesn't it?'

'I'm working with what I've got, Kirsty, which isn't much if I'm being honest.' McLean shrugged. 'The point is, someone found her, somehow. They broke down the door and shifted heavy furniture out of the way to get her.'

'Why go to all that trouble and then just leave her body behind?' McIntyre asked.

'I have no idea, Jayne. Right now, none of this makes any sense at all.'

'I've got that information on the missing girl you were after, sir.'

McLean looked up from his desk to see DC Sandy Gregg standing in the open doorway and clutching a report folder in one hand. He'd gone straight back to his office from the senior officers' meeting, figuring that he could at least make a start on the paperwork while waiting for more information to come in. He'd found it almost impossible to concentrate, and for a moment all he could think of was the dead girl in the basement, but Gregg would have been more specific if something important had come up. And that girl wasn't missing. She was in the mortuary.

'You asked me to speak to someone in Immigration, remember? Couple of days back?'

McLean's expression must have still been blank, as Gregg added 'Before the march? Lad by the name of McKenzie?' And that finally tripped the memory.

'Sandwiches. Got you.' He shook his head to hide the

embarrassment of being so forgetful. He'd meant to follow up on McKenzie when they found out the girl had died recently, rather than decades ago. Somehow it had slipped his mind. Almost as if he was getting old or something.

'Aye, well. Your man McKenzie's on the level, and so's the place he works. They employ a lot of immigrants, but it's all above board.'

'What about the missing girl? You don't think it could be her we found in the basement?'

'I don't know. Dougie – DS Naismith – said it was bit of a sensitive area. Didn't want to poke his nose in too deep in case they all got scared off. That was before yon wee lassie in the basement, mind.'

McLean checked his watch. Not much of the morning left. 'You have your lunch yet?' he asked.

Gregg shook her head. 'Shift ends soon. I'll be heading off home for a bit of peace and quiet. Need to do some more boning up for the exam.'

'Never mind. I'll find someone else.'

'For lunch?'

'To visit the sandwich factory and have a chat with the owner, maybe Mr McKenzie and the other workers if they'll speak to us.'

'But Dougie said . . .'. Gregg stopped speaking before she finished the sentence, so McLean didn't have to interrupt her.

'That was before we had a murder investigation on our hands. And, besides, we need to identify this girl if we've any hope of finding out why she died and who killed her. Or what.'

Gregg nodded her understanding. 'You want me to find DS Naismith for you, sir?'

'He in?' McLean wasn't sure he'd know the man if he saw him. So many new faces, so many old ones moved on or retired.

'Aye. He was just going to the canteen for a coffee.'

McLean stood up, abandoning the piles of paperwork strewn across his desk. 'I'll come with you. Could do with a leg stretch.'

If Gregg knew the real reason was his uncertainty over who DS Naismith actually was, she didn't mention it, simply stood aside to let him exit the room, then fell into step as they both walked up the corridor towards the stairs. He waited until they were almost at the canteen before speaking again, pitching his voice low so as not to be overheard even though there weren't many officers around.

'About that exam. Way I hear it, you just need to turn up and spell your name right and you'll be fine.'

As it turned out, McLean did know Detective Sergeant Naismith. He'd worked with DCI Dexter in the Sexual Crimes Unit, or Vice as everyone jokingly called it. Given that more than half of the city's sex workers were trafficked illegal immigrants, the move to CID liaison with the Immigration office wasn't hard to understand. Naismith didn't look all that much younger than him, his face lean and lined as if he'd spent most of his career walking the streets on the beat rather than in plain clothes.

'It's like I said to Sandy, sir. You have to tread carefully with these people. Pretty much all of them have had a hard time getting here. Most of them look on the police as the enemy, and given some of the stories I've heard, you can hardly blame them.'

'I got that impression from McKenzie. That's why he came to see me. None of the women working in the factory would have dared.'

'Aye, they don't want to draw attention. No' from us, and no' from the folk who brought them here neither.'

McLean cradled a mug of coffee he didn't really need. The canteen was just beginning to get busy with lunch and shift change, but his seniority meant most of the officers were giving him a wide berth. Either that or his reputation.

'How much did you actually find out, then?' he asked.

'The company's called Fresh Food Solutions. They've a couple other places down in England, apparently. I've spoken to the manager of the Newcraighall site before. Rab Boag. He's OK. Takes on folk others might not want the bother with. Treats them fair, for the kind of work they're in.'

'Making sandwiches.' McLean looked up at the canteen serving hatch and the food on display in the glass cabinets. Were those sandwiches made on site? Or did they buy them in as some kind of cost-cutting measure?

'Among other things. There's a bakery across town too, and some big packing and processing factory out in Fife. The scale of it fair boggles the mind. All for a humble sarnie.'

The way he said it made McLean wonder whether Naismith had eaten his lunch yet. The detective sergeant had only a mug of coffee in front of him, but it was possible his plate had been cleared away already.

'What about McKenzie? He's not exactly from foreign parts.'

'Billy?' Naismith raised an eyebrow. 'No. Local lad. And good on him. There's no' many stick out that kind of job for long.'

'Too much like hard work?'

'A bit of that, aye. But when you're the only one speaking English in a line of folk jabbering away in Polish or Syrian or whatever, well, it's hard to find a way to fit in.'

'Why do you think he does, then?'

'I'd have thought that'd be obvious, sir. He's got the hots for one of his co-workers.'

'The one who's sister's missing her child?'

Naismith shrugged. 'Seems the logical explanation.'

McLean took a drink from his mug, then grimaced at the lukewarm, bitter liquid. He put it down on the table and stood up. 'We need to go and talk to them anyway. Maybe I can persuade McKenzie to act as an intermediary. Come on. I'll drive.'

'We?' Naismith's face suggested he'd been expecting to spend rather more time in the canteen and less out in the cold. 'But I've no' had my lunch yet.'

'Don't worry, Sergeant. Where better to get fed than a sandwich factory?'

12

Fresh Food Solutions occupied a modern warehouse building on the edge of an industrial estate in Newcraighall. Whoever had come up with the name for the company had clearly never spent any time on the internet, as the large company logo spelled out FFS in big blue letters. It hadn't taken long to drive from the station, DS Naismith just as nervous a passenger in McLean's expensive and shiny Alfa Romeo as any junior constable. He'd been too agitated to place a call to the manager, so their visit was unannounced. Even so, Rab Boag had met them within minutes of their arrival. With a florid face and constantly moving hands, the manager looked like he probably enjoyed sampling his product a little too much. He spoke constantly, with all the intensity and conviction of a double-glazing salesman.

'We operate to the highest health and safety hygiene standards. All our equipment is inspected on a regular basis and our staff undergo rigorous and continuous training.'

McLean tuned out the corporate spiel as he followed the manager through a noisy warehouse area and up clattering metal stairs to the company offices. A bored secretary looked at the three of them as they entered, but made no effort to move from her desk.

'Coffee, please, Eileen.' Boag opened a door into a large office with a glass wall overlooking what McLean could only think of as the factory floor. He wandered over for a better look, peering down on a wavy line of conveyer belt, white-overalled people hunched over it like legs on a centipede tipped upside down by an inquisitive child. They all wore hairnets, and some of the men sported beard nets too. Other workers wheeled about trolleys of what he assumed were ingredients, feeding the machine that fed the nation.

'Please, have a seat, gentlemen. Or should I say "detectives"?'

McLean turned away from the fascinating view to see Boag already seated at his desk. Naismith stood uncertain by the door, then had to move as Eileen pushed it open with a foot, her hands occupied by a tray.

'I must say, I'm surprised to see you again so soon, Detective Sergeant,' Boag said as the secretary placed three mugs on the desk. She'd not asked whether anyone took milk, just made them that way. McLean hoped she'd not put any sugar in them.

'DS Naismith was making enquiries on my behalf, Mr Boag.' He approached the desk but didn't sit down, forcing the manager to look up at him. 'One of your employees approached me with a story I couldn't ignore.'

'The missing child? I know. But her mother doesn't work here. I don't know how I can help.'

'You employ her sister though.' McLean nodded his head in the direction of the window. 'Out there on the production line.'

'Aye, Rahel. She's been here more than eighteen months now. Good worker. Nimble fingers.'

'Is she in today? I need to speak to her.'

Something like fear flitted across Boag's face, and his gaze darted from McLean to Naismith as if asking the DS to help.

'It's like I said before, sir. They're very wary of the police. Chances are she won't speak to either of us, even if her English is up to it.'

'I don't want you scaring them off. You any idea how long it takes to train up a skilled sandwich maker? How hard it is to get them to stay?'

McLean wasn't quite sure what to make of Boag. Granted, the man seemed happy enough to give work to immigrants and refugees, but something in his tone suggested his philanthropy came more from a desire to cut costs than to help the needy. There was no point going in heavy-handed though. That was the only certain way to make everyone unhappy and ensure he didn't get the information he needed. Time to take a different tack.

'McKenzie. He working today?'

Boag's worried face turned to puzzlement. 'Aye, I think so.'

'Well get him and this Rahel up here. Or better yet, have you got a canteen? Maybe somewhere the staff can take a break?'

It wasn't exactly a comfortable space to catch a few minutes' break from the grind of sandwich preparation. The workers had made themselves a small area in one corner of the warehouse, upside down crates for chairs, a heavy wooden packing case for a table. The stainless-steel industrial-size sink was more designed for cleaning out mop buckets than mugs, but it had been pressed into use for making tea. McLean stared at the handwritten notices taped to the wall for a while before realising the reason he couldn't understand them was that they were written in a variety of foreign languages. It came as a bit of a relief; he'd thought maybe he needed to get his eyes tested.

A quiet commotion at the far side of the cleared space dragged his attention away from the strange, curling script, and he saw Billy McKenzie gently encouraging a young woman to follow him. The two of them were dressed in production-line chic: white plastic wellington boots, white aprons and hairnets, but the woman also wore a headscarf. It made the hairnet seem somewhat redundant.

McLean stood up, but didn't approach. He'd asked Naismith to stay with Boag, up in the office. The fewer people involved, the better. And they knew Naismith was a policeman, whereas he was just a middle-aged man in a suit.

'Thanks for agreeing to speak to me,' he said as they came closer. 'I'm Tony.'

The young woman's eyes widened at his words, but the wariness never left her. Closer up, McLean saw spatters of margarine, mayonnaise and other sauces on her apron.

'You're Rahel, I believe? Please. Have a seat. Billy, you too.' He gestured towards two upturned crates, then sat on a third, making sure there was nothing in between them.

'It is not time for my break.'

'Don't worry about that. I'll make sure Mr Boag doesn't dock your pay.'

The young woman frowned, looked first at Billy, then at McLean 'What is "dock"? Is where boats come and go, no?'

'It means the man'll no' take it out of your wages, aye? You being here and talking to the in—' Billy stopped himself before going any further. Brighter than McLean had given him credit for.

'Tony. Or Mr McLean if you prefer.'

'What is it you want?' Rahel's expression spoke eloquently of how little she trusted McLean. She knew perfectly well he was police, and she wasn't at all happy being here.

'You have a sister, Akka. I understand she has a child, and that child has gone missing.'

Rahel tensed even more at his words, turned to face Billy with a look of pure hatred and spat something in her own language. He recoiled, but at the words as much as the action. Clearly he understood at least some of what she said.

'Rahel, please. This isn't Billy's fault. He's doing what he thinks is best, but even he doesn't know everything.' McLean

74

waited for his words to get through, unsure just how good the young woman's English was. At least she hadn't stood up and walked away, which was something.

'Ideally I would like to speak to your sister. I want to help her find her child.'

Rahel glared at him as if to say she hadn't been born yesterday. Looking at her, he could tell she was very young indeed. Probably not much more than sixteen, whatever her papers might have said. She should have been in school, going to college, not stuck in a warehouse doing mindless labouring.

'I do not know where Akka is.' She wasn't very good at lying either, but McLean was prepared to let it go, for now.

'When did you last see her? What about the child?'

Something like sorrow spread across Rahel's face, and she dropped her head down, looking at her lap. 'I not see little Nala for two months now. Not see Akka either. She working. She always working. They never let her stop. Not like here.'

'Nala is Akka's daughter, I take it?' McLean waited for an answer, but none came. Rahel just stared at her hands.

'Perhaps you can describe her for me,' he said after a while. 'How old is she? What does she like to wear? What colour is her hair?'

He'd not meant to ask that last question, keeping the details simple to start with. Somehow it slipped out though, and as she heard it, so Rahel looked up at him with a different, more calculating expression. She might have been only sixteen, but the intelligence in her eyes was that of a much older woman, won by bitter experience.

'You have found her,' she said, then shook her head. 'You have found someone, or you would not come asking the likes of me.' A pause, then: 'Is she dead?'

He was so taken aback by her directness, McLean didn't know what to say. For a moment the three of them sat in silence, only the background clatter and hum of the factory behind them.

'We have found a dead girl, yes,' he said eventually. 'I doubt very much it's Nala, but we haven't got many leads yet. Neither you nor your sister have reported her missing.'

Rahel opened her mouth to protest, but McLean spoke over her. 'I'm not here to blame you for that. I'm just trying to find out who this little girl is. Then I can find out who killed her and punish them for that.'

She stared at him for long moments, green eyes studying his face as if she were trying to read his thoughts. Her gaze was almost intimidating, and without his training and years of experience, he might have withered under it, turned away. Instead, he merely waited until she was done.

'Nala is five years old. She is all Akka has, even if she didn't ask to be given her. She is not "missing" as Billy says. They took her, to make Akka work harder.' Rahel reached up and pulled off her hairnet and headscarf, eyes staring at McLean even more fiercely now, almost daring him to look away. He had not known what to expect, really, but the thick dark-red locks that tumbled to her shoulders was not it. 'And her hair is the same colour as mine, the same as Akka's. The same as all of our people, if any of them are still alive.'

13

'You should have brought her into the station for questioning. Not pussyfooted around her and her boyfriend while they were meant to be working.'

'If I'd done that, she'd have clammed up and not said a word. At least now I know it's not her niece down in the mortuary.'

McLean stood in the sparsely furnished office on the third floor of the station that Deputy Chief Constable Steven 'Call-me-Stevie' Robinson used whenever he was on this side of the country. Which was far more often than either of them would have liked. Some of the junior officers called Robinson 'Teflon Steve', and McLean felt that was more apt, given the man's skill at remaining spotless when the shit was sticking to everyone else. His network of contacts, connections and friends in high places was so extensive he might have been a Freemason, but McLean had checked the register and been surprised to find he wasn't. Among those contacts, apparently, was a certain Robert Boag, managing director of Fresh Food Solutions (Edinburgh) plc., who had taken very little time in contacting his chum on the force to lodge a spurious complaint.

'So, what? You're going to personally visit every woman in the city who's reported a child missing? Every woman in the country?' Robinson stared at McLean like a headmaster admonishing one of his pupils for a wrongdoing only he could perceive.

'If necessary.'

'Dammit, Tony. That's what detective constables and sergeants are for. You're a chief inspector. You don't go wandering around the city looking for people yourself. You send others to do it, and coordinate the effort from here.' The DCC jabbed a finger at his spotlessly clean and clear desktop to emphasise the point.

'I do understand chain of command, sir.'

'Call me Stevie, please. You're not a constable any more.' Something about the way Robinson said the words made them sound almost like a threat. McLean let it bounce off him. There were worse things than being a detective constable, after all. Being a detective chief inspector, for instance. It wasn't as if he needed the money.

'It was necessary I speak to them myself. McKenzie came here, spoke to me in the first place because everyone else was away on Operation Fundament. I was a familiar face to him, and not to her. It made sense, and it only took an hour.' He didn't add that what he had discovered in the sandwich factory was going to be more than an hour in the pursuing. Nothing to do with the current investigation, so no point bothering Robinson about it.

'Well, just remember before you go swanning off next time. Delegate. You're in charge of too many ongoing investigations to get bogged down in just one.' The DCC leaned back in his chair, dressing-down over. 'Now, how are we getting on with the wee dead girl in the basement?'

'We've still no identification. Forensics have finished up, so we'll have their report soon. I've got some DCs going over all the CCTV from the area and a team doing door-to-door. We'll find something, but without anyone coming forward to identify her . . .' He let the sentence tail off. It didn't need saying just how little they had.

'Well, keep at it. Get the media involved if you have to.'

'We're on that, sir. Not easy, given the condition we found her in. I can't exactly hand out photos, but we're getting an artist's impression made up, and something about the clothes. She had a soft toy with her too. Looked like it was handmade. The social media team are putting together a wee campaign to try and reunite it with its owner. See if it jogs any memories. It's a long shot, but it might pay off.'

'Good thinking, but keep on it. Case like this, it can get ugly very quickly if the media think we're not doing our jobs properly. Nobody likes the idea of a child's death going unsolved.' Robinson gave him a couple of seconds to reflect on this before launching into the next subject. 'Now, about Operation Fundament. Have we charged all the rioters yet?'

'A couple we had to let off with a caution. Too far from the action to prove they were involved. The rest are all processed and awaiting their turn at the Sheriff Court. All bailed, bar one, sadly. They've got themselves a very expensive lawyer somehow. Counter-terror's happy with the result though. Plenty of good intel going forward.'

Robinson rubbed his hands together like a little boy anticipating cake. 'Splendid. Good work all round, and the kind of joined-up cooperation Police Scotland's supposed to be all about.'

'You'll be happy with all the overtime it took then, sir?' McLean tilted his head slightly and smiled as he said it, but even so the DCC frowned at the joke. Then he sighed, his shoulders slumping a little.

'We steal from one budget to fill another. That's what it boils down to in the end. There's never enough money to pay for everything. My job, and your job too, I should add, is to make sure we keep on top of the finances. Think about that before you head out for a wee jolly at a sandwich factory next time.'

★ ★ ★

'Wondered when I might see you. It's been a while.'

McLean didn't think it had been all that long, but Detective Chief Inspector Jo Dexter had aged since he'd last worked in the Sexual Crimes Unit with her, back when it had been based in the old HQ on the other side of town. Now on the second floor of his own station, she sat at a desk much more cluttered than Teflon Steve's, and almost as bad as his own.

'They're keeping you busy, I see. Can you spare a minute?'

'Can you, Tony?' Dexter pushed her seat back until it clattered against the window behind her, stood up and stretched. Something went 'pop' in her back, and she grimaced for a moment before bending slowly to retrieve a packet of cigarettes from the desktop.

'I'm due a fag break. You can talk to me there if you don't mind the smoke.'

McLean did, but he also knew it was the best chance of getting her attention. They fell into step together along the corridor towards the back entrance to the station and the little perspex bus stop that had been put up to keep the smokers happy. Or at least less miserable.

'What's the situation with trafficked sex workers in the city at the moment?' He knew as he said it that the question was way too broad to warrant an answer. Dexter gave him a raised eyebrow, which was more than he could have hoped for.

'Aye, I know. Be more specific. It's only a hunch, but you know me and hunches.'

This time Dexter slowed, looked at him sideways and said, 'Go on.'

'I interviewed a young woman this morning. Name of Rahel. Fairly sure she's Syrian. Certainly Middle East. Her papers are all in order, I'm told. At least, her employer thinks they are.'

'Or knows they aren't and doesn't care. Uses that to his advantage.'

That brought McLean up short. He'd not considered Rab Boag to be that manipulative, but then he'd not imagined the man would be on the phone to the deputy chief constable either. 'It's possible, but it's not her that I'm interested in. It's her sister, Akka.'

'Name doesn't ring any bells, but that's not necessarily surprising.' They reached the door, stepping out into a blast of freezing-cold air swept in off the North Sea by a brisk easterly wind. Dexter had grabbed a coat from the back of her office door, and McLean wished he'd brought his own as he followed her to the smokers' kiosk. At least the SCU shared a station with CID now, so he wouldn't have to freeze for long before getting back to his office and the waiting coffee machine.

'I think this Akka's being forced into sex work. Her sister didn't exactly say it out loud, but I've been reading between the lines all my professional life.'

'Poking your nose into other people's business too. I remember that about you.' Dexter spoke through lips closed around a cigarette as she lit up and took in a deep drag. McLean counted to five before she let the smoke out through her nose. 'Gets the job done, but it's messy too. Why's this of interest, anyway?'

'According to Rahel, her sister has a daughter, Nala, and whoever's controlling Akka's taken the girl away from her to ensure her compliance. She's five years old. I can't hear about something like that happening and not want to fix it. Not in my city. Not in any city.'

Dexter took another drag, then stubbed the half-finished cigarette out in the bin. 'Horrible things'll be the death of me,' she said in a swirl of used smoke. 'And it's too bloody cold to stand out here for long. Come on.'

McLean followed her back inside, along the corridor and into her office again. Technically they were the same rank now, but he still felt like her junior and stayed standing when she slumped back into her chair.

'Akka, you say?' Dexter pulled a pad towards her. 'Sister called Rahel. Those are Christian names.'

'I didn't get a surname. I can try to find out.'

Dexter barked a short, humourless laugh. 'And here's me thought you knew everything, what with your posh education and all. Not Christian names. Names given to Christians. They're derived from the Jewish Rebekka and Rachel. Common – well, not exactly common, but used in some Syrian Christian communities. Nala I don't know. That's unusual.'

'The young woman, Rahel, was quite unusual. At least, to my inferior intellect and experience.'

Dexter raised a cynical eyebrow. 'How so?'

'She had vivid green eyes, for one thing. Almost as if she was wearing tinted contacts, although I doubt that very much. Mostly it was her hair, though. I'm no expert on these things, but I didn't expect it to be quite so red.'

'Red.' Something about the way Dexter said the word at the same time as putting her pen down carefully sent a chill through McLean's gut. Or maybe it was the look on her face. She shuffled through the detritus on her desk until she came up with a thick folder, flicked it open and pulled out an A4 printed photograph. Even upside down, he could see that it wasn't pleasant. When she handed it to him, his fears were confirmed. 'Red like that?'

It was hard to see the resemblance to her sister, such was the damage done to her face. McLean couldn't see the colour of her eyes, because both were swollen shut with puffy, purple bruises. Her nose was broken, lips split and bloody. Someone had taken out a lot of frustration on her. There was no denying the hair though, exactly the same dark shade of red as Rahel's.

'Is she dead?' It was impossible to tell from the photograph whether it had been taken in a hospital or a mortuary. McLean thought he would have heard about a woman beaten to death though.

'Maybe good as.' Dexter took back the photograph and slipped it into the folder. 'She was found dumped in a commercial wheelie bin in an industrial estate in Sighthill. She was naked, nothing to identify her, and no hits on DNA so far. She's in a medically induced coma, might wake up, might not. Doctors aren't giving her much chance.'

'How've I not heard about this? When did it happen?'

'They found her on Sunday morning. Should have pinged up on your daily bulletin. You do read those, don't you, Tony?'

'Aye, mostly. Missed that though.'

'So, you think it could be your girl Akka then?'

He shrugged. 'I couldn't say. Not from a photo like that. Red hair's not exactly unusual in these parts.' Except that he was sure, somehow. Maybe the uncomfortable timing of it. He didn't believe in coincidence, after all. 'Who's leading the investigation?'

'At the moment? Me.' Dexter waved her hand over the cluttered desk. 'You're not the only one short-staffed these days.'

'You want to pass it on to Kirsty? She might be able to do something with it.'

'DI Ritchie? You sure? I'll no' turn down an offer of help, but chances are she's a prostitute battered by her pimp or some John.'

'I'll tap your team for their expertise when I need it then.' McLean reached out and took the folder from Dexter's desk. 'If she is Akka and she and her sister are here illegally, then we're going to need all the help we can get.'

14

'You seen Dougie Naismith anywhere, Constable?'

McLean had popped his head around the door of the CID room, hoping to find the detective sergeant at his desk. Only one person was in though, and as soon as he asked her the question he remembered that he already knew the answer.

'He's away home, sir. Shift ended a couple of hours ago.'

'What about DI Ritchie?'

'Over at Gartcosh, sir. She left me these door-to-doors to deal with. Pretty much all squared away now. Not that there's anything useful in any of them.' DC Harrison tapped at her keyboard a couple of times, clicked her mouse to finish whatever it was she'd been doing, then stood up. 'Was there anything particular you needed?'

McLean had considered just sending a couple of uniforms to fetch Rahel from the sandwich factory and bring her here while be briefed Ritchie. That would have been how he'd have dealt with a local. Refugees and immigrants presented their own unique problems, and, while he might have been in a minority among his fellow officers in the matter, he felt that a friendly and gentle approach usually worked best. There was no point trying to browbeat someone who'd fled a war zone to get here. The only threat they feared was being sent back, and they were skilled at disappearing before it could be made.

Harrison waited patiently, her gaze not quite fixed on him, and McLean realised he'd been staring at nothing, thinking. If he couldn't send Naismith, then the only other option was to go there himself, no matter what the DCC might have said about delegation.

'I need to talk to someone over in Newcraighall. Naismith knows all about it, which is why I was looking for him to do it for me. Apparently it's called delegating.'

Harrison grinned. 'I'll see if I can find a pool car going spare, sir.'

Harrison might have been an efficient detective, but even she couldn't track down a pool car. Of course, she might just have been angling for a drive in McLean's Alfa, but he didn't mention that. She was a better passenger than Naismith, asking intelligent questions as he filled her in on the situation so far.

'So you think Rahel and her sister are refugees, then?'

'I know they're refugees. It's whether they came here through a legal programme or not that I need to find out. Rahel had papers, according to her boss. I've not seen them though, and the way she spoke about her sister suggested Akka's not doing the kind of work a registered refugee would undertake.'

'So they were trafficked here. How come Rahel ends up working in a sandwich factory, apparently legitimate, when her sister's a sex worker? Why not both of them?'

McLean slowed as they approached the turning onto Peffermill Road, retracing the route he'd gone only that morning. A part of his mind knew he should be back at the station, that sending a couple of DCs to fetch Rahel was the course of action he should have taken. He'd not even found Ritchie to tell her about the woman who might or might not be Akka yet, and there were a hundred and one other things he was supposed to be dealing with before opening up an entirely new investigation. And yet he couldn't stop thinking about it.

'That's what I intend to find out. And, if possible, I'll try and get a DNA sample off her to compare with our Jane Doe.' He risked a glance across at Harrison as she sat in the passenger seat, trying to gauge from her expression whether or not she thought he'd lost his mind. Her poker face was almost perfect, but she was fidgeting with her hands.

'But?' he asked after she'd said nothing for more of the length of Niddrie Mains Road. Finally she dragged her eyes away from the view to the front and looked at him.

'Isn't it all a bit nebulous?' she asked, then added 'sir' for good measure.

'Nebulous, tenuous, a distraction from what I should be doing. All of these things and more.' McLean indicated, waited for a gap in the traffic, and then pulled over into the car park of Fresh Food Solutions. It wasn't much changed from earlier, but then there was no good reason why it should have been. 'From a psychologist's point of view, you could say I was looking for distractions. I like to think of it more as seeing connections where you wouldn't expect them to be. Maybe seeing connections other people don't even notice. That's the job, after all.'

Harrison had no answer to that, but they'd arrived anyway and the time for philosophising was over. She followed McLean through the front door and into Reception, where he was surprised to see Rab Boag leaning over the receptionist's desk, chatting. Not as surprised as the manager was to see him though, judging by his expression and hurried movements.

'Inspector. You should have called.'

'It's chief inspector, but don't worry. And it's nothing serious. I just wanted to have another quick word with Rahel. Something's come up that might concern her.'

'Rahel?' Boag's gaze flicked away from McLean, to the

receptionist, and then back again. 'She's not here. She left.'

From where he was standing, McLean could hear the noise of the factory floor, production in full flow to meet the needs of the lunching population. Tomorrow's lunches, maybe. Unless people picked up sandwiches for their supper these days. He'd done it on occasion, after all.

'End of her shift?' Somehow he had a feeling that wasn't the case, and Boag's slowly shaking head confirmed his suspicion.

'No, I mean left. Handed in her notice not long after you and Sergeant Naismith were here. A shame, really. She was a good worker.'

'Did she say why?'

Boag shook his head again. 'No, no. I tried to talk her out of it, but she insisted. We had to work out her wages and pay her in cash. Most irregular.'

Too much detail: McLean knew the man was lying. 'I still need to talk to her. Do you have an address, a phone number?'

'I . . . I can't hand out details like that. Not to the police. What if the other workers heard of it?'

'I can get a warrant, if it helps.' McLean doubted that he could. What would be the justification, after all? Sometimes the threat was enough to encourage cooperation. But not this time.

'What about McKenzie? He leave too?'

Boag stiffened as if someone had poked him with a cattle prod. 'Nothing but trouble that lad. Thought I was doing him a favour, taking him on despite where he comes from. Those care home boys are all the same though.'

'So he's not here either.' McLean folded his arms over his chest and stared at the manager. 'Don't you find that a bit odd? That I come and speak to them this morning, and by lunchtime they're both no longer your employees? Did they really leave, Mr Boag, or did you encourage them to go?'

'I really must protest, Insp— . . . Chief Inspector. I've been nothing but helpful to the police whenever they've asked. Speak to the deputy chief constable if you don't believe me. That boy was always trouble, and it seems some of it's rubbed off on young Rahel. A shame, as I said. She's a good worker. Now I have to find two replacements, and train them up. And we've got a big new contract that's going to mean adding an extra shift.'

McLean tuned him out. The mention of the DCC was a none-too-subtle warning, and there was nothing more to be gained here now. Well, maybe one thing.

'I'll let you get back to your sandwiches then, Mr Boag.' He stared at the receptionist as he said this, and she blushed deeply, turning away. 'Just tell me what Rahel's surname is, OK? That's not against your employer's ethics is it?'

The question seemed to take Boag by surprise, and for a brief second McLean imagined that the man didn't actually know. Then he shook his head as if dislodging a different thought.

'I'm never very good at pronouncing these things. Rahel's bad enough.' He turned to the receptionist. 'You've got it on the file there, Elspeth?'

'Aye, Mr Boag. I've got it here.' She tapped at her keyboard, bringing up the record. 'Here we go. Rahel Nour.'

15

The address Billy McKenzie had given them when he'd spoken to McLean earlier was not in a good part of town. Hardly surprising for a lad working on the production line in a sandwich factory, but not somewhere McLean felt all that happy parking his Alfa. Not for the first time, he wondered whether it wouldn't have been a better idea just to buy an old second-hand Ford. Something reasonably reliable and yet also unremarkable. On the other hand, he couldn't really see himself in an ordinary car.

'You reckon he'll be home, sir?' Harrison asked as they parked outside a grey-harled tower block. The clouds overhead threatened more snow to add to the dirty slush collecting on the pavement and smeared against the windward side of the building.

'Only one way to find out.' McLean climbed out of the warm cabin and into a lazy cold wind. 'Only, let's make it quick, aye?'

He'd been expecting semi-derelict council flats, judging by the outward appearance of the block, so it was with some surprise he noticed the clean glass-walled atrium, and the neatly painted sign by the front entrance.

'Inchmalcolm Tower. A Dee Trust Property.' Harrison read the words out loud even though McLean could see them well enough for himself. 'Heard of them. Don't they do, like, halfway house accommodation for care home kids? Give them support and a place to stay when they're old enough to be looking after themselves?'

'I've no idea.' McLean tried not to think about the invitation he'd received a couple of days earlier, the charity fundraiser for this very organisation. Coincidence? He'd keep an open mind for now.

They had to buzz an intercom, and an elderly man who introduced himself as the concierge without being able to pronounce the word let them in. He wore a fleece jacket with 'Dee Trust' written on it in a logo that must have cost a fortune to have designed.

'You here about the fight on the fourth floor?' he asked as he led them back to a reception booth that reminded McLean of university halls of residence more than anything.

'No. Unless it involves Billy McKenzie,' McLean said.

'Billy?' The concierge laughed. 'No chance of him getting into a fight. Don't think he's in, mind. He'd be at work now.'

'Not according to his boss, he's not. Can we go up?'

'Sure. He's in 6A. You'll maybe want to take the stairs, mind.'

'Lift not working?' McLean looked at the metal doors across the hall from Reception. The lights were on, and numbers up to twelve spread across a panel above them.

'Och, it's working fine. Just someone had a wee accident in there this morning. I've cleaned it up, but it still smells a bit.'

'Stairs it is then.'

McLean had to pause for breath by the time they reached the sixth floor. At least the view from the window was good, looking out over Lochend and Meadowbank towards Arthur's Seat. The other side of the building would have a spectacular panorama of the Firth of Forth, Fife and the North Sea. It would bear the brunt of the weather, too.

A dark corridor off the landing led to six front doors. 6A was, perhaps predictably, at the far end, looking out over the Forth. McLean listened at the door for a while, but heard nothing. He knocked twice, then listened again. Buzzy pop music filtered in from the flat across the hall, making it hard to tell if anyone was moving around inside.

'Billy? You in there? It's Tony McLean. We spoke earlier this morning.'

Nothing, and then he thought he heard a thump, maybe some muffled cursing. A few moments of silence underscored by an annoyingly catchy tune, then the lock clicked and the door swung open.

'Aye? You no' caused enough trouble already you have to come here for some more?'

Billy McKenzie looked a lot less amiable this time. He wore a tight-fitting, army-style T-shirt that clung to his frame and showed more muscle than McLean had appreciated before.

'Can we come in?' he asked. 'This is my colleague, Detective Constable Harrison.'

McKenzie flicked his gaze briefly to the DC, then back to McLean. He waited a moment before answering, but there was never any doubt he was going to agree. It was all just posturing.

'Aye, fair enough.' He stood back, opening the door wide for them. 'Come on in then.'

For all that it wasn't the best part of town, the view from Billy McKenzie's tiny living room was quite impressive. The Dee Trust had clearly spent a bit of money on the flats too, as the wind barely rattled the glass in the windows, and McLean couldn't feel any draughts at all. He remembered a similar block from an investigation a few years back, a nasty case that had ended in the death of a detective sergeant. That flat had been cold and miserable even in the summer.

'I've no' any tea or anything,' Billy announced as they stood in the small space. He didn't have much in the way of furniture either, just a couple or armchairs that might have come out of a skip, arranged so they faced a small television on an old wooden table. McLean tried not to notice the numerous boxes with the FFS logo on them stacked in the corners.

'It's not a problem. We'll not be long, anyway. I reckon you can guess what this is about.'

'You've spoken to Mr Boag, aye?'

'He said you quit. Rahel too.' McLean perched on the arm of one of the armchairs as Billy slumped into the other. Behind him, he trusted Harrison to stay silent and take a note of everything said.

'He's a lying bastard, so he is.'

'So you didn't quit then?'

'Oh, aye. I quit. Told him where to shove his job and no messing. But Rahel . . .' Billy shook his head slowly, eyes going slightly out of focus as he stared at something no longer there. Then he snapped his gaze back to McLean. 'He sacked her. Called her up to his office and told her to get her things. Didn't even pay her what she was owed for the week.'

'That's a serious allegation. If he's treating his employees that way then I'm sure the authorities will want to know about it.'

McKenzie shook his head again. 'Can youse even hear yourself? "The authorities". Like they give a fuck what happens to a refugee, ken?'

'But you do, Billy. You care for her, right?'

'I . . .'

'It's not a bad thing. Not a weakness. Quite the opposite. You stood up for what's right. There's plenty who'd not do that.'

'Aye, well. Heat of the moment, weren't it? Regretting it now. This place is cheap.' He flung up his arms, hands wide to

92

encompass the entirety of his domain. 'Still costs money though, and I can't even get dole now, can I?'

'What about Rahel? Where's she gone?'

Billy stiffened in his seat, but whereas before he had held McLean's gaze with a steely glare of his own, now he looked away.

'I don't know. She went before my shift ended. I didn't even have time to say goodbye.'

'And yet you're sure she was fired, that she didn't quit?'

'Aye. Elspeth in Reception told me when she gave me my wages. But I knew before that. Rahel wouldn't have quit that job. What else would she do?'

'Are you sure of that, Billy? Not even for her sister, Akka? Not even for little Nala?'

Again, the young man flinched with each name, and he was finding the floor surprisingly interesting. His voice had quietened too.

'She wouldn't have quit.'

'Well, hopefully we can help her with that, if we can find her. And it's important we find her, Billy.'

'Oh aye? So you can send her to that detention centre? Round up her sister too and then kick them out? Back to their old home?' Now Billy looked up at him again, and there was fire in his eyes. 'There's nothing left, Mr McLean. Her whole town was shelled until there was only dust. I've seen the pictures. That whole country, it's fucked. You can't send them back there. You can't send her back there, ken?'

McLean let the silence grow a little before speaking again. It wasn't a perfect silence, the tinny pop music from the next-door flat made sure of that. But it was enough space for McKenzie to regain his composure.

'Look, Billy. You might find this hard to believe, but I'm not interested in sending Rahel or her sister back to Syria. I'm not going to pass their names on to anyone who might be. That's not how I work. I do need to find Rahel and speak to her though. It concerns her sister anyway.'

'What about her? Have you found her wee girl? Have you found Nala?'

It was McLean's turn to shake his head. 'No, I'm afraid not. Tell me, Billy. Have you ever met Akka?'

'Who, me? Naw, man. She's . . .' He stopped as if his brain had only just caught up with his mouth. 'No. Truth be told, I don't even know Rahel that well. No' as well as I'd like, ken?'

And that was it, McLean knew. He'd built up Billy's relationship with the young woman, because that was how Billy had painted it himself, but in the end it was just an infatuation and no more. Chances were he had no idea where she lived, let alone where she might be now. He stood up, fishing around in his jacket pocket until he found a business card.

'It's very important we speak to Rahel, and soon. This is my mobile number, it doesn't go through some police switchboard or anything. If you see her, or she contacts you, please tell her to give me a call, right?'

Billy's eyes were wide again as he reached up and took the card. 'An' you swear she's no' in any trouble?'

'Rahel? No. Not from me, anyway. We think her sister might be, though. And we're very worried about the child.'

'Where the hell have you been, Tony? I've been trying to get hold of you for hours.'

Back at the station, and McLean had barely sat down before Detective Superintendent McIntyre had appeared at his door. Her state of agitation wasn't quite as great as the DCC's had been that morning, but it wasn't far off.

'Sorry. Did I miss something important?'

McIntyre stared at him as if he were wilfully missing the point, which was fair enough, since he was.

'I was following up on something, Jayne.' He fidgeted in his chair like a schoolboy needing to be excused. 'And, yes, I could have given it to a constable to do, but then I'd have had to do it myself afterwards anyway.'

'You took a constable with you as it was.' McIntyre stepped fully into the room, made as if to close the door and then stopped herself. 'A certain young female detective constable, no less.'

McLean tried not to sigh, but it wasn't easy. 'DC Harrison was the only one about. I'd have taken DC Stringer or Lofty Blane or any of a dozen others. I'd even have taken Grumpy Bob if I knew which unused office he was kipping in right now. I know, I know. Station gossip and all that, but to be honest I'm surprised there is any, given how few actual detectives there are here day to day.'

McIntyre dropped heavily into one of the armchairs by the window. 'I know we're short-staffed, Tony. That's the only reason Stevie Robinson doesn't kick up more of a fuss about you acting like you're still a DS. He knows as well as I do that we can't really afford to have too many good detectives stuck in offices doing nothing.'

'Maybe he could try and streamline some of this paperwork then.' McLean flicked a hand at the stacks of folders taking up almost all of the available area on his desk. 'Some of this is just chasing targets to keep the politicians happy, and you know how much I care about what they all think.'

McIntyre leaned forward in her chair, her expression serious now. 'I know what you mean, but we have to play their game. Which reminds me, you should have received an invitation to a charity do in the North British.'

'The Dee Trust?' McLean couldn't hide the surprise from his voice. 'Aye, I did. Chucked it in the fire. Why?'

McIntyre gave him a face that would have done his grand-mother proud. 'You can't do that, Tony. You have to go.'

'Like fuck I do.'

'No, really. There'll be people there who expect to see the police represented. That's your job now, as much as poking your nose in where it's not wanted. More, really.'

A cold wave of something that wasn't quite anger washed through him as McIntyre spoke. Had it come from anyone else, he'd most likely have told them exactly what they could do with their job, but he respected the detective superintendent, always had. If she said he had to go, then it was going to be very difficult not to. Not impossible, but difficult.

'If it's that important, then why not Call-me-Stevie himself? Or you, for that matter, Jayne? Why not the chief constable, whoever it is this week?'

'Because there's a rota? Because sometimes seniority has perks?' She grimaced as if even she didn't believe that. 'But mostly because Jane Louise Dee specifically invited you.'

The cold in his gut turned icier than the street outside. 'And I'm supposed to just roll over and do what she says now, am I?'

McIntyre rubbed at her face as if she hadn't slept in days. 'No. And you don't have to enjoy it either. But you do have to go. Turn up, drink the free champagne—'

'Nothing is free where that woman is concerned.'

'Don't drink it, then. Just be there, OK?'

Closer to impossible now. McLean couldn't recall the last time McIntyre had sounded quite so serious, and quite so scared.

'You know who she is, right?' he asked.

'She's the richest woman in Scotland. Fuck's sake, Tony. She's the richest woman in the world. You don't say no when she asks you to be involved in her charities. You don't even have to make a donation, just go. Be seen.'

'I . . .' McLean was going to say he'd think about it, meaning full well that thinking about it was all he'd do, but he was interrupted by the arrival at the door of Detective Constable Stringer.

'Sorry to disturb you, sir,' he started, then noticed McIntyre sitting on her armchair across the room. 'Ma'am.'

'What is it, Jay?' McIntyre asked before McLean could get the question out.

'Just in from Control. They've found a body out Braid Hermitage way. Another wee girl.'

16

Snow flurried from a sky the colour of broken slate, the light fast receding from the day. McLean glanced at his watch, wondering where the time had gone. Two visits to a sandwich factory and yet somehow he'd managed to miss lunch.

Blackford Hill disappeared into the gloom, lowering over them like a curse as they drove along Braid Hills Drive, DC Stringer silent in the passenger seat. At least he didn't fidget like Dougie Naismith. It didn't take long to find the point on the road nearest to the crime scene: a line of squad cars and forensics vans were playing havoc with the traffic.

McLean parked well back, then took his time changing into walking boots and heavy coat. He'd even remembered to put a hat in the back of the car, but wasn't sure whether he could face the thought of everyone remarking on it. Chances were he'd be made to change into a thin paper suit by the forensic team before he was allowed anywhere near the crime scene anyway.

'You know who's crime scene manager?' he asked DC Stringer as they walked along the roadside towards the centre of activity.

'No, sir. Sorry.'

'Never mind. See if you can track down whoever reported the body. I'll go have a look myself.'

Stringer's look of relief suggested he wasn't all that keen on consorting with the dead. McLean could understand, even if part of him wondered why someone squeamish would ever apply to join the police, let alone become a detective. He watched the young man work his way through the crowd of uniforms and forensics technicians, and was about to go and find someone to show him the body when a familiar voice piped up behind him.

'Forgot your hat again, did you?'

He barely recognised Emma, clothed as she was in heavy-duty overalls and with the hood pulled up over her head. At least she wasn't wearing a mask this time. She held up her camera and took a quick photograph of him, the flash ruining his eyesight for a few blinking moments. By the time he'd recovered enough of his wits to pull the hat from his pocket, she'd turned away and wandered off. An improvement on her normal cold shoulder at work, but only a small one.

'Ah, Tony. You're here. Good.'

In among the mess of squad cars and dirty Transit vans, McLean hadn't noticed the British racing green Jaguar of the city pathologist. The man himself approached from the verge, where a narrow path had been beaten through into the trees. His assistant, Doctor Sharp, followed along behind.

'Is it, Angus? Is it really?'

Cadwallader shook his head. 'No, you're right. It's a bloody nightmare.' He looked McLean up and down as if only then noticing the overcoat and walking boots. 'Not been down there yet, I see.'

'I only just got here. Only heard about it half an hour ago.'

'Fair enough. You'll need to see for yourself though. Grab a suit and I'll go find Jemima to sign you in.'

'Jemima—? Oh, Doctor Cairns. Is she CSM here?'

Cadwallader grimaced. 'If by that ugly abbreviation you mean, is she in charge? – then the answer is yes. Get a suit on, Tony.

You need to see this, and I don't think anyone will thank you for contaminating the scene more than it already is.'

He remembered the Hermitage of Braid from his childhood, of course. McLean had spent many a happy summer's day making dens in the trees that clung to the steep slopes leading down to the Braid Burn. In winter it was less welcoming, the leaf litter dusted with a light coating of snow that made it even more slippery to walk on. Fortunately for him and Angus, the forensic team had been busy creating a safe path, and had even strung a rope handrail between the trees.

The gloom deepened as they descended into the dell. Not much light left in the day anyway, but the broken-finger branches cut it further still. The two of them weaved a twisty path, continuously downwards, until they finally reached a small clearing. McLean could hear the burn babbling away in the background, not too distant. A footpath followed its course, if his memory served. It had been a while since he had last come this way. This place was like many of his dens though, screened from view by whippy saplings and squat rhododendron bushes. Frost rimed the ground to either side of the marked path, but even so McLean could see the discarded needles, the used condoms, beer cans and plastic cider bottles that marked this place as very different from the childhood world of adventure he remembered.

Forensics had erected a tent towards the far end of the clearing, and it glowed from the arc lights within. A few white-suited technicians stood outside it as if reluctant to enter. They moved aside as Cadwallader and McLean approached, faces pale in the cold. McLean took a moment to steady himself. There was something about the trees, the greying sky overhead, the sombre atmosphere that weighed heavily on him. Knowing there was a dead child inside the tent didn't help either.

'OK then,' he said, his voice flat, all echoes absorbed by the watching woods. 'Let's get this over with.'

The air was warmer inside the tent, heat from the lights trapped by the synthetic fabric. It had melted the frost on the ground and leached a slightly unpleasant odour from the soil. Without his prior knowledge, McLean might have been able to fool himself that the small form lying in the middle of the covered space was merely sleeping, except that nobody would sleep outdoors in the winter, and certainly not barefoot. She was curled up on one side, almost foetal, hands drawn up to her face. She wore old, hand-me-down clothes caked with mud and smears of snow. A thick black woolly hat covered her head, pulled down past her ears and almost over her eyes. From where he stood he couldn't see much bare skin except her feet, and her tiny fists bunched into her mouth and chin as if to ward off the bitter cold. What little he could see was dark like weak tea.

'It's hard to tell, but I think she's been moved after she died.'

'Died? Or was killed?'

'Impossible to say without a more thorough examination. I'm inclined towards the latter. I don't think she's been moved far either. Just enough to make it look like she's gone to sleep.'

Cadwallader inched his way around the body until he was on the other side of it from McLean. He crouched down with much popping of knees, and reached out a hand to the girl's face. As he gently shifted one hand, McLean felt a coldness grip his gut that had nothing to do with the ice outside. The skin beneath her hand, where the air hadn't yet reached it, was far paler than her cheek.

'You're thinking what I'm thinking, aren't you, Angus?' McLean crouched down beside the tiny body, and for an irrational moment he had an urge to gather it up into his arms. This little girl had barely been given a chance at life before it had been snatched brutally away.

'I'm saying nothing until I've got her back to the mortuary,

Tony.' Cadwallader shook his head slowly from side to side. 'Not going to make that mistake again.'

'Let's not go jumping to any conclusions, aye?'

As opening gambits went, it was an unusual one. McLean had just briefed the senior officers about the second dead girl, the silence as he finished a clear indication as to what everyone was thinking. What everyone was dreading. Deputy Chief Constable Robinson had broken first, and his words struck a chord.

'We don't have an ID on the first girl yet, do we?' DI Ritchie flicked through the notes McLean had cobbled together, or more accurately the notes DC Stringer had cobbled together on his behalf. The detective constable wasn't quite as thorough or quick as Harrison, but he'd done an OK job of it. Including post-mortem photographs of the first girl was maybe edging towards the kind of conclusion Call-me-Stevie was trying so hard to avoid though.

'Nothing from Missing Persons, nothing from the DNA database. But then that's hardly surprising. There's not that many minors on it, after all. Our best guess is illegal immigrant or refugee. Someone who thinks they'll be shipped back home if they speak to the police, anyway.'

'Did Angus say how long he thought the second girl had been dead?' This from Detective Superintendent McIntyre, sitting at the head of the conference table, since they had convened the meeting in her office.

'You know what he's like.' McLean waggled his hand to indicate the pathologist's reluctance. 'And after the mistake with the first girl, he's being very cautious. Can't say as I blame him, really.'

'What about the skin. You can't deny there's a similarity there. What's causing that? It's not the cold.' Detective Sergeant Grumpy Bob Laird was the most junior officer in the meeting by rank, the most senior by experience and age. As ever, he saw straight to the heart of the matter.

'Angus is baffled. Tom MacPhail is baffled. Even Tracy Sharp hasn't a clue, and there's not much gets past her. They've sent samples off to the hospital and the university to try and work out what it might be.' McLean flicked slowly through the collection of photographs from the scene at Hermitage of Braid. 'The one thing I think we can be sure of is that this second death happened recently. The body was cold, but there was some snow on the ground underneath it. That means it happened no more than three days ago. That's when we had the first snowfall.'

'And we don't know what killed her yet?' Robinson asked. 'What if she just caught a fever or something? If she's here illegally, her family might not have wanted to turn to the authorities for help. Then when she died they couldn't think what else to do with her.'

McLean turned the last photograph face down so that he didn't have to look at it any more. 'That's very possible, sir. It's possible the same thing happened to the other girl, too. But if that's the case it leads to another question, doesn't it.'

'It does?'

'We'll know more once Angus has done the post-mortem, but the first girl died of multiple organ failure, as if she'd been poisoned or something. If the same is true of this girl, then it's more likely some infectious agent. Of the two options, I know which one I'd prefer were the case.'

The silence that followed his pronouncement did nothing to allay McLean's fears. It lasted far longer than he would have liked too.

'Do we need to get Disease Control involved in this?' Ritchie asked.

'Christ, I hope not.' Robinson slumped back in his seat a bit too theatrically. 'Last thing we need is the press going on about some immigrant flu.'

'At the very least, we need to tell them what's happened. I'll get on to Angus, check who he's sent samples to already.' McLean drummed his fingers on the desktop in frustration. For all his moaning, the DCC had a point about the press. 'As to your second point, sir, I'm surprised they're not all over it already. We got lucky with the first body. I was the one who found her, remember? And we've kept a lid on things for now. This new one? It was a couple out walking their dog who found her. We can ask them not to talk to the press, but there's no way it's not leaking out in the next twenty-four hours. Sooner would be my guess. It'll be all over the papers in the morning, probably doing the rounds of the online news sites already.'

'OK then. We need a strategy.' McIntyre pulled together all the pages of her copy of the report like a headmistress shuffling papers at assembly. 'Priority has to be to identify both of these children while we wait to hear from Angus about what killed them. Kirsty, I want you to liaise with Disease Control and keep on top of the medical side of things. The sooner we know how they died, the better. That's the first thing the press are going to want to know, after all.'

'I'll take that as my cue, Jayne.' Robinson leaned forward and gathered up his report too. He wasn't quite as skilled at shuffling it together as Detective Superintendent McIntyre. 'We've missed the evening news, but we'll have something for the late bulletin. We'll set up a press conference for tomorrow morning, so any new information to me before seven, OK?'

Galvanised by the decision, the DCC stood up, meeting over. One by one they filed out of the room.

17

'Thought you'd like to know that's Sheila Begbie given her statement, sir. She's in interview room one, if you want a word.'

McLean looked up from his desk, eyes tired from too much reading of small type. DC Harrison stood in the open doorway to his office.

'Wasn't she coming in earlier?' He hauled himself out of his chair, not quite sure why he felt so weary.

'She was going to, but with the wee girl found down in the Hermitage, everyone was out. I gave her a call, asked if she could maybe make it later in the day.'

'Well, it's certainly later in the day now.' McLean checked his watch. He ought to have been wrapping things up and heading home himself, if he wanted Emma to actually speak to him for a change. 'Not sure why I needed to know, mind you.'

Harrison frowned. 'I thought you asked to see her when she came in.' She turned and looked out of the doorway into the empty corridor, as if there might be some answer to her confusion there. 'Did you not say that?'

'It's possible. I don't remember. Never mind. Let's go and see her, since she's here.'

The detective constable said nothing as they walked to the

stairs, then down to the ground floor and the interview rooms. McLean could almost hear the cogs whirring in her head though. He had no memory at all of having asked to see Begbie when she came in, but that didn't necessarily mean he hadn't. The artist's impression of the wee girl had come through now, so it would be interesting to see her reaction to it first-hand anyway. He'd like to know if she was hiding something.

'Thank you for coming in, Ms Begbie. I understand you've already given a statement to the detective constable.'

The short, round woman he'd met the day before seemed somehow different. He couldn't exactly say how, but he'd imagined her as older than she looked, more dowdy. She wore a different cardigan, and a lighter skirt, but still what he would class as sensible clothes. The interview room was small and stuffy, and her perfume almost stung his eyes as he and Harrison entered: a slightly sickly mix of something floral and a deeper, more masculine musk. At least, he assumed it was her perfume. Someone else might have been in here before her and left the place stinking. Nobody ever opened the windows in the winter.

'Aye, that's right,' Begbie said. 'No' much to add to what I told you before, but at least it's all down on paper now.'

'Indeed.' McLean took the chair opposite her, Harrison sitting beside him. 'There have been a few developments in the past twenty-four hours though, and I had a couple more questions if you didn't mind answering them?'

'Not at all. Ask away.'

'We're looking for some refugees. Possibly Syrian or from that region. Wondered if their names were familiar to you. Rahel Nour, Akka Nour and Akka's five-year-old daughter, Nala Nour?' McLean studied Begbie's face as he said the names, looking for any tic of recognition. Either she had never heard of them or she'd be a very good poker player.

'Can't say as I know them, no.' She shook her head slowly.

'There's a fair few Syrians been arriving in the past year or two, mind. Hardly surprising, given what's happening in the Middle East right now.'

'OK. What about this girl?' McLean held a hand out and Harrison passed him the artist's impression. He studied it himself for a moment before turning it over to Begbie. 'Do you recognise her?'

Again there was nothing in the woman's face to suggest she did.

'Is this her? The poor wee thing you found in the basement?' Her eyes glistened with tears when she looked up at McLean after a long time studying the picture. He nodded once.

'Have you seen her before?'

'No. No. I think I'd recognise her. There's no' many that young come through the door.'

McLean took the picture back. 'Well, thank you for looking at it anyway. And if you hear anything please get in touch. I know you think all we want to do is round these folk up and send them back where they came from, but that's really not the case.'

Begbie stared at him for longer than was comfortable, and there was something about that gaze McLean found deeply unsettling. Only years of training kept him from breaking eye contact, the second time that had happened with her.

'You know, I actually believe you? You see more than most, Inspector, even if sometimes you don't admit it. You care more than most too. As does this one here.' Begbie nodded at Harrison sitting beside him. 'I was grateful for the call earlier. It's not a long walk from the office, but the weather's not kind right now either. I daresay other officers would have been less thoughtful.'

An awkward silence filled the room for a while. McLean couldn't remember the last time he'd been thanked by someone brought in to give a statement.

'Well, as I said, we appreciate you coming in. I'll see you to the door.'

Begbie smiled as she stood up, not so much being led from the interview room as striding out ahead of him so that McLean had to almost skip to keep up. She didn't slow until they reached the door through to Reception.

'Here, let me.' McLean clicked the button that activated the electronic lock from inside, then pulled the door wide for Begbie to exit. 'You're OK walking? I can arrange a lift if you want.'

'Thank you, Inspector, that won't be necessary. Enough that you've freed me.'

It was an odd expression, and odder still when she held out her hand to shake his. Ingrained politeness kicked in, and McLean did as expected. Her grip was warm and surprisingly strong, and like her gaze she held it for a little too long for comfort. Then, with a nod, she released him, turned and walked out of the building.

McLean's phone buzzed in his pocket as he stepped out of the station. He almost ignored it, shuddering at the icy cold that had settled in with the dark. Overhead, the clouds were orange from reflected street lights, and too low for his liking. It had been a long day, a harrowing one at that, and all he wanted was to get home. Still, he dug out the handset, thumbed the screen and clamped it to his ear.

'Aye?'

'Is that any way to greet an old friend, Inspector? Or should I say Chief Inspector? Going up in the world.'

He cursed himself for not checking the number before answering. There were few ways the day could have got worse, but this was one of them. On the other hand, Jo Dalgliesh, one-time reporter for the *Edinburgh Tribune* and general pain in the arse, had a knack for catching him unawares. Just one of her many annoying traits.

'What do you want, Dalgliesh?' McLean found the key fob with his free hand, plipped the button to unlock his car. It flashed its lights at him as he approached.

'Maybe a wee ride in that flash new sports car of yours. Or I could buy you a drink?'

He let the hand holding his phone drop away from his face, looking over to the gates where the car park exited onto the street. Sure enough, an all too familiar form stood under one of the lights, just outside the station itself. Cutting the call and shoving the handset back into his pocket, McLean tramped over.

'Can't drink and drive. You know that. And, as you pointed out, I've got a flash new sports car, which I'm just about to drive home.'

Dalgliesh made a show of checking her watch. 'As if you'd be going home at this hour.' She had an electronic cigarette in one gloved hand, and was wrapped up tight in her trademark long leather overcoat. She'd wrapped her neck in a thick woollen scarf, and sported a knitted hat that was probably the colours of one of the Edinburgh football teams, although McLean wasn't sure which was which and the orange light made it hard to tell anyway.

'You been waiting out here long?' he asked, noticing the shiver that she tried to suppress. She'd always been stick thin, but a narrow escape from a slice of poisoned chocolate cake had left her frail, too. McLean couldn't forget either that the cake had been meant for him.

'Och, a wee whiley. Not so long as I'd freeze my bollocks off.'

'Come on. There's a place round the corner from here. I'll buy you a coffee.'

'Fuck that. There's a perfectly good pub across the road. You can have coffee if you want, but I'll be needing something a lot stronger.'

★ ★ ★

The pub across the road from the station was, inevitably, full of just-off-duty police officers. McLean had spent enough of his time, and his money, in there to be known and welcomed, even if it had been a while since his last visit. Stepping through the door with Dalgliesh didn't quite silence the place like a saloon bar in a TV Western, but it wasn't far off. He led her straight to the bar, making sure there were plenty of sergeants and constables around to hear their conversation. At least that way there was a chance some of the rumours circulating on the next shift would be true.

'Actually, I will have a coffee.' Dalgliesh leaned against the bar on tiptoes, peering over it like a schoolgirl at the shiny new barista coffee machine that McLean was sure hadn't been there before. 'But ask them if they can maybe put a wee dram in it, aye?'

He ordered, getting a raised eyebrow from the barman, but no more comment than that. 'I know you'll just keep pestering me until I've told you what you want to know,' he said while they waited for the drinks to be made. 'So what's this all about then?'

Dalgliesh shoved her electronic cigarette in her mouth, chewed it a couple of times, then took it out again. 'You were much more fun when you weren't so snarky, you know?'

'I'm sure I was. But I'd quite like to get home at a reasonable hour.'

'Aye, OK. Fair enough. Wee birdy told me youse lot were down the Hermitage this afternoon. Full works. Forensics teams all over the place and your pal Angus there too. Only call him out when there's a dead body, aye?'

'You know the score, Jo. If we've not issued a statement to the press it's for a good reason.'

'So there is a dead body.'

'Come off it, Dalgliesh. You already know more about what's going on than that, or you'd not be pestering me for details. Get to the point, will you?'

'Word is you found a wee girl hidden away in the trees. No' there very long, ken?' Dalgliesh chewed on her cigarette a bit, and McLean knew she was studying his face for a reaction.

'Why do you even bother asking me these questions? You already know the answers before you come and speak to me anyway.'

'Got to check my facts now, Tony. Can't be making stuff up like the tabloids.'

He resisted the urge to remind her that the *Tribune* was a tabloid, and perhaps only marginally clear of the gutter on a good day. Dalgliesh in a friendly mood could be a useful ally, but the opposite was also true, so it was best not to upset her too much.

'I can confirm that we've found a body in the Hermitage. I can't confirm any details beyond that until we've identified the body and informed the next of kin. You know how it is, Jo. The last thing we want is for someone to find out their loved one's died from an article in the paper.'

'Aye, I ken that. Just wondering when you were going to come clean about the wee girl you found in the basement a couple of days back. No' sure how much longer I can sit on that one. Not now another's turned up deid.'

McLean paid for his coffees, sniffed them to see which one had alcohol in it and seriously thought about handing Dalgliesh the other. It gave him time to consider his reply, as did the fuss she made about adding sugar and cream.

'Look. We're preparing a press briefing for tomorrow morning. The deputy chief constable's going to be heading that up, so believe me when I say we're taking this very seriously. Never thought I'd hear the words come out of my mouth, but I'm grateful you've not gone with the story earlier.'

'Aye, well. Checking my facts. How is it you don't know who she is? How come you've no' asked us for help wi' that?'

McLean opened his mouth to reply, then bit back his words.

They'd been waiting for an artist's impression of the girl in the basement, since they couldn't use a photograph. Why had that taken so long? More importantly, why had he not chased it up sooner?

'It's early days. She doesn't match anyone on the missing-persons files, and we couldn't exactly run a photo of a dead girl's face in the news, could we?'

Dalgliesh looked sceptical as she slurped noisily at her coffee, but said nothing more.

'We're not trying to cover anything up here, Jo. There's . . .' He searched for the right word, knowing anything he said would just feed her insatiable curiosity. 'There's complications. It's not straightforward. Not that death ever is.'

'There's something linking the two, isn't there?' Dalgliesh's face lit up in a smile of purest delight.

'There are things we have to investigate further before we can go public with this. Things we have to rule out first.'

'Like foul play? You think they were murdered?'

McLean shook his head in frustration. 'It's not a question of what I think, Dalgliesh. It's about finding evidence, working out what's happened and why. We haven't got positive IDs for these two—' He almost said 'dead girls', but managed to stop himself. 'We don't know who they are or how they died. When we do, we're not going to keep that a secret. And in the meantime the deputy chief constable is going to hold a press conference at seven tomorrow morning. Your news editor should have had notification of that by now. I'll see you there.'

He picked up his coffee, meaning to drain it and walk out. It would have been more dramatic with a beer. The dark liquid was much less appealing, especially at this time of the night, so he put it back down again.

'Tomorrow morning, Jo. Then you'll know just as much about all this as we do.'

18

Outside in the cold air, McLean played the conversation over in his head and cursed the day journalists were invented. He jogged back across the road, avoiding the traffic that seemed to get heavier and faster as the conditions deteriorated. Back in the car park, his Alfa waited to take him home. Or he could go up to his office, see who was still in the station and let them know about Dalgliesh, maybe phone everyone else who needed to know. He couldn't pretend the meeting hadn't happened. They'd been in a pub filled with off-duty police officers, after all.

Sighing to no one but himself, McLean trudged back into the station and up to the third floor. He stopped by the small incident room that had been set up for the investigation into the first dead girl on his way. It was almost empty, just a couple of night shift constables either manning the phones or using the room to get some peace and quiet. Both the DCC and DI Ritchie's offices were empty, but he found Detective Superintendent McIntyre still at her desk.

'Thought you'd gone home, Tony.'

'Me too. Ran into an old friend in the car park.' He told her about Dalgliesh and their chat over coffee.

'Well, it was bound to happen sooner or later.' McIntyre pulled off her reading spectacles and placed them on top of the report she'd looked relieved to have been distracted from. 'I'm surprised it's taken them this long, to be honest. And good of Dalgliesh to come and speak to you first.'

'What can I say? We have history.'

McIntyre smiled the distant smile of the exhausted. 'Time was you'd not have given her a chance to even talk.'

'Aye, well. People change. It doesn't help much that the story's going to blow up in our faces tomorrow though.'

'You want me to tell Robinson?' McIntyre picked up her spectacles again, reached for her phone.

'If you don't mind. I reckon he'll shout less at you. I'll give Grumpy Bob and Kirsty a call though. Might as well warn everyone. But I really need to get home.'

'Everything OK?' McIntyre leaned back in her chair, switching smoothly into 'mother' mode. She wasn't that much older than him, McLean knew, but it seemed to come naturally.

'It's . . .' He shrugged. 'Call it a work in progress. Helps if I come home at a reasonable hour every now and then.'

'Well, get out of here then, and get some sleep. Six o'clock start tomorrow.'

McLean grimaced, nodded his head and walked to the door. McIntyre spoke again as he was about to leave.

'You can't do everything yourself, Tony. Sometimes you have to ask for help.' She picked up the phone and began tapping in numbers. 'Trust me. I've been there.'

McLean parked his Alfa next to Emma's car, noticing that it was covered in a light dusting of snow, the windscreen iced up. That at least meant there was a chance she was home, and the recent change in her attitude towards him gave him some hope. Her quip at the crime scene at Hermitage of Braid had been almost friendly, although she'd disappeared swiftly enough after making it and he'd not seen her since. Perhaps he'd not go so far as to call it a thawing in their strained relationship, but it had been a while since she'd been outwardly hostile.

Mrs McCutcheon's cat eyed him from her spot in front of the Aga as he entered the kitchen and dumped his briefcase down on the table. The warmth of the room was always welcome, but he could smell no scent of cooking to go with it. Not that he expected to be waited on; Emma was her own person, not his wife, nor his servant. He worried that she might not have been feeding herself properly. Even a couple of slices of toast would have made their presence felt if she'd made them in the past few hours.

'Anyone home?' He ventured a half-shout as he walked across the hall towards the front door. The day's letters were stacked neatly on the sideboard, so someone had looked through them since the postman had been. No answer came, and when he stuck his head around the library door, the room was empty, television switched off although the light was still on. The fire hadn't been lit, and despite the clanking and gurgling of the massive old boiler in the basement, the temperature inside was only marginally warmer than out. He beat a hasty retreat to the kitchen and the Aga.

The takeaway menus pinned to the noticeboard by the phone tempted him with their siren song, but McLean resisted. Instead, he rooted around in fridge and cupboard. The bread had been fresh once, he was sure. Just not recently. At least it wasn't spotty. He opted for scrambled eggs on toast instead of a sandwich, pondering the day's events as he ate.

Of all the things that had happened, the reappearance of Jo Dalgliesh in his life was, on balance, the worst. True, she could be useful at times, but more often than not she was as welcome as a fart in a spacesuit. He could do without the public scrutiny her breaking the story would bring, although it was inevitable that someone would have broken it sooner or later. Lucky, perhaps, that it had been her. Other journalists might not have given him any warning, and they'd all be fire-fighting as the media wound itself up into a frenzy. A dead girl – Christ, two dead girls. Never mind that they had no idea who they were or what they had died of. The press were going to have a field day.

'Thought I heard a noise.'

McLean looked up to see Emma standing in the doorway. She was dressed in fleece pyjamas with a dairy cow motif printed on them, big fluffy slippers on her feet. Her tousled hair and puffy eyes suggested she'd been in bed.

'Sorry. I didn't mean to wake you up.'

'You didn't. Couldn't sleep. Kept seeing that poor wee girl in the woods. She looked so cold.' Emma shuffled over to the Aga and heaved the kettle onto the hotplate. 'Tea?'

McLean had imagined a wee dram somewhere in his near future, but tea would do at a pinch. Tomorrow was going to start early and go on for a long time. Best to face that with a clear head. 'Aye, please.'

He watched as she went about making them both a cuppa. Neither of them said anything until she had sat down across the table from him.

'Looks like you've got another one of those invitations.' Emma nodded at the pile of letters McLean had dropped onto the table and forgotten about. Sure enough, slotted between a gardening catalogue addressed to his late grandmother and an expensive-looking letter bearing the crest of Edinburgh City Council, another hand-delivered envelope addressed to them both. This time he was able to study the wax seal on the back more closely, seeing the intricately twined letters J, L and D. There was some stylised creature in the background too, most likely a serpent, although it was so tiny he could hardly tell. He fetched his eggy knife from the plate and used it to slit the top of the envelope. Inside, the card was identical to the last one.

'I'd a feeling one of these would turn up.'

'You did? Why?' Emma tugged the card from his unresisting grip and peered at the writing on it, her face turning to a scowl when she saw her first name written there again.

'Jayne McIntyre told me I had to go. Said it was important I represent Police Scotland, now that I'm a high and mighty chief inspector.'

'And you always do what you're told, right.' She dropped the card onto the table, then cradled her mug for warmth. She looked thin and tired, but there was a wry smile on her face too. Something McLean hadn't seen in a while.

'Well, if you'd lit the fire I'd chuck it. Still, there's always the recycling.' He reached out for the card, but before he could pick it up, Emma spoke again.

'Or we could go.' It was almost like a dare.

'Really?'

'Yeah. Why not? It's not like you have to bid on any of their stupid charity auction stuff, anyway. And it's been ages since I've been out anywhere posh.'

McLean sipped his tea, waiting for the punchline in Emma's joke. Only, it never came. Her excitement at the idea was palpable, and it made her look more alive than he'd seen her in months.

'OK. We'll go,' he said. 'But you'll have to wear something a bit more fashionable than cow-print pyjamas.'

19

'Why'd you have to speak to that bloody reporter? And in a pub full of police officers too? What the fuck were you thinking?'

Six o'clock sharp in the small conference room, and McLean wasn't at all surprised to find the DCC in a towering rage. He'd woken to the radio bulletins going on about the two dead girls, police incompetence and rumours of a cover-up. Over a hasty breakfast he'd looked at some of the online newsfeeds and seen even more lurid speculation about both serial killers and mysterious epidemics. He'd not seen that morning's *Tribune* yet, but no doubt Jo Dalgliesh had done her best to spin the story for maximum outrage. That was all people wanted these days, after all.

'If I'd refused to speak to her, she'd have written the story anyway. At least this way I was able to find out more or less how much she knew before it went to print.'

Robinson stared at him as if he had two heads. Perhaps the DCC wasn't used to people answering him back when he was giving them a bollocking, but McLean had been ranted at by more violent people than Call-me-Stevie. It was too early in the morning to get riled up, and Emma's more cheery disposition had left him in a good mood.

'We knew this was going to happen, sir,' he continued. 'Sooner or later the press were going to find out about the girl in the basement. We were going to have to tell them today, start using them to try and track down who she is. A second body . . .' He shook his head, unsure whether he wanted to go on.

'It's still bloody irregular talking to a reporter off the record in the pub. We sack constables for doing that, you know.' Robinson was a bit calmer now, but still agitated.

'That's because constables who mouth off to the press are either doing it for backhanders or don't know better. I'm a chief inspector, as you keep reminding me, sir. I made a decision based on the situation that was presented to me. And I made sure all the senior officers involved in this investigation knew about it as soon as it happened.' He glanced across the room to where Detective Superintendent McIntyre was pretending to read a report. She had spoken to the DCC the night before, he knew. It was just that instead of using the time to reappraise what he was going to say during the press conference, Robinson had spent the night fretting.

'Where are we then? What do they know, and what don't they know that we do?'

'Judging by the newsfeeds, they know pretty much everything and are having a lot of fun making up everything else.' McIntyre picked up a small remote control and pointed it at the projector slung from the ceiling. A portion of the conference room wall lit up with the image from her laptop computer, a web browser page displaying the breaking-news section of the BBC Scotland website. 'The less sensational reports have two separate deaths, a few days apart, neither body yet identified but both young children.' A click and the screen changed to a tabloid website. 'Clickbait sites reckon there's some terrible new virus that's targeting the young.' Another click, another site. 'Or that it's a side-effect of vaccinations.' Once again. 'Or possibly alien abduction and experimentation.'

'Enough, Jayne.' Robinson slumped against the table, his wrath expended.

'I hadn't got to the one where they say it's all a conspiracy by the Freemasons and something calling itself the Brotherhood.'

'All that in less than twelve hours? I'm impressed.' McLean looked at the latest screen McIntyre had displayed. He didn't recognise the site or the name of the person who had authored the piece, but that was hardly surprising. 'Maybe we should pay them to do our job for us.'

'It's not funny, McLean.' Robinson growled out his surname. 'What the hell am I supposed to say to those ghouls in there?' He didn't point or nod his head, but McLean knew well enough what he meant. Even now the assorted members of the press would be descending on the station like flies on a carcass, filing into the largest conference room, anticipating salacious detail they weren't going to get. Outside in the street a line of trucks festooned with aerials and satellite dishes were already buggering up the rush hour traffic.

'I know it's old-fashioned, but we could try the truth. I'll go in there and tell them everything we know so far. Appeal to the public for help and we can shut down all this nonsense before it gets the wind up its tail.' He waved a hand at the web page pretending to be news that was plastered all over the wall.

'You'll go nowhere near that conference room and you'll speak to nobody without my express permission.' The edge of anger was back in the DCC's voice. 'You've done enough damage as it is.'

McLean opened his mouth to complain, then realised what he was going to complain about and shut it again. Not speaking to the press suited him just fine, although deep down he knew that it wasn't going to be that easy.

'Go see your friend the pathologist,' Robinson said. 'We need answers as to how these two girls died, and we need them now.'

He wasn't sure whether the DCC had meant it literally when he'd told him to go and see Angus, but McLean took the opportunity anyway. It meant running the gauntlet of reporters outside the station, doing their pieces to camera with a snow-clad Arthur's Seat in the background for good visuals. Luckily no one seemed to notice as he slipped out of the back door, collar on his overcoat pulled up like a spy. It didn't take long to walk to the mortuary, and the cold air helped to clear his head, sharpen his thoughts.

Cadwallader was already prepped for the post-mortem when McLean let himself into the observation theatre. He'd seen one small girl opened up to reveal her innermost secrets this week already, had no great desire to get too close to a second one.

'I'll just watch from up here if you don't mind,' he said as the pathologist looked up at him. Doctor MacPhail was there too, no doubt to corroborate any findings, and he waved uncertainly at McLean before returning to his stool beside the X-ray viewing screens.

The examination didn't take long, thankfully, and he was able to avoid seeing the worst of it by leaning back in his seat and staring at the ceiling. From a distance, he couldn't hear properly what Angus said, although at one point the pathologist asked Tom MacPhail for his opinion on something. McLean let most of it wash over him, chasing thoughts instead. Who was this little girl, and who was the one they had found in the basement? How could a parent lose a child like that and not kick up a fuss? How terrified for your own life would you have to be that you would keep silent? Or how little did you actually value the life of a young girl? That was always a possibility, if as he suspected both children were illegal immigrants. There was every chance their parents weren't even here in Edinburgh, might not even be still alive. And there was a chance too that a young female life was not worth preserving in whatever foreign land they had come from.

There were those in his own country who almost certainly felt the same way.

'You still with us, Tony?'

The words cut through McLean's musing, and he looked up to see Angus Cadwallader staring at him from a couple of paces away. His green scrubs were remarkably clean for a man who had just performed a post-mortem, and for a moment McLean thought he might have changed already. That he was rubbing his hands on an off-white towel gave the lie to that idea quickly enough.

'Just trying to get my head around what's happening here.' He stood up stiffly, hip aching from where it had been broken several years earlier. It did that when the weather was cold, he'd noticed. Or when there was a storm coming.

'You and me both.'

'That bad, is it?'

'At least. Come and have a look.'

McLean hesitated. 'Not sure I'm in the mood to see another dead wee girl, Angus.'

'That's not what I'm going to show you. Bad enough I have to myself.' Cadwallader turned away and set off towards the open-plan office that stood adjacent to the examination theatre. Glancing back at the stainless-steel table, McLean saw Doctor Sharp busy sewing the dead girl back together again, destined for a long stay in the cold mortuary and then final rest in an unmarked grave. He shook his head to try and dislodge the uncharacteristic lump that had appeared in his throat, then followed his old friend away from the grisly scene.

'How much do you know about ancient Egypt, Tony?'

McLean had found himself a seat that didn't face the glass looking out onto the examination theatre. This meant that he had to watch his old friend as he stripped off his scrubs and clambered into a tweed suit, but that was preferable to the more intimate and horrifying scene playing out behind him.

'I saw a documentary once, I think. And I went on an educational cruise around the Mediterranean when I was about ten. We visited Alexandria, took a bus down to Cairo and Giza. Mostly I remember wee boys begging for sweets, meeting the Gully Gully Man, and feeling terrified when we were taken into a pyramid somewhere in the desert. I was convinced the entrance was going to collapse and we'd be trapped there for ever.'

Cadwallader looked at him as if he were a total stranger. 'I had no idea. You're full of surprises. But trapped under a pyramid for ever? That's . . . kind of appropriate to what we're looking at here.'

'It is?'

'Aye. The wee girl you found in the basement, and that poor thing out there. Both of them have undergone some kind of process that's begun to mummify them. Their skin, well, I don't really know how to describe it. Not exactly tanning. You see, the ancient Egyptians preserved the bodies of their dead because they believed they would need them in the afterlife. They were very skilled, knew things we haven't even begun to rediscover about how to stop flesh and bone from rotting away.'

'You're saying they've been mummified?' McLean stole a glance over his shoulder towards the examination table, but Doctor Sharp had finished her work and was wheeling the body away to its lonely cold store.

'Part-mummified. And only their skin, as far as I can tell.'

'But . . . That makes no sense, surely?'

Cadwallader took off his spectacles and polished them with a grubby handkerchief. 'Tony, none of this makes any sense. The Egyptian mummies had all their internal organs removed before the preservation process began. They'd use a wee hook through the nose to scoop out the brains. These two girls both had all their organs still inside them, only something was making them fail. Their hearts gave out, but their kidneys, liver, spleen, pretty much everything else looks like it belongs to an eighty-year-old, not someone who's only eight. I'd say they might have suffered from progeria, except that it's incredibly rare and outwardly they don't show the classic signs.'

'But they died, you say? They weren't killed?'

'I don't know. Something killed them before their time, for sure. But was it a person, or was it some disease I've not seen before? Something my colleagues at the Faculty of Medicine, even the Centre for Tropical Veterinary Medicine, haven't seen before? Something we can't find any toxin for in their blood? I'll admit it: I can't say why they died. I can say that the unusual preservation of their skin seems to be an after-effect though.'

'So they both died of the same thing.'

'Exactly so.'

'Are they related, the two girls?'

Cadwallader shook his head. 'Not closely, at least. We're still waiting on the full DNA analysis of the first one, and that poor wee thing—' He waved a hand in the direction of the now empty examination theatre. 'Her sample's only just gone off. Blood tests say they're not related though, and physically they don't look much alike.'

McLean hadn't seen much of the young girl in the Hermitage, and now he slightly regretted not getting a proper look at her during the examination.

'Have you got photos of them both? Their faces?'

'Should have. Hang on a minute.' Cadwallader sat down at a computer, reached for the mouse and started swiping and tapping with all the dexterity of a silver surfer. McLean waited as patiently as he could, wondering whether his old friend would find the photographs before Doctor Sharp came back and did it for him.

'Here we are, look.' The pathologist leaned back in his chair and let McLean see the screen. An examination table photograph of the first girl's face filled it, leaving nothing to the imagination. Her eyes were closed, cheeks thin and hollow. She looked darker than he remembered, as if whatever had started to tan her skin was still working its evil magic. The tangle of wiry black hair framing her head looked almost wig-like.

'And this is the one we just examined.' Cadwallader clicked the mouse and another photograph appeared. This girl looked a touch less malnourished, although her skin had that same waxy quality as the other girl. It was tanned, but less so than the previous image. What struck him most about her though was her hair.

'How did I not notice that at the crime scene yesterday?' McLean pointed at the screen as if his old friend would know immediately what he was referring to.

'Notice what?'

'Her hair.'

'Oh, that. She was wearing a woolly hat, remember? Pulled down over her ears. What about her hair? I mean, it's cut short, aye. A boy's cut, but that's not so strange these days.'

McLean stared at the screen, mind racing as it tried to find a place for this piece of the puzzle to fit. Failing badly. There were too many unknowns, and too many coincidences that made no sense. But most of all there was this young girl, dead and shoved away in a cold storage unit in the city mortuary. This little girl with hair as red as the setting sun in the desert.

20

McLean climbed out of the passenger seat of his Alfa at the main entrance to the Hermitage, leaving DC Harrison to lock the car as he walked over to the main gate. He was pleased to see it closed and a uniformed constable making sure nobody slipped in unawares. At least that much procedure was being adhered to. A couple of cars parked further up the road were most likely journalists looking for a photo opportunity. He just hoped they had enough bodies on the ground to keep them from contaminating the crime scene.

'DI Ritchie here, is she, Constable?' he asked as he showed the young man his warrant card.

'Aye, sir. She's up at the crime scene.'

'Any trouble from the press?' McLean waved a hand at the parked cars.

'No' so much. Think this cold weather's keeping them away mostly. Could be creeping in the back way, mind. There's more ways into this place than I reckon anyone knows.'

He was right. A network of official and unofficial paths criss-crossed the park, and there were ways in from gardens of nearby houses, his own included. You could walk in along the Braid Burn, from Blackford Hill and the golf course. Closing the whole area off would have required far more manpower, and expense, than they could afford. Ritchie was experienced enough to prioritise working the immediate area around the crime scene itself. They could expand the search outwards if nothing came up from that. At least the weather was in their favour. In the summer the Hermitage would have been bustling with people. But then, in the summer someone might have seen what had happened too.

He left the constable behind and set off into the park, Harrison following in silence. The still air had a dampness to it that made the chill feel even colder than usual, their breath steaming as if they were dragons.

'Used to come down here when I was a boy. It's a great place to hide out. Well, in the summer anyway.'

Harrison said nothing as they walked down the wide footpath alongside the Dean Burn, but he could see the sideways glance she gave him out of the corner of his eye.

'Of course, that was a long time ago. I don't suppose parents would let their kids go wandering off into the woods all day during the holidays now.'

'Kids today probably wouldn't want to. Why come here when you can hang out at the play park drinking Buckie and swearing at the passers-by?'

McLean raised an eyebrow at Harrison's cynicism, but said nothing. They walked on down the footpath for a while before she spoke again.

'Your place isn't far from here, is it, sir?'

'No.' He stopped to get his bearings. Things had changed since he'd come here regularly. The paths were better maintained for one thing. The city felt closer, too. Before, this had been a jungle. His own adventure playground. Now it hummed with the noise of not-too-distant cars, and peering through the leafless trees he could see buildings where thirty years ago there had been none. Thirty? McLean corrected himself. More like forty.

They walked a bit further, rounding a bend in the path to be confronted by a couple of bored-looking uniformed officers. Crime scene tape had been rolled out between the trees to the side of the path, a marked way leading to the clearing where the young girl's body had been found.

'Morning, sir. Constable.' One of the officers turned as they approached, smiling as he saw them both. Police Sergeant Reg Clark. McLean knew him from his early days with Lothian and Borders, surprised that the man hadn't retired already.

'Busy, Reg?' he asked.

'Hardly. The main entrances are locked down, and the weather's doing the rest for us.'

'Forensics still in there, I take it?' He peered through the spindly trees, just about seeing the white shape of the tent in the gloom.

'Aye. Reckon they'll be done by the end of the day.'

'What about the area search?' He turned in a slow circle, not seeing the undergrowth crawling with coppers.

'No' sure sir. DI Ritchie was here a wee while ago, sir. I think she lost the plot a bit when she found out we'd only a handful of constables to work with and most of them were guarding the gates.'

'She still here?'

'Think she got a call back to the station.'

McLean glanced over to the trees again, then up at the purple-grey clouds low overhead. There was a scent in the air of more snow on the way, which would make any search pointless. They wouldn't have daylight for much longer either. A whole day wasted.

'I know this part of the glen though.' He turned on the spot again, dredging up old memories long forgotten. 'Used to come here as a boy, and I'm sure there's an old walled garden near here. Overgrown, but the stonework's still in place.'

Police Sergeant Reg looked doubtful. 'Couldn't rightly say, sir.' He turned to his colleague. 'You know anything like that, Tim?'

'Sorry, sir. Never even heard of the place till yesterday. My usual beat's the other side of the city.'

'Never mind. I'm sure I'll find it. Just need to pretend I'm seven years old again. Come on, Harrison.'

McLean left the two uniformed officers to their puzzled expressions and set off down the path again. Harrison took a moment to catch up. 'What exactly are we looking for, sir? I thought we were coming to review the crime scene.'

'I was hoping to get some news from Kir— . . . DI Ritchie about the area search, but it seems that's not happened yet. So I'm improvising.' McLean walked on a bit, staring up into the trees. Then he stopped, turned and headed back the way he'd come.

'You saw the girl, right? Yesterday, when she was found?'

Harrison's face had been ruddy with the cold, but now it paled. 'No, sir. I wasn't part of the team. I saw the photographs though, at this morning's briefing.'

McLean frowned at that, then realised he'd missed the briefing because he'd been at the mortuary. It didn't matter, he'd catch up when they got back to the station.

'What do you remember from the photographs then?'

Harrison paused a moment before answering. 'She was better dressed for the cold than the girl in the basement. Had a woolly hat on, and a coat that would go some way to keeping her warm for an hour or two. No good for spending the night out, mind you. Not when it's like this.'

'And she was barefoot, right?'

'Aye, there was that. Makes me shiver just to think about it. Poor wee thing.'

McLean remembered his own, similar reaction the afternoon before. 'So how did she get there? No way she walked on bare feet through the woods. Not for any great distance, anyway. Angus thought she'd been moved, at least to position her after she'd died. So was she brought here and dumped? Where did she come from? Who brought her and why?'

'Is that not what the forensics team are trying to find out?' Harrison looked back up the path to where Sergeant Reg and Constable Tim were stamping their feet against the cold.

'Not going to learn anything from there, I don't think.' McLean walked a few more paces, then pushed aside some heavy rhododendron bushes leaning into the footpath. Behind them, a narrower path led into the woods. 'This, on the other hand, looks much more promising.'

Behind the bush, the path widened. Like everywhere else, it was covered with a thin dusting of snow, but it also looked like people had come this way recently. No more than fifty yards away from where the dead girl's body had been found, the undergrowth was too thick to see through once they stepped off the main route. The noise of the city seemed to mute too, an odd silence settling over them as the pushed on. And then McLean began to see what his memories told him should have been here. A low wall, crumbling masonry climbing up to an empty archway. The path stopped there, and beyond it lay the ruins of a small walled garden.

'I knew it was here.' He couldn't keep the little boy shout of triumph out of his voice, but it was short-lived. Stepping through the arched gateway was not the magical experience of his youth. Rhododendron bushes had taken over much of the area beyond, but here and there were cleared patches, stones arranged in neat circles to contain fires, scraps of cloth tied to branches where larger sheets had been hung to make rudimentary shelters and torn down in a hurry. The more he looked, the more he saw signs of organised habitation. People had been living here, camping here, and recently.

'Sir, I think you need to see this.' Harrison's voice wavered slightly as she spoke. McLean turned to where she was standing, just inside the arch. The wall there was higher than the rest of the overgrown garden, almost as tall as he was. The soft brown sandstone had been worked with great skill by the masons who originally built the garden, but time had worn away the edges, and generations of visitors had carved their names, dates, and other graffiti into it. Someone had carefully chipped out an entire block to make a small alcove, the stone around it decorated with intricate symbols. And inside it they had placed a pair of shoes.

Small shoes.

Like a child might wear.

21

S tuck in traffic as it grumbled along Nicolson Street, McLean couldn't help noticing DC Harrison stifle a yawn and rub at her eyes. The car was pleasantly warm after an hour or two out in the freezing air and gloom of the Hermitage, and he felt the weariness tugging at him too.

'Late night? I hope that flatmate of yours isn't keeping you awake at all hours.'

Harrison almost poked herself in the eye, flushing slightly as she looked away. 'Sorry, sir. Nothing like that.' She shook her head slightly. 'Well, it was a late night, aye. And Manda was involved. She got us tickets to the circus, see? Thought it would be all over by ten, but it was past midnight when we left.'

'Circus?' McLean remembered the tents on the Meadows that had appeared overnight like mushrooms after rain. 'Never took you for the clowns and elephants type.'

'They don't do elephants any more. Scottish government banned live animal shows a couple of years back. This was different. There were clowns, true enough. But there was more, too. The trapeze artists were amazing. The whole thing . . .' Harrison's voice trailed away as if she was overwhelmed by the memories. Then all of a sudden she turned to face him, laid a hand on his arm.

'You should go, sir. You should take Emma. She'd love it. Don't think I've ever seen such a magical show.'

McLean looked down at his arm, then straight at Harrison. For a moment her face was that of a pre-teen going to a party, all excitement and wonder. Then she realised what she was doing and swiftly withdrew her hand.

'That good?' McLean tried a smile to ease the tension that had suddenly filled the car.

'Sorry. I—'

'No need to apologise. I might even take your advice. We don't get out much, Emma and me. It would be nice to do something together for a change, rather than just meeting up at crime scenes.'

The traffic started moving again, which eased the tension and gave McLean something to do. He concentrated on driving until they reached the station, and Harrison kept her thoughts to herself. She only spoke again when they were approaching the building.

'You want me to chase up Dougie Naismith and Billy McKenzie, sir?'

It sounded to McLean like the request of a constable who didn't want to get roped into any more strenuous activity before shift end, particularly not dealing with the paperwork their discovery of the walled garden would generate, but it also reminded him they were still no closer to identifying either of the two dead girls yet.

'Aye, do that. Might be worth getting McKenzie in for a chat, if you can. Show him those artist's impressions we got of the two wee girls and see if they jog his memory. Could maybe show him the photo of the woman we think might be Rahel's sister.'

'You think he's holding back?' Harrison looked sceptical. 'Wasn't he the one came to us first?'

'He did. But he knows more than he's telling us. He's

protecting Rahel too. Most likely because he knows she's here illegally and he doesn't want her sent home.'

'The power of love.' Harrison flushed a little as she said it.

'Thanks for that, Constable.'

'For what?'

'The earworm. That's two songs I'm not going to get out of my head for hours now.'

Harrison's face spoke eloquently of her ignorance on matters musical, at least as far as eighties power ballads went. Then again, she'd probably not been born then.

'I tell a lie. Three songs.' McLean checked his watch, wondering as ever where the time had gone. That day, and the past twenty-something years. 'Team meeting's at half four. Get yourself some lunch and then bring McKenzie in. Naismith can help with the interview if you can find him.'

A curious mashup of Jennifer Rush, Frankie Goes to Hollywood and Huey Lewis and the News rumbled around his head as McLean descended into the depths of the station. He didn't listen to music as much as he once had, not helped by his entire and extensive collection of vinyl records having perished in the fire that had destroyed his Newington tenement flat a few years back. He'd replaced some of them, but it still struck him as odd how a simple, throwaway expression could bring ancient memories bubbling back. Of the three songs, he thought he might have had a twelve-inch single of one, back before the fire. He wasn't going to admit to anybody which one it had been.

The corridor leading to the Cold Case Unit office was dark when he approached, lit only by the meagre daylight reaching down a lightwell at the back of the station. He almost turned back, assuming that no one was in, but then he heard a voice from behind the closed door. Opening it, he found ex-Detective Superintendent Duguid holding court to Grumpy Bob and

Inspector Tom Callander from uniform. The animated conversation dropped away almost immediately, and McLean had a small inkling of what a headmaster must feel every time he steps into a classroom full of boys.

'Am I interrupting something?' He meant the words as a joke, but judging by Duguid's face he might not have quite hit the mark.

'We were just discussing the investigation, Tony.' Callander stood up perhaps a little too swiftly, and despite being comfortably McLean's senior in years, he looked the most ill at ease of the company.

'That's handy. I was hoping to get some CCU input anyway. That's if you're not too busy.'

Duguid glared, but McLean had known the man long enough to see it for the ruse it truly was. Judging by the stack of archive boxes behind his desk, and the heap of old-fashioned report folders piled on top of it, they were hunting around for something new to get stuck into.

'What were you after? And what's your budget?'

'We've got two dead girls, both died in the city in the past few days. And now the press have got hold of the story and are beating us around the head with it. What do you think the budget is?'

'Fair enough.' Duguid leaned back in his chair and cupped his hands together like an amateur dramatic society Shylock. 'But, as you so rightly point out, McLean, the two of them have died in the past week. That's not exactly cold, now, is it?'

'These two aren't, no. But that's not to say there haven't been other cases in the past. We need to go through the archives, and particularly missing persons records for girls in the five-to-twelve age bracket. My memory's not what it used to be, but I'm sure there was something a year or two before I joined up. Two or three girls went missing and were never found.'

'Aye, I remember that.' Grumpy Bob had been slouching in his seat, but now he sat up straight, leaned forward and began tapping at his computer keyboard. 'I wasn't long out of uniform myself. Early nineties, I think it was. They found some clothes in the woods north of Edgelaw Reservoir. Out Temple way.'

'They found one of the girls, too. She'd run away with a travelling circus, hadn't she?'

All eyes fell on Inspector Callander, who just shrugged. 'I read it in the *Courier*, back when I was in Dundee. Half of Tayside Police got shunted down to help you lot with the search. I was stuck on traffic duty.'

'You're forgetting one other thing, McLean.' Duguid's growl wasn't angry, but it wasn't exactly friendly either. 'Those three girls were all reported to the police within hours of their going missing. No one's come forward to claim either of these two yet.'

'Well, it might be nothing, but it's worth looking for anything that might be similar, and since you've got the archives all digitised now . . .'

Duguid made a noise that might have been a cough, or might have been a laugh. It was difficult to tell with the ex-detective superintendent. He seemed to take great delight in being miserable though, which might have explained why he kept on coming back to work even though he'd retired over a year past.

'There was one other thing.' McLean pulled out his phone and thumbed the screen to bring up the photographs he'd taken at the walled garden. He flicked through them until he found the one of the small alcove in the wall, the pair of shoes neatly placed within it, and the swirling sigils carved into the stone all around.

'I'll send you copies of these so you can get a better look at them. Crime scene photos should be on the system soon too. This is a shrine, though, and those are the shoes taken from the wee girl we found in the Hermitage. This was just a hundred yards or so from where we found her.'

'You're sure they're hers?' Callander peered at the screen with myopic eyes.

'Forensics will tell us soon enough, but I'm pretty sure. At the moment I'm more interested in these carvings.' He indicated the squiggly lines and curls with his index finger as Grumpy Bob crowded in for a better look. Duguid hadn't moved from his seat across the room.

'I want you to try and find out what these symbols mean, whether they've been found at any other crime scenes in the past. Anything, really, that might give us a lead.'

Duguid finally moved, scraping his seat back as he stood up and walked slowly across the room. He grabbed the phone from McLean's grasp, fished spectacles out from the breast pocket of his tweed jacket and slid them onto his nose. Then he reached in and pinched at the screen, zooming the image and moving it around with all the skill of a teenager.

'These are old,' he said after a while.

'They looked freshly cut to me.'

'No, I mean ancient, like old writing. Hieroglyphs and what-not. You don't need us, McLean. You need a history professor.'

22

McLean didn't notice the group of people walking towards him from the reception area until one of them spoke. He'd been too busy tapping his fingernail against the back of his phone absent-mindedly as he climbed the stairs back to the part of the station occupied with the present day.

'Chief Inspector, sir. I was hoping we might find you.'

Still not quite used to being called chief inspector, it took him a moment longer than was perhaps polite to realise that the words were addressed at him. He looked up, somewhat surprised to see Detective Sergeant Naismith in the corridor. Behind him, flanked by two uniformed constables, was Billy McKenzie.

'I was told you wanted to have a word with this lad. Had him brought in.'

McLean opened his mouth to ask Naismith why he hadn't gone and fetched the lad himself like he'd been asked, then realised that the message might have got itself garbled along the various links down the chain of command. Either that or the detective sergeant was a lazy sod. Something about the way Naismith stood made him think it was probably the latter. The man looked absurdly pleased with himself when in fact he hadn't done anything at all.

'Thanks for coming in, Mr McKenzie. It's very helpful.'

McLean spoke past Naismith at first, only turning to the detective sergeant when McKenzie had shown he recognised him.

'Show him to interview room one, will you? I'll be there in a minute.'

Naismith looked puzzled for a moment, as if he couldn't understand why the criminal wasn't being thrown in the cells to sweat for a bit. Then he nodded, adding, 'Aye, sir', before turning his attention to the two constables.

'Put him in room one.'

McLean couldn't quite suppress the smile from his lips. He'd known this was exactly what Naismith would do.

'I don't think it takes two constables to escort a man who's helping us with an important enquiry. You can show him there yourself, Sergeant. And wait with him until I get there.'

To his credit, the detective sergeant managed to keep his irritation mostly concealed. McLean stood aside to let him and McKenzie pass, then dismissed the two constables and went in search of someone he felt he could trust. He found her clumping up the stairs from the station back entrance. Detective Constable Harrison's smile was an uncertain one, as if she knew already what was coming next.

'You busy, Constable?'

It was an unfair question, given that she was a detective constable and he a chief inspector. To her credit, she only shrugged. 'It can probably wait, sir.'

'Good. I've got Billy McKenzie in interview room one. Reckon it's time to explain to him just how serious the situation is.'

'There's printed photographs of the two girls in the incident room, sir. You want me to put together a wee folder and bring them for him to look at?'

'Do that, will you? And if you can get one of the young woman DCI Dexter was talking about too. The Jane Doe in the hospital?'

Unlike Naismith, Harrison was quick on the uptake. 'It'll take a minute or two to get one printed off, sir. Is that OK?'

'Fine. I'll go and have a chat with McKenzie for now. Not sure leaving him with DS Naismith was a good idea.'

Harrison opened her mouth, possibly to voice an opinion about that, then closed it again, figuring correctly that a nod was better comment. McLean set off back up the stairs, then remembered something else.

'One more thing, Harrison.' He turned to face her again, noticing that she hadn't moved. Could she anticipate him that well?

'Coffee for McKenzie?'

'Make it for all of us. And biscuits, if you can find them.'

'I've not done anything wrong, you ken? I've just been trying to help.'

McLean sat at the table in interview room one, looking across at an increasingly agitated Billy McKenzie. He wished DC Harrison would hurry back with the coffee; somehow her presence seemed to calm the young man down. Unlike the looming bulk of DS Naismith, standing by the door.

'You're absolutely right, Billy. You've not done anything wrong, and you are trying to help. Believe me when I say you're not in any trouble here.'

'Then why'd you bring me here in a polis car? Why'd you send those two constables round my place to pick me up? You think they don't notice stuff like that?'

'They? Who would notice? And why would it matter?' Naismith's voice dripped with sarcasm as he asked the question, and his attitude explained a lot of McKenzie's unhappiness.

'Sergeant, could you maybe step outside? This isn't an inter-rogation. We're not recording this and I don't need corroboration for anything Mr McKenzie might tell me. Perhaps you could go

140

and find out what's taking Harrison so long with those coffees.'

Naismith looked like he'd been slapped, pausing a little too long before giving McLean a tiny nod. He threw McKenzie an angry glance, and then did as he'd been told.

'I'm very sorry, Billy. When I asked for you to be brought to the station, I meant for a plain-clothes officer to fetch you. I can see how it would look to the Dee Trust, having you hauled out of one of their flats by a couple of uniformed constables. They subsidise your rent, I take it?'

'Aye. It's a halfway house, y'ken? Take us from care homes and set us up. It's free to start with, and there's folk there to help you find work, learn how to use the laundry machines, stuff like that. When you get a job, they expect you to pay something, but it's no' much, ken. No' like renting.'

'You grew up in care, then?'

'Aye. Fostered a few times, but . . .' McKenzie stared at his fingernails for a while, then straight at McLean with an intensity that was shocking. 'The last place, mind. Before I turned sixteen and could get oot. That was proper nasty, like. I'd 've been better off on the streets, but then they told me about Inchmalcolm Tower, the Trust.' He shook his head a couple of times, and went back to studying his fingernails. 'It was good there. An' wi' a job an' all. No' sure what's gonnae happen now. Specially if they think I'm in trouble with the polis.'

A noise at the open door disturbed them both. McLean looked round to see DC Harrison bearing a tray with three mugs of coffee on it, along with a plate of chocolate biscuits she had to have stolen from somewhere. There was no way a packet of those could remain hidden in the station for any length of time.

'Sorry it took so long, sir. Canteen's filling up with frozen constables in from the Hermitage.'

McLean had been concentrating on the mugs and the biscuits while Harrison spoke, but even so he noticed the way McKenzie stiffened at the final word. A gambler might have considered it a definite tell.

'Here you go, Billy. And tuck into the biscuits. If you don't, then some thieving constable will.' He placed one of the mugs down in front of the young man, then waited for Harrison to sit before continuing.

'I'll have a word with the building manager, let them know what's been going on and that you're not in any trouble with us. If there's anything I can do about your job too, I will.' He let that sink in for a moment, waiting for McKenzie to lift his mug to his lips before speaking again. 'Has Rahel been in touch?'

The tell was more obvious this time, now that he was looking for it, the twitch so pronounced, McKenzie almost spilled coffee down his face. He disguised it by taking a bigger gulp than was wise, then coughed when he found it too hot.

'I know what she thinks of the likes of us. We're the face of authority, the folk who'll send her home.' McLean shook his head even though he knew that he really should report any illegal immigrants he encountered in his work. 'I don't want to do that, but I understand why Rahel won't believe me. We still need to talk to her though.'

Billy said nothing, staring through hooded eyes. If half his talk of coming up through the care system was true, then he had no great love of the authorities either, nor any reason to believe them.

'Constable, have you got that file?' McLean turned to Harrison, who produced the folder he'd asked her to put together. Taking it from her as if it were an unexploded bomb, he placed it carefully down on the table, unopened.

'What I've got in here is not pretty. I wouldn't normally show this kind of thing to a member of the public, but given what's happened, I think it only fair you know just how desperate we are to talk to Rahel. The things you will see in here are very upsetting. I just want to warn you of that. OK?'

Billy's nod was almost imperceptible, his gaze darting from unopened folder to McLean's face and back again. McLean waited a moment before lifting up the cover and pulling out a sheaf of high-resolution photographs.

'This is a young girl we found in a basement just off the Royal Mile a few days ago. The day you first came to see me.' He laid out two pictures, one from the crime scene and one from the mortuary. 'This is a young girl we found in the Hermitage yesterday morning. As you can see, her shoes are missing. We found them in a wee shrine a hundred or so yards away.'

Billy tensed again as McLean mentioned the Hermitage. His face had gone very pale, but there was no spark of recognition on it as he looked at the two dead girls. McLean gave him a few moments to take in the unpleasant details before laying out the final photograph in front of him.

'And this is a young woman found dumped in a commercial wheelie bin up Sighthill way. She's not dead, but we don't know if she'll survive. She was beaten so badly, whoever did it must have thought they'd killed her. The doctors have got her in a medically induced coma. We can't identify her, Billy. Her DNA's not on our records, and she was naked when she was found. Our best bet is that she's been trafficked here, sold into prostitution.'

McKenzie stared at the photographs for a long time, but didn't reach out to pick up any of them. McLean let the silence settle, interrupted only by the muted sounds drifting in from outside.

'You think that might be Akka,' he said eventually, indicating the photograph of the comatose young woman with a slight nod. 'That's why you need to speak to Rahel? To get her to identify her sister? If this is her?'

'It's probably not. But her hair's the same colour, her skin tone is similar. Hard to tell if they share any distinguishing features, given how badly beaten up this poor girl is, but she's much the same size as Rahel. I have to look at the possibility, at the very least.'

McKenzie stared at the pictures for a while longer, and McLean could see the conflict inside him written across the young man's face. Young man? He was still a boy, really.

'I cannae make any promises, ken?' he said at last. 'But I'll try an' speak to her. See what she knows.'

23

Darkness had fallen outside by the time the deputy chief constable stepped into McLean's office and closed the door behind him. He was the last to arrive at the meeting, and the rest of them had been waiting impatiently to get started. Not that there was a great deal to discuss beyond their lack of progress so far.

'Sorry I'm late, everyone. Unexpected call from the CC. Wanted an update on the press situation. Seems he's being hassled for progress updates by the politicians, so I hope you've got some good news for me.'

By unspoken agreement, they had left the chair at the head of the conference table free. Robinson slumped into it with such a sigh McLean could imagine he'd walked here all the way from Strathclyde Region, not taken the lift from the car park and ambled down the corridor.

'We found the girl's shoes, sir,' he said.

'Is that all? I take it they didn't have a name tag in them? Nothing useful like an address slipped under the insole?' Robinson didn't hold back with his sarcasm.

'Forensics spent the afternoon processing the walled garden where we found them. I think DI Ritchie has more information on that.'

The deputy chief constable's sneer lifted, but only a little as he switched his attention from McLean to Ritchie. 'Walled garden? I thought the girl's body was found in a clearing.'

'It was, sir. But there was a walled garden nearby. Tony— . . . Chief Inspector McLean led us to it.' Ritchie tilted her head in McLean's direction. 'We'd have found it eventually, I'm sure, but local knowledge is always useful. Looks like it's been used as a camp, and our best guess is a group of refugees hiding out from the authorities. Can't think it would be much fun living there in these conditions though, which might explain why it's been abandoned.'

'And how exactly is any of this helping us to identify the dead girl? Either of the dead girls, for that matter?'

'We know nobody's come forward to claim either of them, sir. We're not getting any hits for DNA either. Best guess is they're the children of illegal immigrants, probably trafficked. They're never going to come forward if they think they'll be shoved in a detention centre, or, worse, shipped back to whatever war zone they've fled from.'

Robinson stared at Ritchie for an uncomfortably long time, then turned his attention to McLean. 'You think that's likely?'

'Can you think of any other reason someone wouldn't come forward about a missing child?'

'Well, they might have killed them, for one thing.'

McLean shrugged. 'It's a possibility, of course. But local children that age will be missed from school. They'll have friends, neighbours. People notice these things, especially once the story's in the papers. We've had artist's impressions of both girls doing the rounds all day, and we've been running multiple social-media campaigns on the toy we found. Not had a contact yet that wasn't some crazy looking for attention.'

Robinson rubbed at his face, still weary from that long walk down the corridor or ground down by yet more bad news. 'Illegal immigrants. Brilliant. The press are going to have a field day with this. Coming over here, killing their children. Christ, what a nightmare.'

'We're still not entirely sure how they died, sir,' McLean said, eliciting another groan from the DCC.

'Well, what exactly do we know then, Tony?' Robinson stared at him for a moment, then looked at the other detectives present, one by one. 'What exactly do we know?'

The light dusting of snow from earlier in the day had been turned to grey slush and pushed to the kerbside by traffic. McLean drove slowly through the city, heading for home and the hope that maybe Emma would be there. If she was talking to him, so much the better.

Bright red brake lights slowed him as he left Sciennes and moved onto the Meadows. He couldn't drive through the park now without leaning forward over the steering wheel and peering up into the sky. It wasn't snowing any more, but the clouds were low, reflecting back the orange of street lamps. The ancient trees clawed at the night with bare branch fingers, but no dead bodies fell into their grasp this time. Shivering at the memory of that case, he tried to piece together the images of that snowy night over a year past. They'd drugged him, that much he remembered. Or, at least, the doctors told him they'd found levels of the stuff in his blood that would make a racehorse groggy. He'd gone to a house and uncovered what could only be described as a hipster opium den, ironically enough, but that was another detail he'd gleaned from reports after the investigation had been concluded. There'd been something about a helicopter, advanced stealth technology the military didn't want anyone knowing about. And there'd been Mrs Saifre, otherwise known as Jane Louise Dee.

Her philanthropy – the Dee Trust – didn't fool him. McLean knew her for the evil creature she was. But she couldn't have been there when he'd fallen from the sky, drugged, into a miraculously deep snow drift. They'd found only the body of the pilot, and according to the tabloids Jane Louise Dee had been hosting a gala dinner in New York that night. Not her, and yet even in his madness he was sure.

A blast of car horn woke him from his musing. McLean saw that the traffic had begun moving again, and hurried to catch up. Glancing to the side, he saw the circus tents pitched on the frozen grass of the Meadows. Saw, too, that the slowing in the traffic was because some drivers were turning off into an improvised car park alongside. Quite how that had got past the city council, he had no idea, but as the car in front turned off the road, he decided to follow.

There was something about the lights, whirling in the darkness, that took him straight back to his childhood. Or maybe it was the smell of old canvas, greasepaint, diesel generator smoke and candyfloss. It seemed to be having the same effect on the other people here. Mostly couples, he saw, although there was the occasional lone figure like himself, and a young family clustered together at the ticket office. Locking his car, McLean wandered over, taking in the sights and sounds. It was easy to forget he was in the middle of Edinburgh: the circus seemed to exist in its own little world.

A neatly painted sign outside the office listed show times for the big top, and prices that took McLean back to his childhood all over again. He'd expected to pay at least fifty pounds for two tickets, was prepared to pay a lot more. Seeing the place, feeling the atmosphere, he knew deep down that Emma would love it. If the numbers on the board were correct, he'd get change from a five-pound note.

He was already pulling out his wallet, waiting for the young family to finish whatever they were doing and step out of the way, when the doubt hit him. What if Emma didn't like circuses?

Some people hated them, after all. And when would be a good time to bring her? Not tonight, obviously, but would a weekday evening be better than a weekend afternoon? What shift was she working these days? He could phone her, he supposed. Ask. But as he thought it, so he realised he couldn't remember the last time he'd spoken to her on the phone. They never talked that way. Never much talked at all, since that horrible night in the summer.

'You wanting a ticket then, pal?'

The accent pulled him back to the present more than the question. McLean looked up to see a young man standing at the window to the ticket booth, staring at him. Acne spots scarred his face, and his thin hair was the pale ginger more normally seen in these parts than Rahel's flame red and that of the frozen little girl. Behind him, at the back of the small ticket office, a young woman closer to his stereotypical image of someone who might work at a circus sat on a wooden stool and stared at her fingernails with total indifference.

'Just wanted to see the show times,' he lied, putting his wallet swiftly away. 'How long are you going to be here for?'

'No' sure. Week or two, maybe.' The lad turned away, directing his question to the young woman. 'Irena? How many more shows will we be putting on, like?'

The young woman dragged her attention from her fingers and looked up with a toss of her head straight out of an eighties pop video. Her hair fitted the image too, tumbling from her head to her shoulders in waves that wouldn't have looked out of place in a shampoo commercial.

'We? So you are one of us now, Roy?' Her words were heavily accented and mocking, but her smile was genuine. McLean wasn't quite sure what was going on between the two of them, nor did he much care. For the life of him he couldn't understand why he'd even thought of coming here in the first place.

'We still here for a while yet.' The young woman, Irena, jumped down from her stool and wandered over to the sales window. 'Plenty time for you and your special one to see the show.'

clues from the scene. Most of the rubbish strewn around looked like it had been here a while, built up in archaeological layers. The body lay on the top, which meant it was recently added to the rest of the discarded and unwanted detritus, but nothing else looked fresh and new.

'What have we got here then, Tony?'

McLean turned awkwardly on the spot, knowing all too well the bollocking he'd get from Jemima Cairns if he stepped off the safe path despite her pessimistic appraisal of the scene so far. Dressed in rather more comfortable-looking white overalls than his own, Doctor Tom MacPhail lugged a small leather case of instruments, none of which would be any help to the patient.

'Morning, Tom. Angus busy, is he?'

MacPhail shrugged. 'He lets the rest of us out from time to time. If we've been good.' His grin faded as he looked past McLean at the poorly lit body. 'Least that's what he tells us. This our poor unfortunate?'

McLean leaned back to allow MacPhail past, shining his torch on the prostrate figure. 'That's him, aye. Not had a chance to look at him closely yet.'

'Probably for the best.' MacPhail crouched down by the body, looking around it without touching anything. 'Keep that light on him, can you?'

McLean did as he was asked and watched as the pathologist carried out his initial examination, aware all the while that this wasn't the sort of work a detective chief inspector should be doing. On the other hand, Kenny Stephen's initial thoughts about the body had been spot on. He might have been looking at an adult male rather than a female child, but the condition of his skin was too similar to that of the other two bodies to ignore. McLean was willing to lay good odds this wasn't an old man who'd dropped dead of a heart attack.

24

The flagstone pavers glistened with icy moisture, reflected in the cold clear morning light as McLean stood on the corner of Broughton Street and a tiny, narrow alley that appeared to have no name. He'd grabbed a lift from a squad car, speeding across town with the full blues and twos, but even so the forensic van had beaten him to this new crime scene. White-overalled technicians had begun the painstaking task of creating a safe path to the body, and that there was a body was pretty much all he knew so far.

'I called it in to Control already, sir. Thought you'd want to have a look for yourself though.' Police Sergeant Kenneth Stephen leaned against a damp stone wall outside a café that had remained closed despite the prospect of cold and thirsty police officers and forensic technicians to swell its coffers throughout the day.

'Any particular reason, Kenny?' McLean asked. 'Not that I don't trust your judgement in these matters.'

'I saw the report on those two wee girls you found. This is similar.'

McLean felt the cold seep into his gut. 'Similar how? I was told this was a man's body they'd found.'

'Aye, but his skin's all dry and . . . Well, it's probably best you see for yourself. Just as soon as they let you in.'

'Get yourself a suit, and he's all yours.' McLean turned to see Jemima Cairns approaching. Beyond her, the first wave of technicians were filing out of the alley.

'Has the duty doctor been?' he asked. 'Pathologist?'

'Aye, and no. Not yet. He's dead, if that's what you're after. Go see for yourself. I'm not making any promises we can come up with good answers for you.'

By the time he'd located a set of white paper overalls, signed for them and pulled them on, half of the forensic team had gone. Uniformed officers, under Sergeant Stephen's expert guidance, had secured a wide perimeter and were making enquiries of the offices, shops and flats in the immediate area. McLean didn't expect much to come of that, but it had to be done. He had been anxious to get to the scene and view the body before it was disturbed, but now he found himself reluctant to enter the dark, narrow alley. It wasn't fear that held him back, so much as guilt. True, Stephen had called him about the discovery, but this was a job that should have been given to a detective sergeant, or an inspector at a pinch.

'You're just being daft,' he muttered under his breath, drawing a quizzical look from a nearby forensic technician.

'You wouldn't have a torch I could borrow?' he asked to cover his embarrassment. He expected to have to sign for it, then get an invoice for the loan in among the paperwork this new crime would inevitably generate. Instead the technician leaned into the van and came back with a heavy-duty flashlight.

'Just give it back when you're done, aye?'

'Thanks. I will.' He hefted the torch, looked around the increasingly busy street, took a deep breath and stepped onto the clear path to the body.

* * *

It had probably been a mews entrance, just wide enough f coach and two, back in the days when Edinburgh had been a of horse-drawn transport. Then the far end of the alley wo have opened onto a courtyard of some form, stables and stores and a shed to keep the carriages in. All that had g swallowed up by later development and the unstoppable adv of the internal combustion engine. Now the alley was a end. A place where wheelie bins lived when they weren't or pavement for collection day.

You could be forgiven for thinking there'd been no collec for weeks, such was the rubbish strewn over the alley. Un cobbles made walking tricky, not helped by the very narrow the forensic team had marked out all the way to the wall back. There, a mess of old black bin liners, damp card boxes and discarded fast food containers piled up again stonework, a modern-day sandbank washed up by the ti human laziness. And sprawled across it, like a shipw mariner, lay the body of a man.

McLean fiddled with the torch until he worked out turn it on. The beam was suitably dazzling, picking ou in sharp relief as he stepped closer. The man lay on staring up at the thin strip of sky overhead with sightl His arms hung limp at his sides as if he had just fallen b into the heap of rubbish and died. His white hair and leathery skin gave him the look of an old man, but were what McLean would expect someone in thei to be wearing. Lumberjack shirt over a plain whi chunky leather jacket, tidy jeans turned up neatly at th black leather boots that had hardly been worn jud state of their soles. Hipster chic it was called, or sor that.

Playing the torchlight over the nearby area, he cc Cairns meant about them not getting much in the w

'This might interest you more than me.' MacPhail reached up towards him with something in his hand. McLean diverted the torch to reveal a thin billfold wallet, and when he opened it up he found a driving licence.

'Maurice Jennings.' He squinted to read the tiny letters in the poor light, unable to hold wallet and licence and point the torch at the same time. 'Local boy, by the address. And he was twenty-four.'

'Twenty-four?' MacPhail rocked back on his heels. 'I'd have added forty to that.'

McLean played the torch over the dead man's face again. Quite apart from the dry, leathery quality of his skin and the shocking white of his hair, the dead man looked shrunken in his clothes, as if he'd borrowed them from someone much bigger. Everything about him shouted great age, except his choice of clothing and the date on his driving licence, but as McLean flicked the torch from tiny passport-style photograph to withered old face, there was little doubt they were the same man. Just the same man several decades apart.

'You going to hazard a time of death? Maybe a cause? I'm guessing this is suspicious, at the very least.'

MacPhail clambered to his feet with a lot less creaking and groaning than his old boss, Cadwallader. 'Time would be late last night, can't be more specific than that given the circumstances. Cause is I haven't got a fucking clue. And as to is it suspicious? You tell me, Tony.' He looked back down at the dead man. 'You tell me.'

25

The phone call came in as he was walking back to the station from Broughton Street. He pulled the handset from his pocket and stared at the screen for a while. The number wasn't in his contact list, and the bitter cold wind whipping in off the Forth made him wish he'd remembered the pair of gloves currently locked away in his Alfa. In the end, curiosity got the better of him and he thumbed accept, ducking behind one of the stone corbels on North Bridge to try and find some shelter.

'McLean.'

'Insp— . . . Chief Inspector McLean?' A woman's voice, vaguely familiar although he couldn't quite place it.

'Yes. Who is this?'

'Oh, aye. Sorry. It's Sheila Begbie, from House the Refugees?'

McLean turned his back on the traffic, hunching against the stonework as a bus rumbled past. 'What can I do for you, Ms Begbie?'

'See that wee girl you found in the basement underneath my office? Well, I've got another one here. Only she's a lot more lively.'

For a moment, he couldn't understand what the woman was saying. 'I'm sorry? You've got a young girl with you? Is that what you mean?'

'Aye. Found her here when I opened up this morning. No idea how she got in, mind, but she was in the kitchen, hiding in one o' the cupboards wi' a packet of biscuits she'd stolen.'

McLean stepped out of the shelter, walking as swiftly as he could up the slope towards the Royal Mile. The offices of House the Refugees were less than ten minutes away. 'Do you know who she is?' he asked.

'No idea. She's no' from these parts, though. I can tell youse that. Hasn't got a word of English to her, and her face, well. You'll understand if you see her.'

'I'm on my way to you now. Shouldn't be long.'

He killed the call, then flicked through the menus until he found DI Ritchie's number. It went straight to message, so he tried DC Gregg. Again no answer – well, at least he could tell McIntyre he'd tried when she bent his ear about it later. He swiped through the contact list again, finally finding DC Harrison's number.

'Sir?' She answered on the second ring. McLean couldn't decide whether or not that was a good thing.

'You at the station, Constable?' He glanced at his watch, still early in the day. He'd barely sat down in his office when the news about the dead man in Broughton Street had come in.

'At my desk. Was there something you needed?'

He told her about the call he'd just received, all too aware as he related the tale that he was looking for a female officer to deal with a child, not someone specifically trained in working with children.

'I'll understand it if you don't think you'd be any help,' he said into the silence on the line after he'd finished.

'What? Oh, no. Sorry, sir. Just put the phone down while I was grabbing my jacket. I'll be there in ten minutes.'

McLean ended the call, hunching his shoulders against the wind as he trod carefully down the Royal Mile. It didn't take long at all to reach the narrow stone house, but instead of going inside, he ducked down the close to the door he'd stumbled upon just a few short days ago. Someone had secured it with a new padlock and hasp, and crime scene tape still fluttered around the frame. Without the hordes of forensic technicians and uniformed officers, the close felt bigger than he remembered, more sky overhead. A locked gate at the end opened up onto a small garden, and the only other door led into the basement of the building opposite. Apart from the tiny kitchen window, neither house had any windows looking out over the close itself, although indentations in the stone walls suggested they might once have been there.

'Why did you come down here?'

He hadn't meant to speak the question out loud. Nevertheless, it was an important one. If the girl had got into the basement through the hole in the floor above it, there would have been no sign of her out here. Whoever had broken the door down must have been looking for her, but how had they known where to find her? The walls were solid here, and thick. There was no way any sound from inside would carry through. No windows to show a torch light, and they'd not found one in among the girl's scant possessions anyway.

'Looking for anything in particular, sir?'

McLean turned swiftly, a sharp jab of pain shooting up his hip. DC Harrison stood at the entrance to the close, ballooned in a massive padded jacket, her head mostly engulfed by a big black woolly hat with a pair of pompons on it that looked like cartoon ears. The tip of her nose almost glowed it was so red with the cold.

'Just thinking. Wondering, really. It can wait though. There's more important matters to attend.' He joined Harrison in the street, and together they climbed the half a dozen steps to the front door of House the Refugees. McLean reached out and pressed the button on the intercom. No voice answered, but the electronic lock clicked, and they both stepped inside.

McLean's brief interactions with Sheila Begbie before had left him with an impression of a small, angry woman. That was perhaps an unfair assessment, given the circumstances of their meeting. She was still small, but when she greeted them in the front office it was with a friendly smile tinged with relief.

'Thank God you're here. Thought it might take a while longer and I'm getting desperate.'

McLean opened his mouth to speak, but a howl of rage like a trapped animal erupted from behind the closed door through to the kitchen. Begbie flinched. 'She's been screaming her head off ever since I called you.'

'And you've no idea who she is?' Harrison asked.

'I don't recognise her, no. And she won't speak any English to me. Mind you, she won't speak much at all. Just keeps on yelling like that.' As if to emphasise the point, the anguished howl ebbed away into a low sobbing.

'Perhaps we should call someone from Social Services,' McLean said.

'Let's see if we can't talk to her first, sir?' Harrison walked over to the door, knocked on it lightly. The sobbing stopped, replaced by an attentive silence.

'Is it OK if I come in?' Like most English speakers addressing a foreigner, Harrison enunciated her words slowly and clearly, as if talking to an imbecile. There was no answer, so she gently opened the door.

'I'm not going to – ooft.' She staggered backwards as something small and child-shaped barrelled through the door and straight into her. Begbie stood open-mouthed in astonishment, but McLean was already moving, ready to cover the door to the hallway and the outside. It wasn't necessary though: Harrison had caught a hold of the tearaway, pivoting around and pinning her arms behind her with a skill that suggested much practice.

'Hold still, you wee . . .' She wrestled with the girl for a moment, sinking down onto her knees so that their heads were at the same level, and twisting her around until they faced each other. 'We're not going to hurt you, OK. We're here to help.'

Either she was lulling them into a false sense of security, or the words sunk in. The fight went out of the girl as if she'd been switched off. There was a moment's pause, and then she flung her arms around Harrison's neck and buried her head into the detective constable's shoulder.

'Hey, hey. It's OK. It's OK.' Harrison patted the girl gently on the back, then looked up at McLean with a 'What do I do now?' expression on her face. He had to admit he didn't have much of a clue.

'Ms Begbie, have you got anything to drink in the kitchen there? Not coffee or tea, something . . .' He nodded his head towards the girl to indicate what he meant.

'Aye, there's some wee cartons of juice in the fridge. I'll away and fetch one, will I?' Begbie edged around the room, not wanting to upset the girl. It wouldn't have mattered as she still had her head buried in Harrison's shoulder, clinging on to her for dear life. From where he stood, McLean couldn't see much about the girl other than that she was shockingly dirty. Her hair could have been any colour, it was so matted and greasy. It hung down to her shoulders in a badly cut mess, all too reminiscent of the dead girl they'd found in the basement below. She wore an odd mismatch of clothes, bulked out in layers against the cold, and he couldn't really ignore the smell that filled the room.

'Here you go, sweetie. How'd you like something to drink, eh?'

Begbie reappeared from the kitchen with a small drinks carton, the straw already popped into the foil circle in the top.

She crouched down beside Harrison and the girl, and held it out to be taken. For a while nothing happened, then slowly the girl relaxed her grip on the detective constable and eased herself away. She looked first at the two women, and then over her shoulder at McLean. Her face was just as dirty as he'd expected it would be, but the look in her bright green eyes was fierce, defiant and hard to meet. He held it though, aware that he was being judged. After a moment that was only seconds but felt like minutes, she nodded ever so slightly, then turned away and took the offered carton of juice.

Harrison rocked back on her heels and stood up, her knees making barely a sound. The benefits of youth, McLean supposed. He stepped away from the door, pulled one of the chairs out from the wall and sat down, his every move followed by those huge, judgemental eyes. The girl drank greedily at first, but then slowed as if unsure whether or not she'd get any more. Finally she took the straw from her mouth and held the carton to her chest like a treasured memento of better times. McLean tried to guess her age, but her odd assortment of clothes, terrible dirtiness and worldly-wise expression made it all but impossible. Five going on fifty was his best guess.

'Hello,' he said after a few heartbeats of pause. 'I'm Tony. What's your name?'

The girl frowned at him, shook her head slightly, then turned to Harrison.

'Janie.' She pointed at herself, then turned the finger towards the girl. 'And you?'

The girl shook her head again, the motion working its way down her entire body as her gaze dropped to the floor. And then she spoke, her voice a mumbled whisper that nevertheless sent a chill through McLean.

'Nala.'

★ ★ ★

It took a long time for the team from Social Services to arrive, but McLean and Harrison stayed with the young girl all the while. She said nothing more than her name, seeming to understand very little English but relaxing in tiny increments as it became clear they weren't going to hurt her. More biscuits and cartons of juice from the kitchen helped with this too, so that when the time came for her to go, she was only slightly hysterical. In the end, Harrison had to accompany her outside to the car.

'Why do you think she came here?' McLean asked Sheila Begbie once they were alone. The charity worker had slumped into the chair at her desk, and was no doubt hoping everyone else would go away so she could get on with the day's work.

'I'd have thought you'd be asking how she got in here. That's what's been bugging me.'

'It's a puzzle, I'll grant you that much. But she was in here, so she must have found a way. I don't believe for a minute this was just a random choice though. She came here for a reason. She knew about this place. That suggests to me she's been here before.'

Begbie's angry face came back. 'I told you I didn't recognise her.'

'Oh, I believe you, Ms Begbie. Given the state of her, I don't think I'd recognise her if she was my own child. But we know she's not local, and we know what your charity does. You must have refugees coming in here, looking for help getting themselves settled, understanding the system, that kind of thing, right?'

'That's pretty much what we do, aye. Only we don't get many folk in here. This is just the office for our admin, fundraising, that kind of stuff. We're not exactly geared up as a walk-in centre. This is the wrong part of town for that, anyway. Too much going on. And things like that march the other day don't help.'

McLean glanced out the window to the near-empty street beyond. He'd not thought about the march in a while. His team had only been logistical support, after all. It was in the hands of the anti-terror boys now.

'Those marchers last weekend were sympathetic to the plight of these people though. That's what it was all about, wasn't it? Helping out those displaced by war? Putting an end to the wars so the people don't get displaced to start with?'

'Aye, and those folk you arrested are all about peace and love, right enough.'

McLean was so surprised by the bitterness of Begbie's tone, he almost missed the import of what she said.

'How do you know about that? We haven't exactly advertised it, and you told us you weren't here that day. Office closed, if I remember your statement.'

'The people I deal with on a day-to-day basis, Chief Inspector, you think they don't notice when the neo-Nazis come to town? You think they don't know what the polis are up to? It's no accident you don't see them most of the time. They're scared of you.'

'Of us? The police?'

'Aye, the polis more than most. Where they've come from the polis are the most corrupt of all. They're working with the traffickers, the folk who run the boats across the Med. Some of these people have had to bribe polis men all the way across Europe just to get here. And when they do reach here, it's no' exactly the promised land.'

'But . . .' McLean had been going to say 'we're here to help them', but his brain caught up with his mouth before the words came out. He shook the idiot thought away, recalling the few interviews he'd looked in on. The expensive lawyer finding technicalities and loopholes to get his mouth-breathing clients off the hook. Of all the angry idiots they'd arrested, only one was in custody, and him only because they'd goaded him into trying to assault one of his interrogators. The sort of people Sheila

Begbie dealt with wouldn't even have been granted the courtesy of an interview before being shunted off to some detention centre while the Immigration Services found the most heartless way to send them back to the horror they'd fled.

'You understand.' Begbie had been sitting, but now she stood up and crossed the room to where he stood. McLean had faced down hardened criminals, stared across interview room tables at psychopaths. He'd stood up to Jane Louise Dee, perhaps the most powerful and influential woman on the planet, on more than one occasion. And yet he could feel himself wither under the intensity of Sheila Begbie's stare. It wasn't cruel, or particularly intimidating, just that it held him like a rabbit when an eagle screams overhead. For a moment it was as if she could read his every thought, and the frustration at how the men disrupting the march would get away with it bubbled up again, unbidden.

'But you're bound by duty. To protect and to serve all, regardless of how much or how little they might deserve it.' She shook her head and the contact broke.

'I'd better be getting back,' McLean said. 'Thank you for calling us about the girl.'

Begbie looked momentarily confused, as if she'd forgotten all about her. Then she shook her head once more, smiled. 'Look after her, Chief Inspector. And don't worry too much about the haters.'

26

'He was only twenty-four. Fit as a fiddle. Loved playing football with his mates, drinking down the pub. How can someone so full of life end up like . . .'

McLean sat in the reception area of the City Mortuary with Mr and Mrs Jennings. The parents of the young man whose body they had found that morning seemed not much older than him, but then there was no good reason why they should have been. No parent should outlive their child though, it went against the natural order of things.

'We'll find out what happened. You have my word.' McLean leaned forward in his uncomfortable plastic chair, wondering where Grumpy Bob had got to. He'd brought the couple to the mortuary, and was meant to be fetching them both a coffee. 'Detective Sergeant Laird has already spoken to Maurice's fiancée, but it would be very helpful to me if you could answer a few questions too.'

'Oh God, poor Tricia.' Mrs Jennings had almost stopped sobbing, but now she started up all over again. Her husband had his arm around her shoulders and pulled her tight to him.

'What do you need to know?' he asked.

'When was the last time you saw your son?' McLean flicked a

glance in DC Harrison's direction, pleased to see that she had taken out her notebook.

'What's today? Thursday? Must have been Saturday afternoon. He went on that march down the Royal Mile, you know? Fighting against the racists or whatever it was they were on about. Not sure I really agree with him. I mean, yes, we don't want to turn people away if they're in need, but we've only room for so many. And as for jobs . . .'

'Did he come to your place, or did you visit him? On Saturday?' McLean tried to move the subject away from immigrants and refugees, all too aware of exactly where it was going. Mr Jennings might have looked like a man in his fifties, but his attitudes belonged to an earlier generation.

'He came for his tea. Always does on a Saturday. Trish goes to see her mum in Peebles, and Maurice comes home for his tea.' It was Mrs Jennings who answered, her voice surprisingly strong.

'And have you spoken to him since then?'

'Oh, aye. He was on the phone yesterday evening. Got tickets for the Hibs match next week. Wanted to know if I'd go with him. Loved his football, did Maurice.' Mr Jennings shook his head like a man coming to terms with a sudden, dramatic change in his circumstances. 'Guess there'll be two empty seats now.'

'Do you know what he was doing in Broughton Street last night? Would he have been walking home from somewhere?'

'Aye, he was in the pub, right enough. That's where he phoned me from.'

'I don't suppose you happen to know which pub? And what time?'

Mr Jennings sniffed, then rubbed at his nose with the back of his hand. 'Probably that one on the roundabout, what's it called? Barrel and something? It's only a short walk back to his place. Trish'd probably know for sure. As to when?' He reached into his pocket with his soiled hand and pulled out a not particularly smart phone. After tapping at the buttons for a moment, he held it up so McLean could see. 'Nine thirty-eight p.m.'s when the call came in. We didn't speak long, but I could hear the background noise. He was definitely in a pub.'

'Thank you.' McLean glanced over at Harrison to check she'd written the time down. 'Just one last question, and I hope you won't take it the wrong way. Understand I have to ask this so we can get the best possible picture of what happened. I don't want you to think I'm pre-judging your son, but was he ever one to get into arguments when he'd had a drink or two?'

Mr Jennings held McLean's gaze for long moments before answering, the silence punctuated only by the quiet sobs of his wife. When he finally spoke, it was with a sigh.

'He's a good boy, generally speaking. But he's competitive. That's why he likes the football so much. Good at it too. I can't say hand on my heart that he's never got into an argument down the pub, but I've never seen him wi' a black eye or grazed knuckles, you know?'

'He's a good boy. Wouldn't hurt anyone, unless they tried to hurt him first. Or hurt someone else who couldn't stand up for themselves.'

McLean hadn't been expecting Mrs Jennings to speak, even less so the force behind her words. Her husband put his arm around her again, hugging her tight to him. They were strong together as a couple, which was just as well. They were going to need that strength in the coming days.

'I'm sure he was, Mrs Jennings. I'm very sorry to have to bring it up at all. I don't think I need to ask any more questions just now, but we'll be in touch as soon as we know any more. Thank you.' McLean stood, trying to ignore the twinge of pain that shot up his hip. Grumpy Bob chose that exact moment to reappear, bearing two paper cups of fine-smelling coffee. 'Detective Sergeant Laird will see you home. If you need anything, don't hesitate to call us.'

'I hope you got all that, Constable. My memory's not what it used to be.'

McLean turned up the lapels of his coat to keep the flurrying snow off his neck as he and DC Harrison trudged back up the hill from the mortuary towards the station. They had left Grumpy Bob behind with Mr and Mrs Jennings, partly to see them home safely in the atrocious weather and partly because it was unwise to try to part him from a freshly brewed mug of coffee.

'All in my notebook, sir.' Harrison patted at her chest with a well-gloved hand. 'If you don't mind me saying, though, I was surprised you interviewed them back there. I'd have been worried about coming across as insensitive.'

'I probably was, a bit. But sometimes you have to be. A time like that, some people want to talk. They've just confirmed their son's the poor bugger laid out on that trolley and they need to make some sense of that. Recent memories are strong, and gut feelings too.'

Harrison stopped walking, and when McLean turned to face her, he could see the horror written across her face.

'Isn't that a bit heartless?' she asked.

'Completely.' McLean dug his hands into his pockets, searching for warmth there but finding none. 'If they'd been more shocked, more emotional, I'd not have pushed it. But they were looking for a bit of sympathy, a shoulder to cry on if you like. I did my bit, and Grumpy Bob will do his. Meantime we gather as much information about Maurice Jennings as we can, as quickly as we can. That way we can find out where he was, where he was going, who he met with. All the stuff that's important in tracking down his movements up to and including the point where he dropped dead on a pile of uncollected garbage in a back alley off Broughton Street. OK?'

Harrison shrugged. 'When you put it like that, sir? Yes. I guess I've never seen it done so . . .' she paused a moment, searching for the right word. 'Clinically?'

'Cynically might be more accurate, but the result's the same. We've got some useful information without upsetting the recently bereaved.'

'So what's next?' Harrison trotted to catch up with him, and the two of them continued towards the station.

'If his dad's right, Jennings was in the Cask and Barrel at nine thirty-eight. We can check that with his fiancée, but it's as good a place as any to start. The alley where we found him's in the wrong direction for going home, so chances are he went somewhere else afterwards. Trace his movements from there first. With any luck we'll get a hit on CCTV somewhere along the line, and when Angus has finished his examination and come up with a cause of death we should have enough to send to the procurator fiscal. If we're very lucky that'll be the end of it.'

They'd reached the station car park, and McLean glanced sideways at his Alfa as they passed. A light dusting of snow covered its black paintwork, which meant leaving later would be more complicated and time-consuming than he would have liked. At least the thing had an all-weather mode that tamed some of its more wild characteristics, but he couldn't help being a little jealous of the DCC's massive four by four, parked a few bays closer to the back door. More so of the days when he could just walk home in five minutes.

'You think there's more to his death than meets the eye?' Harrison asked as she opened the back door for him. Slow off the mark, McLean was still wrapped up in his thoughts.

'Thanks. And yes. There's enough that's odd about it staring you in the face, after all. His skin cured like that? Like those two wee girls? That's a fairly big red flag right there. Then there's where we found him and how he was laid out. If you're feeling unwell, you don't wander down a dark alley and collapse on a bed of bin bags. You call for help. Phone your parents, maybe a pal you've been out drinking with. No, this death is very suspicious.'

'So what next then, sir?'

'Next? We trace Jennings's last movements. Speak to his close friends, especially any he was drinking with last night.'

'And the girl in the woods?'

'Much the same, really. Try and find out where she came from, who was with her before she died. We'll need to get the press in on that, run the pictures of both of them again. Even if they'll give us a kicking for it.'

'I'll get on it. Lofty and Jay should be working through the CCTV footage by now, too. Let you know if we come up with anything useful.'

'Thanks.' McLean glanced at his watch, only slightly surprised to find that it was way past lunchtime. 'I guess I'd better go and shuffle the budgets to help pay for it all.'

27

A gentle knock on the open door dragged his attention from the stack of mindless paperwork he'd been sifting through half-heartedly while he let his mind wander the dark corners of the rapidly converging investigations. McLean looked up to see DC Harrison in the doorway.

'Something up, Constable?'

'It's the CCTV from Broughton Street, sir. I think you need to see it yourself.'

McLean stood up, closing the nearest folder with a feeling of relief. It would still be waiting for him later, but at least he didn't have to feel guilty ignoring it for now.

'Lead the way,' he said, and followed her out of the room. There was no point asking her for details; if it had been something she could tell him, she would have done.

The blinds had been pulled down, and the viewing room was dark when they entered. DC Blane sat at the console, head bowed as he peered at a blurry image on a still screen. He turned around at the noise, rubbed at his eyes for a moment, then struggled to his overlarge feet.

'Sir.' He didn't quite salute, but McLean could almost see him trying to suppress the urge.

'You don't need to stand up every time I come into the room, you know.' McLean smiled after he'd spoken, hoping the detective constable would understand it was a joke. Blane was a good detective, especially when it came to technology, but his social skills needed a lot of work. 'Where's this footage I have to see then?'

'Oh, aye. Sorry, sir. Of course.' Blane turned back to his console, bent low and began tapping at the buttons. 'Just need to rewind a bit. Ah, here we go.'

It took him a moment to get his bearings, but soon enough McLean worked out what he was seeing. The city centre was well served with CCTV cameras, and Broughton Street had enough to keep even Big Brother happy. This one was up the hill towards York Place and St Mary's Cathedral, looking north, and it had a high enough resolution to make out a fair bit of detail.

'You can't quite see it from this angle, but that's the entrance to the alley where we found him, sir.' Blane pointed at the screen with a finger as big as a passing taxi.

'What time is this?'

'Quarter to eleven last night, see?' The finger moved slightly, revealing a timestamp ticking up at normal speed. 'I'll just go forward a wee bit.'

McLean watched the screen as the images sped up. It wasn't anything unusual for Broughton Street on a winter weeknight when there was snow in the air. Mostly taxis and delivery vans on the road, the pavements relatively clear. Come the summer and the festivals, the place would be awash with people.

'Here's our boy.' Blane tapped a key and the video slowed down as a man stepped out of a doorway. Maurice Jennings had the decency to look up, almost directly at the camera. He was accompanied by two other men, and they all seemed to be having a friendly conversation for a minute or two. Then he patted one on the shoulder, waved off the other as they turned away and walked up the hill. He watched them go, then shoved his hands in his coat pockets and set off in the opposite direction. That was when McLean noticed another figure maybe twenty yards further on and directly in front of the entrance to the alley. Tall, and completely dressed in black clothing that looked more like robes than a coat, he appeared to be staring into the alleyway, swaying slightly as if he might be drunk. He made a motion with his head that reminded McLean of nothing so much as a dog testing the air for a scent, and then for no obvious reason, he grabbed Jennings by the throat and dragged him into the alley.

'Jesus. What brought that on?' McLean noted the time on the screen. Just a minute past eleven.

'No sound on these cameras, more's the pity sir.' Blane tapped the console and the video spooled forward at double speed for a while. When he slowed it back down to normal, ten minutes had passed. 'This is him leaving. Whoever he is.'

The figure in black came out of the alley as if he hadn't a care in the world. He walked up the street towards the camera, and the closer he came, the more convinced McLean was that he was wearing a black robe. What he'd taken for some kind of strange hat looked more like long, straggly black hair, and his face was obscured by the kind of wild beard most hipsters would run a mile from. Even though he knew it was stupid, McLean found himself willing the man to look up as he neared the camera, and finally, just before he disappeared from view, he did.

'I take it that's what you wanted me to see?' he asked as Blane froze the image at the perfect moment. Neither he nor Harrison said anything, but then they didn't really need to.

The man's face was difficult to see, blurred by motion and the darkness of the night. Most of it was wild hair and ragged beard anyway, but some trick of the light made his eyes blaze twin points of fire.

McLean left the detective constables to keep trawling through the CCTV footage in search of more images of the fire-eyed man, intending to go back to his office and its insurmountable piles of paperwork. At least mindless bureaucratic tasks let his thoughts percolate, and this case was shaping up to be just as headache-inducing as all his others. Some quiet time alone might help make some sense of it all.

Halfway down the corridor, his rumbling stomach reminded him that breakfast had been a very long time ago, lunch something that happened to other people. Only slightly guiltily, he looked around to make sure nobody else needed him, then headed off in search of something to eat.

He had almost finished a plate of congealed lasagne that had obviously not appealed to any other officers earlier in the day when a familiar figure appeared at the door. DC Harrison wore the expression of someone not sure whether or not they should disturb the boss at his very late lunch.

'Looking for me again, Constable? Or were you after a cup of tea?'

'Umm . . . Both?' Harrison looked at McLean's unappetising plate. 'Neither?'

'It was probably nice at midday. Gone a bit rubbery now.' McLean pushed the remains of his meal to one side and lined up his knife and fork. At least he'd eaten a few mouthfuls. Enough to stop his stomach rumbling, but not so much that he'd feel like having a snooze later.

'We found something else in the CCTV footage that might be interesting. Not sure though.'

'I'm intrigued.' McLean took a final gulp of cold coffee, then shoved plate and mug back onto the tray and took them to the serving hatch. Harrison didn't exactly fidget as he moved, but he could tell she was keen to get on. He waved an arm at the door, then followed her out.

The station appeared relatively empty as they climbed the stairs and walked back to the CCTV viewing room. A brief glimpse in the major-incident room revealed a small crowd of mostly admin staff moving bits of paper about, but no detective sergeants or inspectors.

'Where is everyone?' McLean asked, then remembered Ritchie was going to be coordinating door-to-doors down Broughton Street. He didn't want to think what that was going to cost in man-hours, but he'd sanctioned it. 'All out conducting interviews, I suppose.'

'Aye, sir. Kirsty reckoned it'd be quicker if we got more people out there.'

McLean had noticed before the way all the female members of the team referred to Ritchie by her first name, often even to her face. He doubted very much that any of the junior detectives would call him Tony when they were talking about him behind his back, and even Grumpy Bob had started calling him 'sir' the moment he'd been promoted to inspector. It worked for him, so who was to say Kirsty didn't prefer the informal approach?

The viewing room was dark when they stepped inside, the only illumination coming from the large screen. Harrison must have left it on pause, as it showed a still image of Broughton Street in the dark. It wasn't the same camera as before, judging by the angle.

'Is this better footage?' McLean asked peering at the blurry image and wondering whether he ought to get his eyes tested.

'It's a better angle, but not as clear.' Harrison pulled out a chair and sat down in front of the control console. 'There's plenty of cameras in the street, but most of them point the wrong way. A couple of them are pretty much live feed only. They record about an hour at a go, then write over it. Only any good if someone notices an incident and backs up the initial recording. We didn't find the body until quite a few hours after he died.'

While she was speaking, Harrison worked the controls so that the image rewound swiftly. McLean searched the screen until he found the timestamp. It was counting backwards rapidly, but he couldn't help noticing it had started at around half past one in the morning. Long after the attack on Jennings that they'd seen on the other camera.

'Why so late?' he asked, but Harrison had stopped the recording again. This time the timestamp was saying it was only nine o'clock in the evening.

'See here, sir?' She pointed at the screen with a finger much daintier than DC Blane's. 'It's not easy to make out, but this looks like a small person working their way along the street. Keeping to the shadows.'

McLean pulled out the other chair in front of the screen and sat down, leaning forward until he could see what Harrison was pointing at. She put the video into slow motion, and sure enough something, or someone, crept along the street. Every so often it would stop, and if you accepted that it was a person, they must have been looking around to see whether or not they were being followed. Finally the shape reached the entrance to the alleyway, looked around one last time, then disappeared into its dark maw.

'That's about the time Jennings was phoning his old man, from what I've heard.' Harrison pointed to the timestamp, now reading nine forty. 'Nothing much happens until just before eleven. I think you've seen this bit, from the other camera.'

She fast-forwarded the video until the point where a man less easily identifiable as Jennings walked down the street. The cloaked figure was standing at the entrance to the alley as before. From this new angle it was even more evident how he appeared to be sniffing the air, searching for something. McLean thought he was prepared for what came next, but even so he gasped when the figure turned on Jennings, grabbed him by the neck and dragged him into the alley. It was so brutal, so unprovoked.

'Can we get any more detail on the attacker?' he asked, but Harrison just shook her head.

'Not from any of the cameras I've looked at so far, sir. Kirsty's team are going to be asking all the pubs and shops, but I doubt we'll get anything clearer than the first footage.'

The video spooled forward a while longer, and the cloaked figure emerged, striding up the hill and out of shot. McLean slumped back in his chair. 'So we've not really got any more to work with then.'

'Not for Jennings, sir, no. But there's this.' Harrison tapped a button and the image jumped. For a moment McLean thought nothing much had changed, but then he saw the timestamp had moved to half past one in the morning again. At first nothing moved, the street as quiet then as it would ever be. And then something emerged from the alleyway.

'Is that the same thing we saw going in at half nine?' McLean peered at the screen again. Definitely going to need an eye test soon.

'Not a thing, sir. A person. I'm sure of it. See?' Harrison switched screens, the image reverting to the one McLean had first seen earlier in the day. It was much clearer, but set further back from the action. Even so, he could see the tiny figure as it scurried up the road, stopping frequently to look back.

'I think it's a child, sir,' Harrison said, and at the suggestion McLean could see what she meant. There was only one way in and out of that alley, which meant whoever it was had hidden in there while Jennings was killed. Stayed with his dead body for hours in terror of being found.

'I think it might be the girl we found at the charity place.' Harrison tapped at the console and zoomed the image in. Not clear enough to make out any features, but enough to see the shape and type of clothes, the unkempt mop of dirty hair. 'I think it might be wee Nala.'

28

'Tony. You're late.'

As welcomes home went, it wasn't particularly warm. McLean would have been happy to have been shouted at, given how little communication he and Emma had managed over the past few months. She stood in the kitchen, clearly anxious, and it was only as he noticed how well she was dressed that the penny dropped.

'The charity thing? That's tonight? Shit. I'd forgotten.' It was true enough, although a little voice at the back of his mind told him that he'd probably wanted to forget in the hope it would just go away.

'That much is obvious.' Emma glanced up at the clock above the door. 'You've got fifteen minutes to get changed. Taxi will be here at half six.'

'Taxi?' McLean still held his car keys in one hand, and rattled them between his fingers.

'Well I'm not driving there, and I can't imagine you'll cope without a drink.' Emma bustled across the kitchen and took his briefcase from his unprotesting grip, turned him around and pulled off his overcoat, then pushed him towards the door through to the main hallway. 'Come on. Chop chop.'

McLean did as he was told, surprised when Emma followed

him through the house, up the stairs to the bedroom. He felt tired and sticky after a long day at work, but there wasn't really time for a shower if the taxi really was booked.

'Why are you so keen to go?' he asked after he'd splashed water on his face and done what he could with his hair. Emma had already been through his wardrobe, and for a horrified moment he thought she was going to make him wear the full kilt and Prince Charlie. Relief at the simple dinner jacket and bow tie was tinged with a degree of horror at the thought of having to be sociable. Would anyone there know who he was?

'Well, for one thing I've never been invited to something quite so grand before. Gives me an opportunity to get dressed up in something a bit more fashionable than forensic-technician white, don't you think?' Emma twirled, and the hem of her ankle-length dress splayed to reveal splashes of brighter colour in the pleats of the dark red material. She'd done something with her hair, too, although McLean couldn't have said exactly what. And she was wearing make-up, which he couldn't remember her doing in a while. More than all of these things though, she was almost giddy with excitement.

It reminded him of when she had been recovering from a head injury, a few years earlier. For a while she'd regressed to something like a teenager, which had been utterly exhausting. Although his tiredness might have had as much to do with the case he'd been working on at the time.

'You look stunning,' he said, aware that an answer had been required. It was true too. There was a glow to her he'd not seen in far too long. The smile she gave him suggested that he'd said the right thing. It was true this evening's event was everything he disliked about Edinburgh society, and it was hosted by someone he'd less like to spend time with than a convicted child abuser, but if it was a way to bridge the gap between him and Emma, then he'd give it his best.

'Not these, I think.' He held up the shiny black trousers that went with the dinner jacket. He hadn't worn them in at least a decade, and there was every chance they'd be much tighter around the waist than he remembered.

'No?' Emma frowned, her stillness muting the colour of her dress once more. 'What's wrong with them?'

'Too boring.' McLean dropped them back onto the bed and rummaged through the wardrobe until he found what he was looking for. His grandfather's old tartan trews had a bit more space in them, and were far better suited to the occasion than some stuffy old evening wear.

'Much better.' Emma laughed, then turned serious again. 'Now hurry up and get dressed. We don't want to be the last to arrive.'

It wasn't too bad, at least to start with. McLean felt a bit self-conscious as an officious-looking man in a too-tight black suit and tails announced Emma and him to the crowd swelling the largest ballroom of one of the city's most prestigious hotels, but when it was clear none of them were paying any attention, he began to relax a little. It had been many a year since last he'd been to any formal event like this, but at least he had some experience. Judging by the way she clung limpet-like to his arm, a rictus grin fixed on her face, Emma did not, and neither had her initial enthusiasm and excitement for the evening survived the harsh reality.

'Who are all these people?' she kept on asking as they cut a slow path through the great and the good, or at least people who considered themselves great and good.

'I really have no idea,' McLean said, and then almost immediately spotted the deputy chief constable listening intently to something being shouted into his ear by one of the country's senior members of parliament. Seeing both men seemed to trip some switch in his brain, and he soon started recognising other people, either from their appearances on the news or from the kind of police briefings they would be very surprised to find themselves included in.

'Oh my God. Isn't that . . . ?' Emma tugged on his arm and pointed at a young man standing over by the dais that had been set up at the front of the room.

'I have absolutely no idea who that is,' he said.

'Sure you do. He was in all those films.' Emma took a step towards the man, then stopped herself. 'He's much shorter in real life.'

McLean couldn't help laughing, and after a moment's frowning, Emma joined in.

'It's Tony, isn't it? Detective Inspector? I never forget a face.'

The woman who approached them was hauntingly familiar, but McLean couldn't place her. Judging by the way Emma choked on her laugher, her eyes widening in surprise, she could.

'It's chief inspector now, but I try not to make anything of it.' McLean held out a hand and the woman shook it gently. There was something other-worldly about her, and he knew he'd met her before, but still that name eluded him.

'You don't remember, do you?' She smiled, and then he did. Must have been five years ago, at least.

'Miss Adamson. Sorry, it took me a while.'

Her smile broadened, lighting up her face. 'Vanessa, please. You know, it's such a rare thing these days, to meet someone who doesn't know who I am. Or at least who they think I am.' She turned to Emma. 'He's clearly not going to introduce us. I'm Vanessa.'

'I . . . I know.' Emma shook her head. 'Sorry. I'm Emma. Emma Baird. I had no idea you knew Tony though. He never said.'

'He interviewed me about my neighbour. They'd just arrested him for burglary or something. It was all very exciting.' Adamson turned her attention back to McLean. 'Are you here bidding, or are you one of the lots?'

'I'm here under sufferance, if I'm being honest. My boss told me I had to represent Police Scotland or something. But he seems to be doing that all by himself anyway. I don't even know what's being auctioned, so I doubt I'll be buying anything.'

Adamson pouted at him. 'Not even me?' She must have read the look of confused horror on his face as she added: 'You can bid for the chance to have lunch with me and young Nero over there.' She waved a hand in the direction of the man Emma had pointed at earlier. 'And a visit to the set where we're filming.'

McLean was about to ask, 'Filming what?', but stopped himself when he realised he should already know.

'Oops. Gotta go. Can't keep my director waiting.' Vanessa waved back at an elderly man who was motioning with his hand for her to join a group of people close by the dais. 'Good to see you again, Insp—. . . Chief Inspector. And you too, Emma. Ask him about the time he interviewed me in my nightie.'

And before McLean could say anything more, she was gone.

'Is there something you want to tell me, Anthony McLean?' Emma glared at him as they stood in the middle of the crowded ballroom. For all the chatter of conversation, the muddle of people in too-fancy dress drinking champagne and eating canapes, they could have been alone.

'I'm sure I don't know what you mean.' Even as he said it, he knew it was a weak protest.

'How is it that you don't recognise Nero Genovese but are on first-name terms with Vanessa Adamson?'

'I'd hardly say we're on first-name terms. And as for the bloke, I've never even heard of him.'

Emma glowered at him for a while, but then relented. 'That much I can believe. But Adamson? She's Hollywood royalty. How on earth do you know her at all?'

'Must have been, what? Five years ago? She was next-door neighbour to Fergus McReadie. Remember him? IT guy and part-time cat burglar. I seem to recall you were the one who proved the bank statements he'd planted in my flat were forgeries.'

Emma's face went blank for a moment as she cast her mind back. 'Oh. Him. The Obituary Man.'

'The same. She lived next door, so we spoke to her when we were searching his apartment. And, yes, she was only wearing a nightdress at the time. I wasn't alone though. Grumpy Bob was there, if I remember right, and MacBride. And Detective Constable Kydd . . .'

McLean stopped talking. He'd not thought about Alison Kydd in years. She'd pushed him out of the way of an oncoming truck, saved his life even as she'd lost hers. What a stupid waste of a life. And what a stupid waste of time being in this room with all these people who couldn't give a damn.

'What are we doing here?' he asked. 'I mean, really?'

A waiter passed, bearing a tray laden with glasses of champagne. Emma took two, handed one to McLean and lifted hers high.

'We're here to enjoy someone else's hospitality. And to get out of the house for a change. Cheers.' She clinked her glass against his, then took a long sip, spluttering slightly as the bubbles went up her nose. McLean held his own glass up to the light as if it were a fine vintage needing close scrutiny before drinking, but truth was he didn't much feel like champagne. Didn't much feel like enjoying any of the hospitality paid for by the Dee Trust, however much good work they might do.

'Detective Chief Inspector. I'm so glad you came.'

McLean didn't need to turn to know who was speaking this

time. The voice cut through him like a rusty saw, bringing with it snippets of garbled memory. The last time he had seen this woman, she had drugged him, shoved him in a helicopter and told the pilot to drop him somewhere out in the Firth of Forth. Except that memory had the quality of a dream, a nightmare. In that memory Jane Louise Dee had died, but here she was as alive and untouched by the long arm of the law as ever.

'And this must be Emma. Tony, you really should introduce us.'

As she swept past him, McLean felt a blast of cold air and the faintest whiff of something bad. Rotten eggs, perhaps. Or a blocked drain somewhere in the basement. Jane Louise Dee, otherwise known as Mrs Saifre, grasped Emma's hand in both of hers, as if it were the most precious of gifts. She held on for just long enough to be uncomfortable before finally relinquishing it and turning to McLean himself.

'It's such a pleasure to see you again. How long has it been now? Three years? All that unpleasantness with poor old Andrew out at Rosskettle.'

McLean had no intention of shaking Mrs Saifre's hand, but she had much more ambitious ideas anyway, sweeping in and planting kisses in the air beside both his cheeks. Her youthful looks were all artifice, he knew. She had to be nearer sixty than fifty. And yet placing her alongside Emma it would be easy to assume Mrs Saifre was the younger woman. Her flawless pale skin was framed by straight black hair that fell past her shoulders. She wore a dress of red so vibrant it was almost vulgar, perfectly matched by her lipstick, and carried a small patent-leather bag looped over the elbow of one long-gloved arm. Unwelcome air-kiss over, she stepped back and eyed McLean up like a side of beef hanging in a butcher's shop.

'I do love a man in tartan trews. You look very fetching, my dear.'

McLean opened his mouth to protest that he wasn't her dear and that if he had any say in the matter he'd arrest her on the spot. Before he could get any words out, Saifre had turned her attention back to Emma.

'Darling, I'm so dreadfully busy right now, with this charity do and everything. But I would so like to get to know you better. Tony's told me absolutely nothing about you. How like him to want to keep you all to himself.'

'Umm . . . OK?' Emma took a step back as she spoke, but Saifre closed the space between them without appearing to move.

'Good, good. We'll have tea some time soon then. When the menfolk are at work.'

It was such an unexpected expression, especially coming from someone who had built her own international business from nothing, that McLean almost laughed. Instead he turned his disbelief to a question that had been nagging him for days now.

'The Dee Trust. How long's that been a thing?'

Saifre cocked her head to one side, as if searching his face for any hint of sarcasm. McLean was well practised at hiding it.

'The charity's been in existence for decades, Tony. My involvement goes back a few years. We rebranded recently, refocused our efforts.'

'And what is it exactly that you do?' McLean indicated the room full of partying people with a shrug and a dismissive wave of his hands. 'Apart from raffling off lunch dates with film stars?'

'The money goes to good causes. You've seen us in action out at Inchmalcolm Tower, I understand. That's a halfway house, for youngsters coming out of care and heading into the wide world. So many damaged lives. We do what we can to help them mend.'

'Very laudable.' It was McLean's turn to search Saifre's face for any sign of disingenuity, but if anything she'd had even more practice than him.

'So can we rely on you for a bid? Maybe a lunch with the delectable Miss Adamson. I saw you two chatting earlier.'

'We'll see. I'm always happy to support a good cause. Just like to know where my money's going.'

'Don't we all, Tony. Don't we all.' Mrs Saifre reached out and touched his arm, gently. A shock ran through him so sharp and so sudden he could scarcely hide it. Like static from a cheap polyester rug, he twitched involuntarily. And in that moment the room changed. It was no longer an elegant ballroom filled with wealthy people drinking and eating and shouting at each other. Now it was more like a Hieronymus Bosch painting, an image straight out of hell. A blink, perhaps a short gasp of surprise, and everything was back to normal.

Everything except Mrs Saifre, whose expression was wary now.

'Well, this affair won't run itself. I must be away.' She nodded towards McLean's glass of champagne, still full. 'Drink, eat. Enjoy the party. And if you feel the urge to bid on something, don't be shy.'

And then she strode away, perfectly balanced on ridiculous high heels, disappearing into the appreciative crowd.

'Well. She was . . . strange.'

'Don't be fooled. She is the most evil person I've ever met. If she's fronting this charity then there has to be something in it for her.' McLean caught the eye of a passing waiter, who proffered his tray still holding a dozen full champagne glasses. Adding the one he'd still not drunk anything from made a nice round thirteen.

'You not feeling well?' Emma took another gulp of her own drink, emptying her glass just as the waiter disappeared into the crowd.

'I'm fine. Just don't want anything she's paid for.' McLean

saw the quizzical frown Emma gave him. 'Call me old-fashioned if you like.'

'Well, it's a shame. If I'd known you weren't going to drink we could have saved on the taxi.'

'And found somewhere round here to park? At this time of night?' McLean grabbed another glass from the next passing waiter, handing it to Emma and relieving her of her empty one. 'Come on. Let's go and see what they're flogging to raise funds.'

They pushed through the crowd until they reached the front, where a couple of large boards bore the logo of the Dee Trust. Printed beneath was a list of fairly predictable experiences and prizes, each with a lot number beside it. A weekend in a famous golfing hotel sounded like something they'd have to pay him to do, rather than the other way around. If he was tempted by anything it was the day of race training with a Formula One star up at Knockhill, but the only really notable offering in the auction was the lunch with the Hollywood couple, and a chance to visit them on the set of their latest blockbuster movie, currently filming in Aberdeenshire. A couple of phone calls and McLean reckoned he could have that for free, although that wasn't the point, of course.

'Anything take your fancy?' he asked after Emma had spent five minutes gazing at the boards.

'Not really.' She drained her glass and plonked it down on the dais. 'And this champagne's shite. I've had better Cava from M&S. What are we doing here?'

McLean suppressed the urge to say that it was her idea to come. That might be true, but even he knew that saying so wouldn't win him any favours. He looked out over the crowd, expensively dressed and ready to spend ridiculous sums of money on rubbish just because it was for a good cause. A salve to their consciences so they could sleep at night in their warm beds and million-pound homes. What would they make of the camp out in the Hermitage, people living outdoors in sub-zero temperatures because they had nowhere else to go? Because they'd been bombed out of their homes by a war none of them had asked for. What would they all think about a little girl lying dead in a city basement, another curled up in the snow? The answer was obvious enough: they wouldn't think about them at all except to tut and look for someone other than themselves to blame.

'You want to go?' he asked, all too aware that his failure to mingle and press the flesh would not go unnoticed by the deputy chief constable. McLean found it hard to care.

'Yeah.' Emma took a step closer to him and slid her arm through his. 'Let's get out of here before they all start braying.'

29

The taxi took them through a city quietened by the bad weather. McLean still wasn't sure of Emma's mood, although she'd seemed closer to him that evening than in all the months since her miscarriage. She stared out the window, wrapped up warm in a fur coat that had belonged to his mother and which was about as far from politically correct as it was possible to get. He was happy to relax into his seat and just watch her, grateful their driver wasn't the chatty kind.

'Thank you.' Emma spoke to the glass first, then lazily turned her head to face him. It was hard to tell in the darkness, but she looked happy for a change. Tired, too.

'For what?'

'For agreeing to accept the invitation. For taking me to something I never thought I'd experience, even if most of it was dire. Meeting a film star though, that was pretty special.'

'Would you have preferred it if I'd bid for that lunch with her and the other fellow? What was his name again? Hadrian something?'

'Nero Genovese, as well you know. And no, he's not my type. Vanessa seemed nice though. Down to earth.'

'Oh, Vanessa, is it? And here's me thinking you were starstruck.'

Emma thumped him on the arm, but only playfully. Then she leaned in and shared her warmth with him. She smelled of champagne and shampoo and some very expensive perfume. It made a change from white-paper overalls and whatever unpleasant stench the latest crime scene brought them.

'I was surprised she remembered me, to be honest.' He slid an arm around her shoulders and enjoyed the moment of peace.

'You have that effect on people, Tony. Your problem is you don't realise it.'

They sat together in companionable silence as the taxi drove down Clerk Street. When it turned onto Summerhall and approached the Meadows, McLean was surprised to see the circus still lit up, the car park full.

'Took my wee girl to see that yesterday afternoon. Brilliant show, it was.' The driver took that moment to start a conversation.

'Don't think I've ever been to a proper circus. One with performing animals and all that. We used to go to the funfair when it came to town, but that's not the same.' Emma pulled away from McLean the better to peer through the car window.

'They'll not have any animals. Not any more. They brought in rules last year, remember?'

'Aye, I do now. Probably for the best.'

'Still, we could go and have a look.' McLean glanced at his watch, surprised at how early it was. But then they'd hardly stayed at the charity fundraiser any longer than was strictly necessary. Probably not even that. 'If you want.'

'Yeah. It'll be fun.'

'Drop us off here, can you?' McLean asked the driver, and he and Emma climbed out into the cold night air. He envied her the coat, and even more so the decidedly unladylike boots she'd been hiding under her long dress. Tartan trews were smart, not exactly warm, and the shoes that went with his outfit weren't really designed for walking on frosty, snow-rimed grass.

The ticket office was still open when they approached, and the young woman behind the glass seemed to recognise McLean.

'You come back then? I knew that you would.'

'Really?' He cast his mind back to the last time he'd been here. The enthusiastic young local lad had served him, and this one had been more interested in her fingernails.

'It's Irena, isn't it?' McLean made a fuss of getting his wallet out of his jacket pocket. 'Roy not working tonight?'

The young woman's gaze tightened for a moment, peering at him as if she were trying to read his thoughts. McLean simply smiled back until she relented.

'He is working the ropes. No, how you say it? Learning the ropes? Some day maybe he be great acrobat.' Irena smiled at some joke only she knew. 'If he loses his fear of falling.'

'I'm sure he will.' McLean glanced around the ticket office, looking for a programme of events, or even a board with show times on it. Judging by the crowd of people milling around, there was still plenty to see. 'Is there a performance this evening?'

'Is started already, but this is no matter. You will enjoy.' Irena pressed buttons on a machine of the kind McLean had last seen in a cinema when he was five years old, producing two narrow tickets cut neatly from a roll.

'How much?' He pulled out a twenty-pound note, but the young woman simply waved it away.

'You came back,' she said enigmatically. 'For you is free.'

In sharp contrast to the charity fundraiser, the circus felt like a place at ease with itself. McLean took his unexpectedly free tickets and together he and Emma walked through the crowds towards the big top. He recognised the young man and would-be acrobat, Roy, standing at the entrance, deep in conversation with an older woman who looked like she had come from central casting to act the part of a witch in a children's pantomime.

'Sorry, sir, ma'am. Show's already started.' The young lad stood straighter than many of his contemporaries out beyond the confines of the circus. He couldn't have been working here long, probably came looking for a job as soon as it arrived. Run away to join the circus. Somehow the phrase felt more familiar than the obvious cliché, as if McLean had heard it used recently. If he had, he couldn't think where or when. It showed some initiative on the part of the lad anyway. And a certain amount of trust on the part of the circus to take him on too. Judging by the way his companion tutted and pushed him gently to one side as she stepped forward, he still had much to learn.

'Irena has given you her blessing. You can go in.' She held her hand out and McLean stared at it stupidly before remembering the two thin strips of cheap pulp paper the young woman in the ticket office had given him. He passed them over, noting the dark henna tattoos all over the old woman's skin, swirls and dots and patterns that must have had some meaning, although what that might be he had no idea.

'All our hands tell a story, if you know how to read them.' She reached out and grabbed him with a swiftness and strength that took McLean by surprise, holding both of his palms upwards as the two tickets tumbled forgotten to the ground. Then, as quickly as she had taken hold, she released her grip and turned to the young man.

'Roy, show our guests to their seats.'

The young man snapped to attention like a scolded cadet. He pulled back a heavy canvas flap and motioned for McLean and Emma to go inside. The bright lights of the ring made the dark entranceway like a cave, an uncomfortable feeling not helped by the soft ground underfoot. There was a warmth to the air like breath, too, and the noise of the show grew ever louder as they neared the edge of the ring.

McLean knew it was just an illusion, his senses playing tricks on him, but the tent felt much bigger inside than out. Rows of benches surrounded a circle big enough to fit his entire house into. Overhead, wires had been strung between two tent poles, each as thick as a stout man at their base. Ropes disappeared into darkness overhead, and a pair of acrobats in matching outfits performed a routine that had the entire capacity audience on the edge of their seats. There was no safety net, he noticed. How had that got past health and safety? For that matter how had any of this ancient-looking setup been approved by anyone, least of all the council? And yet here it was. The only concession to modernity he could see was the lack of caged animals.

They took seats at the back, high up and yet still with a perfect view of the action. There were clowns and tumblers, yet more acrobats on the high wire, displays of skill that were hard to believe even though he watched them with his own eyes. McLean hadn't realised quite how tense he'd been, but as the show built to its climax, so he found his shoulders relaxing. Emma's closeness and warmth were something he'd missed too. Just being with her, sharing this experience. He couldn't remember the last time they'd done anything like it.

He wanted it to go on for ever, to be trapped in that strange place of wonder. The moment was such a perfect release from the stress of the job, the anguish over Emma's miscarriage and his own feelings of guilt about it all. He wanted to forget the still nameless little girls, forget Maurice Jennings and all the other endless worries that assailed him. Just to be here, lost in a spectacle he'd not seen since he was a boy, made him wish that he were still that boy. Before the world turned ugly and complicated and mean.

But he wasn't a boy any more. The world moved on, and so did the show. It might have been forty minutes, it might have been an hour, but all too soon it was over.

30

A subdued calm filled the audience as they filed peacefully out of the big top, show over. McLean felt it like a warm but refreshing breeze, and a tiny, cynical part at the back of his brain wondered what the circus master might have been pumping out through the air conditioning. Except that there was no air conditioning as far as he could tell. The whole circus looked like something that had been stuck in a time warp since . . . when? He could only think of childhood; before his parents had died they'd taken him to the circus, and maybe his grandmother had too. But even then it had been more funfair and less show. The memories that this place brought him were of things he had read about in his childhood rather than things he had actually experienced.

'That was quite magical,' Emma said as they sat and waited patiently for the rest of the audience to file out. She leaned in close and kissed him gently on the cheek. 'Thank you.'

'Thank me? You were the one who suggested it.' McLean stared up into the murky shadows high up in the marquee, more visible now that the house lights had been raised. 'It's really not what I was expecting.'

'No, me neither. It was, I don't know, like some kind of dream. An idea of a circus. Nothing like what I remember as a kid, but then I guess that was all dodgems and shoot-'em-ups and trying to impress boys by drinking cider round the back of the freak show tent.' Emma rubbed at her eyes with a thumb and forefinger as if she was trying to ease a 25-year-old hangover. 'Must have had a glass or two too much of that cheap champagne. How're you feeling?'

'I didn't drink any, remember?' McLean stood, offering a hand to help Emma to her feet. She swayed a little, leaned into him again, then caught her balance before setting off down the steep narrow steps to the ground.

Outside, there was far more to the circus than the main show in the big top. The tents and caravans had been arranged in a wide arc, forming an alleyway of sorts with attractions on either side. People took their time ambling between the stalls, buying food and trinkets, trying their hand at the sort of sideshow games that McLean had only seen in museums. A couple of times he started to glance at his watch or reach for his phone, but something stopped him. As if the circus represented a bubble of calm and it wouldn't allow the world to intrude until it was ready.

'Well if it isn't my two favourite lovebirds.'

They had been walking in silence, hand in hand, just enjoying each other's company and the strange sights of the circus. As he heard the words, McLean almost felt a shudder of annoyance that someone had broken their perfect moment. At the same time, he recognised the voice and was unsurprised when Emma broke away from him, turned and ran towards the figure a few paces behind them.

Madame Rose, part-time medium and dealer in antiquarian books and occult curios, was a big woman at the best of times. Perhaps because she had been born in the body of a man, perhaps because she was so much larger than life. Dressed in a coat and hat that must have single-handedly diminished the local mink population by a satisfying percentage, she looked enormous.

Emma trying to wrap her in a hug was both comical and a little dispiriting, given that she had forsaken McLean's embrace in the attempt.

'Rose. It's been months. Where have you been?' Emma was like a little child all of a sudden, and McLean couldn't help but remember the first time the two of them had met. Back then Emma had been very much like a child, recovering from the attack that had left her in a coma.

'It's not been that long, surely.' Madame Rose wrapped a massive arm around Emma's shoulders and steered her back to where McLean stood. 'Although I have been out of town a lot over the autumn.'

She raised her eyes heavenwards, and as if on cue a few soft flurries of snow fell out of the orange-painted darkness overhead.

'Autumn's long gone,' McLean said. 'And it wasn't the best of times, as you know.'

'Aye, I know.' Rose squeezed Emma's shoulder before releasing her back to him. 'But what brings you to the circus? I wouldn't have pegged you as a clowns and acrobats man, Tony.'

'Don't blame me. It was Emma's idea.'

She thumped him gently on the chest. 'You brought it up. I just thought it would be more fun than that dull charity do.'

'Which was also your idea, I seem to recall.' McLean smiled as he said it, worried that Emma might not see the joke. Her frown was cut short by Madame Rose.

'Well, never mind. It's good to see you anyway. And since you're here, there's an old friend of mine I'd really like you to meet.'

Something about the way she said it made McLean suspect this was the real reason Rose was here in the first place. Either that or his natural cynicism had finally managed to overpower the feeling of peace and ease that filled the circus. He found that he didn't much mind. Anything that prolonged the moment was good; he wasn't so naive as to think that Emma's change of mood would last for ever. Looking around, he could see the crowd beginning to thin, people finally drifting away to their homes and their beds. Directly behind where they were standing, a hand-painted sign above an ornate canvas tent that wouldn't have looked out of place in a souk read 'Madame Jasmina – Fortunes Told'. No guesses as to where they were going then.

The inside of the tent lived up to the promise of its exterior and then some. McLean held open the flap for Emma and Madame Rose to enter first, then stepped into a dark, warm space like a womb. Scented candles filled the air with aromas of the east, and everywhere was draped with heavy rugs depicting weird scenes in red weave. In the middle of a surprisingly large room, a round table was arranged with four chairs, almost as if Madame Jasmina had been expecting all three of them to join her. If that was the case, then her own absence must have been for dramatic effect.

'Please, Tony, Emma, have a seat.' Madame Rose indicated the two closest to the exit. 'I'm sure Jasmina will be along soon.'

'I'm not sure I need my fortune told right now.' McLean pulled a chair out for Emma to sit, but stayed on his feet.

'Perhaps wise, given what the future holds for you.'

Madame Jasmina appeared from the shadows at the back of the tent. McLean was only slightly surprised to find that she was the same old woman who had told Roy to let them into the big top show after it had already started. She was dressed for the part of fortune teller, even more so than Madame Rose, who at least brought a kind of Morningside chic to the bangles and volumin-ous robes.

'I was expecting you earlier, Rose,' she said, ignoring McLean and Emma now as if she had forgotten they ever existed.

'And I wasn't expecting you at all, Jasmina. But as ever it's a pleasure. Even if it's never good news that brings you back to the city.'

'Shall we sit?' Madame Jasmina waved a hand at the table, and this time McLean felt almost compelled to do as he was asked. Rose dropped into her own chair a little more heavily than was ladylike.

'Perhaps some tea.' Jasmina strode to the back of the tent, pulled the hangings aside and shouted something in a language McLean didn't understand. There was a familiarity to the cadence of the words though, the patterns and rhythms reminding him of the little girl they'd found in the office of House the Refugees. He would have asked what language it was, but the fortune teller had already taken her own seat, reached out and grasped Emma's hands before he could form the question.

'Your troubled past is written clearly, my dear.' She turned Emma's hands over swiftly, then ran a finger across one palm. 'Your future is more clouded, but less tragic. What you wish for is beyond anyone's gift, but what you will have is more than most can hope for.'

'Really?' Emma pulled her hands away, wiping them on her coat. 'Is that the best you can do?'

'Would you prefer the sugar-coated version I give to the paying customers? Your heart's desire will be yours before the year is out, and all that rubbish?' Jasmina's English might have been heavily accented, but it was fluent and laden with very local sarcasm.

'What does Rose mean, "it's never good news that brings you back to the city"?' McLean asked. Madame Jasmina turned her attention on him with all the swiftness of a snake striking.

'You see to the heart of things. I have heard that about you, Anthony McLean.'

'And you have heard my name too. All very impressive. I did enjoy the show, and I thank you for the tickets. But if you have something to say to me, or something to ask, just get on with it. Rose will tell you, if you don't already know, that I'm not the most patient of men.'

Madame Jasmina bowed her head in understanding. 'Of course. Where I come from there are formalities. Ways of doing things that are perhaps unnecessary, but give us a certain sense of calm and order. As a man who deals with the chaos, I can understand, you might not appreciate the subtle approach. But at least take tea with us.'

She waved towards the back of the tent, and the darkness shifted, shadows coalescing into the form of a young woman bearing a tray set with tea things. The delicate china cups, iron kettle and teapot were of only passing note. McLean's attention was almost entirely on the one bearing them towards him. She was better dressed than the last time he had seen her, but there was no mistaking that flame-red hair.

'Rahel?'

31

To her credit, the young woman didn't run. Neither did she drop the tray in surprise. McLean could see it in her eyes though. She was as much set up for this as he had been. For a moment she simply stood and stared at him, like a wild creature caught in the hunter's spotlight. Then Jasmina barked something at her in that oddly musical language and she hurried to put the tray down on the table.

'Rahel has just joined us recently. I believe you have met her before, Anthony McLean.'

'I prefer Tony, really. Or Detective Chief Inspector if we're being formal.' He waited for Madame Jasmina to open her mouth to speak in reply, then interrupted her. 'Tell me. What is that language you use with her?'

'You would know it as Aramaic, but the truth is more complicated than that. Why?'

'I've heard it spoken before. Just recently. A young girl with hair the same colour as Rahel's here. A girl calling herself Nala.'

Now Rahel did drop the tray. Fortunately for her it was just an inch off the table top. Still, the rattling of cups and teapot brought a frown to Madame Jasmina's face. She turned to Rahel and spoke more words in that ancient, flowing language. McLean could understand none of it, but he caught the name Nala spoken by both women, and Akka too.

'Where is she?' Rahel asked in her accented English. 'Where is Nala?'

'She is safe.' McLean considered the last time he had seen the young girl, led to the care worker's car by DC Harrison. 'Social Services are looking after her until we decide what's to become of her.'

'What is to become of her? She should be with her mother.' Rahel's voice boiled with anger, and was it a trick of the lighting in this strange tent that made her green eyes appear to glow from within? She clenched her fists, and for a moment McLean thought she was going to pick up the tea tray and throw it at someone, but Madame Jasmina reached out and closed one bony hand around the young woman's wrist. At her touch, the light in Rahel's eyes dimmed, her shoulders slumped.

'I quite agree. She should be with her mother.' McLean stood up. It was too awkward talking up to the young woman. 'We've been trying to find you, Rahel. I've been trying to find you exactly because of that. Have you spoken to Billy recently?'

'Billy? Why would I speak to him?'

'I don't know. I thought maybe you two kept in touch.'

The faintest of blushes reddened Rahel's cheeks, confirming McLean suspicions. He could get annoyed with her for avoiding him even when she knew he needed to talk to her, or he could let it slide and make the most of this situation others had engineered for them.

'It doesn't matter. You're here now, and I've some bad news, possibly. About Akka.'

The flush drained from Rahel's face in an instant, and for a moment McLean thought she was going to faint. 'Where is she? What have you done to her?'

'We haven't done anything to her.' McLean struggled for a

way to put his gut feelings and suppositions into words. Speaking the ideas only underlined how tenuous they all were. 'A woman matching her description was found badly beaten on the outskirts of the city. She's in the hospital, unconscious. We can't identify her, but you might be able to.'

Rahel stared at him, mouth hanging slightly open as she processed what he had said. Before she could reply, Madame Jasmina reached out and took her hand, spoke softly to her. Something like resolve spread across the young woman's face, and she stood up straight.

'I will come with you to hospital now.'

McLean was somewhat taken aback. It was late in the evening and he'd not planned going anywhere other than home as soon as he'd assured himself Rahel wouldn't run away. On the other hand, the Western General would be quiet right now, and it was unlikely DCI Dexter would complain if he managed to positively identify her victim.

'OK.' He stuck a hand in his pocket and pulled out his phone, ready to call a taxi. Madame Jasmina stopped him with a wave of her gnarled hand.

'A moment, please, Anthony McLean.' She turned to Madame Rose. 'Perhaps you, Emma and Rahel could give us a moment. There are matters of great importance I must discuss with . . .' She looked back at McLean, a mischievous glint in her eye. '. . . the detective chief inspector.'

'You are a good man, Anthony McLean. Rose says so, and that is enough for me. But your actions here tonight confirm it for me. I am . . . happy it is so.'

McLean pushed down the impatience that gnawed at him, even if he couldn't stop himself from glancing back towards the exit where Emma, Madame Rose and Rahel had left. Searching for a distraction, he took up his cup and sipped at the tea.

'People seem to be very free and easy with talking about me behind my back,' he said after a couple of sips. 'I much prefer it when they're direct, and tell me exactly what it is they want of me.'

Madame Jasmina dipped her head in understanding, but took a few moments to drink some of her own tea before speaking again.

'Of course. There is a time and a place for niceties, and maybe this isn't it. So tell me. What do you know of the djinn, Detective Chief Inspector?'

'The what?'

'The djinn. Some call them genies, but that name robs them of the fear and respect they deserve.'

'Genies? As in magic lamps and three wishes?' McLean put his cup back down on the table, ready to leave. A shame, as the tea had been very good. But there was only so much of his time he could waste, and he'd rather spend it at home than with this wizened old lady, especially given the improvement in Emma's mood.

'So quick to jump to conclusions. Rose told me that too.' Madame Jasmina poured more tea into his cup, then topped up her own. 'As to Emma. She is healing from a great many misfortunes. It is hard on one body to carry two souls. You must give her the space she needs.'

McLean resisted the urge to scoff at the old woman's words. He'd had enough experience of Madame Rose's vague prognostications and seeming ability to read his mind to know better than to rise to that bait.

'These djinn, then. I take it they don't travel around on flying carpets.'

Madame Jasmina allowed a small smirk to crease her old face at that, but it didn't last long. 'Indeed not. The djinn are an ancient race. They walked the earth long before mankind, and will no doubt still walk it long after we are gone. By and large they leave us be. They do not need anything from us, and we have little to gain from them.'

'I'm going to have to stop you there,' McLean interrupted. 'I know Madame Rose believes in all this occult stuff, but if you've spoken to her about me at any length you'll know that I don't.'

'And yet it exists all the same. And you might protest, Anthony McLean, but you have met it time and time again. Faced it down and defeated it. Only this evening you met with Atargatis. I can smell her on you like the odour of decay. But she has no power over you.'

'Atar—?' McLean shook his head. If there was some point to all this, then interrupting would only mean it took longer to get there.

'She is older even than the djinn. And some of them worship her as a goddess, do her bidding. I cannot fathom why, but the reason is unimportant. The result is all too clear.'

'It is?'

'Look around you, Anthony McLean. Do you not see the signs? War is everywhere. Chaos and evil. It drives good people like Rahel from their homes, tears children like Nala from their mothers. It follows the desperate as they flee, and it finds fresh fields in this new land. New soil in which to sow its discord.'

'I thought you were going to get to the point. What is it that you actually want from me? Why am I here?'

'You are here because you wanted to see the show, are you not?' Madame Jasmina raised an ancient eyebrow. 'And as to what I want from you, well, I'd call it a favour.'

The old lady put down her teacup, then reached forward with the same hand, palm down, and laid it directly in front of McLean. When she lifted it up again, a tiny brass casting lay on the table, although he could see no way how she could have been holding it before. That was the magician's skill, though.

'This is a talisman, a thing of great power if you believe in it, a lump of base metal if you don't. You will find the one responsible for the dark deeds unfolding in the city this winter, and when you do, it will not be what you are expecting. All I ask is that you give it this.'

McLean stared at the tiny object for a moment, then looked back up at Madame Jasmina. She wasn't smiling now. This was no joke to her, and something of the setting, the tea, and even the relaxed atmosphere of the circus made him realise that she was completely serious.

'And what happens when I do?' he asked.

Now the fortune teller smiled. 'Would you believe me if I told you?'

'Probably not. But you've found Rahel for me, so I owe you one.' McLean leaned forward and picked up the tiny casting, surprised at both how warm it was and how heavy. The light in the tent was not good, and his eyes were tired from a day gone on far too long. Even so he could see clearly the intricate etching and scrollwork, the carefully formed handle and tiny spout for a wick. A patina of age coloured the surface, shiny where it had been handled most, dull everywhere else. Solid, and too tiny to actually work, it was nevertheless quite clearly a model of an ancient brass lamp. The sort of thing he might expect to find in a Damascus edition of Monopoly, if such a thing existed.

'If I polish it, will I get three wishes?' He held it up on the palm of his hand, unsure whether he shouldn't just hand it back. And yet doing so felt somehow rude.

'Wishes always come at a cost, Anthony McLean. I think you already know that.' Madame Jasmina stood up, and McLean reflexively did the same. It felt only natural to close his hand around the tiny trinket, then transfer it to the pocket of his tartan trews. He felt the warmth of it against his leg, soothing the dull ache in his hip that was his constant companion these days.

'Come, let us see what Emma, Rose and Rahel have been up to.' Madame Jasmina led McLean towards the exit.

'I can't remember the last time the circus came at all. Not this circus, at least. And not here. We get the funfair every summer, and there have been shows like this one during the Festival and Fringe, but—'

'There are no shows like this one. I can assure you of that. And the last time we were here was twenty-five years ago. It was young girls the creature was after that time too, although it preys always on the vulnerable, the ones who won't be missed. We managed to save one of its victims. I had thought we had killed it too, but in truth you can never kill something like that. Only send it back to where it came from.'

McLean remembered then where he'd heard of someone running off to join the circus recently. The conversation with Dagwood, Grumpy Bob and Tom Callander in the Cold Case Unit, before they'd realised the young girl in the basement had died only recently.

'You know about the two young girls we found? About Maurice Jennings?'

Jasmina's gaze dropped, her face stony. 'The man . . . complicates things. He should not have been a victim.' She shook her head vigorously. 'No, that is not the right way to say it. None of them should have been victims, but I do not know why he was one. The beast. It has never taken such a life before. Always it has preyed on the young, the innocent. Those who cannot protect themselves.'

32

The Western General never truly slept, but it had entered a period of night-time quiet when McLean arrived with Rahel and Emma in tow. He had only briefly contemplated suggesting Emma take a taxi home on her own, and decided swiftly to keep that idea to himself. It helped that she seemed to have formed a bond of sorts with the young refugee. He could only guess at what Madame Rose had told the two of them while he'd been discussing Middle Eastern mythology with Jasmina.

They must have looked an odd sight, the three of them walking the empty hospital corridors. McLean in his tartan trews and formal jacket, Emma in a long fur coat, and Rahel with her angry red hair and matching attitude. Nobody commented, of the few folk they saw, so maybe being outlandish was the best way to remain incognito.

A lone uniformed constable sat on a chair outside the room where the young woman who was almost certainly Rahel's sister lay. McLean didn't manage to see the title of the book he was reading before he scrambled to his feet, slipping it into a pocket as they approached.

'Detective Chief Inspector, sir. Nobody said . . .'

'At ease, Constable.' McLean racked his memory for the name. 'It's Sullivan, isn't it?'

'Sir.' The young man nodded, smoothing down his jacket with hands that didn't quite know what they were supposed to be doing. He tried to keep his gaze on McLean, but couldn't help darting glances at his two mismatched companions.

'The young woman.' McLean waved a hand at the door. It had a thin glass panel let into it, and beyond he could see the corner of a bed surrounded by intensive-care machinery. 'She's still unconscious, I take it?'

'Aye, sir. No' really sure when she'll wake up.'

McLean couldn't help noticing he'd said 'when', not 'if'. He hoped it was more than just youthful optimism and innocence.

'I need to see her,' he said. 'More importantly, this woman needs to see her.' He pointed at Rahel with an open hand. 'It's possible she may be able to identify her.'

The constable nodded, then produced a clipboard and pen from behind his chair. 'You'll have to sign in, sir.'

McLean did as he was asked, adding Rahel's name to the very short list of people who had visited that day.

'I'll just wait here,' Emma said, and peering into the room beyond, McLean could hardly blame her. There wasn't much space to start with, and most of it had been filled with life-support apparatus. The bed in the centre of it had been rigged up with a traction frame, wires and supports holding limbs in what looked like very uncomfortable positions. At first he thought that there were only limbs, as the young woman's head was almost totally engulfed by pillows and half obscured by bandages. He had seen photographs of her taken not long after she'd been found, bruised, bloodied and caked in filth. Somehow, cleaned up and kept alive by gently humming machinery, she looked worse.

'Akka?'

Rahel's uncertainty was understandable. She stood close to McLean, just inside the room, not daring to go any closer at first. Then she took a step, another, each one a hardening of her resolve, until she stood at the head of the bed staring down at the comatose young woman.

'What happened to her? Who did this?'

McLean edged around the bed until he was standing beside her. 'We found her on an industrial estate, out Sighthill way. Whoever did it left her for dead. It's only luck she was discovered in time.'

Even as he said it, he questioned the use of the word. There was nothing lucky about this poor wreck of a human being.

'Is this your sister, Rahel? Is this Akka?'

Rahel nodded, reached out a hand towards the bed, then clenched her outstretched fingers into a fist and withdrew it again.

'She'll get the best possible treatment. If anyone can help her it's the doctors working here.'

As if hearing his voice for the first time, the young woman in the bed let out a low moan, so soft it was almost inaudible. The eye not covered by bandages flickered under its closed lid for a second or two, then she fell still again. If the humming and beeping machinery registered anything, McLean couldn't tell, but it was a positive sign nonetheless.

'Come.' He laid a hand gently on Rahel's shoulder, half expecting her to shrug it off and refuse to be parted from her sister. Instead, something seemed to go out of her and she allowed him to steer her from the room.

'Why does it not surprise me to find you wandering through my hospital in the dead of night.'

They had barely reached the end of the corridor, McLean, Emma and Rahel each silent in their own thoughts as they walked to the entrance and hopefully a taxi, when they were interrupted by a familiar voice. McLean had known Doctor Caroline Wheeler for many years now, and he couldn't ever recall a time she hadn't looked tired. Now was no different, although given the late hour it was hardly surprising.

'I could say the same for you, Caroline. Do you never sleep?'

Doctor Wheeler's smile took too much effort to last long. 'It's been known to happen. Once or twice a year.' She turned to Emma. 'It's good to see you looking so well, Em. And Tony, the trews suit you. Maybe you should wear them more often.' Finally, she looked at Rahel, part hiding behind the two of them, and her eyes widened in surprise. 'Ah.'

'Rahel Nour, this is Doctor Caroline Wheeler.' McLean made the introductions. 'And judging by the direction she was walking, I'm guessing she's been looking after your sister.'

'Sister. Yes, of course.' Doctor Wheeler nodded to herself. 'You've been to see her, I take it?'

'Just now, aye. Maybe not the best time, but . . .' McLean stopped speaking, not quite sure what else to say.

'Will she wake up?' Rahel asked.

'That is a very good question. And one to which I have no answer. Not right now.' Doctor Wheeler had a clipboard with her, and she peered at it intently for a while. McLean knew a prop when he saw one.

'She's in better condition than when she arrived here. That much I can tell you. We've set her bones, cleaned up her wounds. She's going to lose one eye, I'm afraid.' Doctor Wheeler let out a long, weary sigh. 'Well, actually she's already lost it. We had to remove it to stop infection getting in. She's going to be here a long while yet.'

'But you don't know if she will wake up,' Rahel said. 'Why do you do this for her? Who will pay for it all? I have no money.'

'We don't charge for our services here. Not if we can help it. And as to why I do this, it's my job.' Doctor Wheeler shrugged.

'Akka's in good hands here, Rahel,' McLean said. 'She'll get the best medical attention she can, and we're guarding her in case anyone comes looking for her. She'll be safe, but we still need to find out who did this to her.'

'I'm away on my rounds now, but I'll let you know the moment anything changes with the patient.' Doctor Wheeler turned her attention from McLean back to Rahel. 'Akka, did you say? And you're Rahel. Rahel Nour. OK. I'll get the records updated. Nice to know she's not a Jane Doe any more.'

McLean opened his mouth to speak, but a buzzing from Doctor Wheeler's pocket interrupted him. She pulled out a very old-fashioned-looking pager, peered at the message scrolling across its tiny LCD screen with a worried frown.

'Good to see you, but I have to go.' Without any further ado, she hurried off up the corridor towards the intensive-care unit, leaving the three of them alone again.

'What's that about?' Emma asked, then stepped swiftly out of the way as a pair of orderlies hurried by, pushing a trolley laden with expensive equipment. Shortly afterwards a couple of nurses rushed in the same direction.

'Something's up. Best we leave the experts to deal with it.' McLean directed the two women towards the entrance hall as yet more hospital staff rushed past.

'I go back to circus now?' Rahel's question was almost hesitant, as if the implications of her situation were beginning to sink in.

McLean pulled out his phone and checked the time. Almost midnight. Tomorrow would start early with a morning briefing, and while Rahel's identification of her sister wasn't immediately relevant to his own cases, he was sure she had information that would be. Could he risk losing her again?

'Would you stay there if I took you? Would you talk to us tomorrow, on the record? At the police station?'

Rahel stared at him, her green eyes defiant. And then she seemed to deflate. He'd thought her in her late teens, but now she looked more like a fourteen-year-old pretending to be sixteen.

'Are you going to arrest me? Will you send me back there? To the war?'

McLean opened his mouth to assure her he had no such intention, but Emma beat him to it. She put an arm around Rahel's shoulders and pulled the young woman into an unresisting hug.

'Nobody's arresting anyone, and they're certainly not sending you away. It's too late to go back to the circus now. Come on. Let's all go home.'

The sharp taint of exhaust fumes from the departing taxi hung in the crisp night air as McLean unlocked the back door and flicked on the lights. When he turned to let Emma and Rahel in, it was to see the younger woman staring up at the dark house, her face a picture of disbelief.

'Come on in. It's too cold out here to stand about on the doorstep.'

Still staring as if she couldn't quite believe what was happening, Rahel allowed herself to be steered indoors by Emma. When they stepped into the kitchen, the heat from the Aga was a welcome relief, and without thinking McLean set about filling the kettle and putting it on to boil. Only once he'd done that did he glance at the clock over the door, seeing it was closer to one now than midnight.

'Is many people living here? They are all asleep?' Rahel's gaze darted from fridge to table to sink and back to McLean, never resting anywhere for long.

'Just me and Emma,' he said, then felt something move at his feet. 'And the cat.'

Mrs McCutcheon's cat, usually nowhere to be seen whenever a stranger arrived at the house, had sauntered in as if she had not a care in the world. She sniffed the air, then walked boldly up to Rahel and nudged her hand.

'Oh, hello there, puss.' Rahel crouched down and rubbed the cat behind her ears, getting a deep rumbling purr in response. McLean wasn't sure whether to be jealous or relieved, settling for a bit of both.

'Anyone want a cup of tea?' he asked, hoping the answer would be no. He'd need to be at the station for six o'clock, which didn't leave much time for sleep.

'I'm too knackered for tea. Think I'll head to bed.' Emma walked over to the Aga and removed the kettle from the hob. 'Rahel, I'll show you where you'll be sleeping, OK?'

Rahel straightened up, looked around the kitchen one more time. 'I can't believe . . . How big is this house? It is like a palace, no?'

'Don't get too comfortable now,' McLean said. 'This is only temporary. Until we can work something out. I still need to ask you questions. A lot of questions. About how you got here, about Akka and the others. And we'll get you to see the young girl we found, Nala. If we can identify her as Akka's daughter, that opens up all manner of possibilities.'

'Nala.' Rahel's eyes widened at the name, the young teen showing through the hardened exterior again. 'I must see her. I have to protect her.'

'She's safe where she is. Trust me.' McLean recalled the CCTV footage he'd seen, the look of fear on the little girl's face when he'd arrived at the charity offices. Could he really be sure she was fine in some care home right now? He had to believe that she was.

'Get some sleep, OK?' he said. 'We'll talk tomorrow, and then you can see her.'

33

'**W**hat the fuck did you think you were doing taking her back to your house? Why didn't you bring her here the moment you found her?'

McLean had been preparing himself mentally for this bollocking ever since Emma had offered Rahel a place to stay. It was irregular, to say the least, but, even so, he was surprised at the deputy chief constable's anger. It didn't take a genius to work out that something else was bothering Call-me-Stevie, and McLean was prepared to give good odds he knew what that something else was. Or that someone.

'I only found her by accident, and late last night at that, sir. I'd no reason to arrest her, and if I'd tried to bring her in for an interview then, she'd have disappeared again and we'd be no further on with the investigation.'

'And which investigation is that exactly, McLean?' Robinson paced back and forth in front of the floor-to-ceiling glass that made up one wall of his office. 'I thought you were already tied up with the two dead girls and that other bloke. That not enough work for you? Need to go poking your nose into Jo Dexter's cases over at Vice now?'

Definitely something else bothering the DCC. Someone else. McLean didn't want to come over too defensive, but he shoved his hands in his trouser pockets anyway. The warm weight of the tiny brass lamp figurine was strangely comforting, reminding him more of the wonderful show than the strange conversation that had come afterwards. He'd transferred it from the pocket of his tartan trews the night before without thinking.

'Our investigations overlap, sir. Makes sense for us to follow leads when we find them. DI Ritchie's been liaising with Vice so we can share resources. And anyway, I tried to call Jo last night but she wasn't answering her phone.'

Robinson stopped mid-stride, then rounded on McLean. 'That's because she was representing Police Scotland at the Dee Trust charity fundraiser all night. Covering up for a detective chief inspector who thought it would be more fun to bunk off and go to the circus instead.'

'I . . . I was there, sir. At the fundraiser.'

'For all of five minutes, right enough. Jane Louise said she'd spoken briefly to you, and then you were gone before she could introduce you to anyone. That's not the sort of impression you were supposed to make.'

'Impression I . . .' McLean shook his head in disbelief. He hadn't failed to notice the casual use of Mrs Saifre's double first names, which both confirmed his suspicion of what was really bothering the DCC, and dropped the man yet further still in his estimation. 'Sir. It's a miracle I even turned up at all. If Emma hadn't wanted to go and see what all the fuss was about I'd have stayed home. Hobnobbing with the kind of people who like to be seen at that sort of event is not part of my job description. As you already pointed out, I've got the deaths of two wee girls to worry about, and a young man who may or may not be connected to them somehow. Quite frankly I've better things to be doing with my time. And if I want to make a donation to charity, that's my business and nobody else's, OK?'

Robinson went very still, the blood draining from his face as

215

if there were a vampire at his neck. When he spoke, it was quiet, controlled and all the more chilling for that.

'The Dee Trust is not some fly-by-night organisation providing virtue-signalling services to the high and mighty. It's an important – no, it's a crucial part of the city's fight against delinquency. Without the services they provide in places like Inchmalcolm Tower our job would be ten times more difficult to do. You understand that, McLean?'

'I understand that it's private finance taking over public service, if that's what you mean, sir. I also understand what makes your good friend Jane Louise Dee tick, and it's not the warm glow of satisfaction from doing good deeds.'

'Never took you for a socialist. Not with the sort of cash you've got in the bank.'

'Is this an official reprimand, sir? Or are you just pissed off because Mrs Saifre's been bending some minister's ear and he's passed it on to you?'

Robinson's face went from white to red with a swiftness that would have made his GP wince. McLean could almost feel the heat radiating off him.

'You've never had much respect for authority or the chain of command, have you, McLean? Always thought of yourself as better than those above you.'

'Better?' McLean fought the urge to take a step back as the DCC loomed over him. 'No, sir. But I've had experience of your new friend Mrs Saifre before. You want to know what she's really like, then ask Grumpy Bob. Better yet, see if Sandy Gregg will tell you about her house blowing up.'

'I . . . what?' Robinson's confusion trumped his anger, and McLean dared to hope the worst of the tirade was over now.

'We've had run-ins with Jane Louise Dee before, sir. She's very rich, very powerful, and she won't take no for an answer. I know she can be charming when she wants to be, and she's an expert at taking a tiny bit of influence and leveraging it until she owns you. I don't trust her in the slightest, and I don't want to have anything to do with her unless it involves carting her off to a cell.'

Robinson stared at him, the thoughts as clear on his face as they were no doubt muddied behind it. McLean gave him the time he needed, even if he was anxious to get on with interviewing Rahel and tracking down wherever it was Social Services had taken Nala.

'I still find your attitude unacceptable, McLean.' The DCC moved as he spoke, striding back around his desk and dropping into the seat. 'Whatever your personal opinion of Ms Dee, she is still a friend to Police Scotland and has the ear of people who can make both of our lives far more miserable than they already are.'

'As I said, sir—'

'I'm not finished.' Robinson held up a hand. 'I find your attitude unacceptable, but I also trust your judgement. It's been sound in the past. I'll not push this matter further if you offer an apology to the trust for your early departure from last night's event.'

McLean clenched his jaw in frustration, then forced himself to relax. Hard to speak when your mouth was clamped shut. On the other hand, hell would freeze over before he'd apologise to that woman. A swift nod was at least open to interpretation.

'And Rahel Nour?' he asked when he was certain Robinson wasn't going to press the matter further.

'Who?' The DCC looked momentarily confused. 'Oh, yes. Her. You're going to interview her, I assume?'

'Ritchie will. In about an hour.' McLean glanced at his watch. 'Emma's bringing her in, and once we're done here I've arranged to take her to see the young girl we found yesterday. It's possible she's her niece.'

Robinson looked as if he wasn't really listening. Quite clearly the reason for his terseness was nothing to do with McLean giving Rahel a room for the night and everything to do with Mrs Saifre bending people's ears. He waved his hand in dismissal. 'Very well. Keep Jo Dexter up to speed with anything you find out, OK? And when you're done with her, let Immigration know where she's staying.'

McLean almost asked why, but managed to stop himself. 'Sir.' He nodded again, hoped he didn't look like some kind of deranged animal. Robinson stared at him for a moment longer than was comfortable, then picked up the nearest folder from the tiny stack of reports on his otherwise empty desk. Bollocking over.

McLean said nothing more, turned and left the room. It could have been much worse, he supposed. And there was no way he was going to mention Rahel's name to Immigration any time soon.

'Well, this is a fine bloody mess and no mistake.'

McLean had been sitting alone in interview room one. He'd sat in as DI Ritchie questioned Rahel, and was enjoying a rare moment of peace before he had to take the young woman to see the little girl who might be her niece. The detective constables and sergeants, whose stream of queries seemed to follow him through the station, were unlikely to find him here, but Jayne McIntyre knew him better than most. She stood for a moment in the doorway, then walked over and sat down in the chair Rahel had recently vacated.

'Which particular "this" were you referring to?' he asked, and rubbed at his face with weary hands. It was still early in the morning, but last night had ended late and he'd not had nearly enough coffee.

'You tell me, Tony. We've got a young woman in a coma identified as an illegal immigrant by her sister, who is also an illegal immigrant. A detective chief inspector shielding both of them from Immigration Services and muscling in on another unit's investigation when he's supposed to be tracking down whatever it is that's killed two girls and a young man in the past few days. I mean, it's almost as if you're just making it up as you go along. Whatever happened to chain of command? Procedure? I know you never really liked that side of the business, but you used to pay lip service at least.'

'You know what's even worse?' McLean picked up his mug and peered into its empty depths for the hundredth time. Upstairs was a coffee machine with a refill waiting, but also upstairs were all the problems threatening to overwhelm him. Except the one sitting directly in front of him.

'Enlighten me.'

'Yesterday a wise old woman told me there was a genie loose in the city. Not some kid-friendly animation, either. This is evil incarnate, feeding on innocence. And people are sacrificing their children to it because they're terrified if they don't they'll get shipped back home. Imagine that, Jayne. To have escaped a place so unbearable you'd kill your own child rather than go back. To experience such horror you'd believe genies and all that nonsense are real. The only way you can survive is to blame it all on mythological creatures because if you admit that it's men doing these things to each other, then you'll just go mad.'

McIntyre leaned back in her chair and gave her chin a thoughtful scratch.

'When was the last time you had a break, Tony?'

'A break?'

'You know. Time off? A holiday?'

'I don't see what that's got to do with—'

'Not since before Emma's miscarriage, that's when. Not since you were suspended after all that nonsense with Bill Chalmers over a year ago. You've been through the wringer more times than I can count and you just won't stop.'

'I . . . It's not like . . .'

'It's exactly like, Tony. You're the worst kind of workaholic, and it's starting to show. Genies, for Christ's sake. You sound like Madame Rose.'

'Well, I've only you to thank for introducing us. You never did tell me how the two of you met in the first place.'

'Enough trying to change the subject. What are you going to do about this woman, Rahel Nour?'

'Do?' McLean picked up his mug again, but it was still empty. 'I'm going to try to gain her trust enough so she'll tell me who she thinks is responsible for almost killing her sister. I know it's technically Jo's case, but I'm the one with a connection right now. She'll speak to me. Don't think she'll speak to anyone at Vice.'

'And your own cases? What about the wee girls? Maurice Jennings?'

'My gut says Rahel's the key to that, too. Her and the little girl, Nala. I've asked Social Services to set up a meeting. See if Rahel recognises her niece. And the other way round.' McLean twiddled the mug around in frustration. 'I know it's thin, but if we can find out who that girl really is, we can hopefully talk to her too. Right now nobody even knows what language she's speaking.'

McIntyre said nothing for a while, and McLean was happy to let the silence grow. She was right about one thing he didn't want to admit. It was too long since he'd taken more than a short weekend off, too long he'd been throwing himself into his work to avoid having to think about anything else.

'So how does Jennings fit into it then? What killed him and why?'

'You've seen the CCTV?' McLean asked.

McIntyre nodded. 'Not quite sure what to make of it, mind you.'

'Well, here's my thoughts about it.' McLean cupped the mug in his hands, using it as a shield between himself and the detective superintendent. 'Jennings wasn't picked as a target for any reason. From what I've been told he's the sort of bloke who'd step up if someone needed help, but not one to start a fight. He was just unlucky. Wrong place, wrong time. The real target was that little girl, but somehow she managed to hide from the killer. My best guess is Jennings asked the killer what he was doing, maybe saw him acting suspiciously and decided to find out why. Didn't work out quite how he'd expected it to.'

'But why was the killer looking for the girl in the first place? Why was she running about Broughton Street late at night anyway? Where did she come from?'

Now for the hard part. The part McLean didn't want to believe, but which sounded more and more plausible each time he turned it over in his head. 'I think he was hunting her. Like an animal. I think that's what went on with the other two girls too.'

'That's . . .' McIntyre stopped speaking, stared into the distance for a moment, then focused her attention back on him. 'Are you sure you're not taking that old wise woman a bit too seriously?'

'Do I believe in genies?' McLean shook his head. 'Well, I've never met one yet outside of panto season. But I do know we've a growing problem of trafficked refugees. There's exploitation of migrant workers all over the country, and I'm not just talking about sex work. These people are terrified of what they fled from, and terrified of being packed up and sent back. Their gangmasters know that all too well. Who's to say this isn't just another way of keeping their workforce compliant?'

34

Fenton House wasn't quite what McLean had been expecting. The name conjured up images of some Scots Baronial pile, too big for the single family it had originally been built for and now pressed into different service. There were plenty of old country houses spread around Scotland, built off the trade in sugar and slaves, now turned into private schools or boutique hotels. Some were even centres of industry or academia, and some were care homes for people at both ends of life. He had assumed Fenton House would have been much the same, but the monstrous sixties concrete edifice that squatted in the middle of a nondescript housing estate near Burdiehouse was something quite different. The dirty snow on the ground lent it a dilapidated air, not helped by the broken playground swings and bleak tarmac yard.

'Nala is here?' Rahel leaned forward from her seat in the back of the Alfa, neck craned as she peered through the windscreen and up at the four-storey building. McLean pulled into a parking space and killed the engine.

'She's being looked after here until we can find somewhere more permanent for her. It's standard procedure.' He opened the door and climbed out into a bitter easterly wind that promised yet more snow. 'Come on. Let's go see if she really is your niece.'

The front door to the block was locked. Beside it, a small plaque informed McLean that Fenton House was run by the Dee Trust. Just how far did that woman's influence reach? Beside it, the intercom system had a single button. It took far longer for someone to answer than he would have liked.

'Aye? Whit is it?' The nasal voice whined through the speaker, even more tinny than it would sound face to face. Not a good start.

'Detective Chief Inspector McLean. I'm here about the young girl Nala. You're expecting us.'

A moment's silence, and then the intercom crackled again. 'Nobody tellt me about no polis. Youse got any ID?'

McLean bit back the 'For fuck's sake' that wanted to escape, fished around in his pocket and pulled out his warrant card. Scratches covered the camera on the intercom panel where someone had tried to clean off some graffiti, but he held the card up to it anyway. There was another long pause.

'Whit aboot theys two?'

McLean looked around to where Rahel shivered behind him. Emma at least had thought to wear a coat, but even so she looked miserable in the cold.

'Are you going to let us in or what?'

'Fine, fine. Just wait in the hall, right? Don't want to upset the kiddies any more'n they already are.' The lock buzzed briefly. McLean yanked open the door and they all stepped inside. It wasn't much warmer, but at least they were out of the wind.

The hall was little more than a glorified porch, lit by narrow windows either side of the door they had entered through. McLean checked the door through into the main building, but it too was locked. Three plastic chairs lined one wall, opposite a corkboard pinned with flyers and NHS medical posters that looked like they were from a different century. It smelled of damp.

'This is where you sent her?' McLean could hear the anger in Rahel's voice, and had to admit he felt much the same.

'I—' he began, but the far door clicked open to reveal a young woman.

'You the polis man?' she asked, as if she hadn't just seen all three of them on the intercom camera. 'Aye, well. Come on in then.'

The door opened onto a wide corridor that ran down the centre of the building, a window at the far end the only source of lighting as far as McLean could tell. At least it was a bit warmer in here, although the smell of damp persisted, along with the aroma of bad cooking that reminded him of meals at his hated boarding school.

'Are you in charge here?' he asked.

'Aye.' The young woman barely slowed as she spoke. 'Well, the day manager. And since there's no night manager at the moment, that means I'm lumped wi' the whole thing.'

'This isn't quite what I was expecting,' McLean said.

'How no?' She stopped, turning on the spot, too close for comfort. McLean resisted the urge to take a step back, knowing full well that was what she wanted him to do. She was a head shorter than him, but he didn't fancy his chances in a fight. He'd seen her kind before, hardened by the sort of upbringing he could only imagine. Her short-cropped hair and thin, silver nose ring only added to the air of hostility radiating from her. She seemed an ill fit for managing a children's care home, but then Fenton House didn't meet his expectations either.

'It doesn't matter. The girl?'

'Aye, this way.'

They walked all the way down the corridor, pausing at the final door. Close up, McLean saw that the window was reinforced glass, no latch to open it. Grime clung to the outside, and a dead plant sat on the windowsill, water stains around the pot showing where once someone had tried to look after it. The young woman pulled a set of keys from her pocket that looked like they belonged in an eighteenth-century gaol rather than a care home for children, carefully selected one and slotted it into the lock on the door.

'She's a wild one, so she is. You'd best be careful.' She twisted the key and turned the handle, pushing open the door to reveal a surprisingly large room beyond. McLean had time to take in a mismatched collection of institutional sofas and chairs, walls painted in muted beige and pastel green, carpet and ceiling tiles equally stained, and a window to match the one at the end of the corridor. A pile of battered toys sat in the middle of the floor, and an elderly woman perched on the edge of an uncomfortable seat. She looked up at them as they stepped inside, her face creasing into a frown. McLean recognised her as the woman who had picked Nala up from the offices of House the Refugees, although clearly she had forgotten him.

'Who—?' she began to ask, then an excited shout rang out from the pile of toys.

'Rahel!'

The young girl sprung up from where she had been sitting on the floor, rushed across the room and threw herself into Rahel's startled arms, jabbering away in a foreign language, crying and sniffing and thoroughly overwrought. McLean stepped aside to give them more room, saw Emma's wide-eyed stare from where she still stood in the corridor.

'Well, I guess that answers that question then.'

'I don't know where you found her, but I'm very glad you did. Poor wee thing's been half off her head since she got here.'

McLean sat on one of the uncomfortable sofas, next to Mrs Eileen Williams, the woman who had been looking after Nala. She was a lot more friendly than the young day manager, Chloe, who had bustled off almost as soon as they had all entered the room. McLean had wondered at the click of the lock behind her, but apparently it was a precaution against other children wandering in unannounced in the middle of a therapy session. There was a latch on the inside to let them out.

'How do you mean off her head? She looks calm enough now.'

The young girl sat cross-legged on the floor, her aunt beside her. They had spoken at length in that musical language of theirs, but now seemed happy just to be playing with the assortment of moth-eaten and half-broken toys that were piled up in front of them. If Nala had lived the kind of life McLean suspected she had, then this was surely some kind of paradise in comparison.

'She started crying almost as soon as that young constable of yours let go of her hand. Didn't let up all the way here. I've tried to talk to her, but she doesn't seem to speak any English. She understands some, though.'

'Did she sleep at all?' McLean looked around the room. 'I don't imagine she's been in here all the time.'

'Och, no. There's rooms upstairs for all the wains. But she wasn't happy on her own. We left a light on, gave her something to eat, some toys. Nothing would settle her. When I came in this morning she was hiding under the bed. Don't think she'd slept a wink. But look at her now.' Mrs Williams nodded towards Nala and Rahel. 'That lassie's her aunt, you say? Seems awful young.'

'Her sister's not a lot older. Let's just say life's not been too kind to the Nour family so far.'

'Is she in some kind of trouble?' This time Mrs Williams pointed at Nala, who had found a headless doll and was making it fly like Superman.

'How do you mean?' McLean asked.

'I'm not stupid, Inspector. She's an illegal immigrant, isn't she? They both are.'

'That's not your concern, Mrs Williams.'

'Oh, but it is. Especially now that you know who she is. An unidentified child we can cope with. A child taken from its parents by a court order? That's something we deal with every day, sad though I am to admit it. But the child of an illegal immigrant is another matter altogether. I'd look after her if I could, believe me. But there are rules.'

'Why don't you call Rose?' Emma asked. She had been sitting so quietly, watching everything unfold, that McLean had almost forgotten she was there.

'Rose?' He couldn't hide the astonishment in his voice. 'Madame Rose?'

'Well I'm sure you know lots of women with that name.' Emma rolled her eyes theatrically. 'Of course Madame Rose. Who else would I mean?'

'But . . . Why? She's not involved in this. She's not related to any of them.'

'She's a trained and registered carer, and Rahel trusts her. We need to get the two of them away from here.' Emma threw her hands up in disgust at the room they'd been locked in. 'Rose can give them somewhere to stay while you get to the bottom of this. And if Akka comes round, well . . .' She left the rest unsaid. Both of them knew the chances of Nala's mother ever regaining consciousness were slim.

'You know a registered childcare specialist who could help out?' Mrs Williams's voice was the most animated he had heard it, and looking at her he could see something like excitement crease her weather-beaten face.

'I—'

'We do.' Emma cut McLean off before he could say anything more. She shoved a hand into her pocket and pulled out her phone, swiped at the screen, placed a call.

'We do,' McLean confirmed. 'Although she wouldn't necessarily have been my first choice.'

Mrs Williams shrugged. 'If the police are happy with it, then I'll no' complain.' She glanced at the locked door, something she'd done a number of times since angry Chloe had left. 'It would make life much easier for everyone.'

35

McLean knew that he should be back at the station, dealing with the assorted investigations under his command, but there was something very soothing about sitting quietly in the dilapidated playroom, Emma by his side, and watching as Nala played with Rahel. Seeing the two of them, it was hard to believe the horrors they had witnessed and the tragedy still unfolding around them. Was this what family brought? The thought of it made his guts clench in memory of what had happened to Emma those few short months before. If she hadn't miscarried, then he would have an infant daughter to care for himself.

The buzz of the intercom boomed loud in the room, cheap, thin walls doing nothing to keep out the noise. Glancing at his watch, McLean saw that somehow half an hour had passed since Emma had called Madame Rose. She couldn't possibly have made it across town that quickly. And yet moments later the lock clicked and the door swung open to reveal an irate day manager.

'Detective Chief Inspector McLean?' She managed to make his title and name sound vaguely disreputable. 'There's a . . . woman here claims . . . she knows you.'

Before she could say any more, Chloe was pushed aside and the imposing form of Madame Rose swept into the room. She couldn't have dressed specifically for the occasion, not given how swiftly she had arrived. And yet she wore an outfit that might have been chosen with the sole purpose of annoying the irritable day manager. A full-length skirt in a dark tweed was set off by a matching jacket tailored to the medium's somewhat bulky frame. Her grey hair looked like it was not long out of the curlers, and her make-up made a benign mask of her face, mouth twitched into a humorous smile. A good foot taller than Chloe, she was everything the young woman appeared to dislike.

'I take it you are in charge of this establishment, Miss . . .' Rose left the question dangling as she looked around the room, eyes finally coming to rest on Rahel and Nala. 'Ah, there you are, my dears.' She strode across the threadbare carpet tiles, then lowered herself to the floor with surprising grace. Even kneeling, she towered over the young girl.

'You must be Nala,' she said, then slipped into the same musical tongue that Rahel and Madame Jasmina had used and the young girl had been jabbering away excitedly in since she had been reunited with her aunt. Somehow McLean wasn't surprised to find Madame Rose fluent in Aramaic. She probably had a passing knowledge of every language spoken.

'This is not how things are done, Inspector. You can't call up some . . . woman and bring her in here like this.'

McLean stood up as Chloe approached. 'I really don't see what the problem is. We were unable to identify the young girl yesterday when she was found in the city centre. That's why she was brought here, so she could be cared for. Now we know who she is, she can go back to her family. I'm grateful to you and the Dee Trust, especially Mrs Williams here.' McLean nodded in the older woman's direction. 'I say that both on a personal level and as a representative of Police Scotland. You've been very helpful, but we can take it from here.'

For a moment he thought the day manager was going to back down, but something had clearly rattled her cage.

'As I understand it, the girl is the child of an illegal immigrant. She and her mother should be in a detention centre.'

McLean studied the young woman's face as she spoke, not quite able to square the image she presented with the words coming out of her mouth.

'Her mother's status is unimportant at the moment, and quite frankly none of your business.'

'Let's just go, shall we, Tony?' Emma's hand on McLean's arm made him realise how tense he had become, and so quickly.

'I'll need the paperwork signed, and I'll have to see . . .' Chloe hesitated again, not so much nodding in Rose's direction as stretching her neck like an ostrich. '. . . her credentials.'

'Of course, my dear.' Madame Rose had been fussing over Nala, but all of a sudden she was on her feet and towering over the young manager again. She produced a thick sheaf of papers with all the skill of a stage magician, shoved them in Chloe's chest. 'I think you'll find it's all in order.'

'Where the hell have you been? I've been trying to get hold of you all morning.'

McLean had seen off Madame Rose with instructions to keep Rahel and Nala safe, then dropped Emma at the forensic-service headquarters before heading back to the station. He knew that someone was going to give him grief for being out of touch, but a quick look at his phone before walking into the major-incident room had shown no missed calls or urgent texts. Clearly the DCC had been using telepathy to telegraph his wishes. Just a shame he wasn't very good at it. His management skills could do with a refresher course too. Nothing like laying into senior detectives in front of the constables. Still, nothing they'd not seen before either.

'Something urgent came up, sir.'

'More urgent than finding out who's murdering wee girls?

More important than a possible outbreak of some unknown disease that kills people in minutes?'

McLean let the tirade wash over him. Robinson wasn't normally given to histrionics, but lately the pressures of the job seemed to be getting to him. That his new-found fractiousness coincided with the return to Edinburgh of a certain Mrs Saifre was a connection McLean kept to himself.

'I've actually been pursuing a lead that might well help solve both of those cases, sir.'

'This would be the young woman you found at the circus, no doubt.'

'Rahel Nour has been very helpful, sir. She's positively identified the woman left for dead in Sighthill as her sister, Akka Nour, and the young girl we found in the Old Town is her niece, Nala. Akka's daughter.'

'And where are they now?'

'Akka is still at the Western General, as far as I know. The doctors aren't sure whether she'll ever regain consciousness. Who knows what state she'll be in if she does?'

'I didn't mean the hooker. What about the wee girl? And the other one?'

McLean tensed at the derogatory term. Robinson really should have known better, but now wasn't the time to point that out. 'I've arranged for both of them to be taken into care. As it happens, I've found a registered carer who speaks their native language. The young girl, Nala, doesn't seem to have much English, even though she was born here, far as I can tell.'

'Bloody immigrants.' The DCC muttered the words under his breath, but McLean heard them all the same.

'Refugees, sir. There's a difference.' Maybe now was the time.

'They're a bloody nuisance is what they are. We're stretched enough as it is without them coming over here and bringing their crime with them.'

The room had turned unusually quiet, a fact made all the more noticeable by McLean's silent count of ten. It was an old habit, born of years working with Detective Superintendent Duguid, DCI Brooks and many other senior officers with a tendency to blame victims for making their lives difficult rather than effectively investigating the actual criminals.

'Was there something specific you wanted to see me about, sir?' he asked once he'd fought down his own rising anger. 'Or did you just want a status update?'

'I can get that from anyone here. Probably more accurate information too, given they're actually working the cases, not arranging care provision for—' Robinson stopped himself before his rant could build up too much steam. 'Operation Fundament. I need an update on the men you arrested at the march. Where are they now? Who's been charged with what? Has the report gone to the PF?'

The march. So much had happened since then, McLean had almost forgotten the small band of neo-fascists who'd tried to disrupt things. And yet it was only a few days since he'd observed the interviews.

'I've not heard from the anti-terror boys, sir. But one of the men we arrested was refused bail. He'll be in Saughton kicking his heels while they set up a trial date, no doubt.'

Robinson pinched the bridge of his nose, scrunching his eyes tight as if someone had just squirted acid in his face. 'Matthew Seaton,' he said.

'That's the fellow.'

'You'll not have seen the news then.'

Cold spread through McLean's gut as he looked from the DCC, around the incident room at the collected uniformed and plain-clothes officers.

'What's happened?' he asked.

'He's dead is what's happened.'

'Dead? How?' McLean tried to remember something, anything, about the case. He could scarcely recall what Seaton looked like, which wasn't a good start. 'When?'

'Late last night. It's all in the briefing note you'd have read if you'd been here doing your job. Seems he picked a fight with his cellmate and came off second best. Whose great idea was it to put a weedy racist bastard with a short temper into a cell with a six-foot-six ex-bouncer from Iraq?'

McLean did remember now, his conversation with DS Peterson from the Anti-terrorism Unit after Seaton's outburst during his interview. How they were going to make him sweat in custody in an attempt to make him give up more details about the organisation he belonged to. If Seaton was dead, that should have been a matter for the prison service, and possibly the anti-terrorism unit, but the fact Robinson was giving him grief about it suggested there was a lot of hand washing going on.

'Don't want to sound like I'm making excuses, sir, but what's this got to do with us? We were just logistical support for Operation Fundament.'

Robinson shook his head. 'Aye, I know. But the anti-terror boys are all tucked away over at Gartcosh. Now I've got some smartarse lawyer shouting about police brutality and how his client was set up from the get-go. He's been briefing the press against us, threatening to sue us, demanding heads on blocks, the works.'

This time McLean remembered the man. More vampire than lawyer. 'Kennedy Smythe.'

'The very same. He's got the ear of some influential people, and they're making my life difficult. That means I'm going to make your life difficult until you sort it out, understand?'

36

HMP Edinburgh, universally known as Saughton, was not a place McLean much enjoyed visiting. There were plenty of men there he was in some manner responsible for putting away, which was a good enough reason to want to avoid the place. Even more so, he found the grim collection of buildings dragged at his soul, as if a great evil had been done here in the distant past and its stain still seeped into the earth.

DC Stringer had been unlucky enough to be at a loose end when he was looking for a spare constable, and the prison appeared to have the same effect on the young man as it did on McLean. He said nothing as they cleared the security gates and parked the car, barely spoke when asked to show his warrant card by the security guard at the entrance. It wasn't until they were in the administration building and heading towards the governor's office that he finally spoke up.

'Never really liked this place much.'

'Me neither,' McLean said. 'I'm surprised you've had much to do with it though. Been here often?'

Stringer hunched in on himself, as if embarrassed. 'My uncle . . . Well, more like three times removed, but family, aye? He's in here. Has been for years. Likely will be for a while yet.'

McLean didn't ask why. The detective constable would tell him if he wanted to.

'Used to visit with my mum. Don't know why she came to see him. Maybe thought it was her duty or something. I'd sit in the waiting room while she was talking to him.'

'That why you joined the police?'

'Aye, in a way. I used to talk to some of the prison officers here, but mostly it was seeing the folk come to visit. Made me want to do something to help. Couldn't stand the thought of coming somewhere like here every day though.'

Stringer might have said more, but they'd arrived at the governor's office. The door was open, and the man himself sat at his desk expectantly. Word had clearly gone ahead of them.

'Detective Chief Inspector. I was expecting a visit. Didn't think it would be so soon, or someone quite so senior.' He stood up and came to meet them both at the door, extending a hand to be shaken. McLean couldn't remember whether or not he'd met this governor before. It had been a while since last he'd visited the prison, thankfully.

'This'll be about Matthew Seaton, I take it. Horrible business.'

'He was attacked by his cellmate, I understand.'

'Mostafa Hussein, yes. Beat him half to death. Said Seaton attacked him first, but it's hard to believe that.'

'Hussein's also a remand prisoner?' McLean asked.

'Yes. He's waiting on a trial date for a charge of common assault. Seems he's here on dodgy papers anyway, so chances are he'll get deported soon as his time's up.'

McLean began to ask more about Hussein's charge, but then the governor's earlier words sunk in. 'Wait. Half to death? Seaton was still alive when you found him?'

'Oh yes. He was badly concussed, but conscious. Hussein's a big man, Chief Inspector. He picked Seaton up and threw him against the cell wall.'

'Where is he now? Hussein, that is? Well, both of them, for that matter.'

'Hussein's in solitary. You can interview him if you want. Seaton was taken to the Western General. He died late last night.'

McLean cursed himself for not taking the time to gather all the information before coming out. Then again, the DCC had demanded action, and just this once he thought the man wouldn't have appreciated him sending a sergeant out to deal with it.

'I see.' He considered his options and the amount of time they would waste. 'Perhaps a quick word with Hussein first. Then I'll need to pay a visit to the hospital.'

The governor hadn't been lying when he'd said that Mostafa Hussein was a big man. He had to stoop through the doorway as two prison guards led him into the interview room, shuffling slowly in shackles. They chained him to the sturdy chair across the table from where McLean and Stringer sat. At least six foot six, and built like a mountain, his greasy black hair hung long and lank to his shoulders, and his face was mostly obscured by a wiry beard that was beginning to show streaks of grey. He peered at the world through hooded eyes that gave no indication as to his state of mind, and while physically he was intimidating, there was no aura of menace about him. Rather, he gave the impression of being a gentle giant, shoulders slumped in tacit acceptance of his situation. Even the knowledge of what he had done, both to warrant being in prison in the first place and once he had got here, did nothing to dispel the feeling of a man who would rather not resort to violence if at all possible.

'You want a lawyer present?' McLean asked once the introductions had been made.

Hussein shook his head. 'It wouldn't make any difference.'

McLean was taken aback by the man's voice. The deep tone was unsurprising, given his size, but the cultured accent and flawless English spoke of expensive education. It clashed both with the physicality of the man, and his circumstance.

'Matthew Seaton. Your cellmate. I'm told you smashed his head against the wall and he later died from his injuries.'

'I shoved him against at the wall, yes. And he banged his head. If he died from his injuries, that was never my intention. I am sorry.'

Something about the way Hussein said it made McLean believe the man. 'Why did you do it then? Why throw him against the wall?'

Hussein paused before answering, looked around the small interview room as he gathered his thoughts. 'I didn't throw him. I pushed him. Maybe a little too hard, but did you meet him, Seaton? Before he was sent here? I don't think I've ever met a more narrow-minded and obnoxious individual in all my life. From the first moment he was brought to the cell, he started abusing me. Calling me names, spitting on the floor at my feet. I couldn't pray for his constant interruptions. But I did my best to tolerate him.'

'What finally made you snap?'

Hussein cocked his head to one side, considering the question. 'He took my Quran. Started tearing pages from it and throwing them to the floor. I have few enough possessions as it is, and this was given to me by my father.'

'So you threw him against the wall and killed him?' Stringer asked, the first words he had spoken since they'd entered the room. Hussein turned his gaze slowly onto the detective constable.

'No. I shoved him in the chest. He fell backwards, slipped on one of the pages and hit his head on the wall. You might call that an act of God, if you like. I never intended him harm, that is not the way of Allah. He was still conscious when they took him away to the hospital.'

Again, McLean had the sense that despite what he'd been told about the incident before, this was closer to the truth.

'What was it that got you in here in the first place, Mr Hussein?'

'I intervened in a fight outside a nightclub. Two men were kicking a young lad on the ground. It didn't seem fair, so I grabbed one by his coat and hauled him off. Unlucky for me, he was an off-duty police officer.' Hussein tried to hold his hands out, palms up, in a gesture of how stupid the whole thing was, but the cuffs around his wrists chained to the table top made it look more like an involuntary spasm. Behind him the two prison guards tensed, one taking a step forward to prevent an attack McLean knew was not coming.

'I'll look into that, Mr Hussein. And I'll be looking into what happened to Mr Seaton after he left your shared cell too. I'd be interested to know whose decision it was to put the two of you together in the first place, although I'll be the first to admit that could just be the luck of the draw. Seems there's been quite a bit of bad luck following you around recently though.'

Hussein dropped his massive hands back onto the table in front of him and lowered his head in a nod as slow as the mountain he resembled. 'There is an ill wind blowing through this country, Chief Inspector. People like Mr Seaton feel at ease spouting their hatred and bigotry. Nobody criticises them, so they grow bolder day by day. You know this, I think?'

'Give the hospital a call will you, Constable? No point heading over there if Mr Seaton's already in the mortuary.'

McLean stepped out of Saughton Prison into the cold winter air with more questions than when he'd entered, not an hour earlier. There was something disturbing about Mostafa Hussein's calm acceptance of his fate that made the injustice seem twice as deep. A better picture of what had happened wasn't hard to see.

Seaton had been put with the man-mountain because Hussein was a devout Muslim and represented everything he despised. The plan had been to rattle Seaton's cage to the point where he'd open up about the gang he ran with, but there was always the possibility that might backfire. Hindsight was such a wonderful thing.

'Body was transported over there a couple of hours ago,' DC Stringer said as he slipped into the driver's seat of the pool car and closed the door.

'OK. Mortuary it is.' McLean leaned back into his own seat, staring up at the slate-grey sky as Stringer drove out through the security gates and slowed into heavy traffic.

'You think he's telling the truth?' he asked after they'd driven in silence for five minutes, progressing only slightly further than a drunk man could walk in the same time.

'Hussein? I don't know, sir. He was convincing though. I mean, he could have denied it, made something ridiculous up, refused even to speak to us. Instead he just accepted it all. Wasn't quite what I was expecting, to be honest.'

'Me neither. Still, his story should be easy enough to corroborate. The prison will have his Quran, so we can find out if any pages have been ripped out recently. Ask the guards if there were any on the floor when they came in. And we'll see what Angus has to say about Seaton's injuries, what actually killed him.'

'It's still manslaughter though, even if it was accidental. He shoved him, the guy died. And if Hussein's here on fake papers then that's not going to help him much.'

'Aye, you're right. Poor bastard. It's not our problem though. Shouldn't really be our incident to investigate either. Reckon we've both got better things to be doing.' McLean stared at the long line of cars, delivery vans and buses snaking in towards the city centre. Somewhere up ahead an accident or some roadworks were doing their best to bring everything to a halt. He pointed to a side street just ahead of them as the car in front inched forward. 'Turn here, OK?'

'Sir?' Stringer had the decency to do as he was told before asking why.

'Not thinking straight. I guess it's been that kind of day. They might have sent Seaton's body to the mortuary already, but we still need to talk to the doctors who saw him when he was brought in. Maybe see if they X-rayed his skull too. Got to be better than sitting in traffic for an hour.'

Stringer nodded his understanding, taking a swift route to the hospital by the back roads over Corstorphine Hill and down towards the Western General. As usual there was nowhere to park once they'd arrived.

'I'll go see what I can find out.' McLean unclipped his seatbelt and pushed open the passenger door as Stringer pulled the car into the kerbside.

'You want me to wait here?'

'No. Let's not waste too much time on this, aye? You head back to the station. Get a statement from the prison and start on the report for the PF. I'll fill in the blanks when I get back.'

37

McLean had spent many a wasted hour at the Western General Hospital. Tucked into the northern corner of Craiglieth, at the end of Ferry Road, it was where his grandmother had spent her final eighteen months, in a coma after her stroke. She'd never recovered, but he'd done his best to visit her most days. It helped that the old Lothian and Borders Police HQ was just down the road at Fettes Avenue, not that he'd ever been based there for more than a couple of weeks at a time.

It had been a while now since his gran had finally died, so he wasn't too surprised that few of the nurses looked familiar and none of them nodded or smiled as he walked past them. Other things besides visiting the coma ward had brought him to the hospital more recently – the previous night's impromptu visit was a case in point – but not with such regularity he expected to be recognised.

'Detective Inspector. Tony. It's been a while.'

There was, of course, always the exception. Approaching an admin desk at the end of the corridor leading to the neurological unit, McLean spotted an older nurse, who had been leaning against the counter and chatting to one of her colleagues. Jeannie Robertson had looked after his grandmother for most of her eighteen months in the hospital, and had even come to her funeral.

'It has indeed.' He returned her smile a little awkwardly, unsure of the protocol for greeting someone you both did and didn't know well. 'So long that it's Chief Inspector now, not that I'm all that fussed about it.'

'I'm sure it's well deserved. But I'm guessing you're not here for a wee chat. The poor fellow they brought in from Saughton gaol yesterday, I take it?'

'Matthew Seaton, yes. Did you see him when he came in?'

Robertson shook her head. 'No. I don't work that unit, and I was on the early shift besides. You'll need to speak to Doctor Wheeler.'

'Actually, I saw her just last night. Please don't tell me she's back at work already.' McLean recalled their meeting and the discussion about Akka Nour's slim chances of recovery. Strange to think that while he'd been confirming her identity with Rahel, somewhere close by Matthew Seaton had been fighting for his life. Was that what the sudden emergency had been?

'Not sure she ever goes home these days.' Robertson let out a sigh. 'Not the only one I know who works all hours though, Tony.'

'I'm trying to be less of a workaholic, honestly.' McLean felt the words sound hollow even to him. 'I don't suppose you know where Caroline is, do you?'

'Caroline is it, now?' Robertson raised a mocking eyebrow, her smile betraying the joke. Then she nodded towards the end of the corridor behind him. 'That'll be her just now.'

McLean turned to see the doctor walking slowly in his direction, her attention almost entirely on a man wearing hospital whites and walking beside her. She didn't see him until she was almost at the admin desk.

'Oh, Tony. We really must stop meeting like this.' She handed a clipboard over to the nurse behind the desk, then turned to her colleague. 'Malcolm, this is Detective Inspector – no, Detective

Chief Inspector Tony McLean. Tony, this is Malcolm Anders. He's our new resident neurosurgeon.'

'Pleased to meet you.' McLean shook the man's hand, surprised to find it slightly damp, his grip limp. Most surgeons he'd met had grips like iron and tried to stare you down as if everything in life was a contest.

'Are you here about the girl, Akka? Only there's been no change yet. Malcolm's been looking over her brain scans to see if there's anything we can do, but I suspect it's just going to be a waiting game.'

'Actually, it was about Matthew Seaton. The man from Saughton who died last night?'

Something like anger flitted across Doctor Wheeler's face, swiftly suppressed. She turned to her colleague once more. 'I won't be long, Malcolm. We can go over Mrs Ogden's X-rays when I get back, OK?'

The surgeon nodded, his face giving nothing away. 'Nice to meet you . . . Tony,' he said, the first time McLean had heard him speak. Clearly a man of few words, he wandered off without saying any more.

'Walk with me.' Doctor Wheeler set off at speed in the opposite direction to the neurosurgeon. McLean hurried to catch up, falling in beside her as she strode swiftly along the corridor.

'Seaton. I take it his death's not straightforward then.'

'Too bloody right it's not. The man should be back where he came from with nothing more than a headache to show for it.'

'I thought he'd fractured his skull.'

Doctor Wheeler coughed out a hollow laugh. 'There was barely a bruise. We X-rayed him, found nothing untoward. Not even a concussion. Not the first time I've seen an inmate fake a head injury just to get out for a wee while. No chance of him escaping, mind you. He was handcuffed to a prison officer most of the time.'

'So why wasn't he discharged? Sent back to Saughton?'

'Procedures.' Doctor Wheeler stopped walking just for long enough to look straight at McLean and roll her eyes. 'We had to keep him in overnight for observation. They provided a guard and we shoved him in a secure room. I gave him a sedative and left him sleeping like a baby. To be honest, I'd forgotten all about him. It was only after we'd spoken about that poor young woman that my pager went off. One of the nurses had checked in to see he was OK, found him dead.'

'Just like that?'

'Just, as you say, like that.' Doctor Wheeler set off walking again, and once more McLean had to rush to catch up.

'So what killed him? How did he die?'

'Honestly? I've no idea, Tony. He had a slight bump to the head, sure. But it was nothing serious enough to warrant more than an ice pack. I can show you the X-rays. They're fine. Christ, I must have looked at them a dozen times since it happened.'

'Was he attacked, then? Did the guard see anything?'

Doctor Wheeler stopped again. 'Ha. The guard? A herd of elephants could have got past him. Nurse tells me he was fast asleep when she stopped by to check on your man.'

One more to interview, and another complication he could have done without. There seemed to be a lot of buck-passing going on with regard to Matthew Seaton. McLean hadn't much liked the man, but that didn't mean his death could be swept under the carpet like this.

'So you don't know what killed him, but it's unlikely it was the head injury he was brought here for. He's at the mortuary now, right?'

'Sent the body off a while back, yes.' Doctor Wheeler stopped by a closed door, and when McLean looked he saw the familiar sign for the Ladies. 'Go see Angus. He'll tell you how the poor bugger died. It wasn't for lack of care here though. I'm sure of that.'

★ ★ ★

'If you're looking for something on the fellow who died last night, I've not had a chance to get to him yet.'

McLean had barely put his head around the open office door before Cadwallader spoke. The pathologist wore a clean set of scrubs, ready for another examination, and a body awaited his attention, laid out under a white sheet on the stainless-steel table in the theatre.

'Didn't think you would have, Angus. I just thought I'd pop in and have a quick look at him. You got someone else ready to go?'

'Aye. Maurice Jennings. You'll not have got the message I was about to do him, then.'

McLean pulled out his phone and checked for messages. 'Damn thing seems to be screening my calls. Still, I'm here now.'

'Right enough. Your other chap's in one of the cabinets if you really want a look.' Cadwallader walked past him and started towards the cold store.

'It's OK, Angus. It can wait. Reckon Jennings is more important.'

'You sure?' The pathologist shrugged. 'OK. Let's get on then. Tracy?'

Doctor Sharp appeared from a small storeroom off the main examination theatre. McLean took that as his cue to step back and let them get on with their job. He tuned out for a while, letting his mind wander over the events at Saughton and the hospital, how Matthew Seaton's death might play out with the press and the inevitable politicking that would accompany their coverage. It bothered him that Hussein was being set up, too. The man was a victim, not a criminal, and yet he was locked away, likely to be sent back to a country that would treat him even worse. No wonder the immigrant and refugee communities in the city were so scared, so easily manipulated.

'Well, I think it's fair to say he didn't die of natural causes.'

Cadwallader's words were louder than his normal dictation to the microphone, and directed at McLean himself. He looked up to find the examination almost completed.

'You sure of that?'

'Well, just look at him, Tony.' The pathologist sighed, then gestured for McLean to move closer. Jennings was still part covered by a white sheet, preserving what little modesty he might have had left. It didn't conceal the rough Y-shaped incision, now being stitched by Doctor Sharp, where his torso had been opened up and his organs removed for perusal.

'What am I looking at?' McLean asked from where he fully intended to remain standing, several feet from the body.

'Well, his skin for one thing. You can see it most clearly on his face and hands, the bits exposed to the air when he died. But see how the rest of him is turning yellow now?' Cadwallader picked up one of the cadaver's arms, bending it slightly at the elbow so that the hand flopped open, palm upwards.

'Is that not what normally happens?' McLean had seen more than his fair share of dead bodies over a decades-long career as a detective. Some were fresh, but after a while they all started to look like mannequins, waxy and unreal. Quite literally lifeless.

'Yes. Of course. Leave a body in the chiller for a week or two and you'll end up with something like this. Maybe not the same colouration though, us Caucasians tend to go whiter, if anything. But there's the thing. Mr Jennings here died less than twenty-four hours ago.'

'I take it you know what he died of.' McLean relented and took a step forward. Jennings's bare skin had turned a dry custard colour he'd more normally associate with the drunk young women hauled into the station on a Saturday night, a spray-on tan as fake as a game show host.

'What he died of, yes.' Cadwallader placed the arm he had

247

been holding up back down on the examination table. 'Every single one of his major organs has failed, some quite catastroph- ically. Of course, the skin is an organ too, so you could say it's all connected.'

'But surely that would take days to kill a man? Longer. He'd know something was wrong, right?'

'You'd think so. The state he was in when he died, it's a miracle he could even walk.'

'And yet he went to the pub. We've CCTV footage of him being attacked.'

Cadwallader snapped off the latex gloves he'd been wearing and dumped them into a nearby bin. He motioned for McLean to follow him into the office just off the examination theatre, leaving his long-suffering assistant to clean up. 'Exactly. So whatever happened to him, it was very swift-acting. And it's carried on acting since he died. Do you know how many things there are that can do that to a body?'

'I'm rather hoping you'll tell me, Angus. I assume you've got some theory?'

'I have indeed, Tony. Here, have a look at this.' The path- ologist pulled a chair away from his desk and tapped at the keyboard half buried in papers, sample jars and other detritus, waking up his computer. McLean leaned in and stared at the screen. It showed what appeared to be a page from some scientific journal. The tiny text made his eyes ache, but the picture at the top of the screen was clear enough.

'Snake venom?'

'Not just any snake venom, Tony. This is rare stuff. I read a paper a while back about Russian work on weaponising things like this during the Cold War, taking something already nasty and making it a hundred times worse. A hundred times quicker. Never thought I'd encounter anything like it here in Edinburgh.'

'And this is what killed Jennings?' McLean scanned what little of the text he could make out. '*Echis coloratus*, the Burton's carpet viper? Isn't it a little off its patch?'

'That or something like it. Only much, much worse. And before you get too worried, no, I don't think the city's crawling with venomous snakes. They'd all be dead from the cold for one thing.'

McLean looked away from the screen, out through the glass wall of the office and towards the covered-up body. 'This is what killed those wee girls too?'

'I'm still waiting for test results, and I'm waiting to hear back from a friend at the Tropical Diseases Centre, but the symptoms are near-enough identical. Someone's got access to a toxin that can kill in an instant.'

'But who would do such a thing? Why?'

Cadwallader leaned against the desk, picked up one of the sample bottles and peered at it as if he couldn't quite remember what it was. 'That's your job, I believe. What puzzles me more is how it was done.'

'What do you mean?'

The pathologist put the bottle back down and pointed in the general direction of the examination table. 'Here's the thing, Tony. I've been over the body out there with a magnifying glass. Both the wee girls too. They've scuffs and scrapes as you might expect, but I can't find anything resembling an injection mark. Not even a bite. These people have all been poisoned with something incredibly powerful and fast acting, but I can't work out how.'

38

'Detective Chief Inspector McLean?'

The walk from the mortuary to the station was a short one, and McLean had made it so many times now he couldn't begin to count the number. Even so, it was unlike him to be so absorbed in his thoughts that he didn't notice the car pulling in to the side of the road. Then again, it wasn't every day he saw his old friend the pathologist quite so perplexed.

'Who wants to . . . ?' He glanced sideways at the car, a stretch limousine with blacked-out windows. Despite the salt and grime on the roads it was spotless and shiny. A heavy-set man in a too-tight black suit stared at him from the front seat, window wound down. 'Let me guess. Jane Louise?'

The car stopped with scant regard for the rest of the traffic or the double yellow lines at the side of the road. McLean considered legging it back to the station; it was only a couple of hundred yards away after all. It would be undignified though, and he wasn't as fit as he had once been. There was the small matter of his conversation with the deputy chief constable to consider too. If Teflon Steve had sold his soul to this devil, then McLean would have to tread carefully when dealing with her.

He waited while the bodyguard opened his door and climbed out, straightened his jacket, then walked to the door at the rear of the car. McLean half expected Mrs Saifre to be sitting in the back, Mafia boss style. Perhaps with some terrified petty criminal with her who she would execute in front of him just to show him that she could. When he saw that the car was empty, he was almost disappointed.

'Mrs Saifre asks that you grant her an hour of your time.' The bodyguard spoke with a cultured accent McLean had missed before. It sounded strange coming from a body that had clearly spent more hours in a gym than the classroom.

'And if I refuse?'

The bodyguard simply tilted his head slightly in an expression that could have been taken as a threat or that he thought McLean an idiot for even suggesting it.

'OK. But an hour is all she's getting. And only because my boss told me I had to.' He stepped into the back of the limousine and sank into a soft, deep seat. The nameless bodyguard closed the door on him, shutting out the noise of the city with impressive totality. The car rocked slightly as he climbed back into his own seat at the front, and McLean thought he might have felt the slightest of jolts. Then the car was pulling back into the traffic and they were off.

The first time McLean had crossed paths with Mrs Saifre she had bought a large house not far from his own. As far as he was aware, it had since been sold to a disgraced Russian oligarch, and was sitting empty while its owner languished in a gulag in Siberia. He expected to be taken to some expensive city centre hotel for his meeting, but as the opulent stretch limousine picked up speed down the Old Dalkieth Road towards Cameron Toll, it became apparent Saifre had other ideas. Out past the city bypass and he was fairly sure he wasn't going to get back to the station in the allotted hour either.

McLean knew the area to the south-east of the city well enough from various investigations down the years. Even so, he was surprised when the limousine turned off a tiny road some-where near Rosewell, through an ornate pair of wrought-iron gates and along a tree-lined drive. He had thought the countryside here was a mixture of plantation forestry and arable farmland, and yet someone had built an enormous mansion, perhaps a hundred and fifty years ago. Surrounded by snow-covered lawns and circled by the dark pine forestry all around it, the place could have been tucked away in the Highlands it was so secluded. That, presumably, was the point.

The car pulled to a gentle halt right outside the main entrance, deep in the shadow of a tall stone tower. McLean waited for the bodyguard to open the door for him, not wanting to know whether or not he'd been locked in for the journey.

'Mrs Saifre will see you inside,' he said in that oddly cultured voice, indicating the wide steps up to a black oak doorway already standing open. 'We'll be here to take you back to the city when you're done.'

McLean climbed out of the car, feeling the chill in the air as the wind dropped off the Moorfoot Hills and flowed straight through him. He wanted nothing more than to hurry up the steps and get inside, where it would be warm, but instead he paused a moment, took out his phone. A couple of taps at the screen brought up the map function, pinpointing his position. He copied it into a text and pinged it off to the station with a request to be picked up in an hour. The bodyguard with the posh voice stood silently all the while, but McLean could sense the frustration boiling off him. He let the man stew, waiting for a response to his text.

'Sorry about that,' he said as the phone buzzed, the screen lighting up with the answer he wanted. Smiling, he shoved it back in his pocket. 'Let's go see what all this fuss is about then.'

★ ★ ★

'Ah, Tony. You got my message. How delightful to see you again. So good of you to come.'

Mrs Saifre met him in a hallway almost as big as his house back in the city. Two enormous fireplaces blazed on opposite sides of the room, doing their best to chase away some of the deep winter chill. Even so, his breath steamed slightly as he spoke.

'I wasn't aware I had any choice in the matter. What do you want?' McLean looked at his watch more for effect than from any desire to know the time. 'The clock's ticking.'

Saifre pouted like a teenager, and for a moment he almost forgot that she wasn't the young woman she appeared to be. Jane Louise Dee was a product of the baby boom and the best plastic surgery he had ever seen. Either that or she bathed in the blood of virgins and refused to go out into the sun. Being evil incarnate was clearly good for the skin.

'Come now, Tony. There's no need to be rude. I'm here to help you, after all.'

'Forgive me if I find that hard to believe.'

'Nevertheless, it's true.' Saifre shrugged, tossing her shoulder-length hair around as if she wasn't quite comfortable with it. 'But let's not talk about that here. This house is rather wonderful, and has a very interesting history behind it. But it's perishing cold in the winter. Please, come through to the drawing room. It's much warmer in there.'

Saifre turned away and set off across the hall without waiting to see if McLean was going to follow. Part of him felt like turning around, heading back out of the door and away. Experience told him it was better to get this unpleasantness over with as quickly as possible. And he couldn't deny that his curiosity wasn't piqued. Just important to keep his wits about him.

'How many houses do you own then?' he asked as he caught up with her halfway down a corridor wide enough to drive a coach and four along.

'In my father's house are many mansions.' Saifre paused at a door, then pushed it open to reveal a large room beyond. 'But this is the only one I own right now.'

'Really? I thought you owned half of Manhattan, and there's the old Dee family pile up in Fife.' McLean stepped inside and was hit by a wall of heat, dry like the desert. Another log fire crackled enthusiastically in a hearth big enough to roast a whole ox, in stark contrast to the winter landscape outside the floor-to-ceiling French windows.

'Corscaidin? Well, I suppose technically I own it. Haven't been back there in years though. It's an orphanage these days.' Saifre shook her head, smiling at some joke only she knew. 'Can't call it that, of course. Not politically correct. It all amounts to the same thing though. Part of the Trust, like Inchmalcolm Tower and Fenton Hall. Society can be so cruel to its children. We do our best to pick up the pieces.'

McLean studied Saifre's face for any sign that she was lying. He had a good eye for the normal tells, the facial tics and little mannerisms that gave people away. And yet the woman standing in front of him wasn't normal. Not in any sense of the word. She could have been lying with her every breath and he wouldn't be able to tell. Easier just to assume that she was, and then try to tease out the truth from what she said.

'Drink?' She broke eye contact and crossed the room to where an antique sideboard stood, not waiting for him to answer. McLean let her pour generous measures of whisky into two crystal tumblers even though he had no intention of drinking. It was far too early in the day for one thing, and he wasn't about to start accepting hospitality from her for another.

'What is it you want, Mrs Saifre?'

'Why do you have to be so formal all the time? Please, Tony, call me Jane Louise.' She swayed her hips with a little too much exaggeration as she walked back towards him, one hand outstretched to pass him his drink. McLean took the tumbler, almost dropping it as her finger brushed his and a jolt of something far more powerful than static electricity shot between them. He took a step back, relieved when she didn't immediately try to fill the gap that opened up between them. Something like puzzlement flickered briefly across her face.

'If it's all the same, I'll stick to Mrs Saifre for now.' McLean fought the urge to look at his finger, even though his mind was telling him it was no more than a blackened stump. 'I find formal works best in this kind of situation. Now, if you could get to the point?'

Saifre dropped herself down into a leather sofa, gave the seat beside her a half-hearted pat by way of an invitation for McLean to join her. He could feel the allure of her as if it were a physical thing, but he knew it wasn't real. She wasn't real. Just a thorn in his side. The pain in his finger from her touch was receding now, but it gave him the focus he needed to resist her glamour.

'OK. I can see you're not going to play, so I'll lay it out straight. You have a problem. Something – someone, I should say – has killed two young girls and possibly a man too. Here, in Edinburgh, in the past week. You're no closer to understanding how it, he, has done this than you are to finding out who he is. What he is, I should say.'

McLean almost took a sip of the whisky. He could smell that it was good quality, heavily peated, just how he liked it. The glass was at his mouth when he noticed the look in Mrs Saifre's eyes, fixed not on him but on his drink.

'If you have information about crimes committed in the city, then withholding that information is a crime in itself.' He pulled the glass away from his lips with more effort than it should have taken. Almost as if he were arm-wrestling an invisible opponent. Placing it down on the nearest table brought a small gasp of relief.

'I'm not withholding anything, Tony. That's exactly why you're here, so I can tell you what I know.'

'And what, exactly, is that?' McLean paused a moment, then added: 'And what do you want in return?'

'So suspicious.' Saifre stood up, placing her own barely touched glass of whisky down beside McLean's, then walked to the fireplace, hips swaying in that exaggerated manner again. She took a slim brown envelope from the mantelpiece, brought it over and handed it to him. McLean was more careful in taking it than he had been with the glass, and he couldn't help noticing that Mrs Saifre was too.

'The Dee Trust looks after all sorts. Lately we've had a fair number of refugee children come to us. Syrians, North Africans, a few Iraqis and others from the Middle East. You'll have noticed it's not the most stable of places right now. They speak to us more freely than they do the police and other authorities, and a lot of them tell us about how they got here. There's a recurrent theme to their stories, and a name that keeps cropping up time and again. All the details we've been able to find about him are in there.' Saifre nodded at the envelope, and for a moment McLean was almost fooled by her act of concern. Then he remembered who he was talking to, how she had brought him here.

'If you know who this person is, then why not deal with him yourself? It's what you've done in the past.'

'What can I say, Tony? After our last meeting, all that nastiness with poor old Andrew Weatherly and his family? Well, it made me think about myself and what I can do for society. The Dee Trust is a small part of that. Life has given me so much. It's only fair I give something back.'

'Forgive me if I take a bit more convincing.' McLean waved the envelope like a fan. 'But if this turns out to be useful, then you'll have my thanks. Next time, though, maybe just send it to the station, or perhaps give us a call. All this being picked up by

256

bodyguards and driven out to the countryside is a bit too cloak and dagger for my liking.'

'Would you have come? If I'd asked nicely? Would you have even looked at that if I'd had Albert deliver it?' Saifre stood a little too close for McLean's comfort, her stare back to its more normal, penetrating manner. 'Or would you have shoved it in a drawer, maybe even binned it? Just out of spite.'

He held her gaze for as long as he could, but it was like staring into the void. For a moment there was nothing but the two of them, no room, no country mansion, no Edinburgh, no Scotland. He was surrounded by darkness and the crackling heat of the flames in the fireplace, falling through blackness with no hope of a snowdrift to cushion the impact when he hit the ground.

And then a buzzing in his pocket broke the moment. Everything snapped back into place, including the scowl on Saifre's face. McLean pulled out his phone, saw a text scrawled across the screen.

'That'll be my lift back to the city.' He folded the envelope lengthways and slipped it into his inside jacket pocket. 'I'll see myself out.'

39

Ice-cold air chilled his lungs as McLean stepped out of Mrs
Saifre's house. The shiver that ran through him might have
been due to the drop in temperature, or it might simply have
been relief at being out of the woman's presence. Woman. Yes,
Saifre was certainly that, but she was something else besides.
Something rotten and festering he wanted nothing to do with.
And yet, like the proverbial bad penny, she just kept on turning
up.

The folded envelope in his breast pocket pressed against his
chest with an uncomfortable heat quite at odds with the winter
chill all around him. Not that it was hot, particularly, so much as
it represented something he'd been fighting hard to avoid. If it
truly contained useful information, as part of him knew it would,
then that would be a favour owed. Accepting it made him
somehow beholden to her, and she knew it. He was tempted to
take it out, rip it up and leave the tearings scattered over the stone
steps, but even he could see just how melodramatic that would
look. And Saifre wouldn't have brought him all the way out here,
given him this intelligence, if it weren't in some way true.
Overlooking it would be as bad as accepting it, and both were
more manipulation than he cared for. Damn her.

'You all done, sir?'

The bodyguard – Albert, McLean assumed – appeared as if from nowhere and hurried to the stretch limousine still parked in the snow-smeared gravel turning area in front of the house. By the time he'd reached the bottom of the stone steps, the well-spoken young man had already opened the passenger door and stood beside it expectantly.

'Not necessary, thanks.' McLean walked on past the car, feet crunching through the thin layer of snow that covered most of the surrounding landscape. Only the low stone walls and occasional leafless shrubs gave any clue as to where nature took over. That and the arrow-straight tyre tracks where the limousine had brought him here from the public road. In the far distance, over the tops of the trees that surrounded the parkland, he could see the Moorfoot Hills painted stark white. Here and there, rectangular strips of plantation woodland cut black scars in the landscape, and as he took them in, McLean realised that the clouds had begun to clear, a thin, weak sun breaking through.

He was halfway to the gates and slightly regretting his actions, when he heard the crunch of tyres on snow behind him. The limousine was quiet, its engine all but inaudible above the sighing of the wind in the trees, but then only the best was ever good enough for Mrs Saifre. As the car pulled up alongside him, he expected the driver's window to wind down and the bodyguard-cum-chauffeur to try to convince him of the folly of walking all the way back to the city. Instead, the car inched slowly ahead of him, and then the rear passenger window opened.

'Really, Tony. You can be quite childish sometimes. What would the deputy chief constable think of this?'

McLean stopped walking, and the limousine continued on for a few feet before coming to a halt. He waited until it had reversed back to where he stood, tempted to then carry on towards the entrance gates and the road beyond. For all that he didn't much care to share the same air as her, Saifre was right though. He was going out of his way to be awkward, to turn down anything she offered him, and Call-me-Stevie would almost certainly give him a bollocking for it when he got back to the station. Well, it wouldn't be the first time.

'I appreciate your offer, thank you.' He bowed his head ever so slightly towards the open window and the pale-skinned woman sitting behind it. As if on cue the sound of an approaching car wafted over the trees from the direction of the road. 'I find when I need to think, walking helps. The rhythm of feet on pavement, you see?'

Saifre stared at him as if he were mad, which was something she probably knew more about than him. Out of the corner of his eye, he saw movement at the gates, a not-so-shiny silver-black shape against the whiteness.

'Besides, I arranged my own transport back to the city.'

McLean set off once more towards the gates, unsurprised when the limousine kept pace with him all the way. His text had only asked that he be picked up, not how or by whom. Even so, he was disappointed to find DC Harrison behind the wheel of one of CID's few remaining pool cars. He'd hoped it might have been Grumpy Bob, or even a squad car out of Dalkieth. He'd also not planned on Saifre following him all the way. The fewer people he brought to her attention the better. He stood by the passenger door, waiting for the limousine to move off. Instead it pulled to a halt alongside, sandwiching him between the two cars.

'The new girl. Detective Constable Harrison, isn't it? I've heard good things about her.' Saifre's smile could have frozen Gladhouse Reservoir solid. 'Well. I can't say it's been fun, Tony. But then you never really were. Say hello to that lovely Emma from me.'

The empty smile and soulless eyes slowly disappeared as she wound up the passenger window, replaced by McLean's own reflection in the blackened glass. And then with a silence so total it was as if he had gone deaf, the limousine slid forward, into the road and away.

'Don't get to drive out this way often, sir. It's kind of pretty in the snow.'

McLean stared out of the windscreen at the narrow road, ragged hedges on either side. There were many words he could think of to describe this part of the Midlothian plain, but 'pretty' wasn't one of them.

'Thanks for picking me up,' he said.

'It's no bother. I needed to get out of the station. Why were you all the way out here anyway?' Harrison slowed for a blind corner, handling the car far more expertly in the snow than the idiots who blocked the M8 every time the weather turned bad. McLean held his hands over the air vent, heat turned up as high as it would go, and fought off the shivers that were still running through him.

'You remember Jane Louise Dee?'

'The tech billionaire? Aye.' Harrison risked a sideways glance at him, and McLean could see the look in her eyes. 'You thought she was involved in that mess with Bill Chalmers last winter, right? Only she was in New York or Silicon Valley or somewhere the whole time.'

'So everyone says.' McLean reluctantly pulled his hands away from the warmth and reached into his jacket for the envelope. 'Well, this time she's most definitely here, in Scotland. That was her in that limousine when you picked me up.'

Harrison said nothing for a moment, the thoughts tumbling all too obviously across her face. 'And she what? Whisked you all the way out here without the opportunity to say no?'

'Something like that. She seems to have the ear of the DCC, so pissing her off pisses him off. I hope he knows what he's getting himself into.'

Another long pause before Harrison spoke again. 'But why bring you all the way out here?'

'To show that she can?' McLean flapped the envelope against his leg, unsure whether or not to open it. 'To give me this.'

'What's that?' Harrison risked another sideways glance, then went back to concentrating on the road as the car slid on a patch of ice.

'You drive, I'll read, OK?' McLean stared at the envelope a moment longer, then carefully unsealed it and pulled out the thin sheaf of papers inside. The front page was a bad photocopy of what looked like some kind of military report, chunks of text effectively redacted with black marker pen, the lines slightly off-level. Even so he could see that the information was useful. Flicking through the rest of it, he felt the chill seep into his guts as the implications of what he was reading sank in. It was tempting to ask Harrison to take him straight back to Saifre's mansion and arrest her for withholding information relevant to their enquiries, messing with their investigation, something, anything. He knew it wouldn't stick though, and of course she wasn't there. Albert had driven her off somewhere else. More to the point he wanted to ask her why, and why now. What was in it for her to investigate this matter and then hand over her findings to the police? To him specifically? She was manipulating him towards something, and it had to be more valuable to her than to them.

40

'You do realise what this means, Tony?'

Detective Chief Inspector Jo Dexter looked like she hadn't slept since the last time McLean had spoken to her, several days earlier. Creases lined her face, and her eyes were crusted at the corners, red from repeated rubbing. Her hair hung in tired ringlets, and the smell of cigarettes hung about her like a curse. All this and more he had taken in without comment, waiting patiently as she read through Mrs Saifre's report. Her shoulders, slumped with the weight of the world before she started, had sunk even further with each page turned.

'And here's me thought your first question would be where I got that.'

'I'll get to that in time. More importantly, this blows away six months of fucking hard work. Who else knows what's here?'

'You, me; the person who compiled it. Oh, and Jane Louise Dee.'

Dexter dropped the report onto her desk, rubbed at her eyes and then stared straight at him.

'Jane Louise Dee? What the fuck's this got to do with her?'

'I have absolutely no idea. Don't know why she's so keen for us to deal with it either. That's not normally her style.'

Dexter went to rub her eyes again, then stopped herself. She pulled open a couple of drawers, searching until she found a tiny bottle. The skill with which she stared at the ceiling, administered drops to each eye, rolled and blinked them, suggested to McLean this was something she had to do on a regular basis.

'I could do without this stress. Plays havoc with them.' She waved a hand in the general direction of her face. 'Doctor says I should give up smoking, but days like these I think it's the only thing keeps me going.'

McLean reached forward across the desk and teased out the last page of the report. It was taken up mostly by a poor quality black-and-white photograph of a dark-haired man with a wild beard. The rest of the report had more detailed information on a gang trafficking people into the country, some for prostitution, some for slave labour and some – the lucky ones who had presumably paid well enough at the outset – to simply be dumped somewhere and left to fend for themselves. How many of them had passed through the doors of House the Refugees, and other charities like it? How much did Sheila Begbie know about the journey her clients had made before they reached her?

'What are we going to do about this?' He tapped his finger against the photograph. 'You got anything on this guy?'

'Omar Mared. Sometimes goes by the name Ozzy Jones.' Dexter shook her head. 'I have diddly squat on this guy. Never heard of him until you brought this in. Never seen his face before, not that you can see much from that. And yet a lot of the other information in here is spot on. Stuff we've been trying to build a case with for months, and it's all here. All inadmissible in court. Fuck.'

'If you can find him though, that'd tie everything together, would it not? And most likely clue us up to how and why those two wee girls were killed. Maurice Jennings too.'

Dexter shuffled through the pages, more for show than anything. 'Aye, that'd be nice. All wrapped up wi' a bow on the

'I'll give you that. Doesn't change the fact that she wants this man Mared found but for whatever reason can't find him herself. She's using us to do her dirty work, even if it helps us in the short run.'

'So you want us to find him then,' Grumpy Bob said. 'Why not leave it to Jo and her team?'

'She's got her hands full dealing with the rest of the information Dee's given us. Not best pleased at how it's buggered up six months of undercover work, either. Reckon she's going to have to move quickly on a lot of the operations this mysterious Omar Mared is meant to be controlling. Might be that the man himself slips through her fingers.'

'You said Dexter's never heard of him?' Duguid asked. 'What if he's not the man in charge? What if he's just some kind of enforcer?'

'You'd still think he'd be on their radar, at the very least. And she wants him found, which almost makes me want to hide him away.'

'What if he doesn't exist at all?' Grumpy Bob voiced the concern that had been niggling in the back of McLean's mind since he'd first scanned the pages of Dee's report a few hours earlier. 'What if it's all a distraction from something else? Divert our attention while she does her own business.'

'That had crossed my mind, Bob, but it's too elaborate even for her. There's a reason why she wants us to investigate this person, and I don't know what that is. Which is why I want you to look into him without raising any suspicions. Find out what you can without setting off any alarms. We can leave arresting him to Jo Dexter. What I want to know is why Dee wants him out of the picture.'

top would be better still. Trafficking, drug dealing, modern-day slavery, living off the proceeds of immoral earnings? Even murder, if what this report says is true. Or the whole thing could be an elaborate set-up. I mean, who is this guy? Does he even exist? How could he be running all this stuff we know about, and yet we've never heard of him?'

'That's kind of what I was hoping you could tell me.'

Dexter paused a moment, her focus sliding past McLean and into the distance before snapping back, decision made. 'I need to speak to my people. We're going to have to do a half-dozen coordinated raids in the next twenty-four hours or a lot of hard work is going to be wasted. If your pal Dee has this information, others do too, and I can't risk losing what we already have. Fuck.'

'Not going to be getting much sleep, I take it.'

'No. And I might have to borrow a few of your constables, too. This needs to be done hard and fast, or these people will just melt away.' Dexter picked up the report and leafed sightlessly through the pages, muttering 'Fuck' under her breath every so often.

'I'll give you all the support I can. Seems only fair, considering.' McLean stood up to leave.

'You want a copy of this?' Dexter flapped the loose pages of the report at him.

'I suppose I ought to. Rather not have anything to do with Dee though.'

'I can understand that. Nothing so annoying as someone trying to be helpful.'

'That's the thing though, Jo. She's never helpful. Not without expecting some heavy price in return.'

He should have gone back to the major-incident room and checked in. After all, he'd been away from the station for most of the day and he was supposed to be in charge. For too many reasons to list, McLean couldn't face the idea of walking into that room, the barrage of questions he'd have to deal with, so very few of them actually relevant to the investigation. This was why he'd never wanted to be promoted in the first place. He thought best on his feet, worked best with a small team of detectives he could depend on. Coordinating something as big as this made his head spin.

There were far better officers to deal with the day-to-day running of an incident room. At least that's what he told himself as he took a route from Jo Dexter's office that avoided it. Instead, he descended into the depths of the building, away from the concrete modernity and into the brick-vaulted Victorian basement. As he went, so the bustle of the station quietened, and his nervous tension with it. And when he stopped at the half-open door to the Cold Case Unit, McLean almost laughed at the thought that he'd be far happier working here with Duguid than upstairs calling the shots.

'You going to lurk out there like a guilty schoolboy or come in and tell me what it is you want?' The ex-detective superintendent's gruff voice startled him – he'd not made so much noise in the corridor that anyone inside would have heard him. When he looked up, McLean saw the man standing by the filing cabinets at the opposite end of the room to his desk. From there, Duguid could see through the gap in the doorway, out into the corridor. How he'd known McLean was standing there was anybody's guess.

'A lot on my mind,' McLean said by way of explanation as he stepped into the room. Grumpy Bob looked up from one of the other desks, doing his best impression of a man who's just popped in for some information and hasn't been down here in the darkness all day. Not at all.

'Something you think we can help with, I've no doubt.' Duguid slammed the filing-cabinet drawer closed and stalked back across the room, a slim folder in one long-fingered hand.

'Depends on how busy you are. I've a name an[d] Could do with tracking a person down.'

'Not a cold case then.' Duguid didn't try to [hide] from his voice. The bear was angry today, which [meant] whatever he had been working on had hit a brick [wall] he'd not be too busy then.

'I had an interesting meeting with a certain Jan[e] this morning. Not something I expected or particu[larly] I can assure you.' McLean gave them the rundown [of what] happened, and the report he'd left with DCI Dex[ter.] Bob's face was as black as a collapsed coal mine, Dug[uid one] that could curdle milk.

'I take it you mean Jane Louise Dee the IT bil[lionaire?] you know her?'

'Aye, we're like this.' McLean held up his han[d, first and] middle finger intertwined. 'Ask Bob about the last ti[me she had a] bath.'

'She's . . . not what you might think.' Grumpy B[ob shifted in] his seat like he had piles. 'And I'd no' trust her to ke[ep an eye on] my pint while I went to the cludgie.'

'Thank you for that image, Bob,' McLean said. '[But that's] the heart of it, I guess. She's a bloody menace, stick[ing her nose] where it's not wanted. The thing is, she has the ea[r of the chief] constable and every lickspittle politician in Holyroo[d on speed] call and she could probably have all of us out of a j[ob. She's] used to getting what she wants regardless of wheth[er it's legal or] not. I know for a fact she was involved in that Bill C[halmers affair] last year, and yet soon as I started mentioning h[er name the] whole thing got shut down.'

'Thought you were off your head on laudanu[m when that] was all going down.' Duguid dropped into his seat [and folded his] arms on the desk in front of him, staring at McLe[an with a look] that defied him to say it wasn't so.

41

'Heard you wanted to see me, Angus. Anything important?' McLean had already pushed through the door into the small office directly off the examination theatre before he realised that the city pathologist was not alone. He was used to seeing Doctor Sharp, Cadwallader's assistant, there, but now the two of them were joined by a third person. A young man with thin, sandy hair that jutted out from his head in a dishevelled mop, he leapt to his feet like a startled ferret.

'Calm yourself, Donald. It's only the chief inspector.' Cadwallader stood, placed a fatherly hand on the young man's shoulder and forced him back into his seat before approaching McLean. 'Tony. What unusually good timing. I was just going over the details with Professor Christie here.'

'Professor?' McLean looked at the young man more closely, wondering how someone clearly not long out of school could have achieved such a lofty status.

'Don't start,' Cadwallader said, then broke into a semblance of a smile. 'We're none of us getting any younger, right enough.'

The young man, Professor Christie, stood up again and turned to face McLean. He was all angles and thin limbs clad in what might be mistaken for running gear. Certainly not the fusty tweeds and leather elbow patches the term 'professor' conjured up.

'Donald. Donald Christie.' He held out a hand for McLean to shake. 'You must be the detective in charge of the investigation.'

It didn't matter that he didn't say which investigation. McLean knew well enough. 'And you must be from the Centre for Tropical Diseases. Am I right?'

Christie tilted his head slightly to one side in assent. 'I've just been looking at the bodies Angus sent me samples from. Fascinating, and ever so slightly alarming.'

McLean's gut clenched. 'Do you know what killed them? Is it something contagious?'

'I—' the young man started to answer, but Cadwallader cut him short.

'Let's all sit down, shall we?' He dragged an office chair from one of the other desks and twirled it around for McLean.

'It's a simple enough question, Angus. You asked me to come over, so what's the story?'

Cadwallader slumped into his own chair and let out a long sigh. 'It's complicated. Always is when you're involved, Tony. Young Donald here's just the icing on the cake, so to speak.'

'OK.' McLean fought the urge to shout. 'The bodies. What killed them?'

Nobody said anything for a moment, Professor Christie looking pointedly at Cadwallader as if asking for permission. Finally the pathologist nodded.

'The two children,' Christie said. 'I think you know already they both died from organ failure. I'm not as much of an expert as Angus here, but basically they shut down. Lungs, liver, kidney, then heart. There's toxins that can do that, and horribly swiftly too. Not something we see in this part of the world. Well, not normally.'

'Toxins?' McLean asked. 'So it is snake venom then, like Angus thought.'

'Normally I'd say so, yes. Venom's my speciality, and why Angus came to me in the first place. From what we can tell, the chemical signature in their bloodstream is . . .' Christie shrugged. '. . . Well, it's very similar to snake bite.'

'Aye, Angus already mentioned that. What was it? Richard Burton's viper or something?'

'Burton's carpet viper. *Echis coloratus*. Nasty wee thing found mostly in the Middle East, although there's a couple of ophidiaria in the UK have breeding specimens.'

'Breeding? Why on earth would you want to breed venomous snakes?'

'I think you've answered your own question there, Tony.' Cadwallader smiled at his joke, but it didn't last. 'There's not much call for antivenin in the UK. We're not exactly overrun with poisonous beasties here, thank Christ. But some of the compounds have medical properties, and some have attracted interest from the military. That's kind of where we're going with this.'

'See, these three victims have all suffered much the same fate,' Professor Christie cut in. 'But normally you'd expect to see an injection site. Bite marks would be obvious. Usually on the hand or face, not many other places a snake can get you when you're fully clothed. But then a snake wouldn't last ten minutes in this weather.'

'Not a snake then. So something else – someone else – injected them?'

'Not injected, no.' Cadwallader hauled himself out of his seat with a groan, crossed the room to the desk where Doctor Sharp was busy ignoring them all, and retrieved a stack of photographs. When he returned, McLean could see they showed limbs, waxy yellow skin, hands and feet. It wasn't hard to tell which belonged to the two children and which to Maurice Jennings.

'I've been over the bodies with a magnifying glass. Even got Tom MacPhail to have a look, and some of the students. There's no injection site on any of them. Whatever this was, it wasn't administered with a needle or a bite. There is this though.'

Cadwallader laid out three photographs that made McLean wince. They all showed close-ups of the victims' faces. Tiny white teeth showed in the slightly open mouth of one of the children, but the other two mouths were tightly closed. All three had that dark beeswax colour and texture, lips flushed and swollen, the slightest discolouration where blisters might have formed, had they been still alive.

'I never noticed that before. Their mouths.'

'It's something that's developed post-mortem.' Cadwallader slid the photographs back together in a stack, only the face of Maurice Jennings still visible. 'I missed it first time around because it wasn't there. Like the skin tanning, I suspect it's a side-effect of the toxin, only its localization suggests that might be where it was administered.'

McLean dragged his gaze away from the photograph. 'The lips? But how? A spray? Something wiped on them? Could that even work?'

'Actually, poisoning someone via the lips is quite easy.' Christie reached up and tapped his own with a single finger. 'Touch them, and people can't help themselves from licking. The skin's more absorbent there too, so you could get a dose that way. It's just . . . well, I don't know how you could make the toxins in the venom so potent. For the wee kids maybe, but a grown man? Normally they need to be injected into the bloodstream in significant quantity. That's why snakes have fangs, after all. And most venoms aren't that effective when swallowed either.'

'So what you're telling me is that this is like a snake venom, only different.' McLean folded his arms across his chest, all too aware that the day was getting away from him and there was still a lot to do. 'It's somehow been applied topically, probably to the lips, and it's potent enough to kill a grown man in a few minutes.'

Christie shrugged. 'At least it's not some airborne disease. We're pretty sure of that.'

'I'll take "pretty sure" for now. Thank you, Professor.' McLean stood up. 'You'll keep me up to speed on any developments, aye? If it's a venom, an antivenin might be useful.'

For a moment, as he walked up the steep hill from the Cowgate back towards the station, McLean thought he was going to be picked up again and carted off to the countryside for more harassment by the deputy chief constable's new best friend. As before, a car slowed to match his pace and pulled in close to the kerb. Unlike the stretch limousine driven by Albert, the polite bodyguard, this car's engine was audible above the general noise of the city, and glancing sideways he saw a slightly more welcome figure at the wheel.

'You wanting a lift, Tony?' Jo Dalgliesh shouted across the empty passenger seat and out through the open window as she slowed to a halt. McLean knew that the station was only a few minutes away, and the weather had improved enough that he didn't mind walking. It was no coincidence the reporter had been passing. She wanted something from him, and might just be persuaded to be helpful in return.

'Sure. Why not.' He pulled open the door and slumped into the low leather seat. McLean had never really associated Dalgliesh with cars; she always seemed to appear on foot and disappear into the crowd the same way. He'd accepted a lift in this one before though, on another day when the snow had fallen heavily in the city. The reporter waited for him to fit his seatbelt before checking her mirror, indicating and pulling out into the traffic.

'Been busy, I hear,' she said without looking at him.

'Always. You know how it is. So what do you want this time?'

Dalgliesh glanced at him sideways. 'Can I no' offer a friend a lift without raising suspicion?'

'You don't want me to answer that, Dalgliesh. Come on. It's only a short way to the station anyway, so get to the point, aye?'

'Fair enough.' Dalgliesh indicated again, then pulled to the side of the road and stopped. 'Word is you've another body. Local man this time, but same MO as the two wee kiddies.'

He'd been out of the loop thanks to Mrs Saifre and her tricks, so McLean wasn't sure exactly how much information about Maurice Jennings had been shared with the press. He was fairly sure that details of exactly how the man had died wouldn't have been made public, and he knew for a fact they were keeping a lid on what had killed the children. Or at least trying to. He said nothing, hoping that Dalgliesh would fill the silence. She didn't disappoint.

'There's a couple of the tabloids working an angle you're no' going to like. Thought I'd give you a heads-up, seeing as we're pals and all.'

McLean nodded his head once, unsure whether he was agreeing with the sentiment or indicating she should go on.

'They've picked up on the two wee kids being foreigners, like. Illegal immigrants. The story goes they were trafficked in with a group from Syria or Libya or somewhere. Doesn't really matter to the folk who read that kind of stuff. Only that they're foreign, probably scrounging off of us hardworking types, aye? And they've come here with their foreign diseases too. Killed a couple of them, and now it's spread to the locals. It's a plague, you see? The Black Death or something like it. Eats up your insides and turns your skin yellow.'

Dalgliesh's car wasn't cheap. A modern Jaguar two-seat coupé, it had enough soundproofing to deaden the worst of the city noise outside. When she finished talking, the silence was even deeper than that, as if everything had stopped in that instant. McLean reached up and pinched the bridge of his nose between thumb and forefinger, started to count to ten, then gave up.

'You know that's all bollocks, right?'

'All of it?' Dalgliesh cocked her head to one side like a confused spaniel.

'Aye, well. The two kids are probably illegal immigrants. Refugees, but trafficked here illegally like you say. That's the best explanation for why we've had such a hard time identifying them. Nobody's come forward to claim them. Nobody's even reported any children missing in the past month. Not within a reasonable distance of here, anyway.'

'So their skin's not turned waxy yellow then? They've not died from massive organ failure?'

McLean shook his head. 'I can't confirm details like that, Jo. Not to a reporter. I can tell you that we've consulted with the Centre for Tropical Diseases and they've told us it's not something contagious.'

'But they did both die of the same thing though. All three of them, I should say.'

'Again, I'm not going to tell you. Not until we have more information.' McLean stared out through the windscreen. 'We have some leads on the dead man, Maurice Jennings. We think he might just have been unlucky. Wrong time, wrong place. Got in the way of someone. Maybe stopped them doing something.'

Dalgliesh took her hands off the steering wheel, guddled about in a pocket and pulled out her electronic cigarette. A faint syrupy smell wafted across to McLean as she stuffed one end in her mouth, but she didn't inhale and the thing wasn't even switched on.

'So he was murdered then, Jennings?'

'It looks that way. That's how we're treating it anyway. So you can understand why I don't want too much detail swilling around in the more lurid press.'

'Aye, fine. I get that. I'm no' interested in that kind of speculation anyways.' Dalgliesh waved the electronic cigarette around as she spoke, then shoved it back in her pocket. 'Can't say the same for some of my colleagues in the gutter press, mind.'

McLean almost made a caustic remark about her being one of them, but managed to stop himself at the last moment. Dalgliesh was a hack, that much he knew. She'd trick the story out of someone, or pay for it with cash or some other kind of leverage, but it was a long time since she'd put her name to something that was an out-and-out lie just to sell newspapers.

'Well, thanks for the warning.' He reached down and unclipped his seatbelt with one hand, popped open the door with the other. 'And the lift. I'll walk it from here though. Wouldn't want to be seen fraternising. No hard feelings.'

'Aye, you're all heart, Insp— . . . Chief Inspector.'

McLean ignored her as he climbed out of the car, but he couldn't deny that her warning was useful. Quite what he could give her in return that wouldn't land him in the shit, he wasn't so sure. And then it occurred to him.

'There is something you might want to look into,' he said as he began to close the door. 'Fellow by the name of Omar Mared, sometimes goes by Ozzy Jones. Apparently he's behind a lot of the trafficking that's bringing these people here in the first place. Got his fingers in the sex work trade and drugs too. Might be behind a woman found beaten almost to death in Sighthill a week ago.'

'Never heard of him.' Dalgliesh's expression suggested she meant it.

'That's the thing. Nobody has heard of him. Nobody except Jane Louise Dee.'

'Wait, what?' Dalgliesh started to ask something else, but McLean closed the door on her, the Jaguar's expensive sound-proofing as effective at keeping the inside in as the outside out. She threw a rude gesture in his direction, but he just waved, then turned and began the short walk back to the station.

42

McLean had been intending to go straight to the major-incident room and get up to speed on the ongoing investigations into the two dead girls. His conversation with Dalgliesh and her information about where the tabloids were going with the story meant that he needed to see someone else more urgently first.

'I was wondering when you might put in an appearance.' The DCC stood at the glass window wall of his office, staring out at the darkening winter skies. He must have seen McLean's reflection at the door, as he didn't turn until after he'd spoken.

'It's been a busy day, sir.' And then some. McLean's stomach rumbled quietly to itself, reminding him of just how long ago breakfast had been, how non-existent lunch.

'And what have you got to show for it, eh?' Robinson's voice wasn't quite as unfriendly as his words, more wearily impatient than angry.

'Connections, mostly. Things that don't quite add up. There's a pattern beginning to emerge, but I've just had some more alarming news.'

'Oh aye?' Robinson slumped his shoulders in resignation. 'Go on then.'

'According to Jo Dalgliesh, some of the more lurid tabloids

are working up the story that there's some new infectious disease or plague going round the city. Brought in by illegal immigrants and what are we going to do about it.'

'And is there?'

Robinson's question surprised McLean. The DCC seemed defeated, weighed down by the troubles of the world. He wasn't his normal, irritatingly upbeat self at all.

'No, sir. I've spoken to Angus at the mortuary, and an expert from Tropical Diseases. Whatever killed those two girls and Maurice Jennings is more like a toxin than an infectious disease. It's acting a bit like snake venom, only there's no way in hell there are poisonous snakes out in the city. Not in this weather.' He waved a hand at the window, where even now more flurries of light snow clustered around the street lamps.

'So how are they getting it?'

'That's one of the things that doesn't quite add up yet, sir. There's an obvious link between the two wee girls, but Jennings is a wild card. If we can follow the movements of the man we think attacked him, that might give us a break. Meantime I'm trying to get as much information as possible out of Nala Nour and her aunt.'

'Nala—?' Confusion creased Robinson's face for a moment. 'Oh yes, them. You never did tell me where you'd sent them both. Not still at your place, I hope. That would be inappropriate.'

'They're both in care, sir. Someone I trust not to lose them.' McLean checked his watch, alarmed at just how late it was. 'I'd hoped to speak to them this afternoon, but most of that's gone already. Could have done without chasing after Matthew Seaton. Or being dragged away by that bloody woman.'

'You could have sent a sergeant to look into Seaton, couldn't you?' Robinson's question seemed genuine, even though McLean recalled all too well the DCC's insistence he deal with the matter personally. Maybe he'd forgotten. He certainly seemed distracted by something.

'I thought it was sensitive enough I'd best handle it myself. Seems I was right, there's more going on there than meets the eye too.'

'Oh good Christ.' Robinson muttered the words under his breath, but McLean heard them well enough. 'Keep me up to speed then. And what about this "bloody woman"? Is that why you went missing all afternoon?'

'Your new best friend, Mrs Saifre. Jane Louise bloody Dee.' McLean told the DCC about his brief trip out to Midlothian. 'If it was up to me, I'd have her hauled in here for questioning.'

Robinson recoiled as if he'd been slapped. 'Are you mad? Bring Jane Louise Dee into the station and question her like a common criminal?'

'I was thinking more like a member of the public helping the police with their enquiries, sir. But common criminal works for me as well.'

'Jesus wept, McLean. Can you imagine the fallout if you tried to do that?' The DCC staggered around his desk and slumped into his chair as if his legs couldn't carry the weight of such a monstrous concept. 'We'd have every lawyer in the land on our backs, not to mention the gutter press making life impossible for us. You do know how many papers she owns, right?'

McLean didn't think it wise to mention these were the same papers planning on raising hell for them already. 'She as good as kidnapped me, dragged me off to some stately home outside the city, handed me a dossier that has to have been obtained illegally and which shows she has information about several ongoing investigations. Information she could have sent us at any time, and yet she chose not to until today. I'd call that both wasting police time and obstructing justice.'

'And I'd call it helping us out when we haven't got a

clue what's going on.' Robinson rubbed at his face with tired fingers. 'If you concentrated on running the investigations you were supposed to be running and didn't spend all your time chasing ghosts, we might not need her help. As it is, I'm not going to worry too much about the state of this gift horse's teeth.'

McLean waited a moment, then pulled out the chair on his side of the DCC's desk and sat down. 'Look, sir. I don't like Saifre, and I don't trust her at all. Anything and everything she does is for her interests and her interests alone. She's playing us by feeding us this information, and I want to know what her endgame is before I do her dirty work for her.'

'What have you done with the intel she gave you?' Robinson squared his shoulders as if remembering how to be a police officer again.

'I passed it all on to Jo Dexter, since most of it's to do with trafficking refugees for sex work. All hell's going to be breaking loose in the next twenty-four hours, so you might want to have a word with the chief constable about budgets.'

'Christ. What did I do to deserve this?' The DCC fell silent a while, and McLean was content not to fill it.

'You still need to work with what Dee has given you,' he said eventually. 'I can see she's playing her own game, but even so she's too powerful to ignore. She owns those papers, after all. If you can find out what she really wants, then maybe we can use that to our advantage.'

McLean nodded. 'Understood. I'll keep you up to speed, sir. We'll weather this storm.'

Robinson gave him a look of grim uncertainty. 'Aye, maybe. But you're not the one who's going to be in front of tomorrow's cameras. Go on, get out of here, will you? I need to make some calls.'

McLean stood up and walked to the door, not stopping as he

opened it and left. The meeting could have gone a lot worse, and it hadn't escaped his notice that Robinson had stopped calling Mrs Saifre by her first names. Maybe they weren't such firm friends after all, and that could only be a good thing.

He didn't even make it as far as the major-incident room before he was interrupted. DC Stringer appeared from the doorway of a darkened room as he walked past it.

'Ah, sir. Have you got a moment? I think you might want to see this.'

Still slightly reeling from his meeting with the DCC, McLean paused a moment before answering. He peered past the detective constable and saw a room filled with mostly blank screens. The unfeasibly tall figure of DC Blane obscured one of the few that was lit up, and alongside him DC Harrison gesticulated with her hands, pointing every so often at an image he couldn't see.

'What's up?'

'We pulled the CCTV footage from the hospital, sir. Just trying to get a handle on when Matthew Seaton died and who was around.' Stringer stepped back into the gloomy room. Not quite sure what else to do, McLean followed him.

'I thought you were just going to start writing up a report for the PF. They've not even done his post-mortem yet. Might be no reason for any of this.'

'I was only going to have a quick look, sir, but . . . Well.' Stringer stepped aside so that McLean could cross the room to the bank of screens. It didn't take him long to recognise the view that Blane and Harrison were arguing over. It showed the corridor in the Western General, late at night. A small group of figures stood frozen by the pause button, and for a moment he thought this might be the start of some elaborate joke. Except that detective constables didn't play elaborate jokes on detective chief inspectors. At least not ones that they could see coming.

'It's ancient red Morrison.' McLean leaned between the two detective constables and stared at the surprisingly clear image of Rahel, Emma, Doctor Wheeler and him in his tartan trews.

'What?' Harrison asked.

'The trousers. My gran was Esther Morrison, so I can wear Morrison tartan if I want. It's much nicer than McLean. That's what you were arguing about, wasn't it?'

'I . . . We . . .' Harrison started to protest, then gave up.

'See. I told you it wasn't McLean,' Blane said.

'Well, once we've all finished admiring my trews, can you explain why I'm in here looking at myself on hospital CCTV and not, for instance, in the incident room dealing with the ongoing murder investigation?'

Blane straightened in his chair, adding a good ten inches to his seated height. 'Sorry sir. This was just the reference point on the cameras for Seaton's estimated time of death. I was looking at the various feeds and spotted you there.' He reached for the controls and tapped at some keys until the image disappeared, replaced by a different corridor. This one was empty, save for a chair beside a door, in which a man sprawled asleep, dropped paperback book on the floor beside him.

'This is the room Seaton was in. As you can see his guard wasn't exactly paying attention.'

'Has anyone spoken to the prison? We'll need to interview him.' McLean didn't envy whoever that job fell to. Prison officers could get defensive at the best of times, and this was most likely a sacking offence. Still, a man had died in his custody.

'Not yet, sir.' Stringer stood on the other side of Blane, his head more or less level with his fellow detective constable despite the fact one was seated and the other standing. 'Seems he called in sick this morning. Maybe understandable given the circumstances, see.'

Blane tapped a button and the image spooled forward.

Nothing moved for a few moments, and then another figure came into view, a person wearing a long, black coat. Male or female, McLean couldn't be sure. The figure had black hair down past its shoulders, but something about it suggested masculinity. It might have been a glitch in the recording or just his imagination playing tricks, but the screen appeared to darken as the figure moved towards the centre of the picture, lines flickering across it like electronic interference. The figure stopped by the sleeping guard, held a hand out to his face, then withdrew it with a flourish of long fingers. A moment later the figure stepped past the chair, pushed open the door and disappeared inside.

'I've run the video a dozen times, sir, and he doesn't come out.' Blane tapped a button, causing the image to leap into fast-forward, eating up minutes on the timestamp until a nurse appeared. He tapped the button again and it returned to normal speed. 'We've spoken to the nurse on the phone. Name's Edna Grayling. She's coming in to give a formal statement tomorrow. She swears there was no one in the room when she entered. Seaton was dead when she found him.'

McLean rubbed at his eyes, feeling the grit in them from a long day that was about to get longer. 'Why is it always more complicated than it needs to be?'

Nobody answered. Presumably that was above their pay grade.

'You said "he". What makes you think that's a man?'

Blane leaned forward and peered at the screen even though the figure was no longer showing. 'I just assumed. First impression, you know?'

'Aye, I thought that too, but is there any footage of him from the front? Anything showing his face?'

'I've not had a chance to go over everything from the hospital yet, sir. Still wading through a lot of the feeds from Broughton

Street too. Can't help thinking they look very similar though. Height, build, black clothing. Something about the way they both move.'

'Bring the video back up again, will you?'

McLean waited while Blane fiddled with the controls, then watched as the black-clad figure walked up the corridor again. That same interference crackled across the screen, dimming the image and making it hard to see anything clearly. Still, now Blane had mentioned it, McLean had to admit there was a resemblance to the figure they suspected of attacking Maurice Jennings.

'It just keeps getting better and better,' he said. 'We got anyone who can do gait analysis on the footage?'

Blane swivelled in his seat and stared at McLean as if he'd just recited something in ancient Sumerian. 'Gait analysis?'

'You know, the pattern of their walking. Sure we used it on that case back in the summer.'

'I know what it is, sir. Just surprised—' The detective constable stopped himself from accusing his superior of being a technological naïf just in time. 'We can get it analysed, yes. Have to send it out though. Might take a wee while to get an answer.'

'Get on it then. And while you're waiting see if you can't find any more footage with this . . .' McLean paused, but now it had been pointed out he couldn't shake the certainty. 'This man. We need to see his face, and better than the Broughton Street footage. We'll also need to speak to everyone who was working at the hospital that night. Someone must have seen him. You can't just walk in and wander where you like unchallenged.'

Except that, whoever it was, that was exactly what they had done. And then vanished into thin air. Why did it all have to be so bloody complicated?

McLean's phone buzzed in his pocket, an occurrence unusual enough for him to fetch it out and peer at the screen. A text message from Angus Cadwallader.

Something you need to see. Come ASAP.

A last look at the black figure, paused with its hand reaching out for the sleeping guard's face. McLean felt a shiver run down his spine. He had a horrible feeling he knew just what his old friend the pathologist was going to show him.

'I've got to go.' He checked his watch. Almost shift end, but then he was the one who controlled the budget now. 'Set up those meetings with the hospital staff for tomorrow. I'll sanction overtime on this if you want it, but don't stay too late.'

Cadwallader met him at the reception desk, the admin staff having knocked off for the day. McLean followed the pathologist through the darkened mortuary towards the main examination theatre, noting the quietness of the place. It wasn't exactly loud at the best of times, but now it felt like someone had dropped a blanket over them, muffling even the squeak of his shoes on the polished linoleum floor.

'I hope this is important, Angus. Emma's not going to be best pleased if I don't make it home before eight.'

'Tracy too,' Cadwallader said. 'But I think you'll find this is as good an excuse as they come.'

They reached the examination theatre, and McLean saw that the table was empty, cleaned down and shiny under the artificial light. All the instruments of the pathologist's trade had been tidied away, and the counter that ran the length of one wall was clear. Even the screens used to show X-rays were dark.

'Your man Matthew Seaton. I wasn't going to do him till tomorrow.' Cadwallader led him past the table and across to the cold store. Stainless-steel doors hid those unfortunate subjects still awaiting his tender mercies. 'I needed to check something before leaving though, so I just had a quick look.'

The pathologist pulled open one door, slid out the shelf within to reveal the naked form of a dead man. McLean knew it was Matthew Seaton because Cadwallader had told him. He only vaguely remembered the man from his interview, but even so the cadaver laid out in front of him was not what he might have expected.

'How is this possible?'

'Do you know, those were my exact words when I saw this?' The pathologist walked over to a nearby table and pulled a pair of latex gloves from an open box, snapping them on with a skill born of considerable practice. Returning to the body on its shelf, he lifted up one arm, turning it so that the hand splayed open, palm up.

'I saw this man when he came in – what? – six hours ago? That was less than eighteen hours after he'd been declared dead, and he was as pale as you'd expect someone born and raised in the Home Counties to be. He's been in this drawer all the time, and now he looks like this.'

Cadwallader laid the arm back down again, unrolling the white rubberised sheet that had partially covered Matthew Seaton's naked body. His skin had taken on the colour of a beeswax candle, and the same unhealthy sheen. When the pathologist pressed gently on the man's chest, the indentations made by his fingers remained in place as if he were made of some child's moulding clay, not dead flesh and bone.

'Exactly the same as Maurice Jennings, and the two wee girls.' McLean said the words out loud, even though Cadwallader already knew and Seaton was past caring. 'Well, that complicates things.'

43

'You really should have had something to eat you know, Tony. Your stomach sounds like an old man who's lost his dentures.'

McLean glanced swiftly sideways at the passenger seat of his Alfa, catching Emma's smile in the glare of oncoming car head-lights. He would have liked time to eat something, since breakfast had been considerably more than twelve hours ago, and toastily meagre with it.

'There wasn't time,' he said.

'And whose fault is that? Really. You're your own worst enemy sometimes.'

'Rose might have something.' He concentrated for a while on navigating the snarl-up of traffic at the end of North Bridge. The sooner all the building work was done to replace New St Andrew's House with yet more shopping malls the better. 'And if she doesn't, there's a great little chipper I used to go to at the bottom of Leith Walk.'

Emma said nothing to that, but McLean could sense the rolling of her eyes even as he kept his own on the road. He'd managed to get home before eight, as promised, but only by a couple of minutes. That had left no time for anything other than wait for her to grab her coat, lock the house and climb back into the car. She'd not said much during the journey across town, but even he couldn't blame the low gurgling noise on the Alfa's V6 engine for long.

'Thank you for agreeing to do this,' he said as he drove slowly along the street, looking for a parking space. As if anticipating his arrival, a van pulled out just ahead of him, leaving a gap more than big enough.

'It's OK. Rose helped me, so it seems only fair I help her back. And, besides, Rahel's nice. Don't think I could go through half the things she has and still be sane.'

Car parked, they both climbed out into the cold night air. McLean looked up at the clouds overhead, low and thick and threatening more snow. It clung to the rough stone of the walls, clumped in slushy piles where the traffic had thrown it to the kerbside. Some of the cars here hadn't moved in days, if the thick layer of white on top of them was anything to go by.

'Besides' – Emma's words dragged his attention back to the reason they were there – 'you're never going to stop working all the hours, so if I want to see you I'm going to have to join in, right?'

She smiled as she spoke, and her voice was light, cheerful even. But McLean couldn't help wondering if there wasn't a bitter truth in her joking.

'I'm trying my best, Em. But you know what it's like.'

She shrugged. 'Aye, I do. Wouldn't stick around if I didn't now, would I? Come on. Let's find Rose's place quickly. It's bloody freezing out here.'

Rose's place turned out to be directly across the road from where they had parked. McLean couldn't pretend to be surprised by that, although the house he saw was not at all what he'd been expecting. He'd been there before, of course, but only ever entered from Leith Walk itself, which actually presented the rear of the house, further obscured by the later addition of shops. He'd only seen a couple of rooms that Rose used for her medium and tarot-reading work too. Coming in from the front showed a far more substantial stone-built mid-terrace property, not much smaller than his own home. The city was full of these vast houses, built hundreds of years ago by wealthy merchants, their extensive gardens long since swallowed up by later development. Leith had been a prosperous port well before Glasgow grew into the city of Empire through its trade in sugar, tobacco and slaves, and that wealth showed in the buildings that remained, even if most of them had been subdivided or turned over to offices.

Rahel met them at the door, opening it almost before McLean had pulled the old brass knob that jangled a slow bell somewhere deep within. She looked different, and it took him a while to realise that this was because she was wearing a long skirt and a pullover that might have been fashionable a decade before she was born.

'You came. Is good.' She stood to one side, letting them both into a wide parlour, closed the door behind them and then enveloped Emma in a warm hug, as if they were old friends reunited after years apart. McLean stood awkwardly to one side until they'd finished.

'Rose is here, I take it?'

'Yes. I show you the way.' Rahel led them through into a large hall, stairs climbing up to two sets of landings underneath a wide glass cupola skylight. Lamps in sconces on the walls cast more shadow than light, and the overwhelming smell was of cat. McLean counted at least a dozen, staring at him from various vantage points as he and Emma followed the young woman up to the first floor. They entered what was undoubtedly a large sitting room, although it was so packed full of what could only be described as stuff that it was hard to tell just how large.

'Tony, Emma. You came. How wonderful.' Madame Rose

would never leap or spring, but nevertheless she stood up with impressive alacrity and crossed the room to greet them. Emma got another hug, McLean was happy enough with a handshake.

'We did,' he said, then noticed the young girl Nala sitting cross-legged on a Persian rug in one of the few areas of clear floor in the room, not far from a fireplace crackling with a real wood fire. 'I'm not so sure this is a good idea though.'

'Pish and tosh, Tony. I know what the rules and regulations say. You have to have meetings with Social Services, set up an interview plan, submit it in triplicate, blah, blah, blah. Or, you and I and Rahel here can ask wee Nala to tell us what she saw.'

Hearing her name, the girl gazed up at Madame Rose and smiled. McLean was fairly sure that was the first time he'd seen her look anything other than scared.

'It's all for a good reason, Rose. I can't use anything she says in court against the people who were after her, or the people who hurt her mother. If word gets out I've spoken to her like this, then any case against them will collapse before it gets anywhere near a court. And I'll likely be out of a job too.'

'And if you drag her into the station, or back to that care home, and set up an interview the way you're supposed to, she'll tell you nothing.'

'Aye, I know. Which is the only reason I'm here.'

Madame Rose raised an eyebrow. 'The only reason?' She dismissed the question with a shake of her blue-rinsed hair. 'It's no matter. Shall we get started? Or would you like a cup of tea first?'

After an hour, McLean was glad he'd accepted Madame Rose's offer of tea. He'd been starving anyway, and the medium didn't seem to mind him helping himself to more of her very fine chocolate cake than was perhaps polite. Watching him eat seemed to put Nala at ease, too, which gave him a good excuse. It wasn't easy coaxing any kind of a story out of the young girl though.

Her grasp of English was poor, and her native Aramaic not much better. Instead, she communicated in a strange hybrid that Rahel translated for them as best she could, and slowly, piece by piece, the dreadful tale began to emerge.

'We came here when the war destroyed our town,' Rahel explained after Nala had fallen silent again. 'There were lots of us, to start with, but we were split up into smaller groups. Sometimes we would be locked away in a house for days, waiting for the right time to move on to the next place. That was when the men started to take interest in Akka.'

'Akka. Mamma,' Nala chipped in, then went back to her drawing. Rose had given her a sketch pad and a box of crayons in the hope that she might use them to help illustrate her story, but so far she had only covered page after page with random coloured scrawls even a trained child psychologist would find a challenge to interpret.

'These men. They were the ones arranging your transport here, I take it?' McLean recalled Mrs Saifre's report. Right now Jo Dexter would be prepping for multiple raids across the city. With a little luck, the entire operation would be shut down. But what would rise up in its place? Something always did.

Rahel's face darkened, her green eyes narrowed in anger. For a moment McLean feared she might even spit on the floor, but she stopped herself, uttering some word he didn't understand but which was clearly the foulest of insults.

'I call them men, but they are worse than animals. Take what they want and kill you if you try to stop them.'

'And one of them is . . .' McLean nodded in Nala's direction, not really wanting to voice the accusation in front of the girl.

'I think is not likely.' Rahel looked at her niece, who had bent down close to the paper and was hard at work on something that took all of her attention.

'Why do you say that?'

'She is not like them. She is like her mother. Like my mother before . . .' Rahel shook her head. 'No. Little Nala came more than nine months after the journey. Her father is here.'

'Any idea who he might be?' McLean knew enough about the work Akka had been put to once she'd arrived in Edinburgh to understand that the girl's father could be almost anyone. How many men had she been sold to? Had she been given any kind of protection?

'I not know. I barely see Akka for years. Just hear things, you know? And sometimes men would bring Nala to us. Tell us to look after her. If we were lucky they even gave money to help. Maybe some food. But we are not lucky people.'

'How did you end up at the sandwich factory?' McLean asked, trying to find a different angle into a tricky subject. He needed to find the people Rahel had been living with, anyone who knew about the two dead girls. He also knew that trying to round up the refugees and illegal immigrants living in squats and slum tenements around the city would only drive them deeper underground. This was his best chance at cracking an impossible case, so no pressure then.

'Akka got me papers. One time, when I had to look after Nala for many weeks. The men gave them to me. Told me to go see Mr Boag.' Rahel managed to make the name sound like a curse, which in a way it was. 'It is hard work there, and very bad pay. Always they threaten us. Keep working or you go to the detention centre. Do not complain or we will tell police where you are.'

Police. McLean was all too aware in that one word how wide the gulf was between him and this young woman. 'What about Billy? Did he not help you?'

'Billy?' Rahel smiled. 'Billy is sweet, but he not know how we are treated. How we live. How we struggle to survive.'

'He knew about Nala though. That's how I found out in the first place.'

Rahel's smile hardened into a scowl. 'He should not have done that. Learning to speak our language. Listening in on us like a spy.'

'He likes you, Rahel. That's why he did it. To impress you.' Rose spoke the words, more effectively putting the young woman back at ease than if McLean had done so. He needed to tread a fine line to get useful information out of her, finer still to find out anything from Nala.

'Your people, Rahel. The ones you came over from Syria with. Are they all still in Edinburgh? Do they all work at the sandwich factory?'

Rahel's head drooped, her chin almost to her chest. 'Not many have papers. They find work where they can. Some have died. Is not easy in the winter when you have no place to live.'

McLean recalled the hastily abandoned camp site in the Hermitage, snow on the ground, thinner where the makeshift tents had been removed. How could these people not reach out for help? What was it that kept them so terrified of the authorities? Did they really believe they'd be sent back to a war zone? Clearly they did.

'I'm sorry,' he said. 'It shouldn't be like this. You fled a war, you should be welcomed, given shelter, and instead you end up being exploited by the likes of Boag, and the scum who beat up your sister.'

He'd not meant to sound quite so angry. Sitting next to him on Madame Rose's ancient sofa, Emma reached out and laid a hand softly on his forearm. He could feel the warmth of her touch, an anchor against the rising frustration.

'I need to know where they are, Rahel. I need to speak to them and find out who's doing this. Who killed those two wee girls and why. If we can't track them down and put a stop to it, then more people are going to die.'

Rahel looked down at her hands, over to the fireplace, at Madame Rose and down at Nala. Anywhere but at McLean. He gave her the silence and time she needed. He knew better than to force the point any more than he already had, even as the urge to be getting on with things, moving forward, gnawed at him like an empty stomach. For a long while it was as if the world held its breath, just the gentle crackling of flames in the fire, the distant, monotonous tock of an old clock. Then, finally, Rahel shoved her hands into her lap, looked McLean straight in the eye and opened her mouth to speak.

'Affit.' Nala interrupted her, surprising all of them as she tore the page out of her sketchbook and held it up for them to see. 'Affit. Look.'

McLean half stood, then got down onto his knees and reached out a hand towards the paper. Nala looked at him suspiciously for a moment and then handed it over. The picture she had drawn was naive, as might be expected from a child of her years. Even so, he could easily understand the scene. A tall, narrow building, more like a tower than a house except that it had five sets of windows for five storeys. A set of steps leading up to the first floor from the road. Standing in front of it were the stick figures of two men, slightly apart but hands held out to shake. One was pale-faced, his top half a blaze of yellow with red dots that was a passable rendition of an overly flamboyant shirt McLean had seen recently. Peter Winterthorne's hair was greyer than Nala had coloured it, but then she had only the crayons Madame Rose had given her to work with.

The other figure stood taller than the old man, his body a mess of black scrawl that McLean took to be a long cloak. More black spiked out from his chin and cheeks, sprouting from the top of his round head in a childish rendition of a scraggly beard and hair, but it was his glowing red eyes that left a chill in the pit of his stomach.

'Affit?' McLean asked the little girl as he pointed at the demonic figure in the drawing.

'Affit.' Nala smiled, and nodded enthusiastically, then said something in her native tongue to Rahel. She let out a quiet gasp, and covered her mouth with one hand.

'I think she means afrit, or demon.' Madame Rose leaned forward in her chair and plucked the picture from McLean's unresisting fingers. She peered at the image, then tugged at a slim chain around her neck to fetch a pair of half-moon spectacles from the depths of her cashmere jumper. 'Otherwise known as a djinn or genie.'

44

Darkness painted the glass window wall of his office black as McLean sat at his desk early the next morning. Nala had presented him with her picture with all the seriousness of a young child. Now he stared at it, laid out in front of him, deep in thought. That the grey-haired man was Peter Winterthorne he had no doubt, which raised the question, who was the other figure? Did the old man know whoever was responsible for killing the wee girls and Maurice Jennings? Or was this just the wild imaginings of a five-year-old, traumatised by the kind of upbringing McLean couldn't even begin to contemplate? And where did Sheila Begbie fit into it all? She'd sworn that she'd never seen Nala before, or either of the other two girls. She could have been lying, but then why call him when she found Nala hiding in her office?

'Thought I saw your car out back. You got a minute, sir?'

McLean dragged his gaze away from the picture to see Grumpy Bob standing in the doorway, clutching a suspicious brown folder under one arm. He stepped into the room and slid the folder onto the desk. 'Going through the archives, looking at cold cases with Dagwood. Trying to find something that might tie in with your wee girls. We stumbled across this one. Not sure why it's not been put on the system, except, well . . .'

McLean turned Nala's picture face down, took the folder and flipped it open. The dense text of an old-style case report blurred his vision. 'You want to give me the executive summary?'

Grumpy Bob shrugged. 'Of course. There any coffee in that machine of yours?' He walked over to the little counter at the far side of the office and poured himself a mug from the freshly brewed pot. McLean wasn't quite sure how he felt about having a coffee maker in his office; it struck him as the sort of unnecessary perk that only served to emphasise the divide between ranks. He couldn't deny that it was a lot more convenient than walking all the way to the canteen, and a lot more palatable than the vending machine one floor down. Nobody ever brought him cake, though.

'Twenty-five years ago, there were a number of unexplained deaths in the city over a couple of months of winter. Don't know if you remember it, sir. Would've been before you joined up, I think, but it was a cold one, and it lasted almost through to May. There was still snow in parts of the Pentlands in June.'

'The unexplained deaths, Bob? The wee girls?' McLean tried to get the detective sergeant back on track before he went full meteorologist on him.

'Right enough. It's all in there.' Grumpy Bob waved at the report with his free hand. 'Three young lads from Eastern Europe died. They'd been out Tayside way picking fruit in the summer, decided to stay when all their friends shipped back home.'

'Twenty-five years ago?' McLean racked his brain for memories of what he'd been up to then, found it harder to remember than he would have liked. 'Were they even coming from Eastern Europe then? I thought the Berlin Wall didn't collapse until eighty-nine . . . oh.'

'Aye, life does that sometimes.' Grumpy Bob sat back down again and slurped his coffee. 'Germany unified at the end of ninety, and that was more than twenty-five years ago.'

'Christ, it was, wasn't it? When did we get so old, Bob?'

'Don't look at me, sir. I'm retiring at the end of the month, remember?'

'OK, so these three young men. What's their story?'

'They were all living in a hostel in Bruntsfield, down towards Lochrin Basin. This was back before they closed the railway marshalling yards, knocked down all the old warehouses and tried to make it posh, mind. Nobody really paid much attention when they died. Three separate incidents, six weeks apart. Didn't see any connection other than they were foreign. Probably why nobody much cared. The only thing that linked them was the hostel. That and what they all died from.'

'Which was?' McLean knew that Grumpy Bob would get to the point eventually, but he also knew there wasn't much time left before the morning briefing. Best to chivvy him along.

'It's in the report there. Internal organ failure. The pathologist reckoned they'd all done some new kind of drug. Funny thing is, it made their skin go all waxy and yellow. Ring any bells?'

McLean opened the folder again, leafing through the pages until he found the pathology reports. Not his grandmother this time, she'd have been close to retirement twenty-five years ago, if not actually gone. Not Cadwallader either, even though he would have started working at the City Mortuary by then. Someone called Doctor Mercer had examined all three dead bodies and declared them as probable drug overdoses, substance unknown.

'Never heard of this pathologist. I'll speak to Angus, see if he remembers them.' He flicked back a couple of pages. 'The hostel. I don't suppose it's still there.'

Grumpy Bob shook his head. 'Whole street's gone, sir. Doubt the bloke who ran it would still be around either. He was in his sixties then.'

McLean remembered his conversation with Madame Jasmina.

The old fortune teller speaking of when last the circus had visited. Twenty-five years ago, the early nineties.

'You ever find out more about those girls that went missing? Must have been round about the same time.' He'd asked them to look into the symbols carved into the stone wall at the Hermitage, too, now he thought about it.

'That's what brought this up. And no, we didn't. The files on the two who weren't found are still open, but nobody's looked into them in decades.'

'And the third one? The one who ran away to the circus?'

'Ishbel Monroe.' Grumpy Bob leaned forward and teased the report away from where McLean had laid it out in front of himself, then flicked the pages until he found the one he was looking for. 'Fifteen years old. She'd run away from a care home. Spent all her life in and out of fostering. Ended up in a place out Burdiehouse way.'

'Fenton House?'

'That's the one.' Grumpy Bob closed the folder and put it back on the desk. 'You know it?'

'I was there just yesterday. If it was anything back then like it is now, I'm not surprised she ran. Do we know where she is now?'

Grumpy Bob shrugged. 'She turned sixteen a month after they picked her up. State no longer had any responsibility for her. I've no idea where she went. Maybe back to the circus?'

McLean glanced at his watch; only a few minutes before he needed to be at the morning briefing, and now his mind was full of this new information. Too many threads, not enough connections. Just the nagging feeling that it was all linked together, somehow. He stood up, reaching reflexively for the folder he'd been reading before Grumpy Bob interrupted him. It wasn't important enough to take with him, and Nala's picture he was keeping to himself. At least for now.

'Make a few calls will you, Bob? See if you can't find her, eh?'

★ ★ ★

'As most of you will already have seen, some of our friends in the Fourth Estate have got it into their heads there's a lethal contagious disease threatening the city.'

McLean sat at the top table, looking out across the major-incident room and a colourful collection of plain-clothes and uniformed officers as the deputy chief constable ended the morning briefing with his customary summary and pep talk. It was one of those frustrating but necessary rituals he had learned the hard way not to try and hurry along or interrupt. Even so, he struggled not to fidget with impatience listening to the man. There was so much to do.

'We'll be having a full press conference in time for the lunch-time bulletins, of course. Drafting in some experts from the university to try and explain the situation. But in the meantime I can't emphasise how important it is that none of you speak to anyone about this case who isn't already in this room. If you're asked anything, refer it up to your superiors. Detective Super-intendent McIntyre will coordinate the media response, and I'm here for the duration too. If you've any worry, even the slightest concern that you might be saying something out of turn, then say nothing. OK?'

A dull murmur of assent rumbled around the room like the threat of a distant storm. For a moment McLean thought Robinson was going to do the full unimpressed teacher routine and press for a more enthusiastic response, but instead he simply stared out over everyone's heads for a moment before dismissing them all with 'Good, then get to it, people.'

McLean stood up as soon as the DCC had finished speaking, but there was no escaping the room in a hurry.

'No sign of Ritchie?' Robinson asked, gazing out over the room. There weren't anything like as many officers present as might have been expected for a major incident.

'She went out with Jo Dexter and the Vice team first thing, sir. That information your friend Mrs Saifre gave us had to be acted on quickly. Reckon we'll be dealing with the fallout for a while.'

'She's no friend of mine, McLean. Bloody nuisance if you ask me, but we can't ignore her. Too powerful, too well connected.'

'And up to something, too. She'll have known full well what we'd do with her information, mark my words. This isn't anything like the end of it.'

'How do you mean?' Robinson asked.

'Well think about it, sir. Sexual Crimes and the immigration team have been working for months on these sex traffickers, the pop-up brothels, and all the other rackets that go along with them. That report forced their hand. They've had to mount a dozen raids simultaneously. Mistakes are bound to happen when we do that, and people who ought to be locked up are going to slip through our fingers. And it's going to make a big hole in the city's sex industry.'

'That's a good thing, surely?'

'Aye, it is. But someone always finds a way to fill the vacuum, don't they. We'll have more girls like Akka Nour trafficked in before the week's out. New faces running the same show. And we won't know who they are. Not for a while, anyway.'

The DCC pinched the bridge of his nose, squeezed his eyes tight shut for a moment. 'Did anyone ever tell you you're a cynical bastard, McLean?'

'Maybe once or twice. Doesn't change the fact I'm right though. Saifre's sown chaos and my bet is it'll be her who most benefits from that.'

'What's next, then? Are we any closer to finding out who killed those wee girls? Do we even have a plan to catch whoever killed them?'

McLean chose to ignore the sarcasm in Robinson's voice. 'As

it happens, we do, sir. And there's a number of people I need to speak to quite urgently. So if we're done here . . .'

The DCC let out a weary sigh. 'You're not going to get a sergeant to do it, are you, McLean.' It wasn't a question. 'Go on then. Get it done. But I want you back here for the press conference, OK? And find me a bone I can throw them so they don't rip us all to shreds.'

45

The Sexual Crimes Unit having borrowed almost all of his team for their early-morning raids, McLean decided it would be just as easy for him to go and speak to Peter Winterthorne himself. He hadn't made it far down towards the Royal Mile when a familiar-looking, low-slung coupé slowed and pulled into the kerb alongside him. He was all for ignoring it, but a sharp toot on the horn changed his mind. With luck, nobody from the station would be looking this way, anyway, and it would be warmer being driven to the office of House the Refugees than walking.

'Hope you liked the positive angle I wrote on youse lot in the *Tribune* this morning,' Jo Dalgliesh said as he dropped down into the passenger seat. 'That's one you owe me, I reckon, after what those numpties at the tabloids are printing.'

McLean rubbed his hands together and blew on them, as much to give himself time to think as for the cold. 'You're all heart, Dalgliesh,' he said eventually, adding, 'Thank you' when she continued to scowl at him.

'Seatbelt.' She scowled some more, and nodded her head towards the door pillar. McLean did as he was told, and only once he was properly clamped in did she indicate and pull back into the traffic. 'Where you headed?'

'If I'd known you were doing a taxi service I'd have called. I was just going to the Royal Mile. Not far.'

'House the Refugees, I take it?'

'I'll not bother asking how you know that.'

'It's where you found that wee girl, right enough. Reckon I might be interested in having a word with Sheila MacNeil Begbie myself.'

McLean was used to Dalgliesh's offhand way of suggesting she knew more about something than he did. It had never occurred to him to ask if the woman running the refugee charity had a middle name, although someone must have written it down when she had given a formal statement. What were the chances the reporter had seen a copy of that? A lot higher than he would have liked.

'Did you have a point? Or are you just being kind?'

Dalgliesh coasted towards some traffic lights, then stood on her brakes when the car in front stopped the second they switched to amber. 'What the fuck're you playing at, idiot? Could have got a bus through there.' She made a rude gesture through the windscreen at the oblivious driver, then turned to McLean. 'Omar Mared. Some ghost chase you sent me on there, Detective Chief Inspector.'

'You didn't manage to find anything, then? Not even Ozzy Jones?'

'Sweet Fanny Adams.' Dalgliesh pulled out her electronic cigarette and shoved it into her mouth, chewing at the plastic for a noisy few seconds before taking it out and shoving it in her pocket again. 'But in an interesting way.'

'How so?' McLean asked, but then the lights changed back to green and for a while Dalgliesh was too busy driving right up the bumper of the car in front to answer.

'Most folk I asked, the answer was always the same. A shrug, a "fuck knows" maybe. Some of them told me to piss off and mind my own business, but they didn't act like they knew and weren't telling.'

'So the name's a bust then. I got fed bad intel.'

'No, no, no. Not so fast, Tony. I don't give up that easy. Especially not if you've been given the name by my boss.'

'Your boss?' McLean frowned. 'I thought the Tribune Group was owned by that Arab sheik. Mohammed Bin something or other.'

'Old news. He sold out to the Saifre Corporation last year.' Dalgliesh swore under her breath, then overtook the car in front as it put its indicator on in the hope a parking space might materialise. She gave the horn a long blast and raised an angry single finger as she shot past, narrowly missing a taxi coming the other way.

'Remind me not to accept a lift from you ever again.'

'Och, you're a wee feartie.'

'Maybe, but I was also in a nasty car crash a year ago. Don't want to be making a habit of it. So, Omar Mared then?'

'Aye, fair enough. It wasn't easy, and your pals in Vice raiding every knocking shop in toon isn't going to help me follow it up either.' Dalgliesh slowed down as she turned the car onto the cobbles of the Royal Mile. They weren't more than a hundred yards from House the Refugees now. 'From what I've found out so far he's a cypher, your man Ozzy. Ha! Cypher, Saifre. See, I only just thought of that.'

'How do you mean, a cypher? He doesn't exist?'

'Well, aye, he exists. But he's more than one man. And no one. You seen that film *The Usual Suspects*, aye?'

McLean couldn't help noticing how Dalgliesh managed to give the word "film" at least two syllables, but he got the reference too. 'Keyser Söze?'

'That's the chappie. Reputation for being a ruthless bastard, but doesn't actually exist. Just stories to keep the local criminals in line.'

'Only it's not criminals with Omar Mared. It's immigrants. Illegal or otherwise.'

'Oh, definitely illegal. Desperate, poor like a Glasgow slum in the fifties, exploited to fuck and back. These people are broken, Tony. They've fallen through the cracks into some dark and shitty underworld and we just go about our lives in blissful ignorance.'

Dalgliesh had pulled into the side of the road, just a few paces up the hill from their destination, but she kept the engine running, indicator clicking away quietly in the background. She stared out of the window as she spoke.

'Seriously, Tony. The stuff I dug up chasing down that name until I found someone who really reacted to it. That's some story. Might even be my retirement fund.'

'But Omar Mared doesn't exist. He's a made-up person used to scare these refugees into doing what they're told.'

'That and more. He's a stone-cold killer according to some. Runs the sort of brothels where you can get anything you want provided your money's good enough. There was this one old Armenian bloke told me Mared runs boats from Libya across the Med. Sank a couple on purpose when the Italian navy was closing in, so they'd go after the survivors and he could escape. Pretty much every shitty thing that's happened to anyone who's fled a war and ended up here? It's all Omar fucking Mared's doing.'

McLean unclipped his seatbelt, but didn't open the door. That Mared wasn't an actual person didn't really surprise him; if he had been then Saifre would just have made him disappear. Or handed him over to the police if that suited her twisted agenda. He was in no doubt that either action was well within her power. But she had sent him in search of the man, so she must have wanted something to come out of his investigations. The question was what?

'You going to speak to Begbie then?' he asked.

Dalgliesh frowned at him. 'I thought you were.'

'I was, but it can wait. I mostly wanted to speak to Peter Winterthorne.' He nodded in the vague direction of the building.

'Winterthorne?' Dalgliesh's frown turned to an expression of puzzlement. 'As in Loopy Doo and the Swinging Sixties?'

'That's the chap. You know him?'

'Aye, well, no. Thought he was deid.'

McLean tried the door before buzzing the intercom, surprised to find it unlocked. The hall beyond was empty, and a note taped to the glass door to House the Refugees read 'Back in five minutes'. Given that he and Dalgliesh had stared at the building for longer than that without seeing anyone come out, McLean suspected it was an optimistic estimate at best.

'You still want to speak to Begbie?' he asked as the reporter pushed in behind him and dragged her feet over the doormat. 'Only it looks like she's not here.'

'She can wait. I'd no mind a wee chat wi' Winterthorne though. Might be a story there to make the trip worth my while.'

'Well, you'll have to wait. This is police business. I can't have you tagging along and making life awkward.'

'Aye, right. He's up here, is he?' Dalgliesh stepped across the narrow hallway and pushed at the door that opened onto the stairs. McLean expected it to be locked, but it swung open as readily as the one onto the street. Before he could stop her, the reporter was thumping up to the first floor.

'Mr Winterthorne? Are you there?' She stopped on the landing, breathing more heavily than McLean would have expected. Her hand went to her jacket pocket and the electronic cigarette she never seemed to actually smoke. When she saw him looking, she stopped.

'First floor's office space for the charity. Least, that's what I was told.' McLean tried the first of two doors that led off the

307

landing, opening it up onto a dusty, empty room lit only by the light filtering in through the grubby window to the front of the building. He could tell just by sniffing that nobody had been in there for a while. Closing it up, he tried the next door, revealing a small bathroom to the rear. Again, it was empty and smelled of disuse. Lifting the toilet seat revealed a series of rings in the bowl where the water had slowly evaporated away. Nobody had flushed any time recently.

'Winterthorne lives on the top two floors,' McLean said as he stepped past Dalgliesh and onto the next flight of stairs. She looked at him as if he'd insulted her entire family, still wheezing slightly.

'Aye, go on then. I'll be up in a minute.'

'You all right?'

'Not been the same since that bloody cake.' She thumped at her chest with a weak fist, coughed a little, making an unpleasantly wet and gurgling sound. 'Serve me right for being so greedy.'

A few years ago, McLean might have made a crude joke about her misfortune, but that was before she'd saved his life from a knife-wielding religious maniac. And, of course, the cake that had poisoned her had been meant for him. It was a wonder she still stuck around.

'Well, take your time, OK? I'll warn him you're coming.'

He didn't bother stopping on the next two landings. It was most likely Winterthorne would be on the top floor, and if he wasn't, then he'd meet Dalgliesh going down. McLean couldn't help noticing the slightly damp and musty smell to the air as he climbed though. It hadn't been there the last time he'd visited, with DC Harrison, but now the whole building felt unused, empty. It was as if it had been closed up and left many years ago, like the basement with its collection of long-discarded furniture.

'Mr Winterthorne? Are you in there?' He knocked on the door that opened onto the large living room. Slightly ajar, it nudged further open at his touch. Straining his ears, McLean could hear nothing from inside, just the omnipresent dull roar of the city beyond the grimy windows. He pushed the door open and stepped in.

The room was much the same as he remembered it from before. Up this high, the neighbouring buildings didn't cast so much of a shadow as they did for the lower floors, which meant the room was light and airy. It was also as cold as the grave. The gas fire was unlit, damp glistening on the fire surround and hearthstone. The saggy old leather armchair Winterthorne had sat in was empty, as indeed was the whole room. McLean cast his eyes over the collection of ancient artefacts, but he couldn't see any difference from when he and Harrison had visited before. He walked over to the window and looked down onto the Royal Mile, half expecting to see the old man legging it up the road. There were few enough people out in the cold weather, and none of them fitted his description.

He met Dalgliesh coming up the stairs as he went down. 'Nobody home.'

The reporter nodded. 'Not upstairs?'

'No. And the place feels . . . I don't know. Empty. Almost like nobody's been here for years. But I was here just a few days ago.'

'He's no' in either of these two rooms.' Dalgliesh pointed at one of the doors on the landing. 'No' downstairs either. Odd that, leaving the doors unlocked for anyone to wander in.'

'What about the office? Did you try the door?' McLean trotted back down the stairs to the main entrance hall, leaving the breathless Dalgliesh behind him. The note was still taped to the glass, and when he tried the handle, the door was locked. Peering in, he couldn't see any sign of life. Although the door at the back that led through to the room where they'd found Nala hiding stood slightly open, no lights were on.

'Curiouser and curiouser, said Alice.'

McLean turned to find Dalgliesh standing just behind him and almost jumped in alarm. He'd not heard her on the stairs, hadn't heard anything as he'd strained to see through the glass. And then a noise at the front door had them both looking round like guilty schoolkids. It swung open, and two figures stumbled in from the cold outside, one supporting the other.

Of all the people who might have entered the building, these two had the most right. It was still a surprise to see Sheila Begbie struggling to hold up Peter Winterthorne.

46

'Chief Inspector? Thank God. Help me, please.' Begbie took a step forward, and McLean saw that the man she was holding upright was unconscious, his head lolling to one side. He took a quick couple of steps across the hall and grabbed Peter Winterthorne under the other arm. He was as light as a feather, his face as pale as the snow still pasted across the Pentland Hills to the south of the city. For a moment, McLean thought he might even be dead, but then he let out a low moan of pain.

'What happened?' he asked, as Begbie shoved keys in the lock and opened the door to the office.

'Bring him in, quickly.' She waved him towards her, then pointed at one of the low reception chairs in the bay window. 'I found him outside in the street. Looks like he collapsed, poor dear.'

McLean set the old man down in the chair. Winterthorne was dressed in a long, dark overcoat, slightly threadbare and buttoned up to his neck against the weather. His lank grey hair made him look like a scarecrow. McLean put a finger to the pale skin under his jaw, feeling for a pulse. Faint, but steady, he would still need medical attention and fast.

'Call an ambulance, will you? We need to get him to hospital.'

There was no response. McLean turned to see why, and

found Begbie standing halfway between the door and the large desk towards the back of the room. It was almost as if someone had flicked a switch and turned her off, so total was her paralysis. He'd seen it before when people reacted on instinct to a crisis, then the world caught up with them.

'Ms Begbie.' He left Winterthorne sprawled on the chair and crossed over to the woman, taking his mobile phone out at the same time.

'I . . . I found him out there.' She shook her head slowly, as if trying to remember what she'd been doing. 'He was . . .'

'It's fine. I've got this.' McLean reached out and placed a hand gently on her arm. The contact sent a shudder through her, but Begbie seemed to rally. She stood a little straighter, looked around as if unsure exactly how she'd ended up in the room, then saw Dalgliesh standing in the doorway.

'Who are you?'

The reporter extended a hand and put on her best fake smile. The thought flitted across McLean's mind that she might have been a vampire, unable to enter until invited.

'Jo Dalgliesh. I work for the *Edinburgh Tribune*.'

If Sheila Begbie had been shell-shocked from finding Winterthorne outside, she rallied quickly at the mention of the city's less reputable daily newspaper. McLean could almost feel the heat radiating off her.

'What do you want?' Four short words, each loaded with anger.

'Well, I've been looking into the plight of refugees and asylum seekers in the city and further afield. Planning on writing up a series of articles about how badly they're being exploited. Not just the folk who bring them over, but the dodgy employers who use them as virtual slave labour. You know some of them are so poor they're living rough outside in makeshift camps? In this winter?'

McLean tuned out. He'd heard Dalgliesh when she was turning on the charm before. From the way Begbie's face softened, the reporter knew exactly the right buttons to press. He was more concerned with Winterthorne. Staring at his phone, he began to tap at the screen to call up Control and arrange an ambulance, but he was stopped by a weak hand on his arm.

'No . . . No doctors. Please.'

McLean stared at the hand, then along the arm and into the face of Peter Winterthorne. He looked close to death, a sallow texture to his skin and clammy sweat matting his hair, beading his forehead. And yet his eyes burned with an urgency hard to ignore.

'You need medical help.'

'I'm OK. Just took a wee turn, is all.' Winterthorne tried to sit up, his grip on McLean's arm tightening for a moment before it relaxed and he fell back into the chair exhausted, his words fading to a whisper as he passed out again. 'Sheila can look after me. She always does. Just, no doctors, aye? They won't understand.'

'Ambulance is on its way, shouldn't be long.' McLean slipped his phone back into his pocket and checked Winterthorne's pulse for the second time in as many minutes. Beside him, Sheila Begbie wrung her hands together like a fishwife.

'He doesn't like doctors. Always been very insistent about that.'

'Ms Begbie, he's a man approaching, if not already, eighty years old. He's had a nasty fall, and it's not the first time recently either. Someone has to look at him or he could very easily die. Where would you be if that happens?'

Begbie tensed, as if she'd been slapped, then turned away from him to address Dalgliesh. 'Can we maybe talk another time? This is sort of important.'

'Quite understand.' Dalgliesh guddled around in her coat pocket, pulling out a slightly tatty business card which she handed over. 'It's shocking the way we're treating refugees right now, and that's before you even get started on why they're coming here in the first place. I'd like to write a longer piece about it some time.'

'Of course. Happy to help.' Begbie took the card, holding it in both hands as if it might explode.

'You fine walking home, Tony? Only I'm gonnae get a ticket if I leave my car there any longer.' Dalgliesh hooked a thumb in the direction of the road.

'I'll be fine. Thanks.' McLean stood up, tensed for a tweak of pain from his hip that never came. 'And thanks for the info too. Let me know if you find anything else.'

'Make it worth my while, aye?' Dalgliesh gave him a half-hearted wave of the arm, then turned and left.

The door had hardly banged shut behind her when the short 'whoop' of an alarm signalled the arrival of the ambulance. McLean was startled both at how close it was and how quickly it had come. Looking past the unconscious old man, he saw the flashing blue light right outside the window, and a paramedic already climbing the stairs to the front door. In moments, the office was full of activity as Winterthorne was checked once again by more professional hands. He stood back out of the way, all too aware of how small the office was once it began to fill up with paramedics and a stretcher.

At the back of the room, the door through to the kitchen-cum-storage room stood slightly ajar. He'd noticed before, and now McLean took the opportunity of everyone else's distraction to nudge it a bit further and slip inside. It wasn't much changed from the last time he'd seen it, when he and DC Harrison had found Nala here. That was a question he'd still not had a satisfactory answer to: why had she come here? How had she known about the place? It couldn't be a coincidence that the other wee girl, still unclaimed and nameless, had come here too. Both had been fleeing something. Was it too fanciful to think that they were being hunted? That some man was playing the part of an ancient evil spirit in a sick game designed to keep Rahel and her people in line? But why had they come here? What was it about this place that had made them think of it as a sanctuary?

The obvious answer was the charity run by Sheila Begbie. And yet she had claimed never to have seen Nala before, let alone the dead girl found in the basement. And then there was Nala's childish crayon drawing.

'Were you looking for something, Chief Inspector?'

McLean whirled around, the blush at being caught like a naughty schoolboy creeping up his neck even though all he had been doing was staring out of the window without actually seeing anything. Begbie stood in the open doorway, and beyond it he could see Winterthorne, tube in his arm, oxygen mask over his pale face, strapped to the stretcher and being wheeled out by the paramedics.

'No, no.' He shook his head as much to cover his embarrassment as emphasise the point. 'Just getting out of the way. That him off then?'

Begbie gave him a look of deepest suspicion, but stood aside to let him leave the room. 'Aye. I was going to go with them. Just so there's a familiar face when he wakes up, ken?'

'That's very . . .' McLean searched for the right word. '. . . good of you.'

'Well, it's like you said. He's an old man. Never been fond of doctors and hospitals. Not since his accident, anyways. He's always been a good landlord, mind, so it's the least I can do.' Begbie raised both arms to encompass the office and the building above it. 'Have to lock up, though.'

315

'Of course.' McLean took a step towards the exit, then stopped. 'You said "his accident". What accident?'

'Oh, years before my time.' Begbie pulled the door to the storeroom closed behind her, locking it with a key that she pocketed. 'You'll read about it all on the internet, I'd imagine. The band was getting back together, recording an album, rehearsing for a tour. This would've been what? Early nineties? Something like that. Then Pete was in a plane crash. Almost died, so they say. Miracle he didn't. But he was out of action for eighteen months, and the whole tour fell apart. Don't think they even recorded that album either.'

47

'You ever find out more about Peter Winterthorne, Constable?'

McLean hadn't much enjoyed the walk back to the station from the offices of House the Refugees, the snow having set in with renewed vigour almost the moment he'd watched the ambulance pull away from the kerb. For such a short distance, he'd got surprisingly cold, and his overcoat was soaked through.

'The Loopy Doo guy?' DC Harrison looked up from her computer screen, self-consciously flicking a lock of hair out of her eyes. McLean hadn't noticed before, but it was longer than he remembered.

'The same.' He told her about the visit, the old man's collapse and odd request about no doctors. As he did so, she pulled her keyboard towards her and started tapping away, grabbing the mouse occasionally as she searched for information. By the time he'd struggled out of his coat, hung it over the radiator to dry, and walked around the desk, she had a Wikipedia page loaded and was scrolling down too swiftly for him to read.

'Here we go, sir.' Harrison stopped scrolling and stabbed a finger at a dense clump of words, half summarising, half reading aloud. 'Seems as well as a rock guitarist and singer, Peter Winterthorne is an expert on Sumerian history and culture. In

1993 he was the only survivor of an expedition to study the remains of the ancient city of . . . I have no idea how to pronounce that.'

McLean read the word twice. Too many consonants and all in the wrong places. He had no chance of pronouncing it either. His understanding of the geography of the area was more up to date though. 'It's probably not there any more. Most of that area was overrun by ISIS or whatever they call themselves. Apparently anything older than their leader is an affront to something or other and they blow it up. They destroyed half of Palmyra, too.'

Harrison looked at him oddly, but he was used to that.

'Aye, well,' she said. 'The plane came down in a sandstorm somewhere in the desert in north Iraq. It was thought he'd died along with everyone else, but some months later he returned to civilisation claiming a nomadic tribe had rescued him and nursed him back to health.'

McLean peered at the screen, trying to absorb the information Harrison left out. As was always the way with the internet, he had to take what was written with a large pinch of salt. If he had the time, he'd probably have chased up the references and dug deeper into Winterthorne's story. Something about it didn't so much ring false as set off his internal alarms.

'That would certainly explain his odd taste in decor, and his mistrust of doctors,' he said, as he read about the injuries the old man had sustained in the crash. He could scarcely imagine recovering from them with all the technology modern medicine could bring to bear. Stuck in a camp in the middle of the desert being tended by nomads sounded implausible at best.

'Have a word with the hospital, will you? Just keep a check on how he's doing. I wanted to talk to him anyway, so it would be good to know when he's back on his feet.'

'On it, sir.' Harrison reached for the phone. 'Will you be in your office for the rest of the day?'

Something about the casualness of the question suggested to him that she'd been primed to ask it. At a guess it was Jayne McIntyre's subtle way of reminding him where his duties lay. McLean glanced at his watch, aware that the morning had gone and lunchtime was fleeing swiftly into the distance now.

'I'll be back in time for the press conference. I've an appointment with an old friend up at the university first.'

'Tony McLean, good to see you. It's been a while.'

McLean studied the man in front of him as he shook hands, trying to see the young boy he had been. Professor William Charnley, or Gobbo as McLean had known him back in his primary school days, had aged well but he had most definitely aged. The battle between hair and forehead had long since been lost, and he wore not one but two pairs of spectacles. The first perched right on the tip of his nose like a diver on the high board summoning the courage to leap. The second had been shoved up into the greying tufts of his receding hairline. Dressed exactly as you would expect of a professor of ancient history specialising in Middle Eastern culture, he looked at home in his dusty, book-lined office in the heart of Edinburgh University's old campus on George Square.

'Fifteen years, I think. Since the last reunion. Swore I'd never go to another one after that.'

'Was it that long?' Charnley let out a low whistle of surprise, and McLean remembered just how irritating it had been when wee Gobbo had done it too.

'I still get the quarterly magazine, but you know what it's like. Just leaf through it to see if anyone I know's died.'

Charnley grinned, running a hand across his head that served only to dislodge his spare spectacles.

'Oh. That's where they got to.' He folded them carefully, then jammed them into the breast pocket of his jacket alongside a number of plastic biros. 'I must say, your call piqued my interest. Just as well I was working this weekend. It's about one of your cases, I take it? You were some kind of police officer, if memory serves.'

'Detective Chief Inspector, for my sins. And, yes, it's a work-related query I had.' McLean shrugged, unsure whether he should be embarrassed about the fact that he had lived in the same city as one of his old school friends for the best part of five decades and only talked to the man once every couple of years. If that. Being sent away to boarding school in England at the age of six had cut him off from a lot of social interaction, and being raised by his elderly grandmother hadn't helped either. 'I was wondering if you knew anything about Peter Winterthorne.'

Charnley let out another low whistle, then leaned back against his desk and pushed his first pair of spectacles back up his nose. 'Peter. Aye. I know him. Haven't seen him in a while, mind you. He used to lecture a module here on Sumerian language, artefacts and mythology. I think most of his students only turned up because he'd been famous once. Most didn't stay the course either.'

'Dull, was he?'

'Oh, quite the opposite.' Charnley stood up again, walked around his desk and flopped into his chair, indicating with an open hand for McLean to take a seat too. 'Peter's lectures were fascinating. But the stuff he was teaching was way out there on the fringes of theory. And he's very intense when he gets going. Frightens the students off.'

McLean tried to square that with the mild-mannered man he'd seen taken away in an ambulance, the man who had quietly answered his questions in formal interview only a few days earlier. If there had been any great intensity about Peter Winterthorne then, he'd been keeping it well hidden. Apart from his unusual fear of doctors.

320

'What about his work in the Middle East? I heard he was in a plane crash and nearly died.'

'Oh that. Yes. Before my time here, of course. I think I was probably still an undergrad myself when it happened. It was very strange, and very sad.' Charnley wiped at his head again, only this time there were no spectacles to dislodge. 'I mean, it was miraculous that he survived, but we lost three great scholars in that crash. People who would have been in a good position to advise against certain idiotic military adventures in the region, if you get my meaning.'

'You think the crash wasn't an accident then? Someone wanted awkward dissenting voices out of the way?'

Charnley shrugged. 'Who knows? It was a long time ago and we can't exactly snap our fingers and make it all not have happened. More's the pity.' He did just that as if to illustrate the futility of such wishful thinking, the noise dying quickly in the echoless room. 'But there were rumours. Always are. And the desert's not kind to dead bodies. They were hard enough to identify as it was, mummified as I heard it. Skin turned to leather by the heat and the dryness. That's why everyone thought Peter was dead too. They found enough bodies, just couldn't say whose was whose.'

McLean perched himself on the arm of an elderly sofa that formed part of a motley collection arranged in a loose square in front of the desk, no doubt for students and their tutorial groups. He wasn't quite sure why he'd come here to ask about Winterthorne, except that he couldn't talk to Winterthorne himself right now. Something had been bugging him about the old man, and hearing Gobbo talk about him helped narrow it down a bit.

'You said Winterthorne's an expert on artefacts and mythology. What sort of things did he used to lecture about mostly?'

'Oh, definitely the mythology. He has a thing about some of the ancient gods and demons. Atargatis and her afrits were favourites of his. I remember one of my students being quite upset when he cornered her after a lecture and expounded his theories about the origins of the djinn.'

And there it was.

'Djinn, you say?' McLean leaned forward the better to hear.

'Oh yes. Poor old Peter. He's obsessed with them. That's how he survived, you see. At least that's the way he tells it now.'

'I thought it was a nomadic tribe who found him and nursed him back to health. That's the story—'

'In Wikipedia, I know.' Charnley laughed. 'And you should know better than to trust everything you read there, Tony. You're as bad as my students. It's a fine enough place to start, but then you've got to do some work to get to the truth.'

'Which is?'

'Nobody really knows how he survived. Not even Peter. Nobody really knows how bad his injuries were, though I've heard everyone else was pretty badly beaten up. Wikipedia goes with the nomadic tribe story because that's as close to Peter's telling of it as makes any sense. He says he was discovered by a tribe, but they weren't nomads, they were djinn.'

'As in genies. Aladdin. Magic lamp and three wishes?' McLean tried to keep the weary sigh out of his voice as he spoke, but might not have been entirely successful. 'Only I've been hearing that story a lot lately.'

Charnley grimaced. 'Not exactly, no. These are more your actual demons in semi-human form. And their thing's more stealing your life essence than granting wishes.'

'So why did they save him, then? Why not leave him in the desert with all his friends?'

'That's the question, isn't it, Tony? And I've asked him myself. Never really got a clear answer out of him, mind.' Charnley held his hands wide in an eloquent shrug. 'All I know is it's not a subject he likes to talk about, and those who knew him before it happened say he came back a very changed man.'

48

DC Harrison interrupted him munching on something called a nutritious wrap, which he'd picked up in a corner shop on the walk from the university back to the station. McLean looked up from his desk as she stood in the doorway, his mouth full of something that needed a lot more butter or mayonnaise, or probably both, to make it moist enough to swallow. He indicated for her to come in, then carried on chewing. When she walked past the chair in front of his desk, over to the coffee machine, poured a mugful and brought it back to him, he could have cheered. If his teeth hadn't been stuck together by something clearly not intended for actual consumption.

'What's up?' he asked once he'd finally managed to wash down the foul-tasting muck with only slightly less foul-tasting muck that was at least warm and wet.

'Did a bit more digging on Peter Winterthorne, like you asked.'

McLean wasn't aware that he had, but he let it go with a nod for her to continue.

'Hospital have got him under sedation still. He's stable, but very weak. They're not quite sure what caused him to collapse. The doctor I spoke to sounded like he'd rather not have to deal with complications, but I guess they're all overworked. Same as us.'

'Which hospital did they take him to in the end?'

'Western General. He's in the ICU there. At least for now.'

'ICU? I didn't think he was that bad.'

'I don't think they really know what's up with him. They just want to keep him in for observation because of his age. ICU's as good a place to put him as any while they wait for their test results to come back.'

'Test results?'

'Aye. There was something about his blood. Some toxin or other interfering with their normal tests.' Harrison pulled out her notebook and flicked to a page. 'They explained it all, but basically his haemoglobin doesn't work properly. Should really be on a daily dose of pills, but of course he's not seen a doctor or been near a hospital since he came back from the desert. Mad old bugger probably self-medicates. Just like my dad. He can't stand doctors either.'

'So he's likely to be there for a while yet? And he's still unconscious?'

'Yes, sir. Not going to get any answers out of him soon, if that's what you were after.'

McLean stared at the second half of his wrap. It was food, and he was hungry, but even so he couldn't bring himself to eat any more. Instead, he drank his coffee, tasting only the tarriness of it having spent too long sitting on the hotplate after it had been brewed.

'Was that all you found out about him?' he asked after a while.

Harrison flipped a page of her notebook. 'Aye, sir. I followed up on the names he gave us. The folk he was meant to be spending some time with in Perthshire?'

McLean nodded for her to go on, picked at something green poking out of the top of the wrap.

'Tom and Maureen Cartwright. I phoned them, got a fellow

called Martin Dunsford. He was very surprised when I asked about the Cartwrights. Hadn't heard their name in a while.'

'So Winterthorne lied to us about his alibi? Made the whole thing up?'

'Well, not exactly. The Cartwrights lived there. Owned the place since the sixties, apparently. But Tom died fifteen years ago, and Maureen's in an old-people's home in Pitlochry now. She sold the house to Dunsford to pay for her care.'

'Did you speak to her?' McLean knew that Harrison would at least have tried.

'Aye, well. Sort of. I spoke to one of the nurses. Maureen's eighty-three and has senile dementia. She's no family and hasn't had any visitors in months.'

'I want a uniformed officer up at the hospital right away. Twenty-four-hour guard on Winterthorne until he's awake and well enough to be arrested.' McLean picked up the wrap again, then dropped it in the bin. 'Meantime I think we need to have another look at that house of his.'

He'd been here before, of course. It wasn't that long since he and Jo Dalgliesh had climbed to the top floor in search of the man himself, but McLean hadn't been considering Peter Winterthorne as an accessory to murder then. He hadn't been looking for clues that might point to whoever it was had hunted down those two little girls and attacked Maurice Jennings just for interrupting his hunt for a third.

'Are we looking for anything in particular, sir?' Detective Constable Blane struggled to fit his overlarge hands into latex gloves as they stood in the little hallway that opened both onto the offices of House the Refugees and the staircase up to the rest of the building.

'Anything that looks like it doesn't want to be found.' McLean pulled on his own gloves, then pushed open the door. 'You and

Stringer start from the bottom and work your way up. Harrison, with me. We'll go to the top floor and meet in the middle.'

The detective constables nodded their understanding, Stringer and Blane each taking one of the two rooms leading off the first landing. Harrison said nothing as she followed McLean all the way to the top, although the climb didn't seem to bother her as much as it had Jo Dalgliesh earlier in the day.

Peter Winterthorne's cluttered, cold and damp living room didn't look much different to how it had the other two times McLean had been in there. The old man's favourite armchair still stood by the unlit fire, the uncomfortable sofa he and Harrison had sat on the first time they had visited still pushed a bit too close to the window. A carved armoire of some dark, unidentified wood stood against the wall opposite the fire, and beside it, an antique pedestal desk was home to almost as much random cluttered paperwork as McLean's own. Leafing through some of it, he saw bills mostly, some dating back years.

'That'll be Loopy Doo then.' Harrison spoke from the other side of the room, and when McLean looked over, he saw her staring at a framed photograph on the wall. Colours faded almost to sepia, it showed five young men in clothes that would have been outrageous even then. Most of them held an assortment of musical instruments, but Winterthorne himself sat jauntily on a bass drum with the band logo painted onto it. He looked different to the old man McLean had last seen being taken off to the hospital, but also recognisably the same.

Another photo hung from the wall alongside the band picture, this time showing an older Winterthorne, dressed more soberly in knee-length shorts, a light cotton jacket and wide-brimmed hat, standing in front of the Monumental Arch at Palmyra. Two other men stood with him, all smiling at the camera. There was no indication of when the picture had been taken, or who the other men were.

'If you were an old man with something to hide, where would you put it?' McLean looked around the room, squaring its dimensions with the shape of the building as a whole. It filled most of the top floor, the rest being taken up by a small kitchen and the stairwell. There were bedrooms and bathrooms on the lower floors, he recalled.

'In the attic?' Harrison pointed upwards at the ceiling, flat and ornately corniced despite the sloped slate roof outside. There was no hatch in the living room, but out on the landing they found what looked like a narrow press cupboard which opened to reveal a set of wooden steps on a hinge. Pulling it out activated a clever mechanism that opened a hatch overhead and levered a handrail into place. Tucked into the cupboard beside the steps was a light switch that must have been been installed at the same time as mains electricity came to the city. It still worked, bright light flooding a surprisingly large, lined attic when McLean flicked it on.

'Looks like this sees fairly regular use.' He ran a finger over the treads of the steep stepladder, coming away clean. The wood was worn smooth and shiny by the passage of feet. 'I'm impressed if Winterthorne climbs up and down here regularly.'

The stepladder creaked and swayed a little as he climbed up it and into the attic. In addition to the lightbulbs, four narrow skylights would let light in during the day. The nearest one showed only black, its bottom edge heaped with snow.

'Wow. This is huge.' DC Harrison climbed up into the room and stood by the hatch, mouth hanging open as she looked around what McLean was trying very hard not to describe as an Aladdin's Cave. A couple of bright-coloured Persian rugs had been laid over the floorboards, and when he bent down to thump a hand against the pile, no dust rose up into the air. Old wooden tea chests had been stacked up against one gable end wall, and at the other a workbench that must have been constructed in situ was arranged with a collection of old glass flasks, brass instruments and other alchemical paraphernalia. McLean approached cautiously, worried both that there might be some kind of Indiana Jones-style booby traps set, and that whatever was in the flasks might explode. There weren't, and it didn't.

'Looks like Winterthorne has unusual hobbies.' He picked up one of the flasks carefully, angling the label to the light. Arabic script flowed in neat black pen; no chance of him reading that. Stacked tidily to one end of the workbench, a half-dozen leather-bound books were also mostly in some form of Arabic, although one appeared to be Latin.

'Christ, that gave me a shock!' Harrison's tiny yelp of surprise had McLean leaving the workbench and hurrying to the far end of the attic. A Samurai warrior lurked in the shadows, although on closer inspection it was only his armour on a custom-made stand. Everywhere he looked there was more stuff, all as clean as you might expect to find it in a museum, and just as valuable. McLean even spotted the bass drum from the photograph downstairs, Loopy Doo painted on in fading pink letters.

'Sir, I think you should see this.' Harrison had moved on from the warrior and was stooped over an old leather trunk, its lid tilted open to reveal neatly folded clothes. She reached in and gently pulled out a long black cloak, complete with hood. Lifting it close to her face for a good sniff, she wrinkled her nose in disgust before recoiling away. 'Eww.'

'What is it?' McLean asked.

'Garbage, by the smell of it. Rotting bodies. Oof, it's nasty.' She proffered the garment to him, but McLean didn't need to get close to catch the smell. He could place it instantly, too.

'Maurice Jennings.'

'Looks a lot like the robe our mysterious figure was wearing in the CCTV footage, sir.' Harrison held the garment at arm's length, letting the hem fall to the floor. It might have been a stage prop, were it not for the stench.

'Smells a lot like the garbage heap we found the body in too.' McLean lifted a hand to his face to cover his nose. Suddenly the attic wasn't so large any more. 'There's one thing bothers me though.'

'There is?' Harrison carefully folded the robe and placed it back in the trunk, closing the lid on the worst of the smell.

'Aye. What does this mean? If Winterthorne's somehow involved. If it was him or an accomplice who attacked Jennings and was hunting down Nala, then why the hell did she come here to hide?'

49

'That's good progress, McLean. If forensics can lift any evidence from that cloak linking directly to Jennings, we'll all breathe a sight more easily.'

Back in the station, and McLean could see the tension ease out of the DCC as he briefed him on what they had found in Winterthorne's attic. He couldn't help thinking that Robinson's optimism was misplaced though. Finding the cloak hadn't made things any less complicated. Quite the opposite: it posed far more questions both about the old man and the true nature of House the Refugees.

'It'll take time, sir. And we've a long way to go to unpick this particular puzzle yet. Too much of it doesn't make any sense.'

'Oh I know that, Tony. But you'll figure it out, I'm sure. And in the meantime I can head off the press with this new development. Shut them up about their bloody plague epidemic. I've half a mind to arrest those two from the tabloids who started that rumour. No bloody help at all.'

'That wouldn't be wise, tempting though it is to just lock up the lot of them.'

'Aye, right enough. Still, we can dream, eh?' Robinson clasped his hands together and rested them on his desk in front of him, like a man awaiting the arrival of food. 'How long do you reckon before we get some answers?'

'Forensics are there now, but only to record and secure the site. They'll get stuck in on Monday during office hours.' McLean saw the complaint coming before the DCC could voice it, half raised a hand to stop him. 'The cloak's at the lab already, sir. That's being fast-tracked and we'll have preliminary results in the morning.'

In the morning. Sunday morning when normal people didn't have to work. He glanced at the window wall, the streetlights and rooftops beyond. It was already later than he would have liked to be still at the station, given the warming in Emma's manner towards him. McLean wanted nothing more than to get in his car and drive home. Spend some quality time doing something other than work. Chance would be a fine thing.

'What about the woman? Begbie? You'll be questioning her again, I take it?'

'Aye, sir. She should be here any time now. I sent DCs Stringer and Harrison to fetch her. I've asked DC Blane to go through the charity records, too.'

'You reckon she's involved?'

McLean's first inclination was to say no. That had been his gut instinct the first time he'd met Sheila Begbie, and he usually trusted his gut on things like that. But then he'd been wrong about Winterthorne. Even if the man wasn't involved in the recent deaths, he'd still lied about his alibi.

'I don't know, sir. Given her line of work, it seems strange that she'd actively help in persecuting refugees. On the other hand, how better to identify suitable targets than to pose as a friend to their cause?'

Robinson nodded, stroking his chin with a thoughtful thumb. 'And the stuff you found in Winterthorne's attic. The potion bottles. Any idea what's in them?'

McLean knew where the DCC was hoping the question

would point, but he had no answers. 'I couldn't read the script on the labels, and there's no guarantee that what it says is what's in them anyway. We've sent photos of the labels and other stuff to a professor I know at the university. He should be able to translate them, hopefully. Meantime the lab boys will analyse whatever's in them and see what it is. If it's some strange snake-venom-derived toxin, then at least we'll know how the wee girls died. And Maurice Jennings too. I'm not holding out for it to be that simple though. Winterthorne's too old and frail to be our man in the CCTV, so he has to be working with someone else if he's involved at all.'

'How is he? Winterthorne, that is?'

'Still unconscious, as far as I know. He's under twenty-four-hour guard too.'

Robinson nodded, opened his mouth to ask something else, then looked over to the doorway. Turning, McLean saw DC Harrison, arm raised to knock on the open door.

'Detective Constable?' The DCC asked.

'Sorry to interrupt, sir. It's just I thought you'd like to know we've got Sheila Begbie in interview room two now.'

McLean glanced at his watch, noting that it was past shift end. He didn't know if Harrison had a significant other she should be spending time with, but at least there was a budget for overtime on this case.

'I'd better go and speak to her then.'

'How long have you known Peter Winterthorne, Ms Begbie?'

Interview room two wasn't as nice as interview room one. The walls needed a repaint for one thing, still bearing the watered-down marks from where a cleaner had tried to get the bloodstains off after one suspect had turned violent. As far as McLean could recall, that had been several years earlier, so there was clearly no rush.

'Peter? I don't really know. I guess, fifteen years maybe? Could be longer.'

'And have you been renting the ground floor of his house all that time?'

Begbie looked around the small room with an expression of unease on her face. It wasn't the deep worry or the paranoid terror that McLean had seen far too many times before, so much as a confusion. She had already waived her right to a lawyer, so it was just him, her and DC Harrison in the room, and yet she kept glancing off in odd directions as if she could see someone else. Or perhaps was expecting someone else to be there and couldn't quite understand why they weren't.

'House the Refugees, Ms Begbie.' McLean spoke again to try and focus her attention back on him. 'How long have you been running the charity?'

'Oh. Sorry. I thought . . .' Begbie snapped her gaze back to McLean, her eyes darting to the far corner a couple of times again before she answered. 'That was the late nineties. There were a lot of refugees from the former Yugoslavia. It's always the same. A bunch of hot-headed idiots start fighting each other, people who should know better keep giving them weapons, and it's the poor innocent bystanders who have to flee for their lives. Some of them ended up here, and they weren't being looked after properly. I worked in a shelter for the homeless down on the Grassmarket, and we'd see more and more of them every day. Barely a word of English. Living in squats or even camped out on Arthur's Seat and places like that. I knew I had to do anything I could to help them, so I set up House the Refugees.'

'And where does Winterthorne fit into all this?'

Again, Begbie stared past McLean, this time into a different corner. She didn't exactly seem mad, or scared, just distracted.

'Ms Begbie?'

'Oh, sorry. Yes. Peter. You were asking me when I first met

him? Well, that would have been much the same time. He volunteered, you see? Just like me. Can you imagine it? Lead singer of one of Scotland's biggest bands of the sixties, ladling out soup for the homeless?'

McLean wasn't sure how being an ex-celebrity, long out of the public eye, made much of a difference. That the man had given up his time for others was telling though. It didn't quite square with the picture he'd drawn of him already. 'So Winterthorne does charity work too?'

'Not so much any more. He's not getting any younger. None of us are. But he's so kind and gentle. The kids love him.'

'Kids? What kids?'

Begbie stared off into the corner again, and this time it looked almost as if she was waiting for someone to answer some question she had asked silently. McLean fought back the urge to look around. He knew there was nobody there, could see easily enough in the large mirror that hid the observation room next door. Finally, Begbie nodded almost imperceptibly, before focusing back on him.

'Sorry. I should have explained how the charity functions. I just assumed you knew. We mostly work with the city housing agencies and a few enlightened private landlords. Even if they've got all the right paperwork, refugees can find it hard to navigate the bureaucracy, harder still to overcome the prejudice against them. We—' Begbie tilted her head to one side as she corrected herself. '—I help them with all of it, from first contact through to setting up home, opening bank accounts, registering with a doctor, everything.'

'And the children?' McLean tried to steer her back on track.

'Well, sometimes I'll have a family come to me and there'll be something wrong. Maybe the papers are for the father, but the rest of them aren't registered. Sometimes children turn up on their own, although not that often. If needs be, we'll put people up in the rooms above the office, on the first floor, for a day or two, maybe a fortnight, while all the paperwork's sorted or we can find somewhere better for them to stay. Peter's very under-standing, doesn't seem to mind at all. I think he maybe gets lonely sometimes and enjoys the company.'

'And was Nala one of those children?'

Begbie stared into the corner again, her eyes widening slightly. 'No. I told you that before, when we first found her in the kitchen. Never saw her before that. I'd have just called in Social Services, but with what happened in the basement . . .'

McLean felt a buzz in his pocket at the same time as Begbie's words trailed away to nothing. He would normally have ignored it, but something made him reach out his phone and check the message that had appeared on the screen.

'OK. We'll wrap things up for now. It's getting late, and . . . something's come up I need to deal with.' He glanced up at the clock. 'I'll have a squad car take you home and we can resume this on Monday morning.'

Begbie's surprise at the swift termination of the interview was matched by DC Harrison's. She had been taking notes to supplement the tape, but now she looked at McLean with one quizzically raised eyebrow.

'You've not been charged with anything, Ms Begbie, but I'd ask you not to travel anywhere before we've had a chance to speak again.'

50

The ICU room was empty by the time he reached it, of course. The sheets had already been stripped from the bed in which Akka Nour had died, and the sharp smell of disinfectant hung in the air like an epitaph. McLean stared into the room, seeing the silent machines and carefully coiled wires awaiting their next patient. He hoped they had more luck than the last one.

'Too much to hope she'd make a full recovery and tell us who beat her senseless and dumped her in a skip.'

He didn't need to look round to know that DCI Dexter had joined him. Her gravelly voice was distinctive enough, as was the aroma of stale cigarettes and Polo mints.

'What a bloody waste.' McLean thumped the palm of his hand against the door frame and turned away from the room. 'Poor bastard came here to get away from a war that had nothing to do with her, and this is the best we could give her.'

'Aye, it fair boils my piss, Tony, but we do what we can.' Dexter scrubbed her foot against the linoleum floor, the squeaking noise both grating and oddly comforting. 'You found her wee girl, didn't you? Her sister too.'

'Yes. I'll go see them in a while. Break the bad news. Need to look in on someone else first.'

'Anyone I know?' Dexter fell in beside him as McLean walked away from the empty room.

'That depends on whether you're into sixties psychedelic rock or not.' They turned the corner to see a uniformed sergeant sitting in a chair beside another door, paperback book taking up his entire attention. McLean recognised him as Kenneth Stephen, who normally worked out of the Torphichen Street station. He must have needed the overtime if he'd not passed this job on to a lowly constable.

'Anything good, Kenny?' McLean asked as they came close. The sergeant looked up, startled, then scrambled to his feet at the sight of two detective chief inspectors approaching.

'Sorry, sir, ma'am. I wasn't expecting anyone this late.'

'Unofficial visit. We were here about the young woman who died earlier today. Just thought I'd pop by and see what was up with Winterthorne.'

'Nothing much.' Sergeant Stephen carefully folded down the corner of the page he'd been reading, closed the book and put it on his seat. 'Doctor's in there with him just the now.'

McLean looked past the sergeant and through the narrow glass panel in the door. It was very similar to the room where Akka Nour had died, only he couldn't see the bed because a white-coated figure blocked the view.

'I'll just go have a wee word then.' He took a step towards the door, only to have Sergeant Stephen block his path. 'Sorry, sir. You'll have to sign in. You too, ma'am.'

'Me?' Dexter shook her head. 'No, I've enough to be getting on with. I'll give you a shout tomorrow morning, Tony. We'll be interviewing a couple of the girls we arrested. The ones who speak at least a little English. Never know, one of them might know something, aye?'

McLean watched her go, waving a hand over her shoulder to wish him goodbye. When he turned back, Sergeant Stephen had a clipboard and pen, ready for him to sign.

'Looks like someone's not had a cigarette in ten minutes,' he said under his breath as McLean scrawled his name in a box too small and the wrong shape for his signature.

'I'll pretend I didn't hear that, Sergeant.' He handed back the pen, then tapped lightly on the door before stepping into the room.

Peter Winterthorne looked far worse than he had when McLean had seen him loaded onto the ambulance just a few hours earlier. His hair seemed thinner and whiter, splayed out over pillows that engulfed his head. The oxygen tube to his nose and saline drip in his arm anchored him to the bed like mooring lines on a beached wreck. A slow beep counted out the beats of his heart in unsteady rhythm. He looked gaunt, almost like he had already died.

'Tony. I wasn't expecting to see you here today.' Doctor Caroline Wheeler stood at the bedside, bent over Winterthorne's prone figure as she fiddled with something at his arm. A nurse McLean didn't recognise stood to one side, and took the small phial of blood the doctor handed her when she was done. 'Get that down to the lab will you, Claire? I'll see the patient gets his medication.'

The nurse nodded, staring at McLean with more interest than hostility as she left.

'How long before the gossip starts up among the nursing staff?' Doctor Wheeler asked once the door had closed.

'Gossip? . . . Oh.' McLean felt the tips of his ears redden. 'No. They all know me from when I used to visit my gran.'

'I'm only joking, Tony. I take it you're wanting an update on the patient. Not much I can tell you about your poor young woman back up the corridor, I'm afraid.'

'I seem to recall you telling me it was touch and go with her the last time. It was always going to be too much to hope she'd make a full recovery, tell us who beat her up.'

'Even so. I was surprised she crashed as hard and fast as she did. We tried to resuscitate, but, well, it was like she just gave up. Same as that man from the prison, Seaton. It's almost as if I'm jinxed or something.' Doctor Wheeler shook her head slowly, her shoulders slumping at the thought of failure. For a moment she simply stood there, then she straightened her back and looked around at Winterthorne. 'Let's hope we can do better with this fellow, eh?'

'Have to admit, I didn't think he was in such a bad way. He'd only taken a wee tumble when we found him.'

'That's what the paramedics told me too.' Doctor Wheeler frowned, reached out and took one of the old man's hands in hers, lifting it and turning it gently. Dressed in a short-sleeved hospital gown, Winterthorne's arms stuck out like thin bundles of sticks wrapped in white parchment. 'The thing is, I can't find any signs of bruising on him. He hasn't even got any obvious bumps on his head. Lots of old injuries, the scars are horrendous and I'd be very surprised if he wasn't taking some kind of pain relief. I guess that might explain it.'

'Explain what?' A horrible thought occurred to McLean. 'He's not been poisoned, has he?'

Doctor Wheeler shook her head just the once and placed Winterthorne's hand back down carefully on the sheet. 'No. Well, if he has, then it's been a long, slow process. There's something in his blood that shouldn't be there though. Do you know if he's on any particular medication? We've nothing on record, and he doesn't seem to be registered with any GP.'

'He's not a big fan of doctors, apparently. I don't recall anything stronger than ibuprofen in his bathroom cabinet, but he had some weird old flasks up in his attic. Might have been something he was dosing himself with, I guess. They're at the lab now. We've fast-tracked them, but it's unlikely we'll know what they are before Monday morning.'

'I don't think he's in any danger overnight. He's stable enough, and it's not as if he's going anywhere. You'll let me know as soon as you've an update on those flasks though?'

'Of course.' McLean took one more look at the old man. From a distance it looked like the bed was slowly digesting him, watched by the sentinel life-support machines around him. 'But I've a feeling it's only going to make things more complicated.'

'Hey, Em. Sorry I'm not home already. You know how it is, right?' McLean had owned his new Alfa almost six months before he'd been confident enough of the hands-free system to make calls while driving. He'd rather have pulled into the side of the road as had been a necessity in his old car. That would have taken up valuable time though, and there was one more thing he had to do before he could finally call it a day.

'It's OK. I'm not there either. Sent you a text, have you not got it?'

It was strange hearing Emma's voice ring loud and clear in the quiet of the car, stranger still to see his phone screen light up where he'd left it lying on the passenger seat. A glance was enough to show the text arriving, if not what it actually said.

'Would you believe it just pinged in? Where are you?' McLean turned off Ferry Road and began to navigate the narrow lanes leading to his destination.

'I came to see Nala and Rahel, at Rose's place.'

He almost laughed, then remembered what had happened and why he was late. 'I'm about three minutes away from you then. I needed to see them both too.'

'Oh aye? Why— ... oh.' Emma was quick on the uptake. 'Shit.'

'Thought it would be better coming from a familiar face.' He slowed down as he approached the house, finding the same parking space as had been empty the night before waiting for him. 'I'll be right there.'

Ending the call, McLean parked and stopped the engine. He paused for a moment before getting out into the cold, staring out at the stone bulk of the house, steeling himself for the task ahead. Telling people their loved one had died was all part of the job. He'd long since lost count of the number of times he'd done it. But that didn't mean it was easy. He was glad Emma was here; she and Rahel seemed to get along, and Nala liked her too. What would become of them once this was all over? Was something like this ever really over? Their lives had been shattered by war, and thrown into turmoil by exploitation. Nala had been hunted like some wild animal by something both less and more than a man, something feral and evil. Something soulless. That was not an easy trauma to recover from.

With a heavy sigh for himself and the family he was about to bring the worst news to, he opened the door and stepped out into the night.

The journey home was a quiet one. McLean could sense that Emma wanted to speak, but also that she couldn't. He might have prompted her, but he was happier with the silence and the churn of his own thoughts. They drove through a city strangely muted, as if it too mourned the passing of Akka Nour.

Mrs McCutcheon's cat welcomed them with her usual suspicious stare. Curled up on top of a pile of laundry that had been set on the warming plate of the Aga to iron, she looked like a casting reject for 'The Princess and the Pea'.

'At least someone's comfortable,' Emma said, finally breaking the silence.

'Cup of tea?' McLean went to pick up the kettle. 'Or something stronger?'

'I'm very tempted by something stronger, but when was the last time you ate anything?'

McLean cast his mind back, unable to say exactly. There'd been half a disgusting wrap as a late lunch, washed down with bitter-tar coffee. Both had been an age ago.

'I'm not really hungry.' He tried to stifle a yawn by shoving a fist into his mouth, but it just made it worse. 'Probably should have something, mind. Maybe some toast.'

He'd been intending to get it himself, but, before he could move, Emma had crossed the kitchen to the bread bin and pulled out a loaf. McLean watched her expertly cut two slices and pop them in the toaster. He beat her to the fridge and the butter though, then went to the cupboard where the jams lived.

'Not really marmalade time of day.' He picked out a couple of jars that were several years past their sell-by date, then found what he was looking for lurking at the back.

'Marmite? What are you, ten?' Emma grabbed the toast as it popped up, then dropped it heavily onto the plate as it burned her fingers. 'Here you go. If you're having that muck you can spread it yourself.'

McLean smiled, sat down at the table and started preparing his meal. For an instant it was almost as if he was ten again, home from visiting a friend and enjoying a late-night snack before bedtime. The nostalgia hit him like a drowning wave, and he clung to the dark-brown glass jar for safety. Turning it around, he half expected it to have been sitting in the back of that cupboard since he was a boy, but they hadn't date-stamped those things back then. This jar was only a couple of years old, apparently.

'Penny for your thoughts?' Emma asked, pulling out one of the other chairs and settling herself down opposite him.

'Oh, nothing much.' McLean knew from her scowl that this was the wrong thing to say. 'Just what you said, about me being ten.' He held up a perfectly buttered and Marmited piece of toast. 'This was a treat back then. I used to love sitting in here for meals, not having to be all proper and formal in the dining room.'

'Must have been lonely. Growing up here with just your gran for company.'

'It wasn't quite that bad. There was old Bill the gardener, and Mrs Robertson the housekeeper. And there always seemed to be someone visiting, staying for a fortnight, passing through. Older folk though, my gran's age.'

McLean took a bite of toast, casting his mind back to his childhood. He'd not thought of it in a long time, never really had any reason to. If Emma hadn't lost their baby, would that have changed? Would he have spent happy afternoons looking after their daughter and remembering how different it had been for him? He guessed he'd never know now.

Emma reached across the table and placed her hand over his. 'When this is over, let's just go away somewhere for a little while. A long weekend abroad maybe.'

'I'd like that. Yes. We should.' McLean took another bite as Emma let go his hand and stood up. She walked around the table until she was standing right behind him, put her hands on his shoulders and leaned in close.

'You mean that?'

He swallowed a half-chewed mouthful. 'Of course. Maybe somewhere hot and sunny.'

'Good.' Emma planted a kiss on the top of his head in a manner eerily reminiscent of his grandmother. Or had it been his mother, earlier still?

'Now finish up your toast. It's time for bed.'

51

Darkness still filled the bedroom when McLean woke, the glowing red digits on his bedside clock telling him that dawn was still some way off. Even so, he felt refreshed and awake in a way he hadn't for many months. Not since the previous summer. Since . . .

He rolled over slowly, enjoying the warmth of Emma as she lay beside him. Barely an outline, she slept on her back, mouth slightly open, snoring in tiny apnoeac gasps. He could have lain there just watching her for hours, but something was niggling at the back of his mind, spoiling the moment.

Quietly, he slipped out of bed and left the room, using the shower in the en-suite off his old bedroom. He had clean clothes enough in there to get dressed, returning to the master bedroom only to retrieve his phone and jacket. Emma had rolled over, stealing his half of the duvet and snuggling into it, but she was still asleep, still snoring.

Downstairs, Mrs McCutcheon's cat lay in her bed of clean laundry. McLean suspected she'd not moved all night, and he couldn't blame her. Outside, the garden was still blanketed with snow, the distant trees skeletal against the glow of the never-sleeping city. Somewhere just a few hundred yards from here people had been camping out in this weather. Makeshift tents cobbled together from plastic sheeting and hidden down in the Hermitage for what little shelter they could get there. How desperate could people be that they were forced to live like that? How terrible were the alternatives? Standing in his warm kitchen in his warm house big enough for dozens to live in comfortably, could he really judge them?

A faint pre-dawn light began to paint the kitchen window as he drank his coffee and munched his way through two bowls of Corn Flakes. He'd not felt all that hungry when he started, eating just because he knew he needed something to get through the coming day. Only when he swallowed the first mouthful did he realise the sensation in his stomach had more to do with emptiness than despair.

'When this is over, let's just go away somewhere for a little while. A long weekend abroad maybe.'

McLean played Emma's words over in his head as he put bowl and mug in the dishwasher, checked he had phone and car keys and stepped out the back door. The irony that he was going to work on a Sunday wasn't lost on him. He really needed to do better than a long weekend abroad. They should have holidays like normal people did, spend time together outside of work. Shared experience, that was the key to a healthy relationship. He knew what he needed to do, it was just the 'when this is over' part that he stumbled on. It was never over.

He almost didn't notice the man, standing between the two stone gateposts where the drive opened onto the road. McLean had plipped the lock on his car, reached for the door handle and was about to open it when something made him look round. A pricking on the back of his neck, perhaps. That indefinable sense of being watched. Leaving the car behind, he walked down the drive, between the dark rhododendron bushes drooped heavy with snow.

'Can I help you?' he asked as he approached. In the half-light he couldn't see the man's face, but something about the set of him, his dark suit and footballer's hair stirred a memory.

'Detective Chief Inspector.' The voice was the giveaway, and as McLean came closer he saw the stretch limousine parked a little way down the street.

'It's Albert, isn't it?' McLean stopped a couple of paces away from the man, who stood in the gateway as if the iron gates were closed, instead of hanging rusty and half off their hinges. He shivered and rubbed his hands together, clearly frozen from a long wait. 'Why didn't you ring the bell?'

'I can't come in.' Albert nodded his head towards the grounds beyond the gate. 'She was very insistent about that.'

'And she wants to see me. Again.'

Albert made a half-bow, half-shrug as if to say don't shoot the messenger. McLean looked back at the house, still dark, Emma hopefully still asleep. 'The house out Temple way?'

'That's the one.'

'You head off now. I'll follow you. Same as before. One hour, and then I leave.'

'I'm so glad you came, Tony. Albert was very worried you wouldn't.'

Mrs Saifre greeted McLean at the top of the steps to her Midlothian mansion wearing something that might have been a twenties flapper dress, or might have been a nightie. He half expected her to be holding an ebony cigarette holder, lit Sobranie tainting the air with expensive tobacco smoke, but her pale hands were empty. When she held them out for a fashionably European embrace, he kept his own hands deep in his pockets. If she was annoyed, Saifre hid it well, glancing past him at his car.

'Still the Alfa Romeo? I always say you can tell a lot about a man by the car he drives. I liked the old one more. It had such a whiff of sixties flair. I did so love that decade.'

'I'd still be driving it if you hadn't ripped it apart.'

Saifre stared at him, her face a perfect mask of innocence. 'I'm sure I don't know what you mean, Tony. I would never be so cruel.'

'And you dropped a ton of rock on the roof of the one I had before, as I recall. What is it you want, Saifre?'

The mask almost slipped, the faintest glimmer of annoyance cracking at the edges of those deep, black eyes. Then, with a theatrical shiver, Saifre turned away from him and swayed back into the house, waving a hand for McLean to follow. He was tempted to leave, just like he had been tempted the last time. He knew who Mrs Saifre was. What she was. A tiny, mad part of his mind screamed 'run' every time he saw her. And yet she wanted something from him. Something she couldn't just take, or get someone else to do. That simple fact kept him coming back. It was a weakness, a chink in her armour he intended to push a knife through, right into her rotten heart.

Still standing off to one side, Albert the bodyguard and chauffeur nodded his head, raising one hand to indicate that McLean should go in.

'How did you end up working for her?' McLean asked.

'Mrs Saifre?' The man looked uncomfortable at being asked the question, but answered nonetheless. 'I guess it was inevitable. I wasn't born into privilege like some. Spent a lot of my child-hood in care. The Dee Trust gave me a scholarship, got me a posh education. Could have been a banker or a lawyer or something, but that didn't pan out. So I went to work for the organisation that had looked after me. Thought I'd pay it back, kind of.'

'You know who she is, though?'

Albert shrugged. 'Nobody's perfect, right?'

McLean shook his head slowly, turned and walked into the house. Albert did have a point. Nobody was perfect, it was true. But at least some of them tried.

52

He found Saifre in the same drawing room she'd led him to the previous time. The fire burned like the souls of the damned, filling the room with a heat that was oppressive after the fresh chill of outside. Even so, he felt a shiver in his spine as he crossed the threshold, as if he had stepped into another world.

'Why did you give us detailed information on someone who doesn't exist?' McLean asked before Saifre could start the whole tiresome rigmarole of offering him drink, food, a hospitality he had no intention of accepting, ever. She stood by the fire, thin as a size-zero model. He knew she had to be at least sixty, and yet it was almost impossible not to think of her as a young woman. That was another frustrating thing about dealing with her. She oozed sexuality in the same way a teenage boy oozed body odour. It was part of her make-up, part of her disguise, and very distracting.

'Doesn't . . . ? Oh, yes. That. I rather thought it was plain as the day, but if your colleagues in the Sexual Crimes Unit can't see it, then maybe not.'

'I don't really appreciate being toyed with. Wasting police time is a criminal offence, you know.'

'So hostile, Tony. I'm just trying to be helpful.'

'Like you were helpful with the Weatherly case and Rosskettle

348

Hospital? Like you were helpful with Bill Chalmers and his little hipster opium den?'

Saifre pouted, dropping herself into a soft leather sofa by the fire. She lifted one hand half off the cushion as if thinking about beckoning him over to join her, then dropped it down again.

'I know you won't believe it, but that wasn't me. Well, not exactly. It's complicated. I'm not interested in that sort of thing any more. I want to help people, the sick and the poor and the needy. That's what the Dee Trust is all about.'

McLean resisted the urge to scoff. He didn't believe a word she was saying, of course, but he had also seen some of the work the Trust had done, and heard the praise sung in its name by some of his more senior colleagues. Praise sung. The thought brought a wry smile to his face.

'What is it you really want, Saifre? What are you trying to buy with all your ill-gotten fortune? Call me a cynic, but I can't believe it's really just a change of heart.' She'd have to have one to change, after all.

'Can I be frank, Tony?' Saifre asked the question of herself. 'I think I can. Omar Mared. Ozzy Jones. You think he's just a name, a bogeyman figure used to keep the city's illegals in line. Trafficked prostitute getting uppity? Ozzy Jones beats her into a coma as a warning to the other girls. Gang labourers organising themselves to push back against the brutal conditions they're being forced to live and work in? Omar Mared takes their children as hostage to their good behaviour. And if they don't give them up willingly he does even worse. You think this is how it works, the same name used by all of the people running these despicable schemes. The trafficking and the work gangs and the child prostitution and all the other horrible things people are capable of doing to other people.'

'And you're going to tell me it isn't so. That Omar Mared is actually a person.'

Saifre tilted her head to one side, the ghost of a smile crinkling the edges of her claret-red lips. 'Well, not a person as such. More a powerful spirit. An afrit, if you like.'

'Don't tell me. A djinn.'

The smile blossomed more fully now, revealing perfect white teeth behind it. 'That's what I like about you, Tony. So much more educated than the average bumbling policeman. Yes, a djinn. A creature of Middle Eastern myth, you might say. But then so am I, if you think about it.'

McLean didn't want to. He would far rather live in a world where Mrs Saifre and her like didn't exist. Where they were just greedy and ruthless, and not obsessed with making excuses for the way they were. God, the devil, demons and angels. Creatures of nightmare and myth. Weak justifications for the horrors men, and women, committed all by themselves. No supernatural influence needed. But there was information to be gleaned here, from this evil woman. Information that might save lives. As such, he would play her game, at least for now.

'I've been hearing a lot about them of late. Djinns, afrits, genies. I thought the pantomime season was over, but clearly not.' He waited until Saifre opened her mouth to speak before interrupting her. 'So tell me, why are you so interested in this mythical being? Why do you want us to find Omar Mared?'

'Are you kidding? Who wouldn't want to find a real genie? I mean, think of the possibilities.' Saifre leaned forward in her seat, elbows on her knees and hands under her chin like an excited teenager. Her enthusiasm filled the room like second-hand smoke at a college party. McLean steeled himself against it, trying not to inhale.

'Possibilities?'

'Imagine it, Tony. The power. The influence. What if you could have three wishes, guaranteed they would come true? What would you want?' Saifre almost bounced as she asked the question, her eyes glinting in excitement. 'How about your and Emma's child born healthy? A happy family life together? Or maybe Kirsty Summers still alive and Donald Anderson nothing but an old antiquarian book dealer who sold you an ancient medical text you thought might make a fun present for a trainee doctor. Or perhaps you might cast your wish back further still. Make it so your parents never accepted that plane ride from their old friend, Toby Johnson.'

McLean said nothing, unsure whether he could speak, even if he could get a word in edgeways. He knew that Saifre had an unhealthy obsession with him, but this was a level of detail that would do a stalker proud.

'Now forget three wishes.' Saifre's tone changed as she spoke, her excitement turning to seriousness. 'Imagine if you could have as many wishes as you wanted?'

'Isn't that what you're supposed to ask for your first one?' McLean found his voice at last. 'Only it never works that way, does it? There's always unforeseen consequences. And anyway, there's no such thing as genies, and wishes are for fools.'

The gleam in Saifre's eyes blinked out as if someone had switched off a light inside her head. 'So remorselessly logical. It really must be no fun being you.'

McLean ignored the taunt. 'So what you're trying to tell me is Omar Mared really is a genie or djinn or afrit, or whatever name you want to call it. Some kind of half-arsed demon preying on the weak. Sounds like someone I need to put away for life, not cosy up to for favours.'

'Oh, Tony. Tony, Tony, Tony.' Saifre walked right up to him, so close her thin shift brushed against the fabric of his suit. He could feel the heat boiling off her body, the tension in her as she stood right before him. His memory told him that she was shorter than she seemed now, her head on a level with his, eyes as black as boiling tar and staring straight at him. For a terrible moment he thought she was going to try and kiss him, and he wondered how easily he would be able to resist this time. No postcard from Emma to lend him strength. Clenching his fists for moral support, he stood his ground. The moment seemed to last an eternity, although it was most likely less than a couple of seconds. Finally, she looked away.

'The djinn are an ancient race. They existed long before mankind came along, and will outlive you all.' She went back to the sofa and slumped into it. 'They keep themselves to themselves, mostly. Human minds can't really comprehend them, much the same as they can't comprehend me and my kind unless we wear these mortal skins.'

Something about the way Saifre spoke convinced McLean that she was completely serious. It shouldn't have surprised him – it wasn't as if you could do the things she did and not know yourself to be evil. As beguiling as it was to accept her for what she claimed to be, he couldn't quite bring himself to take that final step though.

'Sometimes, when the moon is in the right phase or the fates conspire to make it so, when a great storm sweeps the desert and breaks down the barriers between worlds, then the djinn slip into the realm of mankind. It's not always happy when people cross their path, but sometimes they are in a mood to grant favours. Wishes, as you might have it. And so the myths have grown up around them over the millennia.'

McLean let the story wash over him, all too aware of the parallels with what both Madame Jasmina at the circus and Professor Gobbo Charnley at the university had told him. At the back of his mind, his trained detective's thinking asked the question, why? Why was she telling him this? What did she hope to gain from it?

'You know the story of Aladdin, of course. The trapped genie, freed from its lamp, grants three wishes to the poor boy. That's a morality tale as much as anything, but the truth behind it is far less pleasant. There's a very good reason the genie was trapped in the first place, Tony. They might be able to bless people with favours that seem like wishes made true, but they also feed on the souls of men, suck them dry and leave only withered husks behind.'

A cold shiver ran down McLean's back, despite the hellish heat of the drawing room. 'When you say withered husks, you're not being figurative, are you?'

Saifre smiled, and somewhere a thousand hopes were crushed beneath jackboots. 'Now you're getting it.'

The weather had improved slightly as McLean drove the back lanes of Midlothian towards the city, but snow still clung to the verges and drifted through gaps in the tattered hedges. After the stifling heat of Mrs Saifre's living room, he'd turned the fans on high and opened all the vents in his Alfa, letting the temperature drop close to what it was outside. The cold helped to sharpen his thoughts, sluggish after too much time in her dread presence.

She wasn't the devil, and there wasn't a rogue genie or afrit or djinn running loose in the city. It would be so easy to believe her, but then what? There was always a rational explanation, even if it involved other people believing in those things. All he had to do was find that explanation. Find out who was killing children, and how. And why Saifre was interested.

What was it that she truly wanted? The Dee Trust had been going for years, but now it seemed to have attracted her full attention. Either that or she was using it to throw everyone off the scent of what she was really doing. Could it be as simple as muscling in on the Edinburgh gangland scene? Taking control of the people trafficking, prostitution and drugs? Well, she'd been involved in drugs before, even if he couldn't prove it. For someone as wealthy and influential as Jane Louise Dee it all seemed rather low rent though.

The jangling ringtone of his phone broke McLean's train of thought as he approached Straiton and the dual carriageway. He thumbed the button on the steering wheel to accept the call.

'McLean.'

'You driving, Tony? Thought you'd be in the office by now.' DCI Dexter's voice sounded uncomfortably clear and close over the car's expensive loudspeakers.

'Slight detour, Jo. Should be there in half an hour or so.' McLean slowed as the traffic backed up on the approach to IKEA and the Straiton retail park. 'Maybe a little longer. You wanting something?'

'Got someone you need to talk to, but she'll wait until you get in. We're still processing all the folk we arrested yesterday. Have you any idea how inconvenient it was you bringing me that intel on a Friday? Weekend overtime's killing my budget.'

'That's when it was given to me, Jo. Don't shoot the messenger, aye?'

'Fair enough. Looks like we're going to be keeping the courts busy for a while, mind.'

'That's a good thing, right?' He couldn't help but turn it into a question. This was a great outcome for Police Scotland, and would play well with the media. Teflon Steve would be happy, as would the Chief Constable. It was also exactly what Mrs Saifre wanted. Chaos in the city's underworld.

'Aye, well.' Dexter didn't make any more comment than that. 'We've barely made a dent on processing it, and Immigration are all over us like a rash given the folk we've been rounding up. Not a lot of real names, either. But a few are coming up and too many of them are on the database of your favourite charity.'

'The Dee Trust?' For a moment McLean was confused by his

earlier thoughts. He couldn't think why Dexter would be looking into that, or indeed how she'd got access to their records. Then it dawned on him. 'House the Refugees?'

'Aye, them. Your man Lofty Blane's been going through their books. Seems like housing's not the only thing they've been doing.'

53

'I understand you have something you want to tell me.'

McLean sat in interview room three, the one with no window and a heating system that was erratic at best. Across the marked Formica table from him, a young woman fidgeted nervously. She had the pale face and thin, angular features of an addict, but her eyes burned too bright for someone who regularly sought solace in a needle. They were the same vibrant green as Rahel's, almost hypnotic when they stared at him. Fortunately she was more interested in her lap, the table top and her restless fingers.

'I wish for, how you call it? Asylum? I trade you information. The one you seek.'

Her accent was like Rahel's too, something foreign mixed in with a few years of living in Edinburgh. According to DCI Dexter, she was one of nine sex workers, all foreign and most likely trafficked, found working in a nondescript suburban house in Carrick Knowe. Its proximity to Sighthill, where Akka Nour had been left for dead, was what had brought them to McLean's attention. That and her hair. Shaved almost to the skin and covered with a long, raven black wig when she'd been arrested, it was as dark and red as that of the girl they had found in the Hermitage.

'You told us your name is Mandy Cobane.' McLean consulted the copy of the arrest sheet he had laid out in front of him. 'That's not your real name though, is it?'

The young woman stopped fidgeting, crossed her arms and slumped back in her chair. 'They tell me I am Mandy, so I am Mandy.'

'Who tells you that? The men who brought you here from Syria? The men who killed Akka Nour?'

McLean had been hoping the name would spark a reaction, and he wasn't disappointed. The young woman lunged forward, slapping her hands down on the table, her face flushing in something that might have been anger, might have been fear. Was probably both. 'Akka is dead? They kill her? This is why I must have asylum. Is not safe here. Is not safe back home.'

'Nobody's going to send you back home, wherever that might be.' McLean flipped open the folder he had brought with him, a sheet of blank paper covering up the first of the photographs inside it. 'It's clear you knew Akka, so I can tell you that her child, Nala, is safe. She is with Rahel, her aunt. And they're both being looked after by someone I trust implicitly.'

He studied the young woman's face as he spoke, seeing how his words affected her. 'Now, I can call you Mandy, but we both know that's not your name. And we both know it's not a name you particularly like. So what should I call you?'

For a while she said nothing, then the young woman finally turned that hypnotic green gaze on him, almost daring him to argue with her. 'I am Aysha,' she said. 'Akka and Rahel are family. Nala too. I care for her sometimes, when they take her mother away. Only this time they take both of them.'

'You were all brought over here together?'

'No. I was here six months before Akka arrived. If I could, I would tell them to stay home. Better to die in the bombs than live like this here.'

Given what had happened to them, McLean was inclined to agree. Life had not been kind to the people of Rahel's town.

'This won't be easy, Aysha, but I want you to look at a couple of pictures. Two wee girls like Nala. I think you might know who they are, maybe who did this to them.' He pulled out the first photograph, turned it around and laid it down in front of the young woman. Not the artist's impression, this was the least horrific of the pictures taken after the girl had been cleaned up for the post-mortem. She stared at it for a long while, tears welling in her eyes and falling down her thin cheeks.

'Mara was Ishtar's little girl. She was born in the old country. Came over on the boats not more than a year ago.' Aysha reached a shaking hand towards the photo, then withdrew, as if touching it was too painful. 'Ishtar tried to run away, so they took little Mara from her. If she did as they told her, then she could have time with Mara once a week. If not, then it could be months.'

McLean steeled himself against the heartlessness of the situation. Anger would do no good here, even though he could feel it growing. And with it a despair at the plight of these women and children. How sick was the world that it could do this to the weak and innocent? How hateful the men? How utterly soulless?

'This Ishtar. Is she one of the other women in the house where we found you?' he asked after a while.

Aysha shook her head, her voice cracking as she spoke. 'I not see Ishtar in many months. They not let us stay together too long. Always new faces, mix us up, move us around.'

McLean picked up the first photograph and slid it back into his folder, then took the second out, staring at it a while. He knew before he put it down in front of her what the answer would be. The dead girl's red hair and the shape of her face were echoed in the young woman in front of him.

'We also found this one, a few days ago in the Hermitage.'

This time Aysha reached out and touched the picture. She ran trembling fingers gently over the page as if stroking the dead child. She choked on her words, sobs racking her thin body. 'I called her Elia, after my mother.'

McLean almost stood up, meaning to walk around the table and give her a hug. He could feel the loss himself, the echo of what might have been, now no more than an empty hollowness in his gut. Was this why that small, guilt-ridden part of him had felt relief at Emma's miscarriage? Knowing the heartache a child could bring? Was he really that selfish?

'Why? Why would she . . . ?' Aysha clutched the photograph to her, tears flowing freely now as she stared at McLean, her face a picture of purest anguish. Her grief was so fierce, he almost missed her words.

'She?'

'What background have we got on Sheila Begbie?'

McLean wasn't one to run indoors, or indeed outdoors unless strictly necessary. Nevertheless, he walked as quickly as he could to the major-incident room, then back to the CID in search of a detective constable. What if they'd been looking in the wrong place all along? Or, more correctly, what if the truth had been hiding in plain sight?

'Sir?' DC Harrison peered up at him through bleary eyes. She looked paler than usual, either coming down with one of the colds that had been doing the rounds or up late partying the night before.

'Sheila Begbie. The woman we interviewed yesterday, remember? Runs that refugee charity on the Royal Mile?'

Harrison sat up straighter. 'Sorry, sir. A bit groggy this morning.'

'It's OK. We've all been through the wringer this past week. Just get me what we have on file, OK?'

'Yes, sir. We should have her on the system from when you

found the first wee girl. I'll see what I can bring up.' The detective constable covered her mouth to hide a belch as she tapped at her keyboard with the other hand. McLean wondered whether he should keep his distance. He usually managed to avoid catching the periodic lurgies that ripped through the building and disrupted the staffing rotas. More importantly though, he didn't fancy being in the firing line should Harrison lose the battle she appeared to be fighting with her digestive system.

'Rough night?' he asked as she uncovered her mouth to use both hands on the keyboard.

'What? Oh. No. More like dodgy kebab. Me and Manda went to see the circus again, only it was gone so we ended up going to the cinema. Picked up a kebab on the way home. They always say you need booze in your system when you eat those things. Should have had something a bit stronger than tea. Only, I knew I'd be working today.'

McLean barely heard the last of Harrison's words. 'The circus is gone?'

'Aye. Surprised me too. Just a wee sign stuck in the ground. Something about council permits and other nonsense. Can you believe it? Most popular attraction to hit the city in years, and the council tell them to bugger off.' Harrison shook her head at the idiocy of it all. 'Never seen a site so clean, either. If it wasn't for the patches in the snow you'd not know they'd even been there.'

Had he not noticed it this morning? For a moment McLean thought he was going mad, but then he remembered he'd followed Albert in the stretch limousine out of the city, then come back in from the south. He'd missed his normal drive through the Meadows.

'Shame. I quite fancied seeing the show again myself. Emma loved it when we went.' He'd also have liked the opportunity to talk to the enigmatic Madame Jasmina again.

'That's odd. Can't seem to find any record of her.'

'Record?' For a moment McLean's mind was still on the circus and the old fortune teller. Then he remembered what he'd asked Harrison to do for him in the first place.

'We've nothing on the incident file. There should be background here, address and stuff like that.' The detective constable grabbed the mouse and started twirling the little scroll wheel on top of it, her eyes flicking this way and that as she read the information on her screen. After a few minutes, she stopped, turned to face McLean, a look of confusion on her face.

'I don't understand. I filled out the initial data myself, but she's not here. Not even her statements.'

Almost as if she doesn't exist. McLean felt the familiar cold in his gut as snippets of conversations with people he thought mad began to coalesce into something too horrible to contemplate.

'Do a deep search for her. Social Services, council tax, all the stuff you can dig up. Find out who took her home after we interviewed her yesterday, too. We're going to have to get her back in sharp.' McLean glanced at his watch, irritated to find he'd lost a chunk of the morning to humouring Mrs Saifre's whims, even if hers were some of those uncomfortable words.

'On it, sir.' Harrison stifled another belch, then reached for her notepad. 'Should have something together in an hour or so. Will you be in your office?'

An hour was tight for what he wanted to do, but then Harrison would have to be a miracle worker to get what he'd asked for in that time anyway. 'No. I'll find you when I get back. Right now I need to go and see if Peter Winterthorne's woken up yet.'

54

He had been intending to go to the hospital, but McLean realised just how stupid that would have been before he made it as far as the ground floor and the back door to the car park. A quick call confirmed that there had been no change in Winterthorne's condition, Nurse Robertson assuring him he'd be first to know if there was. He had barely sat down in his office when a knock on the open door revealed DC Blane, leading Professor Gobbo Charnley.

'Gentleman to see you, sir. Thought it easier to bring him up, given the circumstances.'

McLean stood again, motioning for them both to enter. The professor scuttled in, marvelling at the space.

'This puts my tiny little office on George Square into perspective. That's some view you've got there, Tony.' He looked around at DC Blane. 'Or should I call you Detective Chief Inspector?'

'We've known each other since we were in short trousers. Tony's fine. Come and have a seat. Not sure if the coffee machine's on, but DC Blane can get you something if you'd like.'

'No, no. I don't need any more coffee just now. And I can see you're busy. Won't take up too much of your time.'

'OK then. What have you got for me?' McLean led the professor over to the conference table, pulling out a chair for him and settling down into another one.

'The Arabic script I was sent yesterday for translation. I know it's a bit irregular working on it over the weekend, but Sunday's my least busy day, as it happens.' Charnley popped open his leather satchel with awkward fingers, and pulled out a series of A4 colour prints. 'I'd love a chance to see the original artefacts some time. I only have a few photographs. The books look especially interesting.'

'I'll see what I can do. Right now though, they're possible evidence so we can't let anyone interfere with them. Were you able to translate the script?'

Charnley spread a sheaf of photographs out on the table in front of him. 'Sort of.'

'Sort of?'

'It's not classic Arabic, although the writing is close. The language is something more akin to Aramaic, but a dialect I've never encountered before. Either it's very old or it's something someone's just made up. It's pretty strange stuff.'

'OK.' McLean tried not to let too much doubt creep into his voice as he picked up one photograph showing the label on a flask. 'What does this one say?'

'That one? Number five.' Charnley consulted a small notebook filled with handwriting that would do a GP proud. 'The closest I can translate that to is "Essence", although if the word is derived from the one I'm thinking of it might also be "Soul".'

McLean peered at the photograph, but this new insight made the flask no less mysterious. Hopefully the lab would have better luck identifying whatever liquid was inside.

'And this one?' He picked up another picture, with several lines of script on it.

'That had me stumped, I have to admit. It seems to say "Water of Sleep" and some kind of warning. Sleep could be the wrong word though. It's all very difficult to translate out of context.'

'What about the books?'

'Ah yes, the books.' Charnley sat up a little straighter, pulling the relevant photographs towards him. 'Quite fascinating. They're incredibly rare alchemies, in the main.'

'Alchemies?'

'Potion books, if you like. Recipes for all manner of things. The alchemists were the first natural philosophers. They were trying to turn base metal into gold, which is a fool's errand of course. But they laid the foundations of modern science too.'

McLean let Charnley lecture him even though he knew his history of science well enough. The man was a professor after all. 'So Winterthorne's a bit of a modern-day alchemist then, is he?'

'These are Peter's?' Charnley held up the photographs, his eyes wide as he leafed through them one by one. 'Oh my God.'

'How does that change things?' McLean asked.

'Well, it's just, he was always obsessed with the myths and legends of the Middle East. The goddess Atargatis fascinated him. Get a couple of drinks in him and he'd lecture you for hours about how she was the real inspiration for later incarnations of the devil. There's some stuff about her here, but it's mostly about her demons. The afrits or djinn.'

Deep down, McLean had always known this would be coming. 'So he believed in genies, then? Believed they really exist.'

Charnley swallowed nervously, and looked around the office in the way a guilty suspect might in one of the interview rooms two storeys down. 'He did, yes. And these books only confirm how far his delusion had gone.'

'How so?' McLean asked.

'Well, I've only translated the pages you photographed, but from what I can tell they're detailed accounts of how to control a djinn, should you encounter one.'

'Control?'

'Oh yes. See here?' Charnley riffled through the photographs until he came up with one showing lines of unintelligible text. 'This describes how one might bind a djinn to one's will by trapping it in mortal flesh. And this one . . .' He scrambled around until he found another equally alien page. 'This one explains how you must let it feed every so often or risk it breaking free and wreaking havoc. It's all nonsense of course, but these notes jotted in the margins here are in English. It looks very much like whoever wrote them thought he was truly in control of some supernatural force.'

McLean said nothing, unsure quite how to process the information. He wanted Winterthorne simply to be mad, but he knew better than to think it could be quite that easy.

'Poor old Peter.' Charnley picked up the nearest photograph and stared at it before letting out that annoying low whistle once more. 'He really did lose his marbles out in the desert.'

'Lost his marbles?' McLean stared past the professor and out through the window to where fresh snow had begun to fall. 'I'm more worried about what he might have found.'

'Lab results just came back on those flasks you found, sir. You'll never guess what's in them.'

McLean had only gone into the major-incident room because he had to pass it on his way back from seeing Professor Charnley out. He'd barely stepped into the room before DC Stringer came bustling up, clutching a freshly printed sheet of paper.

'Water?' He meant it as a joke, but the look on the detective constable's face suggested he'd hit the bullseye.

'How did you know?' Stringer handed him the sheet, a table showing that all the glass bottles had contained purified water and nothing else.

'I didn't.' McLean studied the printout more closely, but there was no ambiguity about the results. No doubt whoever had got themselves geared up in full hazmat suit and locked themselves in a bio-secure lab to carry out the tests would have been a bit annoyed, but it lent strength to the professor's summation of Winterthorne's state of mind. Obsession turned to madness wasn't so unusual, particularly when you considered the old man's background. Creative, lots of drugs in his younger days, fascination with a period of history rich in mythology, major traumatic and life-changing incident. McLean could count the points off one by one and any psychologist would agree with him.

It was just that he'd met Winterthorne, spoken to him. The man had been intense at times, a bit vacant at others, but McLean hadn't got a sense of madness from him. Which either meant Winterthorne's delusion was all-engulfing, or McLean's finely honed detective's instinct was faulty. Or both.

'Is Harrison around? I asked her to do background on Sheila Begbie.'

Stringer gave McLean a nervous look. 'Is that what she's doing? I heard her swearing at her computer earlier. Then she went off to find Lof— . . . DC Blane, sir.'

'Thanks. I'll go see if I can find them in the CID room.' McLean hurried out before someone else noticed he was in there, then used the sheet of paper as a prop to make it look like he was busy reading something until he arrived at his destination. Pieces of the puzzle were starting to fall together now, and while he didn't much like the picture they were forming, he also didn't want any unnecessary distractions to throw off his chain of thought.

He found the two detective constables huddled together at the back of the CID room. Harrison looked like she was winning the war with her kebab, but the crease across her brow when she glanced up and saw him wasn't the most welcoming. Blane hunched over like a timid giant, peering at his computer screen with an intensity more usually associated with young love.

'Got anything for me?' McLean asked it, even as he knew he wasn't going to get the answer he wanted. Harrison stood up as he approached, clasping her hands together like a maid who really doesn't want to tell the king his son's run off with the washerwoman's daughter.

'We were about to come and see you, sir. It's . . . Well, it's complicated.'

It always was. 'How so?'

'Would be easier if other folks worked weekends, but we've been going through the various databases we've access to here. Council tax, rates, the charity commission. It seems that Sheila Begbie doesn't really exist.'

Another piece of the puzzle, the picture ever clearer and yet at the same time just as impossible to understand. At least, not rationally. 'How do you mean?'

'There are no medical records for her. She doesn't have a passport. The address we have for her's a wee tenement flat in Gorgie, but the council tax records show a couple of students living there. Land Registry says it belongs to Winterthorne, too.'

'And the charity? House the Refugees?'

'It's registered, but to Winterthorne. He's behind it all.'

'So who was the woman we interviewed? Who called us about wee Nala when she found her?'

'I don't know, sir. Don't know where she is, either. The mobile number we've got just keeps going to voicemail.' Harrison held up her phone just in case McLean wasn't sure what she meant. 'It's her voice, mind. On the message.'

'Dig out the interview tapes, will you? Did we get video footage? If so, we can pull a photo from it and get her likeness out. We need to find her.'

'That's odd.' DC Blane craned his neck, staring myopically at the computer screen as he spoke. Then he seemed to realise what he had done, leaning back and looking up at McLean. 'Sorry, sir. Just doing a search on the name and this came up.'

McLean walked around the desk until he could see what had caught the detective constable's attention. He'd brought up a news report, and it didn't take much reading to see that it was coverage of Winterthorne's miraculous reappearance from the desert. There was even a photograph of him, looking considerably younger than the man he'd met so recently. An image taken before the crash, it showed Winterthorne flanked by three other people, his arm around one of them. A very familiar-looking woman.

'What's the date on this?' He reached for the mouse to scroll up the screen, but Blane beat him to it.

'Nineteen ninety-four, it says. Before I even went to school. The photo's earlier still.'

'That tallies with the story about the crash, but how the hell can that be Sheila Begbie?'

Blane scrolled back down to the photograph, then past it a bit so he could read more of the text. 'That's not Sheila Begbie, sir. Apparently that's Doctor Eileen Wentworth.' He peered close at the screen again. 'One of the other experts on the expedition, oh, and apparently Winterthorne's wife.'

'It certainly looks like her,' Harrison said as she too stared at the image on the screen. At least she'd met Begbie. McLean couldn't remember whether Blane had or not.

'How did you find that photograph?' he asked.

'A name search on "Sheila Begbie", sir.' Blane continued scrolling down through the text, reading it far faster than McLean could manage. 'Ah, here we go. "Winterthorne arrived at Edinburgh Airport on Tuesday, accompanied by his personal assistant Miss Sheila Begbie. A small crowd of well-wishers turned out to greet him." There's no photo of her arriving, just him.'

'Scroll back to the photo, will you?' McLean waited while Blane brought it back, then expanded it to fill the entire screen. He leaned close, focusing on the faces, paying no heed to the background. There was no doubt in his mind at all. The woman Peter Winterthorne was holding tight with the grin of a happy man spread wide across his face was most certainly Sheila Begbie. But Sheila Begbie as she appeared today, not twenty-five years ago.

A lone uniformed constable stood by the front door to Peter Winterthorne's house when McLean arrived from the station with DC Harrison in tow. He was clearly frozen through, and while the detective chief inspector had little time or respect for PC, formerly DI, Carter, he still had some sympathy for the man. Nobody enjoyed an outdoor posting in this kind of weather.

'Wouldn't you be better off standing inside?' he asked as the constable greeted him with ill-concealed hostility.

'Crime scene manager said I had to be out here.' Carter shivered, his hands shoved deep into his pockets, teeth chattering as he spoke. McLean found he didn't have the energy to argue. He pushed open the door and stepped into the hall instead.

'Did he really used to be a detective inspector?' Harrison asked when the door was once more firmly closed. The office of House the Refugees was empty, the door locked, but the door to the stairs leading up to Winterthorne's flat had been propped open.

'Briefly, yes. That was before he falsified a crime scene report to make his own mistake look like it was mine. I'm surprised they didn't sack him, but he's found his niche now. Come on.'

McLean set off up the stairs, pausing only briefly at the first landing. The full forensic examination of the attic where they'd found the cloak wouldn't happen until Monday morning, but as long as he kept away from there he should be OK.

'Why are we here, sir?' Harrison followed him up the next flight of stairs, close by his shoulder as he looked briefly into the rooms off the second-floor landing. They were bedrooms, but clearly not used often.

'We got distracted the last time. Only gave the living room a brief once-over before we found the attic. Stringer and Blane checked these rooms, but none of us looked at the third floor.' Sloppy detective work, but then none of them had particularly shone during this investigation, himself included. It was almost as if they had collectively forgotten how to do their jobs.

They climbed the stairs to the next landing, fewer doors leading off this one. To the front was a small single room, again looking like it hadn't been used in a while. At the rear, a much larger bedroom was clearly where Winterthorne slept.

'Gloves, I think.' McLean pulled out a pair and snapped them on.

'We looking for anything in particular?' Harrison asked as she pulled on her own pair of gloves.

'Impressions, in the main. What do you see?'

The detective constable said nothing for a moment, her gaze darting around the room as she took everything in. 'It's tidy for a man living on his own. Big bed, too.'

McLean had to agree. The bed dominated one end of the room, a dark-wood four-poster that had to be at least king-size if not larger. Covers neatly pulled up, the pillows on one side were nevertheless creased as if they had been slept on recently. A bedside table on the side nearest the door through to the bathroom held an old wind-up alarm clock with little bells on the top of it, a folded pair of half-moon spectacles, and a small pile of paperback books. A pair of sheepskin slippers tucked neatly under the bed frame suggested this was the side Winterthorne most usually slept on.

'Anything else? About the bed, specifically?'

Harrison stood on the other side, facing him. There was a second bedside table next to her. It too held an alarm clock and a small selection of books. Sitting on top of them, a glass tumbler held about an inch of water.

'The pillows,' she said eventually. 'They've not been plumped up after being slept on. But only on this side.'

'And yet Winterthorne sleeps over here. These are his glasses.' McLean held them up as Harrison turned from the bed and crossed the room to where a large wardrobe stood against the wall. Antique like much of the rest of the furniture in the house, it had three doors, the centre one set with a mirror. Opening it revealed a neat row of dark jackets much like the one they'd last seen Winterthorne wearing, a row of sensible shoes on the shelf beneath. The next door hid trousers and shirts, again clearly a man's. Harrison paused a moment before opening the third door.

'Ah.'

'Starts to make a bit of sense now, although I don't like admitting she pulled the wool over my eyes.' McLean stepped closer to the wardrobe, seeing the neatly folded clothes inside.

Sheila Begbie's clothes.

55

'Why the hell didn't anyone run background on her when you found the first body?'

Early Monday morning, and McLean stood in Detective Superintendent McIntyre's office, feeling for all the world like a schoolboy called up in front of the headmaster even though he's done nothing wrong. She looked more tired than angry, but her accusation cut him all the same.

'That's hardly fair, Jayne. It's barely a week since the march. And we did the same background checks we'd do with anyone in her situation. We had her in here for interview twice, and both times she came of her own volition. If she's played us, she's done it like a pro.' He didn't add that the notes of those two interviews had somehow become corrupted on the system, or gone missing altogether. That was a complication too far for now.

'So we don't know who she is, and we don't know where she is.' McIntyre picked up a sheet of paper from a pile on her cluttered desk, glancing at it briefly before placing it back again with a sigh. 'What do we know about her? Why is she suddenly so interesting?'

McLean pinched the bridge of his nose to stave off the headache he could feel coming on. 'The only reference we can find to her is in an old news report about Winterthorne when he came back to Edinburgh twenty-five years ago. She was his secretary or PA or something. The charity was set up a couple of years later, but Winterthorne's the name on all the documentation, and they've been very low-key for such an organisation. DC Blane's going through their financials right now, but I've a horrible feeling it's just a front for something a lot less worthy.'

'Go on.' McIntyre leaned back in her chair, giving McLean that look he remembered so well from when he was still a detective sergeant.

'I think they've been doing what they say, housing refugees. But they've also been keeping tabs on the traffickers, maybe even working with them. Coordinating them. Helping them, even.'

'You don't think that's a little far-fetched? This Begbie woman's what? Fifty years old, more? Winterthorne's a frail old man who used to be a rock star. Why would they be involved in something like that?'

McLean wanted to say that Begbie had been fifty years old for at least the last twenty-five, but he knew just how mad that sounded. 'I don't know, but that's where the evidence is pointing. I do know that they've both lied to us though, and they know more about the girl in the basement than they told us. We're searching Winterthorne's house from top to bottom now. Probably should have done that on day one. We need to find Begbie, though. She's the key to it all.'

'Stupid question, but you've tried her phone, I take it?'

'It's going straight to voicemail. I've put a request in to triangulate its position, if it's even switched on, but you know what the mobile operators are like.'

McIntyre rubbed at her eyes with the heels of her hands for a moment. 'Would it help if I gave them a nudge?'

'Wouldn't hurt.' McLean thought about it. 'Might be even better coming from the DCC.'

'You really want him to know about this?' McIntyre had

begun to reach for the telephone shoved precariously to the edge of her desk, but pulled her hand back as she asked the question.

'He's going to find out soon enough. Might as well make the best of it.'

'Aye, fair enough. I'll try to break the news to him gently. So, what's your plan of action then?'

'Well, we can't exactly interview Winterthorne. He's still un-conscious and from the way the nurses are talking about him he might never wake up. I've got Sandy Gregg working up a better background on him. See if we can shake out some other acquaint-ances. Problem is he's been a hermit for so long everyone's more or less forgotten about him.'

'And Begbie?'

McLean shrugged. 'Everything we can do. We've circulated her photo. Just have to hope someone spots her out and about.'

McIntyre shook her head. 'No, sorry. I meant how do you think she fits into all this? What even is all this? You've got an eighty-year-old man who's so frail a simple fall is probably going to kill him, and a woman who doesn't exist wearing the face of someone who died twenty-five years ago. Neither of them look remotely like the character you caught on CCTV the night Maurice Jennings was killed, and we still don't know exactly how or why that was done, let alone the two wee girls. How many more are there out there we don't even know about?'

McLean thought about the young woman he'd interviewed the day before, Aysha. The systematic way she and others like her had been brutalised, used up and discarded when they were no longer wanted. Akka Nour thrown into a wheelie bin like so much garbage. 'I don't know, Jayne. We're doing everything we can, but nothing makes sense. Not rational sense anyway. This is much more sinister than an unlikely front for an immigrant exploitation racket.'

'How do you mean?' McIntyre looked up swiftly, her eyes on

him like a raptor sizing up its prey. McLean almost told her about Saifre, Madame Jasmina and all the others going on about evil spirits and ancient, mythical creatures. Perhaps it wasn't so far-fetched to think there was a djinn roaming the city, wearing the skin of a middle-aged woman. America had voted in a former reality TV star as president, after all. And populist politicians much closer to home had created a world where fascist idiots like Matthew Seaton felt encouraged to spout their hateful bile. Why couldn't genies exist too?

'It's—' he started to say, then noticed that McIntyre was looking past him. Turning, he saw the duty sergeant standing in the doorway.

'What is it, Pete?' McIntyre asked.

'There's a . . . person in Reception, ma'am?' The sergeant seemed unsure. 'He . . . I mean, she . . . I think. She needs to speak to the detective chief inspector. Apparently it's very urgent?'

McIntyre was already on her feet and stepping around her desk when McLean turned back to face her. Clearly he wasn't the only one who knew exactly who was asking for him. He could be fairly sure he was the only one with a horrible sense of dread about why she was here.

'Come on, Tony.' McIntyre grabbed his arm. 'If there's one thing I've learned down the years, it's never to keep Madame Rose waiting.'

It didn't take long to walk down to Reception, even if it felt like an eternity. When he saw Madame Rose sitting on one of the narrow plastic seats by the public entrance to the station, McLean was struck by how small she looked, as if she had drawn in on herself. She stood almost before they had stepped into the room, and was halfway to them by the time the electronic lock on the door had clicked behind them.

'Jayne. It's been such a long time.' Madame Rose might have been here with urgent news, but that didn't mean either that she'd not taken the time to make herself presentable, or that she would forgo the social niceties. She embraced the detective superintendent like an old friend, air-kissing in the French style before releasing her and turning to McLean. For a moment he feared he'd get the same treatment, but Rose settled for grasping hold of his hand and squeezing it between both of her enormous paws.

'Duty sergeant said you needed to see me.' He glanced over his shoulder at the glass panel that separated the reception desk from the public, unsurprised to see no sign of the man.

'Indeed I do, Tony.' Rose relinquished his hand, lifting one of hers up to her throat and clutching at her pearls. 'I can't understand how it could have happened. There are wards in place. It shouldn't be possible.'

'What shouldn't be possible, Rose?' McIntyre asked. 'What's happened?'

Madame Rose looked almost too flustered to speak, which only made the situation worse. If ever there was someone who personified control, then it was the transvestite medium and dealer in occult curios. She didn't need to tell McLean what had happened, though. He already knew. Only one thing could have upset her so.

'It's Rahel and Nala, isn't it?'

'Oh, Tony. I'm so sorry. They're gone.'

56

'I thought your gaff was big, sir. But this place . . .' DC Harrison stood in the hall of Madame Rose's house, looking up at the skylight high overhead. 'Wow.'

'Don't get carried away, Constable. We're here for a reason, remember?'

McLean had offered to drive Madame Rose back to her house, but the medium had politely refused, only saying that she would meet him there. When he'd objected, he'd been overruled by Detective Superintendent McIntyre. Harrison had been unlucky enough to be passing as he made his way through the station and out the back to his car.

'Ah, Tony. Welcome, welcome. And you must be Detective Constable Janie Harrison, yes?' Madame Rose appeared on the first-floor landing and walked down the stairs to greet them as elegantly as someone of her size could manage wearing a narrow calf-length tweed skirt. Had she changed since they'd seen each other in the station less than half an hour before? She certainly looked different, larger and more the self-confident Rose McLean knew.

'How did you . . . ?' Harrison began to ask.

'I am a teller of fortunes, a reader of the tarot and consulter of spirits.' The medium put on an even more affected voice than normal as she spoke. 'And I do believe the detective insp— . . . chief inspector may have mentioned your name in passing. Come.' She turned on the spot and led them back up the stairs.

'You get used to her,' McLean said quietly as they followed Madame Rose to the second floor.

'I heard that, Tony.' She paused a moment, not turning to face him, then carried on towards an open door. Beyond it, a large bedroom looked like it had been recently tidied.

'This is where Rahel was sleeping. Nala's room is just through there.' The medium pointed to an adjoining door, also open.

'Have you touched anything?' McLean asked.

'No. She tidied before she left. Both rooms, I'm guessing. Nala wouldn't have done that, so it must have been Rahel.'

'And she didn't leave a note or anything?' McLean walked over to an antique dressing table by the window, its ornate mirror blackened with age around the edges. More modern toiletries formed a neat circle off to one side, a hairbrush trailing a couple of strands of vibrant red hair.

'They left all the things I gave them except the clothes they were wearing. But no. No note.'

'You've no idea where they might have gone either, I take it. Otherwise you'd not have come to the station to speak to me.'

'I'm not even sure when they left. We all had supper together last night, and then I spent the evening in my study. I've just acquired some very interesting fourth-century figurines, and I was so absorbed in studying them I quite lost track of time. It wasn't until they didn't come down for breakfast that I realised they'd gone.' Madame Rose frowned, as if some new insult had been added to her injury. 'That shouldn't be possible. If they walked out the door I should have known.'

Movement in his peripheral vision resolved itself into a large black cat. It sauntered in and wandered up to McLean, sniffing the air around him before moving on to Harrison, and then finally to Madame Rose. From the way it looked up at her and bobbed its head, he couldn't quite dismiss the idea that the two of them were communicating in some silent language. It wouldn't have surprised him. Rose had enough familiars about the house, and further afield, for any unexpected arrival or departure soon to be reported back to her.

'Did Rahel have a mobile phone?' DC Harrison asked.

Madame Rose tilted her head a moment in thought. 'If she did, I never saw her use it. Most teenagers these days are on their phones all the time. Mind completely oblivious to the outside world. I can't say Rahel was like that at all.'

'What about access to a computer? Maybe the internet?'

'Yes, my dear. We have Wi-Fi here. I may surround myself with antiques, but I'm not a fossil. There's a computer in the living room I sometimes use to watch old films.'

'Might I see it? If she tried to get in touch with someone, there may be a trace. Or even just something in the web browser history. It would give us a place to start looking.'

'Of course. Please, follow me.'

'I'll catch up,' McLean said. 'I just want to have a bit more of a look around. See if I can't find anything.'

McLean watched them go, then went back to the dressing table and its collection of toiletries. Pulling out some drawers revealed nothing that hadn't been there long before Rahel had been offered sanctuary, and a cursory glance in the wardrobe was equally unrewarding. The bed didn't look like it had been slept in for months, if not years. When he gently thumped the neatly sewn patchwork quilt, a cloud of dust rose up into the air and hung there like fog. Over by the door through to the next room, the black cat stared at him with idle curiosity, then started to wash its face with a paw.

Nala's room at least looked like it had been used by a child.

The covers were turned down on the bed, and some of the toys he had seen her playing with before were piled up on an old armchair in one corner. Another door opened onto a small bathroom, two new toothbrushes and a tube of toothpaste in an old glass that reminded McLean horribly of his hated boarding school. Everything was just as clean as he would have expected Madame Rose's house to be.

A small waste bin stood between the ancient china toilet and the bath. He lifted it off its lid and peered inside, finding a few discarded cotton ear buds and a scrumpled up piece of paper that looked like it had been torn from a notebook. For a moment, he considered pulling on a pair of latex gloves, but this wasn't a crime scene and the bin's contents weren't particularly unsanitary, so he carefully retrieved the paper and smoothed it out flat on the toilet lid.

Rahel's handwriting was childish, but then McLean was beginning to understand that she was in many ways still a child. Only the hard life she'd lived had aged her past her years, given her the wisdom, and cynicism, of bitter experience. He doubted she'd had much in the way of schooling since arriving in Scotland. The page she'd discarded was a list of sorts. People's names alongside strings of digits, some of which were obviously phone numbers, others which clearly weren't. She had scribbled in additional notes alongside some names, but there wasn't enough light in the bathroom to see them properly. Two entries stood out to his first casual glance. The first was for Fresh Food Solutions, a landline number that must have been who she called to see if there was any work that day. The other one read 'B McK' and was circled in red ink, a red line leading to a mobile phone number. He pulled out his own phone, tapped in the number and hit dial. It rang twice before being answered.

'Aye? Who's this?'

Only three words, but McLean recognised the voice he was

expecting. 'Billy? It's Detective Chief Inspector McLean here. Please don't hang up, OK?'

A long silence followed, but no dull tone of the call having been ended. Finally the voice at the other end spoke again. 'She's no' here. I don't know where she is, aye?'

Something about the way he said it convinced McLean he was lying, but also that he wasn't the first person the lie had been told to. 'Has anyone else been asking about her? Today maybe? Just recently?'

Again a long silence. Normally McLean would have left it to run its course, but sometimes you needed to reassure. 'She was staying somewhere safe. Nala too. I could guarantee her safety here, but I can't if I don't know where she's gone.'

'I . . . I don't know. Where she's gone, that is. If I did, I'd probably tell youse. You're right though, I had someone else ask me about her not an hour ago.'

'Can you tell me who?' McLean noticed movement in the corner of his eye, looked around to see Harrison at the door with a very modern-looking tablet computer in her hands. He held his hand up for silence.

'Aye. Not sure what his name is. He helps oot here at the tower sometimes though. Posh voice a bit like yours, no offence.'

'Does he drive a stretch limousine by any chance? Work for Jane Louise Dee?'

'I really couldnae say, ken?' McLean understood well enough that it wasn't a no. McKenzie was well aware who paid for his halfway-house flat, who his ultimate benefactor was.

'That's OK, Billy. Thanks. And if Rahel gets in touch, please ask her to call me. She and Nala are in considerable danger. I can help them.'

'Aye. I ken that noo. If I hear from them I'll let youse know.'

McLean ended the call, folded the sheet of paper and slipped it into his pocket before turning back to Harrison. 'You find something, Constable?'

'Not sure, sir. I was going through the browser history like I said. There's a few kiddies' videos that must have been Nala, but someone's been searching for information about the Dee Trust too, and it wasn't your unusual friend downstairs.'

'You've asked her, I take it.'

Harrison gave him a pained expression by way of an answer. 'She's . . . Well, if I'm being honest, sir, I'm not really sure what she is. How on earth do you know her?'

'That's a long story for another time, but Superintendent McIntyre's mostly to blame.' He walked out of the bathroom, across the two bedrooms and back out onto the landing, Harrison trailing behind him. Madame Rose was nowhere to be seen again, but that was hardly unexpected. He'd long since given up trying to understand her ways. 'Come on. Let's get back to the station. We're not going to find any more answers here.'

57

'Been trying to track you down for the past couple of hours, sir. Think I understand why the high heidyins get so pissed off when you're not in your office now.'

Grumpy Bob grinned as he made the joke, but there was a hint of worry in his eyes too. McLean could sympathise. There were more than enough things to worry about. He'd sent Harrison off to organise getting pictures of Rahel and Nala out to all patrols in and around the city, so that was at least one of them dealt with. For now. He glanced briefly at his phone, lying face up on his desk. No call from Billy McKenzie yet, although he was certain the young man would be in touch soon. Either him or Rahel herself.

'What's up, Bob?'

'Those runes or sigils or whatever they are, carved into the stone wall down in the Hermitage. You asked me to see if I could find out what they meant.'

McLean leaned back in his chair carefully, aware that it might tip him backwards and onto the floor if he treated it with disrespect. 'And since you gave me the bad news first, can I assume you've found something?'

'Indeed I have.' Grumpy Bob reached into his jacket and pulled out a few sheets of paper, folded down the middle. He spread them out on the table, revealing photographs of what McLean had thought was some kind of shrine, along with pencil drawings of the strange swirls and lines that had been carved into the rock.

'I spoke to a professor up at the university just this morning. Said he knew you and was helping out with something else. He got very excited when I showed him these.'

'Charnley? I'm guessing he doesn't get out much. Seems to know his Middle Eastern history though. What did he have to say about these?'

'Mostly that he was surprised to see something like it over here. Apparently it's an almost exact copy of a wee shrine in some temple far out in the desert. The bit where Syria, Iran and Iraq all run into each other. Not that I'm much of an expert on these things, but isn't that where your wee girl and her aunt come from?'

'Technically, it's Turkey that shares borders with Iran and Iraq. Syria's further west. But yes, Rahel and Akka Nour come from that area. Nala's a bit more of a local, seeing as she was born here in Edinburgh.'

'Aye, well. Anyway. The markings are identical, near as doesn't matter. He even showed me some photos in an old book he had, see?' Grumpy Bob wrestled with his jacket pocket for a moment before pulling out an enormous smartphone, which he proceeded to tap and swipe at with alarming swiftness for a detective sergeant on the eve of retirement. After a suspiciously short time he held the device up for McLean to see. The picture was clear enough, a small alcove hewn into sandstone, symbols carved all around it. The similarity to what they had found in the Hermitage was hard to deny.

'So what's it mean, then? I take it Gobbo told you.'

Grumpy Bob raised a grey and bushy eyebrow at the name, but made no comment. 'Aye, he did. The temple's a ruin if it's even still there and not been blown up. It's pre-Christian. Can't remember who he said it was dedicated to. Atar-something or other.'

'Atargatis? Goddess of fertility.' McLean had heard the name too recently to forget.

'Well, he said protector of the faithful, but I guess a goddess can do what she likes.'

'Indeed.' Like having a detective chief inspector abducted and brought before her. 'Did Gob— . . . Professor Charnley say what the symbols represent? Are they meant to do anything special?'

'Oh, aye. They ward away evil spirits. Particularly aff-somethings. I knew I should have written it down, but the professor said he'd bung it all in an email. Not come in yet, mind.' Grumpy Bob lifted up his ridiculous phone and stared forlornly at the screen.

'It doesn't matter.' McLean picked up his own phone, also blank, and stood up. 'Grab your coat, Bob. We're going on a wee trip.'

The fading light of afternoon had long since given up trying to get down into the depths of the Hermitage. McLean led a silently complaining Grumpy Bob along the path towards the spot where they'd found the second young girl. Not the second young girl, he corrected himself, her name was Elia, after her grandmother. And the other girl had been Mara. Scant consolation to be able to give them names now they were dead; it seemed as if nobody had cared much for them when they were alive.

'Should be in here. You didn't bring a torch, did you?' Crime scene tape marked off the area even though forensics had long since been and gone and the park had reopened to the public. Not that there were many people using it in this weather, and none as the darkness fell among the trees. McLean found the slim penlight he always tried to remember to put into whichever jacket he wore each day, and Grumpy Bob lit up the torch function on his huge phone, casting the snow-dropped leaves in LED white. They pushed through the rhododendron bushes, up a track longer than McLean remembered, until it opened up onto the old walled garden where the makeshift campsite had been.

'Doesn't look like anyone's been back since our lot were here.' Grumpy Bob held up the middle of a loop of yet more police crime scene tape, and McLean ducked under it into the walled garden proper.

The Hermitage was always a haven of quiet, sheltered from all but the dull roar of the city. Stepping into the trees had damped that down yet further. Inside the walled garden might have been the surface of the moon for all the noise he could hear. McLean played his torchlight over the ground, the patchy snow reflecting back in a million crystal sparks. There were footprints, but they had been smoothed off into vague impressions by later falls of powder filtering in from the leafless branches overhead. All sign of the makeshift camp had gone, packed up and taken away by the forensics team. When he found the alcove in the stone wall, the tiny pair of shoes were missing, but the carved sigils still surrounded the space where they had been.

'This it, then?' Grumpy Bob asked. The flatter glare of his phone torch chased away the shadows that had helped define the symbols and letters carved into the stone.

'This is it.' McLean leaned in close for a better look, then ran a finger over the indentations. 'Hold your light over at an angle, can you, Bob? I need to see this better.'

Grumpy Bob did as he was told, but even as the light shifted and the shadows brought out the lines, McLean knew that he was wasting his time. Or perhaps killing it until the inevitable call came through. It wasn't as if they were going to find Rahel and Nala camping out here.

The snap of a twig a distance off rang out like a gunshot in the quiet. McLean looked up, over the crumbling wall, as he tried to work out where it had come from. His eyes were poorly adjusted to the gloom after the light from Grumpy Bob's phone and his own torch, but he thought he could see something moving, over towards the small clearing where they had found the young girl.

Working on memory as much as sight, he forged a path through the bushes towards the spot. The tiny point of his pen torch picked out details in stark light, thin tree trunks rimed with ice, low branches dropped in snow. The ground crunched underfoot and his breath misted the air as the dark woodland pulled in around him.

He almost missed the clearing; only a dangling piece of crime scene tape caught in the light to show him that he was there. It looked different as he played the torch beam across it. The lumbering noise of Grumpy Bob cursing his way through the undergrowth to join him would certainly have scared off any wild animal, even if their combined flickering torch and glaring smartphone hadn't done so already. McLean held up an arm to stop him as the detective sergeant made to step into the clearing.

'A moment, Bob. There's something. I can't quite . . .' And then he caught it, the scent on the almost completely still air. A mixture of a perfume he'd smelled before and a deeper, dryer musk. 'Can you smell that?'

'Can't smell any— . . . oh, aye. I can now. What is that?'

'Not sure. But I've smelled it before, and recently.' McLean played his torch out over the ground of the clearing, towards where the young girl's body had lain. The snow had covered up much of the mess left by forensics and police teams traipsing back and forth, but a fresh line of prints darkened the white.

'Stay here. And shine that great lighthouse beacon of yours over the clearing, aye?' McLean stepped lightly over to the nearest set of footprints, squinting to work out which way the person who had made them had been walking. They appeared at the edge of the clearing closest to the path down below, then meandered across to the spot where the young girl's body had been, circled around it a couple of times. The snow had been brushed away from part of that spot, the ground beneath cleared right back to frosted earth. He crouched down, the light from his torch insufficient to see whether someone had been scraping away at it. Down close, the musky smell was much stronger, the perfume barely a memory.

'See anything?' Grumpy Bob half whispered from the edge of the clearing. McLean could hear the anxiety in the detective sergeant's voice and couldn't blame him. He flashed the torchlight over the retreating footprints, taking a far straighter line back than the way they had come. In the middle of one close by, a dry branch snapped clean in two must have made the noise. Holding his hand out, he measured the length and width of the print against his fingers. The base of the footprint showed the underside pattern of a pair of trainers stamped into the snow.

'Someone's been here.' He retraced his steps to where Grumpy Bob stood. 'Not a child, but small feet. Wearing trainers or something like it. Very interested in the spot where the wee girl was found.'

And then it hit him, both where he'd smelled that scent before and seen someone with small feet wearing trainers. Pink Converse, quite inappropriate for the weather. But that made no sense at all.

'I think I know who it was,' he said. 'But what the hell was Sheila Begbie doing here?'

58

The call came through while they were driving back to the station. For a moment, McLean couldn't quite work out how to answer it, but Grumpy Bob reached over and tapped something on the dashboard. The ringing stopped, there was a brief burst of static and then a voice rang out: 'Hello?'

'Insp— . . . Chief Inspector McLean.' He felt rather self-conscious speaking out loud as he drove. 'Who's this?'

'Aye, it's me. Billy McKenzie. Line sounds awful weird like?'

'I'm on hands-free, Billy. What can I help you with? Has Rahel been in touch?' McLean glanced in his mirror, scanned the road ahead, looking for a place and a chance to pull in. Late-afternoon traffic had blended seamlessly into rush hour, the road too busy to concentrate on driving and talking both at the same time.

'No. Well, aye. Sort of.'

'Billy, I'm trying to help her. I can't do that if you hold back.'

'It's no' that. It's just, she trusts me, ken?'

'She likes you, Billy. But she's young, you know? And she's been hurt badly. We both want to make sure that doesn't happen again, aye?'

There was a long pause, which gave McLean the chance to indicate and turn into a side street. There was nowhere to stop, and two other cars followed him, both sounding their horns as they overtook.

'I don't know where she is right now. But she said she'd come here. Both of them. Just for a while until they can work out what to do next. All the others, the folk that worked at the sandwich factory, the ones in the hostel, none of them will speak to her, see? Not after that thing came for wee Nala. Not after Akka died. They're all afraid.' McKenzie fell silent for a second. 'No, not afraid. Petrified, ken?'

McLean reached for his phone, then realised it was easier to continue with the hands-free. 'After what happened to the other two girls, I can understand.' He looked across at Grumpy Bob, who was keeping perfectly still as well as silent, raised a single eyebrow and got a shrug by way of an answer. So much for that help.

'I'm coming over, Billy,' McLean said after a few moments of silence had passed. 'I may bring DC Harrison with me. Nala's met her, seems to like her. Tell Rahel, and if she wants to leave, then let her, but call me back. I'll be there within the hour.'

More silence, and for a moment McLean thought McKenzie might have hung up. Only the screen on the dashboard showed the call was still connected.

'Aye. OK. I'll see youse in an hour.'

This time the call went dead. McLean gripped the steering wheel as if he were driving a racing car, tensed his shoulders and then tried to relax it away.

'You think it's a good idea going there on your own?' Grumpy Bob asked.

'Not really, no. But I don't see much option. We turn up heavy-handed, she'll just melt away into the darkness and then whatever snapped that branch in the woods back there will get her.'

To his credit, Grumpy Bob didn't immediately call him mad.

The old detective sergeant had seen enough to know better than that. Still, McLean could feel the disagreement in his tense silence.

'I'll see if Harrison's still on shift, OK? It's either her or Emma, and I don't think we've time to go and fetch her.' He hit the indicator, glanced in the mirror and pulled away from the line of parked cars, trying to think of the best way to get back to the station.

'What do you want me to do, then?' Grumpy Bob asked after they had negotiated a maze of side streets and merged back into the almost stationary traffic on Newington Road. McLean had been working out a very vague plan in his head, based on supposition and guesswork. It was that kind of day.

'I need you to get in touch with someone for me.'

Flurries of snow spattered against the windscreen as McLean drove out across Holyrood Park towards Jock's Lodge. Night had fallen completely now, the darkness enveloping his car like a heavy blanket. DC Harrison sat beside him in the passenger seat, fidgeting.

'Something on your mind?'

'I don't know, sir. It's this whole case, I guess. It's . . .' She was about to say more, but the loud buzzing of a phone call blared out through the car's speakers. The screen on the dashboard read 'Caroline Wheeler', and this time McLean was able to locate the correct switch to accept the call without having to take his eye off the road for too long.

'Doctor Wheeler. Caroline.' He spoke louder than normal, still uncomfortable with the technology.

'Ah, you're driving, Tony. I'll make this quick then. Peter Winterthorne is dead.'

The snow grew thicker, smearing against the glass as a gust of wind blew up out of nowhere. McLean had to brake harder than he would have liked, the line of cars ahead of him suddenly slowing as if they too had just heard the news.

'How did he die?' he asked once he'd got the car back under control, ruing the choice of something quite so powerful now that the weather was against him. Fat tyres and five hundred horses didn't mix well with slushy snow.

'From what I can tell, he went into cardiac arrest. Blood pressure dropped through the floor. We tried to resuscitate, but he didn't respond. He was an old man, and very frail.'

'Thanks for letting me know. I take it this happened fairly recently.'

'About an hour. I would have called sooner, but I had to deal with the nurses preparing his body for the mortuary. They had a bit of a shock when they undressed him.' Doctor Wheeler paused a moment before speaking again. 'To be honest, Tony, so did I.'

'How so?' McLean asked the question even though he feared he knew the answer.

'We knew Winterthorne had been in a plane crash and somehow miraculously survived. He had impressive scars from burns and other injuries all over his body when he was brought in, but they were old, healed. I don't doubt they caused him pain and might explain his distrust of doctors.'

'He really didn't want to go to hospital at all.' McLean recalled Winterthorne's last words, the weak hand clutching at his shoulder. Was he in some way responsible for the man's death? No, that wasn't a helpful way to think. 'What was the problem that had the nurses so spooked, then?'

'It was his skin, Tony. I swear I've never seen anything like it. Alive, it was like paper. You could see his veins and sinews through it. Half an hour after he died, you'd have thought he was some kind of ancient Egyptian mummy.'

★ ★ ★

'She's on her way. Just had a call.'

Billy McKenzie met them in the downstairs hallway of Inchmalcolm Tower. He looked scruffier than McLean remembered him, as if he hadn't slept properly since the last time they met.

'You remember DC Harrison?' He nodded at the detective constable by way of introduction. Neither of them had said much after Doctor Wheeler's call. There wasn't much they could say. Nothing seemed to make sense any more.

'Aye. I think so.' McKenzie didn't sound all that sure. 'Youse want to come on up then? Folk get a wee bit nervous if the polis are hanging around down here.'

'Are we that obvious?' McLean asked as he followed the young man to the lift.

'Aye.' He tilted his head to one side. 'Well, youse are. It's the suit, ken?'

McLean had to admit the young man had a point. He'd bought tailored suits in the past, the sort of thing a financier or businessman might wear, but they didn't fare well at crime scenes. It was less painful to bin an off-the-peg number from Marks & Spencer than something that had cost more than the likes of Billy McKenzie earned in a handful of months.

'When did Rahel call?' he asked in an attempt to change the subject.

'No' long before I called youse. She needs help and she's no' getting it from her ain folk. No' like there's any of her ain folk left, mind.'

'How do you mean? I thought there were a group of them working in the sandwich factory.'

The lift arrived with a ping, and McKenzie didn't answer until the three of them were inside, headed upwards. 'Aye, they did. I got a call from that Mr Boag a couple days back though. Ken how he sacked me when he sacked Rahel? Well no' long after that the whole lot of them just didnae show up for work. Desperate, he was. More an' more orders coming in and nobody to make the sandwiches.'

'You went back then?'

'No. I told him to fuck off. Got another job anyways, aye?'

McLean was going to ask him what that job was, but the lift arrived at their floor and the door opened with a loud ping. Even before he'd stepped out into the corridor he could see the two figures standing at the far end. Rahel was holding Nala by the hand, and they both turned to see what had made the noise.

'Stay here.' McLean held out his hand low to stop Harrison from following him. Even at a distance he could see the angry stare Rahel was sending their way, but it wasn't directed at him so much as McKenzie.

'You said you wouldn't tell anyone.' She spat the words out like they tasted of poison. McKenzie took a step forward, but McLean stopped him too. The only way out of the corridor was behind them into either the lift or the stairwell, unless one of the other flats whose doors opened onto the corridor let them in. He wanted Rahel on his side, but right now he imagined she would feel trapped.

'Don't blame Billy. I pretty much forced him into calling me as soon as you got in touch. We need to talk, Rahel. You're not safe. You and Nala both.'

'Nowhere is safe. Not for me, not for Nala. They killed Akka. Used her and then threw her away like trash.'

'I know that, Rahel.' As McLean walked slowly towards them, he noticed the heavy coats both she and Nala wore, the thick woollen gloves. Had Madame Rose given them those? 'We're very close to finding out who did that to her. We will catch them and punish them for it.'

'Will you kill them?' Rahel's question was heavy with disbelief.

'That's not our way.'

'Then why should I trust you?'

'Because at the end of the day you've got to trust someone. Even if just a little.' McLean had covered most of the distance now, just a couple of paces between him and the two refugees. He stopped walking, held his hands out slightly to indicate that he meant them no harm. 'We want the same thing, you and me. We want the evil destroyed.'

'It cannot be destroyed. Nothing can touch it. The others, they try to appease it. Even give their children to it.' At this, Rahel pulled Nala tighter to herself. The little girl still stared at McLean with those piercing green eyes of hers, but remained silent.

'So you're going to run from it, is that what you're going to do?' McLean stepped to one side, turned and indicated the corridor, the lift, the stairs. DC Harrison and Billy McKenzie. 'Where are you going to run to?'

Rahel let out something that sounded half a laugh and half a sob. She sniffed, wiped her nose with the sleeve of her coat. 'I wanted to go back to the circus. They were kind to me there, said I could stay with them if I wanted. They weren't afraid of the evil. Knew how to deal with it. We would be safe there, Nala and me. But when we got there, it was gone.'

The anguish in Rahel's voice was enough to break the hardest of hearts. All the horror and fear, the desperation and hope first raised then cruelly dashed were like a curse visited a thousand times upon her family, the sick revenge of some ancient, twisted, mythical sorcerer. She sunk slowly to the floor, hugging Nala into an even tighter embrace, and this time the sobs weren't mixed with cynical laughter.

'Hey, hey. It's no' that bad, Rahel.' McKenzie pushed past McLean, then knelt down and put his arms around her and the little girl. He said something to them McLean couldn't quite hear, then stood up again, pulling a set of keys from his pocket.

'Come on. Let's all go in, aye?' He slid a key into the lock, twisted it once and pushed on the door at the same time as McLean noticed a smell that hadn't been there before. A mixture of sweet perfume like crushed flower petals and a deeper, more animal musk.

'Wait!' He knew as he shouted the words it was too late. McKenzie's hand was on the door handle, ready to push it open, but something pulled it hard from the inside and he disappeared through the doorway with a frightened scream.

59

McLean moved without thinking, springing forward to where Rahel and Nala stood outside McKenzie's doorway, frozen in shock and surprise. The noise coming from the small apartment was like cats fighting, a high-pitched yowling that sent a chill through his spine. Fighting back the visceral terror, he wrapped his arms around the young girl and her aunt, pushed them away towards the lift.

'Harrison. Get them out of here. Go!'

Something in his voice, or maybe just his touch, broke their paralysis. Rahel hauled Nala by her hand, running down the corridor towards the detective constable. She still stood, open-mouthed, uncertain.

'Take the car. Get them to Rose's place. Or mine if you have to.' McLean shoved his hand in his pocket, pulled out his car keys and lobbed them towards Harrison. Against all the odds, his aim was true and her catching reflex strong. He didn't wait to see them go, but took a deep breath and turned back to McKenzie's apartment.

He inched through into the darkened hall. Light from the corridor spilled across a floor covered with coats, boots and other detritus spilled from a built-in cupboard. Directly across, the door to the living room hung at a crooked angle, ripped from its top hinge as if someone had been thrown bodily through it. A louder scream came from beyond it, spurring him into action.

Crossing the hall, McLean almost fell flat on his backside as his foot rolled on something. He crouched down and found an umbrella, the nearest thing to a weapon anywhere to hand. He scooped it up and trod more carefully, fighting down the urges both to rush to McKenzie's aid and to flee as fast as he could the other way.

All thoughts of stealth disappeared as his phone started to jangle away in his pocket. McLean ignored it, pushed past the broken door and into the living room, umbrella held forward like a fencer's epee. The only light in the room came from a table lamp, lying on the floor where it had been knocked over in the fight. In the semi-darkness he could see McKenzie, sprawled halfway across the room, the broken remains of his coffee table underneath him. His hands and feet spasmed in time with his weakening screams as something dark and indistinct clawed at his chest and neck.

'Get off him!' McLean took two steps into the room and swung the umbrella, surprised when it connected with something solid. Almost impossible to make out in the gloom, a figure in a dark cloak, with lank, greasy black hair snarled at the interruption and turned eyes of burning red on him. The wave of fear almost overwhelmed him, but with the last of his sense, he swung the umbrella back again. This time it connected with the creature's face, snapping it round. He was sure it was going to fall to the floor unconscious, but instead it simply shook its head and slowly stood up to face him.

'You.' One word snarled with all the venom of a Burton's carpet viper. And yet behind the rage, there was a tremor of confusion. McLean took a step back as the creature rose to its full height. He recognised something in that voice, but the figure itself was too indistinct to see, all tangled hair and shadows. Only its eyes were clear, blazing red as if fire burned behind them. Beneath its feet, McKenzie twitched and moaned as he fought for breath, but at least the young man was still alive.

'You're under arrest.' McLean heard the utter ridiculousness of his words even as he spoke them. The shadows moved, stepping over McKenzie towards him, head cocked slightly to one side. He took a step back, uncertain.

'No more wishes, Detective Chief Inspector?' The voice rasped across his mind, but again there was that hint of familiarity in the words, as if he'd heard them spoken, but by another person. Confused, McLean almost didn't notice the figure crouch slightly, tensing for the attack.

Almost.

It lunged at him in a whirr of noise, arms outstretched, those crimson eyes flaming in the near total darkness. There was a smell about it of sewers, burnt hair and something far worse still. Heat boiled off it, and fear too. Paralysing fear that had McLean frozen until the last possible moment. He fell back, whipping the umbrella up again as he did so. The tip of it connected with something and the beast let out a feral howl.

'Die, then.' The shadows spat, and leapt towards him again. McLean scrambled away as best he could, and then felt the wall behind at his back. A claw-like hand speared out of the darkness, grabbed him by the throat and hauled him to his feet. And then, just as it leaned in close for the kill, something flickered in McLean's peripheral vision. A movement, a noise like rushing wind. A cloud of white spray billowed out, catching the creature full in the face.

It let out an agonised scream, tripping backwards in its haste to get away from DC Harrison. She stepped past McLean, arm outstretched and a can of pepper spray in her hand, letting the full volume of it cover his attacker. The creature should have been on the floor, curled in a ball, unable to breathe, but it scratched at its face, pulling out chunks of hair and flesh, throwing them to the floor. And then with a last howl of anger, it turned away, leapt at the window and crashed through the glass into the darkness beyond.

60

'I thought I told you to get Rahel and Nala away.'

McLean struggled to stand upright, his legs weak, head woozy. Harrison ignored him, going first to the window to look out and down, then back to McKenzie as he lay on the floor.

'We need to get him to a hospital fast.' She held a finger to his neck in search of a pulse, then finally looked up at McLean, eyes widening as she did so. 'You too, sir.'

'What? I'm fine.' McLean put a hand up to his neck. It had stung as the creature scratched him, but now it felt numb and warm, almost pleasant. When he pulled his hand away and looked at his fingers, they were slick with blood. 'Oh.'

'Aye. That's about right. Here.' Harrison came over to where he stood, producing a clean white handkerchief from her pocket. 'Hold that tight against it. You've a nasty cut to your neck.'

McLean did as he was told, waiting while Harrison put through a call to Control telling them to send an ambulance. His legs felt strong enough to support him by the time she was done, even if his head was still light, his balance off.

'What about Rahel and Nala though? We need to protect them. That thing—'

'They're OK, sir. Your friend Rose arrived just as we were leaving the building. She's taken them off to her house. I don't think they're going to try to run away again.'

'What about that . . . ?' McLean used various pieces of furniture to help steady himself as he found a path round McKenzie's prone body to the broken window. Leaning as far towards it as he dared, he could see street lights and the surrounding houses through thickening snowfall, but not the area six floors down where the creature must have landed. No way it could have survived that fall though, surely?

A noise behind him had McLean turning too quickly, and he leaned heavily against the wall as his vision darkened. When the spots cleared it was to the sight of an old man. For a moment McLean couldn't think who he was, but then he saw the Dee Trust logo on his fleece jacket, and recognised him from his earlier visit. The concierge who couldn't pronounce the word.

'You'll need to stay back please, sir.' DC Harrison walked towards the man, ready to usher him out, but McLean stopped her with a wave.

'Actually, if you could stay here with Billy, until the paramedics arrive?' A whoop of a nearby siren through the broken window suggested the wait wouldn't be long. 'He's been attacked. I need to make sure his attacker hasn't escaped.'

The old man's eyes flicked from McLean's face to his neck and back again. He nodded once, then stepped past him to where McKenzie lay horribly still.

'Harrison, with me.'

'Sir, you're still bleeding. You need to slow down.' The detective constable caught up with him halfway to the lift, and she wasn't even running. McLean knew she was right.

'Just need to make sure. Whoever that was. Whatever they were dosed up on. There's no way they can have survived a fall from six storeys. Not so they could escape. We need to make sure they're either dead or secured.'

The lift pinged open as they reached it, two paramedics inside.

McLean pointed them down the corridor to the open door. 'He's inside. Deal with him first. I'm fine for now.'

They both looked sceptical, but hurried past nonetheless. He stepped into the lift, Harrison right behind him.

'You really shouldn't be doing this, sir. You should have let them look at that cut. It's deep.'

'It'll be OK. Backup will be here soon. Then we can all go home.'

Backup had arrived in the form of Grumpy Bob by the time the lift opened on the ground floor of Inchmalcolm Tower. McLean tried his best not to stagger as he walked out into the entrance hall, but he might have failed a little. The old detective sergeant said nothing; he didn't need to.

'I know, I know. I've had enough of an earful from Harrison. Can we just get this over with so I can go and sit down?'

'Where are you going, sir?' Grumpy Bob asked.

'Out there.' McLean waved his free hand in the approximate direction of the ground beneath Billy McKenzie's window and the three off them set of for the main doors. 'Thanks for calling Rose,' he added as they stepped outside. The cold air blew some of the fuzziness from his mind, but also reminded him of just how weak and tired he felt.

'Aye, well. If I'd known what was out here I'd maybe have called an armed-response team and all.'

Newly fallen snow made the ground around the side of the tower block slippery underfoot. Perhaps inevitably, the lights that illuminated the front entrance plunged this part of the grounds into greater darkness. Looking up, McLean could see the broken window high above, but the flats below it were either empty or their occupants had gone to bed.

'Careful, sir.' DC Harrison was at his side, a hand to his elbow as if he were a pensioner whose Zimmer frame had been stolen. Only then did the wave of nausea wash over him and he almost fell into her arms. Perhaps looking up hadn't been such a good idea. Or indeed coming out into the darkness in search of some monster with eyes that burned like fire.

'Got to be here somewhere,' he said to cover his embarrassment, all too aware that the words slurred out like he'd been drinking. 'Where's that torch of yours, Bob?'

Light blazed across the yard as both Grumpy Bob and DC Harrison switched on torches. Fat lumps of snow tumbled down through the still air, already covering up the mess of broken glass and window frame beneath Billy McKenzie's flat, and there, lying in the middle of it, a black-clad lump beginning to speckle white.

'Careful.' Harrison inched closer to the body, torch in one hand, pepper spray in the other. It didn't move, even when she prodded it with a foot. She crouched down, clipping the spray to her belt, reached in to roll the body over onto its back, then leapt away with a yelp of surprise when it groaned and started to move. In an instant she had the spray out again, but whoever it was let out a pained whimper and fell still again.

'Sweet hairy Jesus. How could anything survive that fall?' She leaned in again, more carefully this time, and gently teased the black cloth away from the creature's face, directing the beam of her torch at it. 'Oh shit.'

McLean staggered up to see what had spooked her. His neck had gone almost completely numb now, and he could feel his head following suit. How much blood had he lost? Not that much, surely. Behind him he could hear Grumpy Bob on his phone, calling in more backup and another ambulance, and as he looked down at the face of the beast, McLean was strangely unsurprised to see Sheila Begbie's blank eyes staring back up at him.

'She alive?' he asked, forgetting he'd seen her try to move just moments earlier. Then he noticed red spots appearing in the

404

white snow around his feet, spattering off his shoes. A blood-drenched handkerchief tumbled to the ground, and everything turned to rushing black.

61

'Gave us quite a fright there, Tony. How are you feeling?'

McLean opened his eyes, groggy and confused, to find himself looking at Doctor Wheeler as she peered at him closely. For a while he couldn't remember anything, and then it began to come back in disjointed snippets.

'What happened?' His voice sounded croaky and dry, his throat sore as if he'd been shouting.

'Short answer is you went running in where you shouldn't have. Got yourself slashed by something tipped with a nasty poison.' Doctor Wheeler reached a hand towards McLean's neck and he recoiled instinctively.

'Bandage?' the doctor said. 'I need to check your stitches.'

He tried to relax, bending his head slightly so that she could get a clear reach. 'I thought you were a neurologist.'

'Heads, necks. It's all the same thing really. I sometimes feel it's my vocation to patch you and your team up whenever you get into trouble.'

The dull throb of pain he'd barely been aware of flared up livid as Doctor Wheeler examined his wound.

'Ouch. What's the verdict? Will I live?'

'You'll have a scar to impress the ladies with, but I think we've got on top of the infection.' She pressed at his skin again, and the pain was less intense this time.

'How long have I been here?' McLean became aware of his surroundings as if someone had flipped a switch and made them appear. He wasn't surprised by the hospital room, particularly, but the daylight flooding through the window made no sense.

'Twelve hours, give or take. And before you ask, yes, Emma knows you're here and what happened. I left her a message. No doubt she'll be along to give you the telling off you deserve soon enough.'

As if on cue, there was a knock at the door and it half opened. Instead of Emma standing there though, McLean saw the concerned face of DC Harrison peering through the gap. She spoke to Doctor Wheeler first. 'Is he any better?'

'I'm fine, Constable – Janie. Thanks.' McLean looked at the doctor for confirmation. 'I'm fine, right?'

'For a broad definition of "fine", yes, you are. Better than we might have expected given the state you were in when you arrived. You still need to rest. I'll send a nurse to change that bandage, but the wound looks nice and clean.' She laid a hand on his shoulder to push him gently down into the pillows, then pulled it back again as if she felt she had overstepped the mark. Turning away, she walked briskly from the room, a terse 'Try not to let him do anything stupid' to Harrison as she went.

McLean struggled to sit up a bit straighter, his head woozy. The pain in his neck throbbed in time with his heartbeat, faster than he'd expect after so long asleep. The memories were coming back now, but there were still gaps. 'What's the story, then?'

Harrison stood at the doorway, looking unsure whether she should come in or not. 'You collapsed. We thought it was blood loss, but they reckon Begbie must have cut you with some poisoned blade. Similar to what she used on those two wee girls and Maurice Jennings, but less potent. Least that's how it was explained to me. They pumped you full of something to neutralise it.'

'What about Billy McKenzie?' He remembered the young man, the shadow attacking him. Had that really been Sheila Begbie? His memories were jumbled and patchy, but surely she couldn't have overpowered him so easily.

'Same as you, only worse. He's in intensive care right now. I heard something about a full blood transfusion. They're hopeful he'll recover, but he was in a bad way when the paramedics got to him.' Harrison stepped further into the room, shut the door and sat down on the plastic chair beside it. 'Strange thing is, they couldn't find any wounds on him.'

McLean thumped his head back against the pillows, then winced as the cut on his neck reminded him it was there. Two little girls dead with not a scratch on them. Maurice Jennings the same. And now Billy McKenzie fighting for his life. Poisoned? Or was it something more sinister? He remembered the voice of the creature that had attacked him, muttering about wishes. And he remembered all the mystical nonsense spouted by Mrs Saifre and Madame Jasmina. Talk of afrits and djinn. In the desert, maybe. When he was six years old, perhaps. But not now, not in his city. He couldn't allow that.

'Where's Begbie now?'

'In the ICU too. She's not going anywhere, mind. Broke her neck and back in the fall. Multiple fractures in both arms. The doctors can't quite understand how she's still alive. Most of the team wish she wasn't.'

McLean scanned the room as best he could from where he lay. There wasn't much in it apart from the bed, some chairs and a tall white wardrobe. A couple of expensive-looking ICU machines had been wheeled into the corner, but they weren't plugged in, and more importantly neither was he. 'My clothes. They're not in that hanging cupboard are they?'

★ ★ ★

'You sure this is wise, sir? The doctor said you should rest.'

'I know. And she also said you should try to stop me from doing anything stupid. If you want to walk away, pretend you had no idea what I was up to, I won't hold it against you.'

McLean hobbled down the corridor like a man who'd been brought into the hospital unconscious just hours earlier suffering from blood loss and poisoning. His suit hung from him as if it were too big, the cuffs and trouser bottoms still damp and one shoulder of the jacket stained with his own blood. He'd felt grubby putting on old and dirty clothes, but there was something he had to do. If he didn't do it now, he'd start to think about it, and then it would be too late.

'Where exactly are we going, sir?' Harrison almost had to trot to keep up with him.

'The ICU. I need to see Begbie.'

'She's unconscious, sir. They'll be keeping her that way for days, maybe longer. You won't get anything from her.'

'I don't want anything from her, Janie. I want to give her something.'

If Harrison said anything in response, he didn't hear it. McLean was surprised that there weren't many nurses around as they walked up the corridor to the ICU, but he was glad not to be distracted either.

A lone uniformed constable sat on a chair outside the room in which Akka Nour had died; a pleasing symmetry given that, in some way he couldn't yet identify, McLean was sure Begbie was responsible for the woman's death.

'Sir. Nobody told me . . .' The constable leapt to his feet as soon as he saw the two detectives approaching.

'At ease, Constable. I just want to see the patient.'

'You'll need to sign the register, sir.' The constable bent down and picked up a clipboard with a form attached, but no pen.

McLean fetched one out of his pocket, signed and checked the time. Looking at the names listed above his, it appeared Sheila Begbie had been visited mostly by nurses and a couple of doctors whose names he recognised, Caroline Wheeler among them. Two names stood out though.

'Albert Rogers and Geraldine Sellars? Who are they?'

'Aye, them. They came in with the DCC, sir. Way I hear it they're from some private trust. Going to transfer her to a secure medical facility this afternoon. Some new treatment you can't get on the NHS yet. No idea who's paying for it.'

Given what he'd been told of her condition, that seemed a bit extreme. And potentially life-threatening. 'I have a suspicion I know who.' He had a suspicion why, too, even if he didn't want to think too hard about it. 'Are the doctors happy about it?'

'Don't know about the doctors, but the nurses are in a right stooshie. Fair bent my ear about it, an' it's no' as if it's anything to do wi' me.'

McLean looked at the two names again, noting that Robinson hadn't signed the ledger. Perhaps he'd stayed outside. Something bothered him about the first name, though. Albert. It wasn't exactly uncommon, but was it a coincidence that Mrs Saifre's well-spoken bodyguard and chauffeur had the same name? He didn't really believe in coincidences.

'I'll be a couple of minutes, tops. You can watch if you want.'

'That's fine, sir. Long as I know who's been in and oot.' The constable handed the clipboard to Harrison.

'No need. I'll just be a moment.' McLean waved her back as he opened the door and stepped into the room. It was a fair bit larger than the one he'd woken up in, and filled with much more expensive-looking machinery, all of it switched on. Sheila Begbie lay on the bed, her upper body in a Minerva cast and legs immobilised. Once again, he was struck by the similarities with

Akka Nour, although Begbie's tangled hair was grey and black rather than flame red.

'Have to admit, you had me fooled. It's been a while since anyone managed that quite so well.' He stuck his fingers in his trouser pocket as he walked up to the bedside, fishing out the tiny brass lamp Madame Jasmina had given him. McLean wasn't sure he could bring himself to believe in all the mumbo jumbo, but neither could he deny the evidence of his eyes, his own experience. If it was all nonsense, well, no harm done. If it wasn't? Best not to think about that.

Begbie's hand lay on the top of the bed, palm upwards as if she was begging for coins. McLean placed the lamp on it, then gently folded her fingers over. Nothing happened, but then he'd not really expected it to. He turned to see Harrison chatting with the constable on guard duty, not watching him at all.

'Come on then. Let's get back to the station. Write this whole sorry mess up and move on.' He closed the door behind him, signed out on the ledger, then he and Harrison walked away from the ICU towards Reception and the exit. It wasn't until they were well past the first corner that the rush of nurses in the other direction began.

62

'What the hell did you think you were doing, taking an inexperienced detective constable into such a dangerous situation?'

McLean stood in front of the DCC's desk for what felt like the hundredth time in the past week. He'd only been meaning to come into the station to pick up his car, maybe update a few people on what had happened, then sneak out again for the rest and recuperation Doctor Wheeler had suggested he take. News of Begbie's sudden and unexpected death had come in on Harrison's Airwave set long before they had arrived, so it was hardly surprising when he was summoned to explain himself.

'If I'd known it was going to be dangerous, I'd not have gone myself, sir.' He reached up and touched the bandage on his neck very gently. He couldn't see whether it had begun to seep blood or not, hoped that it hadn't. He'd lost more than he could spare already.

'Sheila Begbie, or whatever her real name was.' Robinson paced back and forth in front of his window wall, the red sky of early afternoon not quite throwing him into silhouette. 'You were the last one to see her, before she died.'

McLean said nothing. If it was an accusation, then the DCC was going to have to be more specific.

'What exactly is her role in all this? Was she the one who killed those girls? The other one?' The DCC waved his hand in annoyance at not being able to recall Maurice Jennings's name. 'In God's name, why? And how?'

'I don't know. But I think when we start looking into her dealings in the city a great many things are going to be uncovered. I'd like to discuss the matter with Jo Dexter before anything else. I—'

'No, Tony.' Robinson's interruption was more effective for being softly spoken, a gentle tilt and shake of the head before he looked up again. 'No. You've done enough. Some might say too much.' He walked back across the office, behind his desk, and sat down heavily. Whereas the last time McLean had been here the desktop had been covered in folders and paperwork, now it was clear save for one, which the DCC opened out to reveal a thin sheaf of papers.

'I've been asked to review the way you've conducted this investigation, and I have to say it's not a happy picture.'

McLean clasped his hands behind his back, fighting the urge to say something. He knew what was coming; no need to make it worse.

'With hindsight, it was probably a mistake putting you in charge of such an . . .' Robinson searched for the right word. 'Such an emotional investigation. Two wee girls, and it's only a couple of months since, well.' He fell silent for a moment, struggling to find a sympathetic expression.

'Nevertheless, as a senior officer with many years' experience, you should have been able to deal with it, or know to step aside. You should know how to delegate and when to leave things up to junior officers, but look at you. You were in hospital overnight, unconscious, poisoned. You stink like you've not washed in days and your jacket's covered in blood. Any sane man would have gone home, but you come straight back here.

What's wrong with you, Tony?'

Put like that, McLean had to admit that the DCC had a point. He reckoned the question was rhetorical though, so didn't answer.

'It's no matter.' Robinson shook his head, flipped the report closed and pushed it to one side. 'There's to be an enquiry into the case. Not my idea, I can assure you. But someone's been putting pressure on the politicians, and they've duly passed it on. I think we both know who that someone is, don't we?'

'Jane Louise Dee,' McLean said. 'Let me guess. The secure medical facility they were going to move Begbie to is run by the Dee Trust. Or maybe some other Saifre corporation. No doubt she would have disappeared as soon as she arrived there, and whatever toxic weapon she used would have disappeared with her.' Even as he said the words, McLean knew they weren't true. Saifre wanted Begbie, yes, but for reasons he didn't want to accept.

'Has anyone ever told you how cynical you are, Tony?'

'It's true though, isn't it? Saifre's the one turning the screws. I'll bet she's moving in on the other operations Begbie was involved in, too. The trafficking, the prostitution, the drugs. All the stuff DCI Dexter should be onto right now. This enquiry of yours will put that all on hold, won't it? And by the time you're done, it'll be too late.'

Robinson rubbed his eyes and scratched at a cheek gone dark with stubble. 'It was too late the moment she got involved. You can't hope to beat her, Tony. She's too powerful, too well-connected.'

'That's never stopped me in the past. Won't stop me now.'

'How about a medical suspension then? Will that do?' The DCC pulled open one of the drawers of his desk, took out a sheet of paper. 'The chief constable signed it himself. One month, starting from today. I didn't think you'd be in here for me to give the news to you in person, but there you go.' He slid the page across the desk and McLean reluctantly picked it up, glancing briefly at the typed words. Then he folded it carefully, tucked it in his pocket, turned and walked out of the room.

The same parking space was free when McLean pulled up outside Madame Rose's house half an hour after leaving the station. He sat in the car for a while, staring up at the stone edifice and thinking about what the deputy chief constable had said. Frustratingly, much of it was true, it was just that at the time he'd not had any alternative. None of them had known about Begbie; how could they?

Maybe it was better this way. He'd never take time off voluntarily, so an enforced suspension while they carried out a spurious enquiry into the circumstances surrounding Begbie's death was a good opportunity to break out of the cycle of self-destruction. Maybe he and Emma could actually get away somewhere, like he'd promised.

Thinking of Emma reminded him he'd not told her about leaving the hospital. He pulled out his phone, found her number and hit dial. It rang a couple of times then switched to voicemail, so he left a message, then sent a text as well just to be safe. Only then did he climb out of the car, cross the road and knock on the door.

'Tony, come in.' Madame Rose answered almost immediately, and he had the odd impression that she had been waiting for him while he sat in his car and ruminated. 'Emma not with you?'

'I called, but she's not answering. Probably gone to the hospital to fetch me.'

'Well, you'll just have to make that up to her, won't you?' She stood aside, opening the door wide. 'Come in. We've been expecting you.'

McLean knew better than to ask how, given that he hadn't known he was coming here until half an hour earlier. Madame

Rose was a fortune teller after all. She led him across the hall to the living room, where he was unsurprised to find Madame Jasmina from the circus sitting in an armchair and drinking tea. She stood as he entered, as did Rahel. Playing with her toys on the floor, Nala paid them all no heed whatsoever.

'Rose told me you were a good man, Anthony McLean. She did not lie. Thank you, for what you did. I know it has cost you dear, but the world is safer for your sacrifice.' Madame Jasmina took his hand in both of hers, squeezing it tight.

'You killed her. Sheila Begbie. I led you to her, and then you killed her.'

'The vessel was dead a long time ago. We merely removed the spirit that was using it, sent it back where it belonged.'

McLean wasn't sure he felt any better about things, but Madame Jasmina squeezed his hand once more. 'Your luck will change soon,' she said, then released him.

'Billy. Is he going to be OK?' Rahel approached as if she had been waiting for permission. She was dressed more elegantly than he'd seen her before, no doubt through Madame Rose's influence. It made her look about fourteen, which he guessed was probably her true age. To have seen so much, endured so much in such a short life.

'I don't know. He survived the attack, and they pumped him full of the same antidote they used on me, so the chances are good.' Except that Billy had suffered far worse injuries, far more of whatever toxin Begbie had used on them both. If it was a toxin. If it had been Begbie. He tried to shake away the train of thoughts, and the wound on his neck flared in pain. Why had he come here? He was so tired he could barely stand, wearing clothes that stank of blood and worse. He should have gone straight home, talked to Rose later.

'Thank you. For looking out for us both.' Rahel leaned forward and kissed him lightly on the cheek, then turned away as if embarrassed by her daring. Or disgusted by his smell.

'Rahel and Nala will be coming with us.' Madame Jasmina spoke her words as an inarguable statement of fact. The detective in him wanted to point out that at the very least Rahel's testimony would be needed in the coming enquiry, but he kept that to himself. Someone else would be conducting that, and someone else could try to track her down.

'Will you be going soon? I couldn't help but notice the circus is already gone.'

Madame Jasmina smiled. 'The circus was never there, Anthony McLean. You know that. In your heart.'

He nodded once. It was exactly the sort of enigmatic nonsense he'd grown used to hearing from Madame Rose, but at the same time it was true. He made to leave, then something else occurred to him.

'Why now?' he asked. 'You said you'd dealt with all this twenty-five years ago. Why did it all blow up again?'

'You see to the heart of things. This is why you are a good detective.' The old fortune teller raised a slim eyebrow, her bright eyes focused on him as she paused for a moment, no doubt working out how best to be oblique. 'We did what we could all those years ago, but the creature was well protected. As to why now, the simple answer is that he grew too old to control her any more, the man Winterthorne. It was he who started all this when he went searching for djinn in the desert. No one ever believed he would find one, let alone bind it to his will. It cost him dear. His wife, his best friends, almost his own life. But he found what he was looking for. The one you call Sheila Begbie, the afrit wearing her form, he freed her and she served him. That was his third wish, after it had healed him and taken the form of his dead wife. But you know as well as I do that wishes come at a price. I think you will be finding out what that price was in the days and weeks to come.'

McLean said nothing. There was nothing he could say. It made perfect sense, and it made no sense at all. He took one last look at the odd collection of people, all watching him like sitters for some bizarre family portrait. All save Nala, who acted out her childish games on a motley collection of toy dolls and teddy bears. She seemed happy enough, despite the traumas her short life had dealt. She was safe, and she was alive. That much would have to do.

Madame Jasmina's words still echoed in his memory as McLean let himself into the kitchen much later. Mrs McCutcheon's cat greeted him the same way she always did, by yawning, leaning over and cleaning her arse with her tongue. He ignored her, picked up the kettle, filled it from the tap and put it on the Aga to boil. It was only when he'd gone to the cupboard for the teabags, found a teapot and a mug and taken it all back to the table that he noticed the sheet of writing paper held down by the pepper grinder. Emma's neat handwriting looped across the page, tilted slightly from left to right. He sat down at the table and started to read.

> *Dearest Tony,*
>
> *I'm sorry to do this with a letter, but I don't know when if ever you're going to come home. I can't carry on being the third one in this relationship. Your dedication to your work would be commendable if it weren't so selfish. You let it consume you so utterly there is no time left for anyone or anything else.*
>
> *I have tried my best to be there for you, and I know you've tried to be there for me. But every time it looks like things are getting better, the job takes over again. A psychologist might say you have commitment issues, and I suspect they would be right.*
>
> *I don't know where I will go. Perhaps up to Aberdeen first. My mother doesn't have long, and there'll be things to sort out when she*

finally goes. I might travel again, see some more of the world. I had hoped we might see it together, but I've given up hope of you ever changing.

Goodbye, Tony. And sorry.

Em

The rattling of the kettle on the hotplate dragged his attention away from Emma's words. McLean made himself tea, then sat there and drank it while he read her letter over and over again. At some point Mrs McCutcheon's cat leapt onto the table beside him, nudging his hand with her face until he absentmindedly began to scratch her behind the ears. Her deep purr was reassuring, but it couldn't chase away the emptiness forming in the pit of his stomach, the feeling of being alone in this vast, hollow old house.

Time passed in the slow, steady ticking of the clock over the door, the gentle gurgle of the cooker and the echoing silence beyond. Everything Emma had written was true. There was no real malice in her words, only sorrow.

After a while, the page became difficult to read, the words blurring one into another as the tears welled in his eyes. He put the letter back down on the table, buried his head in his hands, and wept.

63

The click of the door opening woke him from dreams of fire and heat. Of a creature gnawing at his neck that he somehow just couldn't dislodge, however much he flailed and swiped at it. McLean started up straight, knocking over his mug of tea. There was only a dribble left in the bottom, adding the smallest of stains to a table already marked by a hundred years of similar incidents. He looked up, bleary-eyed, to see Emma standing in the doorway. Her hair was a mess, and she'd been crying.

'Em?' He stood, unsure whether to go to her, wrap her in a hug and never let go.

'I went to see Rose before I left for Aberdeen. Rahel and Nala were there. Madame Jasmina too. You know, from the circus?'

He nodded. The lump that had appeared in his throat made it hard to speak.

'They told me what happened. Why you didn't come home last night, didn't call. I waited up, fell asleep on the sofa. When I woke up this morning and you still weren't home I was so angry at you.'

'Em, I . . .'

'Jasmina explained it all. About the djinn, the wish and how she took it away again. But it wasn't like that. I didn't just decide to stop being cold, same as I wasn't really upset at you in the first place. We lost our child. I didn't know how to deal with that. It took time for me to understand you didn't know how to deal with it either.'

'Everything you said though. It's all true. I'm sorry, Em. I never meant . . .'

Emma glanced at the table, saw the letter. She walked across and picked it up, scrumpled it into a ball and threw it in the general direction of the bin. 'It is true, yes. But the truth has many faces, as someone wise told me recently. And besides, I knew all that about you when we first met. Still climbed into your bed, didn't I?'

McLean took two steps towards her, then swept her up into a desperate hug. It didn't last long, Emma's initial enthusiasm rapidly fading. She pushed him away after far too little time. 'Eww. You smell, Tony McLean. When was the last time you had a bath? And what's that all over your jacket? What's that on your neck?'

'Too long, clearly. Blood, and a bandage.' McLean dabbed at his neck with his fingers; the wound was tender, but surprisingly free of pain.

'Oh, I almost forgot.' Emma sniffed, wiped at her nose with the back of her hand, and then shoved it in her coat pocket, pulling something out and passing it to him. 'Madame Jasmina asked me to give you this. She said it was a memento.'

McLean took the object, knowing what it would be before he'd even felt it in his palm. The tiny model of a brass lamp was heavier than he remembered, and more tarnished. Perhaps he'd polish it up some time, but now wasn't the moment. He closed his fist around it, looked past Emma, taking in the battered old kitchen cupboards, the deep sink under a window turned black by the night outside, the gurgling Aga and the old iron kettle sitting on its warming plate.

'How about a cup of tea?'

Acknowledgements

There is always a danger in writing acknowledgements that I will leave out someone important. Not because I don't value the input of each and every one of the people who have helped make this book a thing, but because by the time I get to the point where I'm trying to remember you all, my brain is utterly shot.

Thus I managed to fail entirely in recognising Alan Lewis in the acknowledgments for the last Inspector McLean book, despite him being the villain. Alan, I hope you can forgive me – for this if not for forgetting to wear a tie to work so many times.

This is my story, but an army of helpful people have worked very hard to make it as good as it can be before it reaches your hands. I'm hugely indebted to my editor, Alex Clark, and to Ella, Jo, Jenni and the rest of the team at Wildfire and Headline. My thanks to Mark Handsley for his sharp eyes on the copyediting too.

Thanks as ever to my agent, the irrepressible Juliet Mushens, and to Gemma Osei for being so organised when I am anything but. Thank you also to all my internet friends, the legion of book bloggers and reviewers, and especially the Order of the Crusty Blanket. You may be a time sink, but you also keep me from becoming a complete hermit.

My biggest debt, as ever, is to Barbara, who keeps an eye on the real world when I'm away in my made up ones. I couldn't do it without you.

And finally I would like to thank The Beast from the East, without whom this book would have been finished much earlier. Nothing quite kills the creativity faster than having to dig sheep out of a snowdrift.

Biography

James Oswald is the author of the *Sunday Times* bestselling Inspector McLean series of detective mysteries, as well as the new DC Constance Fairchild series. James's first two books, NATURAL CAUSES and THE BOOK OF SOULS were both short-listed for the prestigious CWA Debut Dagger Award. COLD AS THE GRAVE is the ninth book in the Inspector McLean series.

James farms Highland cows and Romney sheep by day, writes disturbing fiction by night.